THE
ACCIDENT

About the author

Katie McMahon is a medical doctor and writer. Her first novel, *The Mistake,* was published internationally in 2021. Katie has also written articles for *The Age* and *The Quarry.* Katie grew up in Frankston and now lives in Hobart with her family. *The Accident* is her second novel.

Also by the author

The Mistake

THE
ACCIDENT

KATIE McMAHON

ZAFFRE

First published in Australia in 2022 by
Echo
An imprint of Bonnier Books UK

First published in the UK in 2023 by
ZAFFRE
An imprint of Bonnier Books UK
4th Floor, Victoria House, Bloomsbury Square,
London, England, WC1B 4DA
Owned by Bonnier Books
Sveavägen 56, Stockholm, Sweden

A CIP catalogue record for this book is
available from the British Library.

ISBN: 978–1–80418–050–1

Also available as an ebook and an audiobook

1 3 5 7 9 10 8 6 4 2

Typeset by IDSUK (Data Connection) Ltd
Printed and bound in Great Britain by Clays Ltd, Elcograf S.p.A.

Zaffre is an imprint of Bonnier Books UK
www.bonnierbooks.co.uk

For my wonderful mother, Trish

Accidents do not simply 'happen'. They are always the result of an error, either of an individual, a system, or, more commonly, both.

Key Principles of Emergency Medicine (2019 ed.)

The Wise let their Love be a Choice, not an Accident …

Embracing You: A Guide to Life, Love and You

'It wasn't *my* fault!'

Children everywhere

And adults everywhere

It was one of those unimpeachable spring mornings, the type Hobart knew it was pretty good at. The breeze was suppleness and pleasure, the sun obvious but unchallenging. Sandstone buildings shaded electric bikes, school kids scrolled TikTok on buses, and coffee blessed grateful throats. Behind it all stood the mountain, snuggling the little city into the curve between its forest-dim foothills and the wide blue sparkle of harbour.

Four staff members were on duty at the school's drop-off zone that morning. They wore high-vis vests over office clothes. Two had walkie-talkies. Two turned STOP/SLOW signs with a nervous, responsible air. Who could blame them? Cars were bumper to bumper from the end of the narrow street. One STOP/SLOW error would have visited ruination onto many, many bumpers.

Everyone seemed pretty jolly, though. Lots of waving and smiling and mental resolving not to fuss about the little things. In that sort of weather, most of the mums even felt affectionate towards Sandra from the office – there she was, fluorescent-orange jacket neatly velcroed – even though Sandra tended to be hurtfully passive-aggressive if you made the slightest mistake with your kid's photo forms or sports-carnival gear.

That day, it was Sandra's job to harry ('assist') the children out of the cars, and check that the younger ones were right to find their way from the Rapid Drop Zone to the Junior Learning Hub. The senior school kids, of course, knew how to get to their classrooms. Sandra took the opportunity to remind them to put their phones in their bags and keep them there for the duration.

Sandra didn't have a walkie-talkie, so for once, she wasn't the first to know. In fact, she didn't even realise anything had happened until she heard the sirens.

Sirens were rare in that part of Hobart.

NINE MONTHS EARLIER

Chapter One

GRACE

Summer

'Emma,' Grace said. 'We've talked about this.'

Grace both saw and felt stillness settle over her daughter. Then, like a prisoner caught trying to escape, Emma unbent her right knee, stepped out of her lunge and turned to face her mum.

'Emma,' Grace said again. 'Oh, Em. Honey.' Where had *honey* come from? She'd never used that term. It was as if they were in an American teledrama. Maybe she was hoping for the simple, uplifting ending.

'I'm just exercising, Mum!' Emma said. 'Fuck!'

That sort of language might have made Grace smother a laugh, in a parallel universe. Swearing that way just didn't work when your crop-top had slightly too-long straps, and you were standing next to your floating shelf of *Harry Potter* books. 'Emma's going through a phase,' her parallel-universe self could have said, while she sipped a merry glass of wine with a lovably imperfect friend. 'Testing boundaries. Taking risks. Ha-de-ha, I'm dying of stress, pass the bottle, how's *your* mean-ager?'

But nothing much was funny about her daughter at the moment.

'Emma. Sweetie.' What was the perfect combination of words? What phrase set a boundary yet didn't shame? Which sentence strengthened the mother–daughter relationship without endorsing the behaviour?

5

I accept you exactly as you are, but I wish you were different?
I know you can't help it, but you have to help it a bit?
I am here for you, but I'm not sure I can cope?

'I know you're not to blame,' said Grace. Because Emma had an illness. 'I love you. I want to help you. But as you know, our rules are—'

'What are you even talking about? I am *exercising*! God's *sake*!' Emma brandished her phone, where a beautiful twenty-something in false eyelashes and expensive activewear had been paused mid-knee-extension. 'Seven million VIEWS!' She made the last word loudest, the way she'd done since she was a little girl. *I not TIRED. Me more SAUCE.* 'This is what people *do*!'

'I want to help you,' Grace repeated. 'You know you mustn't exercise alone.' Very level. 'You know what the consequence is.'

Pretend you're at work, she told herself. *When a creature is upset, it lashes out. Just turn off a part of your mind and get on with it.*

'You now cannot have your phone till tomorrow,' said Grace. 'You need to give it to me.' She held out her hand.

'No,' said Emma.

Pretend this is a girl you don't know, from a different home, with a different mother. Pretend there's absolutely no way it could be your fault.

'Either you can give it to me, or I will take it.' She stepped towards her daughter.

Emma held the phone out to the side of her body, away from Grace.

'Emma,' Grace said. Emma – foolish, un-strategic, fifteen-year-old Emma – moved back, literally into a corner. She was now standing next to her laundry basket. 'If you don't give your phone to me, I'll need to take it.'

At work, there was a never-needed protocol for physical confrontation, which Grace sometimes skim-read while she waited for her computer to get itself ready for action. She would try to use verbal de-escalation, but if that proved impossible then she would retreat from danger and could dial triple zero, and yes, it might be unpleasant, but a calm voice would tell her that help was on its way, and afterwards there would be no sense that *she* had done anything wrong. She would be the *victim*. The *survivor*. The dedicated professional who'd been threatened while healing (or at least, desexing) the beloved pets of decent, hard-working families. She wouldn't be a middle-aged single mum who had no idea what to do and was in a pickle because of her own bloody stupid life choices.

Emma crossed her arms tight against her chest. Her phone was in something like a fist, almost under her armpit.

'Get. Out. Mum.'

Grace paused, then said, 'I'm coming to take your phone now.'

'I don't consent to this,' screeched Emma. She started to run past Grace, towards the door. Grace grabbed Emma's upper arm, stepped behind her and wrapped her own arms and one leg around her daughter. Emma kicked and scrabbled; a sneakered heel made painful contact with Grace's shin. Grace scraped her fingertips around the phone. Music that made her think of drug dealers and pole dancing and moustaches (that troublingly seemed to be fashionable again) started to thump out of it as she yanked it from Emma's grippy hand.

Grace ran into the bathroom, hesitated and then locked the door behind her. The horrible music was louder in there, and it took her a moment to work out what she needed to do to pause it.

Silence.

Grace's reflection in the mirror looked surprised to find itself calling, calmly, 'Try to take some deep breaths, Em.'

But Emma was already sobbing quiet, remorseful tears. The psychologist had said to let Emma self-soothe, though, because comforting her might reinforce the unwanted behaviour. So, Grace did not speak. (Nobody had really talked about *her* feelings, or maybe it was just that she never properly listened to those bits.)

She turned on the tap, wet one of her hands. Patted water onto her face. She watched as droplets formed larger, odd-shaped puddles on the white vanity. Her kicked shin started to hurt – or she started to notice it – and she sat down on the closed lid of the toilet. She wondered what to do next. She was also thinking: *Please, no. No more.*

∞

Emma had been an easy baby. She slept through the night from very early on, which Grace had believed was due to their home's calm atmosphere and her own additive-free diet. (She at least knew to keep that belief secret.)

Emma smiled at six weeks, sat unsupported at seven months, and soon became – as her kindergarten report helpfully pointed out – capable of hopping on both her right foot and her left foot. Her psychological development seemed fine, too: she Always showed care and empathy, and Usually attempted to resolve conflict in a positive manner. ('Much like us, then, Grace?' Christopher – Emma's dad – had said with a smile.)

Grace had been prepared to feel like an outcast single mum among the Baxter Street Primary School community, but it was quickly apparent that at least a quarter of the preps had separated parents, and that the teacher was too busy wrangling nut allergies to notice – let alone form an opinion about – the fact that Grace and Christopher had never even been in a relationship.

Throughout primary school, Emma wasn't a particularly fussy eater; she tended not to lose expensive runners; she didn't lie or steal or bite, although she did once yell, 'DICK-BOY!' at a fellow Grade

One kid who'd cheated at soccer. ('That was a bit over the top, Em,' Grace had said. And then – non-shamingly – 'So, where'd you hear that word?')

From the age of six, Emma happily spent every second week at Christopher's place; at eight she had a best friend called Nellie; at ten she got a yellow belt in karate and they went out for pizza to celebrate. Her Grade Six report said she was friendly to her peers, and performed As Expected when forming concepts and generalisations. ('What do you think that means?' Christopher had asked Grace with genuine curiosity. 'At the eleven-year-old level?')

It was when Emma was twelve that Grace started to think something was wrong. At first, she told herself she was just being silly. That was easy enough. There was so much stuff about neurotic women and helicopter parents and mothers who thought parenting was the same as their career and (despicably, it seemed) stuck up too strongly for their child's interests. And she was forty-three, and single, and professional, and Emma was her only child. So, from what Grace could tell, she was almost bound to be an annoyingly over-attentive mum.

That was maybe why, when Emma started being a bit funny about breakfast, Grace had told herself to stop worrying. And also, she'd hoped she was wrong. As you did. She'd *hoped* she was neurotic. She'd hoped she was silly. She'd hoped, for the first time in her life, that she was too emotional and her judgement was clouded. She'd hoped that any objective health professional would chuckle and cry, 'Oh no! Grace! That's perfectly normal at this age! Perfectly! Normal! Goodness me!'

But then – Emma had already turned thirteen – Grace had found herself in a GP's office, with her throat closing and then too-suddenly opening as she'd started explaining about the lunches, and the dinners, and all the stuff before bed, and the doctor had slid the box of tissues towards her and said, not, 'Don't be silly, you irrational creature,' but, 'Probably good you've come in.'

And there had been a white plastic step-stool in one corner, and a poster about asthma puffers on a wall, and he'd started talking about risk assessment and mood disturbance as if she'd already known all about it, as if her main priority was finding a good psychologist with a not-too-long waiting list, when really what she had been thinking was: *Are you saying my daughter's got something* wrong *with her? Because let me tell you, mate, there's* nothing, *nothing* at all *wrong with my beautiful little girl.*

∞

'Feeling okay?' Grace said, as they waited. It was four days after the phone confiscation.

The psychologist's office was in a lovely old building, the sandstone-fronted type that everyone said gave Hobart character. Inside, there were quiet corridors, a zigzag staircase with a dark wooden banister, and shinily black-painted doors. Emma's psychologist was behind door number six.

'I'm good. Thanks, Mum.'

Near the chairs where the two of them waited, was a wooden table that always held a miraculously healthy maidenhair fern and piles of pamphlets about things like Feldenkrais movement workshops (Heal from within!), Shakespeare in the Gardens (Experience his most hysterical comedy!) and Bree's Beauty Studio (Achieve your brow goals!).

Often, while Emma was having her solo chat, Grace would find herself wondering how enough people had enough energy to support businesses that provided Feldenkrais and Shakespeare and even, to be honest, eyebrow grooming. All that healing and experiencing and achieving. She had definitely never had a brow goal in her life.

In fact, just how widespread was brow-goal setting?

'Emma,' said the psychologist. 'Grace. Come on in.'

Emma's psychologist – Dr Claire Tait – specialised in eating disorders. She had goal-actualised eyebrows, artfully messy blonde hair and an apparently inexhaustible collection of linen shell tops. She tended to wear them with dull-silver earrings, slim black trousers and wholesome, expensive-looking shoes.

Grace usually wore her work clothes, which involved a dark-green smock-shirt that had *Hobart Animal Care* embroidered in light-green letters on the front, and matching green trousers. Also: pilled black socks and shoes designed for camping. It wasn't so much that Grace didn't care about clothes. It was just that the train of stylish women had swished away from the station right around the time Emma was born, and it was very hard to work out how to get back on board.

'You asked to be squeezed in?' said Dr Claire, with what appeared to be genuine concern. As usual, she was sitting in an easy chair, with a laptop on a swivelling table to her right. Behind her, a large window with leadlight panels along its top opened onto a cluster of silver birch trees. Above them rose the mountain, all unapologetic dolerite and vast wildness. (It was pretty much always around somewhere, though. The mountain – kunanyi/Mount Wellington – was as central, and as complex, as an ageing mother.)

Emma swallowed and seemed about to speak, but didn't, and Dr Claire glanced at Grace, who explained in her most neutral voice that Emma had once again been feeling compelled to exercise alone.

'I see.' Dr Claire nodded. 'Emma?' Her tone was very pleasant. Matesy, almost.

When Emma didn't respond, Dr Claire said, 'Maybe a part of you doesn't want to exercise, but another part is telling you to?'

'At the end of the day, I just think, I have to go to school tomorrow, and … actually, I don't even *think*, I just …' Emma trailed off.

Dr Claire asked a lot of questions, her eyes moving between mother and daughter. Soon, Grace would be sent out. It was surprisingly hard, the way Emma would tell a professional things that she, Grace, wasn't privy to. It hurt her feelings, which was ridiculous.

'And what's going on friendship-wise?' Dr Claire said, at some point.

For the first time, there was a very long silence.

'A few mean kids.' Emma's voice was like a stretching thread of plasticine. She looked at her mum.

'How about if you wait outside, Grace?'

After what seemed like much longer than the seventeen minutes it actually took, Dr Claire invited Grace back in, and as soon as Grace was seated, she said, 'It seems we have some fairly significant issues with bullying.'

Emma's blue eyes were huge and beautiful and surrounded by red skin.

'Oh, Em,' said Grace. Dr Claire was still talking. She was saying things about sense of agency and pervasive problem, but none of her words seemed terribly important right at that moment. 'But what's going on?' said Grace. 'Emma? Sweetie? Is ... how's Nellie? Lucy? How are all the girls?'

'I'm not really friends with that group anymore, Mum,' said Emma. 'I'm not really into the same things as them.' It would have been a horrifying speech, so brave and fake-casual, even without the word 'them'.

'Social acceptance is very important for adolescent girls,' intoned Dr Claire. 'Its absence can be harmful, including in the longer term.'

Grace nodded. *Yes*, she thought. *Thank you. No effing kidding.*

Dr Claire said, 'There was a situation where Emma's schoolbag was placed in the boys' urinal. Fortunately, one of the boys returned it to Emma. Her pencil case has had obscene insults and threats written on it. She received an SMS instructing her to "finish the job", which Emma took to be an allusion to her formerly medically unstable state, an encouragement to end her own life. Texts from young people she previously considered friends, saying, among other things, Kiss.' When Grace looked blank, Dr Claire explained, almost lightly, 'K-Y-S, I meant. It's an acronym for Kill Your Self.'

'Jesus Christ.' Grace spoke quietly, and without meaning to. She wanted to add, *I asked you about this stuff, Emma! Just last week, you said Lucy was fine. Why didn't you tell me?*

She felt like storming into the school office and making a scene. 'How could you let this happen?' she could yell at Min, the pinkish-haired receptionist. 'Take off your CIA-style headset and your fake-perky expression, and lead me to the principal this instant!' (She'd had her doubts about the principal for years, ever since she'd seen him texting during a Year Eight assembly. You could tell from the way he was smiling that it was a non-work-related text.)

Dr Claire was saying things about ongoing fortnightly appointments and sticking with the Family Management Plan approach to Emma's eating disorder. 'But—' She appeared to hesitate, then said, 'Grace, you and Christopher possibly want to consider your options, in terms of Emma's schooling.'

Grace thought about resilience and challenges. She thought about a schoolbag – one with a sparkly 'E' keyring on its zipper, one with a cherished, Christmas-present laptop inside – ending up in a urinal.

If Emma grew up – if she did – and if she ever had a partner who meted out that kind of abuse, Grace would say, 'Leave. Leave now. Leave while you still know it's wrong. Leave, leave, leave, leave, leave.'

Emma was getting out of that school.

Chapter Two

ZOE

Summer

I thought Daniel was acting weird because he was about to propose.

'Zoe,' he said, as he finished wiping the bench. That was one of the weird things. The way he'd jumped up and started cleaning as soon as we'd finished our toast, even though it was Sunday. 'An opportunity has come up for me. A big project.' He made a serious-newsreader face from across the white benchtop.

'Wow, great!' I thought he was about to start talking about grabbing hold of opportunities together forever and all that. I put my coffee down and rested my hands in my lap with as much elegance as possible. This was not a lot. I was wearing an old mauve silk slip, flannel pyjama bottoms and ugg boots.

Daniel draped the cloth carefully over the tap – also weird – and came to sit near me. We were facing the well-swept-by-Daniel outdoor area of our apartment. I thought: *Well, I definitely don't want to end up with his surname. Dickson. Eek.*

'It's a twenty-four-month contract,' he said. 'At least. Working on a dam. Big hydroelectricity scheme.' He clasped his hands, regretfully, on the table. 'Near Vancouver.'

'Wow.' I sat up straighter. I – this was so embarrassing – sort of tossed my hair and adjusted my lips so as to look like the best possible let's-take-on-Canada-as-man-and-wife version of myself.

He still didn't open his mouth, so I said, 'I *love* Vancouver. Well!

I did when I was in Year Eleven. North Vancouver, especially. There was this really amazing op shop, thrift shop as they called it, and – well, anyway. Great!'

I gave his thigh a pat, all supportive-1950s-wifeish, and then left another pause. Hands back in lap, spine still straight, trying to be like Keira Knightley when she was doing that humble, interested expression that made her so beautiful you just wanted to die.

Three people had told me I looked like Keira Knightley. They were being nice, because I wasn't that beautiful. Also, I was much chubbier than she was. Not that I thought being chubbier than Keira Knightley was a bad thing, and of course I realised nobody would ever say, *You look like a plus-size, and also not-as-beautiful version of Keira Knightley.* But that would be truer.

Daniel uncrossed his legs. 'I think it's abundantly clear, Zoe, that it'd be foolish for you to come.'

'How do you mean?' I thought he was going to tell me there weren't many jobs for Australian art teachers in Canada, or visas were going to be a sticking point, or most of all that it'd make our plans for a family tricky, so maybe we should go long distance and meet up in Hawaii or New York sometimes. And that then he'd probably propose on a tropical beach at sunset, or in a romantic bit of Central Park with no rubbish or muggers.

'I think you'd have to characterise our relationship as one that's run its course,' he said. 'If we're being honest.'

Goddy-god-god. 'I beg your pardon?'

'Zoe, we have to face a brutal reality.' He tilted his face up towards me: I'd stood without realising it. My chair had fallen over. 'Sometimes situations evolve, and then you realise … well. Zoe. I wouldn't want to impede your prospects.'

'Why are you using so many stupid words?'

I was suddenly talking in a high, angry way. Maybe it was what people meant when they said *shrieking like a shrew*. As if you weren't allowed to show in your voice that you were hurt or afraid or angry. As if that made you bad. 'What are you actually *saying*?'

'I'm sorry, Zoe,' he said. He did sound sorry. But sorry for *me*, because he was a good, kind man who'd made sure the sink was empty before he smashed up my life. He wasn't devastated. He wasn't upset for *himself*.

I barely realised that I had let my coffee cup fall onto the tiles. The cup didn't break, oddly. Only the coffee spilled. I put a hand onto the back of a chair – not the one I'd knocked over – and properly saw his face. He was watching me with this odd, caring expression, as if he was starring in a 'How to Break Up Well' education video.

'Is there someone else?' I said.

'Nothing's happened,' he replied. But the 'yet' soaked everything in the room.

And then there was a long, tearful time where I screamed things like 'Who is she?' and he answered all my questions in a slow, reasonable way, as if he had spreadsheets that could prove every single point he made. He promised I wouldn't be 'financially disadvantaged', and he said we could keep living together as long as I needed, because the spare room was 'spacious'. As if I cared about the size of rooms. As if he had every right to leave me, because we weren't married, and so he'd never actually *promised* me anything. Even though I was a 24-year-old student when I met him, and now I was a 34-year-old teacher. Even though we had shared friends and a shared lease and a whole lot of other shared things I couldn't even bear to begin thinking about. Even though our lives were, in so many ways, the same life.

The woman was someone from work. She also had an interest in sustainable energy. She was twenty-six. I asked him if she was pretty, and he said, 'Zoe, let's not go down that path.' Like I was being bitchy and insecure and annoying. Like youth and prettiness of *course* never had anything to do with anything. Like these scenarios were always just about abundantly clear and running its course and hydro-fucking-electricity.

When I finished yelling, and he finished being calm and compassionate, I rang my cousin Claire and told her, and she said, 'Really? *Really?*' quite a few times. Then she pulled herself together and said, 'Well, god-goddy-god-god. I'm on my way.'

∞

I stood in Claire's kitchen, with my legs apart and my right thumb in my left fist. Claire was making tea. She had a splodge of greenish clay still clinging to the skin near her hairline, because she'd come to get me without rinsing her face mask off properly.

Claire's partner, T-rex, was moving a pile of his folders and neatly rolled computer cords out of their second bedroom. They were both acting purposeful and hushed, as if they were my assistants, I was the US President, and we were all smack bang in the middle of a serious international disaster that happened to be taking place in a very small North Hobart flat.

'I've opened the sofa bed,' said T-rex. He tilted his head towards the teeny bedroom. 'In case you wanted to lie down, Zoe.' T-rex was called that because he was massively tall – around six foot five – and at one point, he'd apparently had enormous gnashy-looking braces. Also, he was vegetarian.

'Thank you so much!' Something was wrong with my voice. I sounded overeager. Super grateful. As if I was the cousin who had to sleep in the worst bedroom of a manor house and do all the icky chores for her rich, well-bred relatives. Maybe I'd been watching too much *Downton Abbey*. In a normal way I added, 'That sounds fine and dandy.'

Fine and dandy, I repeated to myself. The words began to lose all meaning, but they were the only thing my mind could hold on to. *Fine and dandy. Fine and dandy. Fine and dandy.*

∞

I decided to keep right on working, even though everyone I knew – especially Mum, and my brother's wife in Brisbane, and even more especially Claire – thought I should take sick leave.

'You *are* sick,' said Claire, helpfully, on the Monday morning. 'In a way.'

Claire was a psychologist, and despite the fact that she was sitting on the edge of the bath, squinting at her own lily-white legs and eating peanut butter on toast, she made her voice sound as if she was giving professional advice.

'I'm okay, Claire.' I spat out my toothpaste and frowned into the mirror. 'Life just throws up challenges.'

'You've suffered a *loss*.'

'I'm aware.' I tried to sound breezy, but failed.

'Well.' She held her toast out of the way while she flipped her whole head up and down to boof up her fuzzy blonde curls. 'It's your choice, Zo. But Lofton School is certainly not going to implode if you take the day off. Nobody is indispensab—'

'I *know*.' I banged my toothbrush, hard, on the edge of the sink. 'And you can stop flicking your hair around. We all know it's nice.'

'You sound pretty angry.' Also very helpfully.

'I'm *fine*! This is just a *challenge*!'

There was silence while I noticed that at this time of the day, Claire's mirror showed up a whole lot of lines around my eyes that my own mirror never had. That made me remember we were in her bathroom, I was using her toothpaste – which was the grainy-tasting, health-food-shop type – and she was maybe waiting to brush her own teeth.

18

'Sorry.' I rinsed my toothbrush in a thorough, self-conscious way. 'Sorry. It's really nice of you and T-rex to let me stay here, and I'll … get out of your way as soon as I can.'

'Stay as long as you want, Zo.' She'd finished her toast and was sucking peanut butter off her fingers. 'I got cows' milk for you. Not that there's anything wrong with almond, in my opinion.'

'Oh,' I said. 'Thanks. Thanks very much.'

That was when I started crying. I knew T-rex would be able to hear, but I couldn't help it. The wailing seemed to begin at a tiny point inside my chest, and gush out through all my pores and my nostrils and my throat. And even though a part of me knew all too well that there was nothing to be done except to wait for the pain to be over, that part was very tiny and was standing well off to one side. Most of me was just in agony.

Claire tucked me back into her surprisingly comfortable sofa bed and then she rang in sick for me. I could tell that being right gave her absolutely no pleasure, which was one of the many really wonderful things about Claire.

Chapter Three

GRACE

Summer

'We simply can't consider it, Grace,' Christopher said.

The two of them were drinking – or at least, sitting with – wine on her narrow verandah. Emma was slumped inside at the dining table, a maths textbook open in front of her.

'High school's about learning. Including learning to manage difficult people,' Christopher went on. Then he said some other things, his tone informative, as if he was delivering the finance segment of the TV news.

Grace waited for him to finish. Christopher tended to make the same point a number of times, using slightly different words. He had narrow shoulders that hunched up as he spoke, then lowered when he finished.

She looked at the pot of thyme straggling away on her porch, and thought at least she and Christopher were on amicable terms. At least he cared about Emma, and wasn't violent, or insolvent, or addicted to any one of the many things it seemed a person could be addicted to. Her co-parent, her daughter's father, her one-night stand that had become a multi-year sort-of friendship: he was a good man. This sort of conversation with Christopher was not just a First World problem. It was a very privileged subsection of the First World problem.

'I mean, we need to be the ones who show leadership here,' he was saying now. 'And, yes, I appreciate your concerns, and they're not invalid, but perhaps what's needed is a new skill set.' He paused. 'Michael West's kids are all doing fine there. He and Sarah are more than happy. More than happy, they were his exact words.'

'The psychologist thinks—'

'But does having a psychology degree *actually* give her special insight into Emma? Into schooling?'

'—she says this sort of *abuse* could have long-term consequences, and that—'

'But does it, Grace? Does it really give her any special insight?' Christopher was doing his patient face, as if he was a famous wellness coach, when in fact he was a legal adviser for the Department of Primary Industries.

'It's just Emma was doing so much better.' She'd even allowed herself to hope – in a very secret way, so as not to jinx it – that Emma's illness might be over. The memory of her own ridiculous optimism was what made the tears come into her eyes.

'Now look. Grace. It's natural that, as a mother, you want to protect her from life's bumps, but—'

'Someone wrote on her pencil case about *raping* her,' Grace said. No tears now. Never any actual, falling-down tears. 'So, yes, Christopher, you're right, I want to *fucking* protect her.'

Christopher gave a fastidious little shiver, as if Grace had been rude to a senior citizen. 'This is what I mean,' he said. 'About keeping things rational.'

Grace set her wine in front of her and closed her eyes. She literally took a breath, and then repeated that she wanted to consider a different school.

'Maybe Pardalote?' she said. It was a small school, with a touchy-feely reputation and a focus on student wellbeing. Presumably it was for well-off hippies; she imagined drop-off would be rife with electric cars and rescued greyhounds.

'Absolutely not, unless we want to be paying through our noses for magic fairy drops and circle dancing. Do they even follow the national curricul—'

'*Chris*topher.' Grace held up her hand. 'Please.'

At least some of what she was feeling must have penetrated his brain, because he frowned and let his shoulders relax. He put his wine next to hers and leaned forward.

'Pardalote,' he said, with a perplexed shake of his head. 'I'll consider it.' He held up his index finger. 'Because you're asking me to. But that's all I'm promising.' Then he checked his watch and said he was sorry but he really had to go to indoor soccer or his team would have to forfeit. He drained every last droplet from his wineglass and stood up to leave.

Grace stood too, so they were next to each other, and thanked him for the chat.

'Are you okay, Grace? Because you seem a bit ...' He frowned at her glass. It was still almost full. 'A bit low?'

'Just tired.'

Obviously, that statement was never completely true – and it was very far from the truth on that particular evening – but Christopher seemed to believe her. He nodded once and said she was probably due an early night.

'Understandable,' he added, flicking a thumb at the window in the general direction of Emma. 'All this.'

Grace nodded. It'd be bad enough if that *was* all of it.

'Thanks again, Christopher,' she said.

He wasn't a bad man. He was a very, very good one. It was just that he knew nothing about anything.

'Grace!' said Maria. 'Sorry to grab you as soon as you're through the door, but I've just had' – she lowered her voice – 'Maddie Micari on the phone, you know, from yesterday, and Banjo is worse, not better, so I thought you'd want to see him, and I've squeezed him in, at midday, which makes it very tight, because you've got that extraction, but I thought that'd be all right?'

'Yep, fine.' Grace crossed behind the reception desk, scratched Max the practice cat under his collar, and took her stethoscope and a head torch out of her pigeonhole.

'And also, Olico left a message, and the Revamite Tens are out of stock till the end of the month, I've emailed you a list of alternatives, but we're running pretty low, so you might want to decide this morning.'

'Okay.' Grace bent towards the filing cabinet, flicked through to a manilla folder labelled GRACE TIERNEY and extracted her mail. These days, everything important – certainly all the bills – came electronically, and there was only an ad for veterinarian indemnity insurance and what appeared to be a short novel about a new range of dietary supplements for horses. She gave the drawer the slightest tilt to the right as she knocked it closed, and it shut properly first time. She threw the brochures into the recycling tub.

'And can you let me know what you want to do about the Easter holidays?' Maria was now walking with her down the pale-grey linoleumed corridor. Like Grace, she was wearing a dark-green smock-and-trouser outfit, but Maria – who was sixty-six and indefatigably attentive to grooming – also had large gold hoops, expertly rolled-up blonde hair and tasteful false eyelashes. Grace had often wondered if Maria's fashion choices were related to her hobby (ballroom dancing) or to her former profession (hairdressing). 'I know it's early, but April'll be here before we know it, and we don't want you all away at the same time, zero vets, total disaster, I still have conniptions about two thousand and seventeen.'

'Will do,' Grace said. Certain clients seemed to think vets were rolling in money, but there was no way that she, or her business, could afford for her take the two full weeks off. 'And have we heard from the Masons? About their Saint Bernard?'

'Orlando. He died last night, I've sent you a message, they were really grateful, I told them you'd probably call them, but do the Revamite stuff first, if you wouldn't mind, I have to get the order in by ten, please, can I get you a tea?'

It was tempting to say yes. Even though she didn't particularly want tea right that minute, there was a lot of pleasure in having someone else make her a cup, now and again. They heard a beep and a series of bangs that meant a client was trying to manoeuvre a large cage in through the front door, despite the sign advising that large cages should be brought around the back.

'No, but thanks.' Grace flicked on her room's light and adjusted the thermostat.

'And Renee says that echidna's still not feeding properly, but that's probably just Renee being Renee.' Maria took a dim view of the amount of volunteering Derinya Wildlife Park 'squeezed out' of Grace, who, in Maria's opinion, worked quite hard enough running the business, especially considering she was the single mother of a daughter with *Issues*.

'Thanks, Maria.' Grace reached across her desk to turn on the computer. 'I'll give Derinya a buzz.'

Work, at least, was always eminently manageable.

∞

Grace was on her way out to Derinya to check again on the echidna and to euthanise an injured pelican, when Christopher rang.

'How's she going?' he said.

'Oh, well. You know.'

It had been another horrible morning, preceded by another horrible evening. Ages at the dinner table. The smells of what Grace had learned to call 'purging'.

Christopher said, 'Little Emma. Remember that brontosaurus-shaped hat she used to wear?'

'I do, Christopher.' It was impossible to keep all the emotion out of the *do*.

He said – rather quietly – that he'd been doing some 'solid' research and perhaps the psychologist had a point, but he simply didn't feel Pardalote was a suitable choice.

'Far too eccentric,' he said. Then, tuttily, 'Spelling mistakes on the *website*, and yes, I'm sure they're all very well intentioned, but there's simply no substitute for a proper education.'

Up in front of her, a car hooted and Grace braked automatically.

'So, what were you thinking?' she said.

'Well, Lofton's got to be the obvious choice.'

She had her answer ready.

'It's too big. It's too spread out. They have about a thousand campuses. It'll be full of kids who think Porsches are normal cars. And the mums will all …' Even though she'd prepared for this, she found that she was running out of steam. She actually didn't know what the mums would be like. The phrase *They'll all play tennis* came into her head, but that had to be wrong. No mothers – even Lofton ones – seemed to play tennis anymore.

'There are *three* campuses,' he said. 'And Porsches are excellent cars. Remarkably safe.'

She gave a little nose-clear of laughter, because she was pretty sure he was joking. She said, 'I really don't think—' But she was remembering last winter, when Emma had insisted on running in the garden every evening after her so-called dinner. Nothing could convince Emma to stop, and one Thursday she had collapsed onto the cold, dark lawn.

Grace had had to call an ambulance. Grace had had to check for a pulse. The emergency-department specialist – a Dr Tristan O'Leary – had told them Emma was 'medically and psychiatrically unstable'. Grace had said, *No fucking kidding* out loud, that time.

'Grace? You there?'

Grace replied with some things about Catholic schools, or single-sex schools, but Christopher was having none of it.

'Fine,' she said in the end. 'Let's look at Lofton. If you think.'

Oh, God.

Christopher said very good, he'd arrange a tour and put it in the joint calendar. They were about to hang up when she said, 'Christopher?'

'Yeah?' He sounded as brightly cautious as a new employee.

'You're a really good dad.'

'Well. Thank you. That's certainly very nice of you to say, Grace.'

'It's true.' Then she said she had to go, and after she hung up, she pushed the thought of Lofton away, and instead reflected on the pleasure in Christopher's voice for a whole block of nose-to-tail traffic. He'd sounded so earnest. So very *gratified*.

She herself didn't have a dad, even though several people had told her, *But of course you have a father, Grace*, as if that was a remarkable piece of wisdom that had never before occurred to her. But she'd never known who or where the man who helped conceive her was, and as far as she remembered, she'd literally never cared. (In fact, she kept waiting for the urge to know to strike her, but here she was – forty-bloody-six – and it still hadn't.)

Which she knew made a neat little parcel out of the situation she found herself in. Those *but of course* people probably thought she had an absent father and low expectations and no male archetype and a subsequent inability to form fulfilling emotional attachments.

Grace thought that was rubbish. Plenty of people without dads ended up with nice, normal partners. Plenty of people without dads didn't do what she did.

People did worse things. They presided over companies that killed dolphins. They screamed racist insults at football players. They chucked their parents in nursing homes and stole their money and never visited.

But sometimes it struck her that she didn't actually know any of those people. She wasn't friends with any of them. *She* was the worst person she knew.

∞

'Hiya,' said Grace. She put the bathroom-bin bag into the main kitchen bin and rinsed her hands. 'Emma?'

Emma didn't reply. She was busy deploying her thumbs.

'Em, your dad and I have been thinking,' Grace said. 'Emma! Can you put that thing down for five seconds, please?'

'Fine.' Emma's tone was that of an oppressed woman who'd spent selfless years fighting for justice and would continue to do so despite any number of imbecilic interruptions. She laid her phone patiently on the coffee table, and then let her overworked hands dollop onto her lap. 'What, Mother-dear?'

'Your dad and I have been thinking,' Grace repeated. She took a seat on the couch next to her daughter. Afternoon sunlight slanted in, making the black television screen too bright to look at. 'About your school situation.'

'Yeah?' A bit of the poise went out of Emma. Grace felt she had her full attention for the first time that day.

'We both, your dad and I, are very concerned …' Emma was staring at her with a face like a tree trunk. Where had her tender-hearted girl gone? The girl who used to say, *Mummy, now I'm going to give you forty or more kisses?* The girl who'd wanted so much to be an Ancktarticka scientist? '… about the bullying.'

'Okay.' Emma turned her eyes down to her own lap.

'So, we're thinking about Lofton. For the, you know, they seem to have quite a good set-up. Lots of music and a lovely arts program and good pastoral care.' As if that would sell it to a teenager. Not that Grace was trying to sell it, as such. 'We just thought you might be happier there. That's the main thing.'

'Have you already decided?' said Emma. There was an astute flick in her voice that even *Grace* could tell was one hundred per cent Grace.

'No. Not at all! Your dad and I simply want to meet with them, to ask questions, and we're also wanting to know what you think.'

'Well, I think I'm never going to be like *you*.'

'Pardon?'

'You know, Mum, I'm never going to be like you. I don't even want to be. Even if I could!'

'What do you mean?' God, it was true that your kids could gut you quicker than anyone.

'The way you *work* and …' Emma flicked her eyes accusingly at the stove. '… *cook*. Even everything you *cook* is perfect. Nutritional and … No judgement, Mum, but I personally don't particularly *need* to be like that.'

'It sounds as if you're feeling—' she started.

'And I'm not just a fifteen-year-old girl managing an eating disorder, you know. I'm *me*!' She sounded as if she'd just listened to a podcast. One about honouring your feelings and not being defined by others' expectations.

'I know that.' Grace made her voice as gentle as she could, and hopefully in a non-condescending way. 'Would …?'

'I'm not your *project*. No one's going to give you a prize if I turn out amazing. I know you think I'm dumb, and a *loser*, but *I* just want to Turn. Out. Normal.'

'I don't think you're "dumb" at all. And you're not a loser.' This was so unjust. She had never pressured Emma to achieve academically, had always told her that doing her best was what mattered, and lately, she hadn't even said that. 'I just … just … I want you to, you know, to fulfil your potential, and … and to be happy, and to … to get away from those … *bitches*, those absolute *fucking* little bitches, and stay *alive*.'

Grace heard her own loud breathing in the silence. She knew she wasn't supposed to talk like that. She was the mother. The parent. The one who was supposed to be calm, accepting and reflective. Also stable and balanced and present. She should have said something like, 'It sounds as if you're feeling I pressure you?'

Emma was still looking down at her lap, but not sitting up straight anymore. She was nodding, tiny, fast nods.

'Please, don't *you* cry, Mum,' she said, after a moment, in an astounded, and very small, voice. She put her hand on Grace's back. 'It's all right.'

Grace cleared her throat and made her mind zip past a memory of Emma, lying on the emergency-department bed with a pale-green drip in her left arm and a series of circular white stickers across her breastless chest. She pictured instead a psychologist-approved tall, steady tree, and waved her hands around in a way that indicated nobody should worry about silly old her.

'I'm fine,' she said, as soon as she could.

Outside, they heard the man across the road wheeling his bin along the driveway. When he finished, Emma took her hand away.

'Hey, Mum?' she said presently, and in a different sort of voice.

'Yes, sweetie?'

'Are you ... Do you ... Do you have a partner?'

'Pardon?' Grace said. Where on earth had that come from? She was still only just pulling herself together.

'I was just *won*dering.' Defensively.

'Oh. Well.'

Grace once had overheard two of the other vets laughing about how their kids sometimes asked them questions they were unprepared for. Questions about *sex* and erections, and goodness, even pornography! Grace had wondered what they were on about. She'd read the *Smart Choices: Communicating with Your Kids About Sex* guidelines, and it wasn't rocket science: answer the question that was asked, be honest about what you didn't know and leave pauses for the 'young person' to ask more. She'd first talked with Emma about sex years ago, and – as per the handbook – more than once. She'd used the proper words: penises and vaginas; sperm and eggs.

'I guess I ... I don't ... I mean, you probably remember how I used to go on the odd date and things. I just never really met the right person, I guess,' Grace said.

She'd always hoped that as Emma grew up, they'd develop a confiding, woman-to-woman relationship. But how old did your daughter have to be before you admitted to being in love with a married man? To being the other woman, to being an unforgivable bitch, to feeling sick with shame, or else horrified by your lack of shame, every single second of every single day? These, unfortunately, were not among the handbook's cheery-font FAQs. 'Why do you ask?'

'No reason,' said Emma. She gave her mum a quick sideways look. 'No judgement. Just wondering.'

'Are you bothered that I'm single or something?'

'No.'

'Because you seem a bit—'

'Mum! I was just *ask*ing.'

'Okay,' said Grace, meekly. But after a few seconds she added, 'Because if someone's said something—'

'*Mum!*'

'It's nobody's business, is all I was going to say. And if anyone has anything to say about ... that subject, you can tell them exactly that.'

'Nobody's even asking, Mum.' Emma shook her head at the ceiling, as if the idea of her mother's romantic life being of interest to one single other normal person on the planet was beyond ridiculous.

'Anyway.' Grace cleared her throat with admirable – though, obviously, unappreciated – steadiness. 'What do you reckon? About changing schools? About Lofton?'

In her head, Grace could still hear the regularly irregular beep of that heart monitor. She could still hear Dr Tristan O'Leary as he spoke with a competent sort of relentlessness about Emma's critically low potassium levels and her risk of cardiac arrest.

'If you think,' Emma said. She flipped her ponytail with an imitation of nonchalance that caused an actual, physical throb in the region of Grace's own heart. Her voice was like a confession when she said, 'Yes, actually, Mum. Yes. Please.'

CORONIAL COURT OF TASMANIA
GENERAL INFORMATION

In circumstances of unexpected, violent or suspicious deaths, and in instances where the cause of death is unknown, the coroner is required to investigate.

The coroner's court is not an adversarial, but rather, an inquisitorial one. As such, the coroner's role is to make various findings, without apportioning blame for the death.

The coroner makes findings of fact from which others may draw conclusions.

Chapter Four

IMOGEN

Autumn

This was how the emergency department looked.

There were always people moving across the floor. The floor was off white, and it had a pleasant, subtle glow that hardly anyone noticed. On that floor were yellow A-frame signs, non-ironically saying DANGER CLEANING IN PROGRESS, non-ironically telling us not to slip over as we walked – always as quickly as we could – between the person who'd just had the heart attack and the person who was coughing up the blood.

There were cubicles, with curtains that were closed only when something was going on behind them: a spinal tap, a blood test, the giving or procuring of fluids or of information. These curtains adequately blocked sight but inadequately blocked sound. Most of the time they were open, and the patients in the cubicles sat in their beds, facing towards the staff station, which was a horseshoe-shaped desk the size of a classroom. Inside the horseshoe, the other doctors and I calculated drug doses, asked if anyone knew where spare batteries for an ophthalmoscope might be kept, checked computer screens and frowned.

I had formed the opinion that it was a fallacy to think that stress and pressure brought out the best in people, that facing hardship together forged bonds. You only had to read the data about childhood illness and parental divorce to realise that my opinion was correct.

Or you could just spend an hour in that staff station. It was not a very nice place.

∞

'I'm leaving now, Tristan,' I said. Dr Tristan O'Leary was one of my bosses. He was an emergency-department consultant physician, a specialist in emergency medicine, a king of the staff station, of every single cubicle, of the waiting room and the triage desk and the ambulance bays. I was still a resident, which meant I was a lowly junior doctor, and Tristan was nicer to the nurses than he was to me. 'Thank you for today.'

It was fourteen minutes past six, and I'd already removed my ID badge because I was due to have dinner with Nick. I had clothes with me, and they were hanging in the staff toilets. In case you were wondering, there were no staff lockers.

'Imogen.' Tristan had been smiling while talking on the phone to the haematologist, but now he'd stopped. His grey irises snapped and flicked at everything he saw in me. 'Can you take a seat, please?'

I sat. There were frayed remnants of Blu Tack on the edge of the computer screen in front of us, and over Tristan's shoulder, I could see the renal registrar looking something up.

'You've been back with us for over a month now,' Tristan said. 'How do you think this shift has gone for you?'

'Fine, thank you.'

This was apparently one of the informal debriefing sessions my Orientation Manual had alluded to. 'I'm getting excellent learning opportunities here, Tristan, and I obviously still have a way to go, but I'm very grateful.'

I knew how I needed to respond. The Southern Tasmania Hospital was the only public hospital in Hobart, and thus the only place where I could train in emergency medicine. 'And eager to improve!' I added.

One of my early performance reviews – from my internship – had said I needed to develop the skills to communicate appropriately within the cultural framework of medicine. I therefore had worked hard to develop that competency, even though there were clear flaws in that very cultural framework.

'You're punctual and polite – thank you for that. And you obviously have a very good grip of the basics. Excellent theoretical knowledge, in fact.'

I nodded. I sensed there was a 'but' coming. When people's main point was a negative one, they slowed down their opening, complimentary sentences. That might not be empirically proven; I had nonetheless observed it.

'But we need to talk about your time management.' A man – a cardiologist – walked out of one of the cubicles in front of us. Tristan gave him a joking half-salute and then turned to me. 'We generally expect residents to see about ten patients a shift. You've being seeing about six. Six yesterday. Seven today.'

'Oh.' I didn't realise anyone had been watching me in that way. The day before, when I'd left – at seven thirty-three – nobody had even said goodbye.

I got my Sick feeling. A long time ago, someone asked me if I might be able to give that feeling a name, and even though nowadays I knew all about fight-or-flight responses and emotional arousal, I still called it my Sick feeling.

Tristan was looking at me. He had the balls of his feet on the floor, and he was swivelling his chair just a little way from right to left. It made a squeaking sound, like a tiny blade cutting through a green stick. His knees were at least forty-five centimetres apart.

'Um?' I said. I could feel the sweat under my arms, and it was difficult to remember anything useful. 'Um, yesterday?' I said something about the lady with the pancreatitis who'd taken a long time because there was a delay with her bloods, and a 52-year-old man with acute renal failure, who'd had multiple co-morbidities.

'I'm aware some patients are complex,' Tristan said. 'But in general, we expect you to see about ten patients a shift.'

'I'm very sorry. I—'

'The issue,' said Tristan, 'is the ability to form a suitable management plan in a timely way. Theory is all very well, but a doctor at your stage needs to be able to see the wood for the trees, so to speak. To make clinical decisions.'

I nodded. Due to my Sick feeling, I was unable to produce a well-structured reply promptly enough.

'Is there any way this department could better support you to manage your workload?'

I wanted to say, 'By being *nicer*,' but I shook my head and smiled hard. Responding positively to constructive criticism was item four on the list of competencies for emergency-department residents. 'Thank you for your feedback, Tristan.'

'And your lady in twelve, the one with the chest pain. She's on her infusion already, right?'

'Not yet.' I hadn't been sure whether to utilise the standard acute coronary syndrome protocol, because the trials on which that protocol was based were conducted on Caucasian males over forty-five, and this patient was a 44-year-old Malaysian woman.

I wished to explain my logic, but Tristan stood up so quickly that his maroon wheelie chair rolled back.

'That should have been started twenty minutes ago. Let's go. Right now.' He whipped his thumb and forefinger through the air, to imply I should walk quickly. I had to pass right in front of him. The renal registrar glanced up from her drug chart at us. 'Where're you at with her bloods and her chest X-ray?' Tristan said.

At that moment, I simply couldn't remember what was happening with them. I'd ordered lots of bloods and chest X-rays that shift. Maybe I hadn't been focused enough. Maybe my blood sugar was low. I hadn't eaten lunch. I felt so Sick.

'All that's getting "handed over", is it?' Tristan stopped walking and folded his arms. They were thin and black-haired, like him. 'So the night team can sort it out for you?'

He didn't wait for an answer. He started walking again. I had to move fast to keep up.

'You need to chase her bloods and her chest X-ray, and probably ring cardiology before you go.' For every task, he hit the air with his forefinger. 'And at some point very soon, I think you'd better sit yourself down and review this department's chest-pain protocols.' He muttered something about them being more than clear.

'It's just ...' I stopped. 'I'm supposed to go to a dinner.' I only had the courage to speak because I'd been looking forward to seeing Nick so much.

Tristan stopped too. 'A dinner?'

His face made my Sick feeling worse.

'Nothing!' I said. 'Sorry!'

It was 8.42 pm when I finished. I came out of the locker room, carrying my clothes in their dry-cleaning bags, and decided to wait for the right moment to say goodbye. But then I heard Tristan handing over to the night consultant.

I didn't quite hear everything, let me make that clear. But they were definitely talking about my patient in twelve, and I thought they might have been discussing me. The other consultant definitely said, 'Jeez, that's a worry.' Then he shook his head and said, 'And, mate, did you tick all the boxes on her "supportive feedback" form?'

Tristan said something I couldn't hear, but then he laughed and his voice got louder. '"Don't be so bloody stupid, or your patient'll die." Remember when feedback was that simple?'

They both laughed more.

I decided not to say goodbye. I just turned around and walked to my car, and thought about the phrase 'so bloody stupid'. It was hard to believe anyone would be saying that about me. I got ninety-nine-point-eight on my Year Twelve score! I graduated from medicine with first-class honours! I'd done research into molecular genetics at Oxford University! I was the first to admit I wasn't cookie-cutter pretty, because I had unfortunately inherited the Banks nose, and I also had my dad's legs, and intractable cystic acne to contend with. But I definitely wasn't stupid!

Maybe I'd misunderstood. I must have done. I very often got things of that nature wrong.

∞

Pleasant activity scheduling could be therapeutic when circumstances were difficult, so I baked some brownies on my day off. This used up ninety minutes, and taking them to the hospital helped demonstrate I could work as part of a team.

'Good morning!' I said to the doctors' area in general. I had decided to conduct my shift in a positive frame of mind. I would see ten patients and do so competently and cheerfully.

One intern looked up and nodded, but as usual, everyone else was too busy to chat. This was an example of how constant challenges failed to produce cohesive relationships. However, I put those negative thoughts aside, and by noon, I was four hours into my shift and had seen four patients, so I was on track!

'Imogen?' It was Tristan. His calm arms made me think of a poisonous underwater plant. 'Your lady in four?'

'Yes!' I stood up straighter. 'She's just waiting for her neurosurgery review.'

'Good. You've spoken to neurosurg?'

'Yes, Tristan. About—' I consulted my watch '—fifteen minutes ago, and they—'

'She's had her CT?'

'She's up there now.'

'Okay.' He swivelled his chair away from me, then flipped it back. With a telephone receiver in his hand, he said, 'Her creatinine was normal?'

I swallowed. Patients needed to have their creatinine checked before CT scans. An abnormal creatinine could cause the scan to damage their kidneys.

'Yes,' I said. If I didn't know it to be physiologically impossible, I would have said that the *yes* came out of my mouth without me actually making a decision to say it.

Because even though I'd sent off the creatinine test – it was a simple blood test – I had forgotten to check the result.

Not because I didn't know it was important! Of course I knew a CT scan could be dangerous if the creatinine was too high! It was just that I'd been focused on this patient's vomiting, her oxygen saturation, her medication chart. She had a lot of allergies and potential drug interactions. And I'd had to get onto my fifth patient!

Tristan nodded once and started dialling a number before I could say anything else.

My mouth felt empty and huge. Perspiration ran down my rib cage. I edged past the intern, who made it clear she was irritated at having to shift her chair forward to make room for me. 'Sorry!' I told her, not even stopping to consider that, despite the fact that she'd eaten at least one of my brownies, she wasn't being a particularly good team player.

I picked up a different, random patient's drug chart, and walked at a casually brisk pace over to the computer furthest from Tristan. My little fingers were shaking, and I had to try three times to type in my password. At one point I accidentally said, 'Please,' out loud, and a nurse flicked her cloggily mascaraed eyes towards me.

I managed a professional kind of smile. I wanted to say, *Did you happen to notice the patient in four's creatinine?* Or maybe even, *Please, can you please, please just* help *me?*

Instead, I pointed at the screen and said, 'Slow today.'

She made an uninterested tightening of her lips and snapped her eyes down to the green plastic kidney dish of her own concerns.

The computer screen still said: 'DR IMOGEN BANKS. Please Wait A Moment.'

I found myself wondering who was in charge of the grammar of computer messages. Maybe I could do that job. Maybe I could do a job where I didn't have to hurry very much. Where I could think more deeply. Where I could breathe at a lower rate.

Maybe Ms Erica Hobbs, my high school careers-guidance counsellor, had been right. Maybe I would have been much more suited to being a laboratory-based scientist. A theoretical clinician, she'd said, as if I was foolish enough to believe that that was a widely used term.

Please, I said now, inside my head.

In case Tristan happened to glance over, I stared at the file in front of me and frowned thoughtfully. It was fanciful to believe you could hear your heart pound, but my heart was beating more strongly than was usual.

Just as the nurse marched off, with her kidney dish held blamelessly in front of her, the columns of my patient's results appeared on the screen.

I scrolled down, with my face adjusted to appear as if I was showing a standard level of interest.

Her creatinine was sixty-eight, which meant it was completely normal!

'Well, looks like she'll be just fine,' I said, to nobody in particular. I didn't mean to speak out loud, but as it happened, I sounded responsible and smart, like a stereotypically heroic doctor, in a stereotypically supportive staff station, on a stereotypically characterised medical television drama. 'Just fine,' I said again.

I clicked the screen shut, slid off my stool and walked away as if nothing much had happened.

∞

When I left the building, the dusk air was properly cold. I had four days off now, and I refused to allow worries about work to intrude. I was going to go home, make tea and maybe even send a casual message to Nick.

As I walked towards my car, the mountain, purple-dark and silent, presided over all the nice things other people were doing. Jogging. Yoga classes. Dinners.

It was irrational to imagine it was watching me.

Key Principles of Emergency Medicine (2019 ed.)
W.J. Olsen et al.
Chapter 51

Workplace systems

As we have seen, emergency medicine is practised in a complex and high-pressure environment, where competing priorities must be managed within a time-critical context.

The responsibility for minimising negative outcomes lies with all practitioners.

Nonetheless, it may be unrealistic to expect continuous flawless performance from human beings.

Chapter Five

GRACE

Autumn

The heat pump was juddering an unreliable-sounding hum, which was odd, because that particular serviced apartment was so anonymously efficient that even the people on the front desk seemed like machines. The juddering felt incongruously *human*.

'Nice,' Ben said, after a while.

'Yep.'

You could load a lot into a *yep*. When she was in her twenties, Grace had read in a magazine that it was one of the things men disliked about women, the way they loaded their *Yep*s and their *No*s and their *Well, if you really think so*s. The article had been called something like 'What Never to Say to Him', or maybe 'How Not to Turn Him Off'. She'd studied its magenta-coloured dot points so she wouldn't make unattractive communication blunders.

'Gracey?' Ben turned his head to look at her. 'You okay? What's going on?' His warm hand made a shell over her waist.

She stayed silent, under the unpleasant breeze of the heat pump, and thought about what she could say.

He moved closer. 'What, Gracey?'

She could dissolve into tears – quiet and heartbroken and forlorn, brown eyes brimming soulfully – 'Oh, Ben … Ben …'

She could yell, 'It's over as of now!', leap to her feet and then throw the multi-jointed black table lamp at his head. A naked redhead, outraged; it'd be memorable, at least.

She could use her most assertive and calm tone to say, 'I'm feeling deeply conflicted about my situation, and that emotion is manifesting as anger at you. Do you have a response you'd like to share?' Then she'd cross her hands serenely above the rumpled sheet and smile an enragingly dispassionate smile.

'What do you *think?*' she said, in the end. She was going with passive-aggressive and martyred, God help her. Magenta communication tips be damned. On that magazine's next page, there'd probably been turquoise guidelines about giving him his best blow job ever while not being a sexual traffic cop.

She sat up, and in an angry way.

Ben shook his head, as if he had absolutely no idea what he was supposed to think, but he would think it, if she would only tell him, because he was an obliging sort of fellow even if he did have a wife.

'Hey. Please don't be sad,' he said. 'Come here.' He reached out again. 'Don't get dressed. Come sit next to me.'

She turned around a bit and watched him organise himself, so he was leaning against the bedhead. He reminded her of a prestige-watch ad, all tall and broad, all vigilant green eyes and serious dark brow and pleasing angles. The lines on his face – the deepening folds between his nose and his lips; the remarkably horizontal stroke that nowadays scored his chin – served to make him more impressive, not less. Meanwhile, she was struggling against practically mandatory, apologetic thoughts about how droopy her boobs were nowadays.

'Gracey?' he said, as soon as they were settled next to each other. 'I've always been honest with you, Gracey.' He meant before, back when they were only twenty-one. When lying to get a girl into bed would have been considered perfectly acceptable, and yet he'd still been honest enough to tell her he wasn't ready for a relationship and not sleep with her.

She found herself nodding, like an appliance on a timer.

Ben reached out and touched her cheek, and she closed her eyes. Rested her face in his palm. Tears fell; he disappeared them with his thumb.

'Ah, Gracey,' he murmured.

Her eyes were still closed, her face still in his hand. It was one of the first times she'd properly cried in front of him. (She was not a crier. She was what was once called courageous, and was then called spunky, and was now called resilient.)

'I'm very honoured,' he said, trying to make a joke. Then, serious and sad, because he wasn't a complete idiot, he said, 'It's always been ... so fun, and easy and – sorry, not easy in a bad way – just easy, together. Always. And you're so smart.'

'God, Ben.' She looked at him, and her voice sounded much less bleak than she felt. 'You know better than to call a woman "smart" when you're in bed together. You say that sort of stuff *before* she sleeps with you.'

He laughed. 'Case in point,' he said.

She didn't think she'd said anything particularly smart, but whatever. She cleared her throat.

'Ben, I think I'm probably going to move Emma to Lofton,' she said. 'So we really ... We can't ... We really have to ...' What did they really have to do? Try, yet again, to end it? Make even surer it stayed secret?

Ben didn't reply straight away, and she wondered whether it was possible he'd forgotten what school his own children actually attended. Surely not. It would be taking his important, absent-minded dad schtick that bit too far.

'Seriously?' he said, in the end. 'Lofton?'

'Yes.'

He said he wasn't sure that sounded like a very good idea.

She said it wasn't exactly her first choice, either, but bullying was an issue, and there were only so many schools in Hobart, and Emma's mental health came first. Of course she meant that last part, but she also hated the lofty way she sounded, as if she knew she was playing an unbeatable trump card.

'The psychologist reckons get her out.' And why had she referenced the psychologist, as if she needed some sort of professional sign-off? Was it because she deep-down believed the bullying said something about Emma's lack of strength? Her lack of likeability? Was it because she knew Ben's daughters were the sharp, shiny kind who would never, not anywhere, not in a thousand years, be bullied?

'And *Christopher* and I think she might do better somewhere different.' It was so much easier when you spoke as if you were part of a couple, when your sentences were all about We Think This and We've Decided That.

'But he won't agree to Pardalote, or to anywhere Catholic, or to anywhere single sex, or …'

'Don't cry, Gracey.' Ben rested his hand on her leg, and – apparently with mild but genuine difficulty – recollected that Lauren was off at uni now, and his youngest, Tom, was in Year Eight, but Jasmine was in Year Ten, same as Emma. He told Grace all that as if it would be news to her, and then wrapped up with, 'Still. Our paths probably won't need to cross. And if they do, it won't be the end of the world.'

'I know.' She tried to smile. Back to her jovial-mistress self. 'We'd be extremely discreet, talk nicely to the headmaster, and definitely not pash behind the canteen.'

'Stop it,' he said, very sharply. 'It'd be awful, seeing you there. Quite apart from the kids. Christ.'

As he spoke, he covered her hands with both of his. She felt a rush of pleasure – delight, in fact – that her unacknowledgeable presence would cause him so much pain. And yes, yes, she knew that was pathetic.

After a while, he sat away slightly and said, 'Ah, Louise is there fairly often.'

Louise Buchanan. Who apparently wasn't as *smart* as Grace, or as *fun* as Grace, but whom he had married anyway.

'I've been thinking about that,' she said.

Louise Buchanan would be just involved enough in her kids' education. Not overbearingly. Not annoyingly. That was the marvellous sort of person Louise Buchanan seemed to be. The Coolest Interior Designer in Hobart. The Most Innovative Woman in Business (Creative/Design Category 2020). The Prettiest and Most Appropriately Involved Mum at Lofton.

'Of course. I ... you know. I'd stay out of the way. Out of Louise's way. And out of your way.'

Ben squeezed her hands. 'Not too far away,' he said.

But then he got up to go.

∞

It was the Friday of the Lofton meeting.

'I've got a good gut feeling,' said Christopher, as he picked up his jacket off the back seat and felt in his trouser pocket for his phone. 'Academic results excellent. Not—' he held up a placating hand '—that that's our priority.'

'Let's just see,' said Grace. She scanned the Lofton carpark. God. 'You sure you don't want to reconsider Pardalote? Or Saint—'

'I think we've discussed all that fully already,' said Christopher. (At least he refrained from adding 'Grace'.)

They walked along a nice little path with gravel and face-high

47

fronds of a native plant. Christopher said the smell made him think of when Emma was born. It also grew outside the hospital.

'We're here to see the principal,' Grace said to the receptionist in the front office. 'Mr Dankworth?' What a name. 'Regarding our daughter.'

'Certainly,' said the office lady. Grace had thought she might perhaps be especially intimidating, like one of the women behind the Chanel counter, but the Lofton office lady was just like all the other school-office ladies Grace had ever seen. She smiled proficiently and ushered them through a glass gate towards a large office.

'Mr Dankworth'll be right with you,' she said.

'Thank you, Sandra.' Christopher was a great believer in reading name tags.

'Not very snooty so far,' Grace said, when they were seated on black twill chairs that appeared to be from Officeworks. 'It's kind of disappointing.' Her voice was low, but Christopher said, 'Shhhh,' fretfully, as if she might get them in trouble. *Ben would have laughed*, she thought, for perhaps the seventeen thousandth time.

Principal Dankworth himself chose that moment to enter the room. He seemed far too young, and far too hip, and Grace had to remind herself he was probably about the same age as she was and that his shirt was in fact ironed. It was just that he was wearing skinny trousers and no socks. Grace felt ... not exactly scandalised, but certainly disconcerted. Were there no proper grown-ups left in this world?

Principal Dankworth said to call him Corey. He talked about Lofton's student-centred paradigm, and then said their luck was in because there was one spot available in Year Ten from next term. They had a slick tour of the school – the Integrated Learning Space (big room, many windows) and Break-out Collaboration Spaces (small rooms, also many windows) – and they met Emma's prospective English and mathematics and pastoral-care teachers.

'Welcome!' the pastoral-care teacher said.

Her name was Zoe Morello, and she had an attractive tattoo near her right wrist and a charming little sprinkle of cocoa-powder freckles on her nose. She had a big, comfortable bum and big, adorable breasts and very shiny, very dark hair, and Grace thought: *If I weighed the same as Ms Morello, I would look blubbery and stodgy, but Ms Morello is like a goddess of the harvest or something.*

Ms Morello, in fact, appeared to be altogether lovely. The whole place seemed pretty great, actually.

And this was Hobart, where Grace's former next-door neighbour had grown up next to her slightly odd accountant, and where Maria knew Grace's hairdresser from their sons' old football club, and where, presumably, quite a few people sent their kids to school with their secret lover's (or maybe even secret lovers') kids. Perhaps it was simply the price you paid for the small city with its short bloody commutes and nice bloody views and clean bloody air.

Her flippancy was shameful.

But still. This school would almost certainly be better for Emma, and so she, Grace, would just have to find a way to make it work. She looked at Ms Morello and managed to ask something sensible about digital-technology policies.

If she truly had a bad gut feeling, she placed it very firmly to one side.

Pursuant to *Coronial and Other Act 1991*
Section 16(IV)
[EXCERPT] [DRAFT]

Grace Tierney, a 46-year-old veterinary surgeon, was driving her red 2016 Mazda3 hatchback on the same road in the opposite direction. She was on her way to the Lofton School, where ...

Chapter Six

ZOE

Autumn

'Want a wine?' Claire said. It was after work and we were in her tiny, whole-food-in-glass-jars kitchen.

'What's wrong?'

Claire had the expression that meant she had something to discuss. You'd think she'd have a good poker face – for when her clients told her about awful things – but I'd never seen it.

She handed me my drink.

'What's wrong?' I said again. I could also tell – from the cheerful way she was doing up the wine lid – that it was something bad.

God-goddy-god.

My first thought, and I knew I was being too man-focused, was that it had to do with Daniel. That he was getting married, or that Rhianna, his new *girlfriend*, the passionate-about-sustainable-energy engineer, who just so happened to be from Vancouver, was pregnant.

I leaned against the cupboard, drank a massive swallow of wine and tried to do deep breathing. My floral dress with the nipped-in waist was too tight, though, despite its elastane. Maybe Daniel would still love me if I'd worn more eco-friendly clothes? But he'd never seemed to *want* me to be more into sustainability. Apart from the baby thing, I'd honestly believed he'd been completely happy with me. He'd *seemed* completely happy with me.

'You know, Daniel and I had sex in the shower, sometimes,' I said.

'And I'm talking, within the last six months.' I took another drink. 'Not just in the early days.'

'Well, you had that shower-over-bath arrangement. Makes it more doable.'

'Yep.' I nodded morosely and slugged more wine. 'Anyway, what?'

Claire stood up even straighter, with her excellent, good-self-esteem-type posture. Her goldy-floss hair was in a loose plait, and she was wearing a linen shapeless sac thing that she'd sewed herself. It looked like it had cost about nine million dollars.

'T-rex and I put in an offer on a house yesterday, and it's been accepted.' She swallowed. 'We didn't want to tell you till we—'

'That's wonderful!' They'd been househunting for ages, but everything cost gajillions. I'd sort of thought it was never going to happen. 'I'm so happy for you!' Where would I go? How would I cope? 'Really fantastic!'

'It needs *so* much work.' She puffed out her cheeks as if she was worried, but Claire *loved* that kind of work. 'The mortgage is ridiculous. We're not going to be able to eat for at least the next twenty years.' Her grimace was the sort you gave when you heard a barbecue you'd been dreading just got cancelled due to bad weather.

'No! It's awesome!' But there was a bit of a break in my voice this time. I put my glass down on the counter and turned my head to stare at it, as if I could tell the difference between colours of sauvignon blancs and cared about that stuff.

Claire let her cheeks go back to their normal shape. She took two steps across the kitchen and wrapped her hands around my elbows. Her eyes were all shiny. 'It's really crappy timing, though, for you. Sorry.'

I looked at her properly. 'I'll be fine,' I said. Of course I would. Fine and dandy.

'Move in with us, obviously.'

I did a thanks-but-I-don't-know gesture with my head. Staying in their unit was one thing. I could pretend we were zany and urban, and that I was just in the middle of a youthful, Bridget Jones–type setback. Moving into their first proper house with them would feel pathetic.

I pushed the word 'spinster' away like it was a disturbing news article, even though only a few months before I'd announced that it was a dumb, outdated label made up by olden-days men. '*Tot*ally,' Claire had answered, and she'd added something about gender stereotypes, and I'd said, 'Totally!' a couple more times, and we'd both nodded wisely with our smugly partnered mouths full of vanilla slice.

Even though I truly believed all that about spinsters, I still didn't want to *be* one. Shame on me.

I grabbed my wine and took a huge, young, urban slug. 'It really is great, Claire. I'm stoked for you both. Honestly.'

She still had her hands on my elbows, and she kept one there while she picked up her drink again. Our feet were almost touching. 'Thanks, Zo.'

'Bloody Daniel,' I said suddenly.

'Bloody Daniel,' Claire agreed. She drank more wine and said, 'He was always so arrogant and ... *superior*.'

'Really?'

'Like he was doing us all a favour,' she said. 'And he had such a chubby *arse*, you know?'

'Yes!' I didn't feel in the least hurt on behalf of Daniel, or his arse. I just felt bitchy pleasure. 'It was so sort of *pointy*.'

'Totally.' She squinted into the air. 'Unusual on a man.'

We laughed.

'Him, fuck.'

'Him, fuck.'

That was how we swore sometimes. It was from when we were teenagers and Claire's parents tried to make her do German classes.

She did not go to one single lesson. She told them: 'German, fuck. Lessons, fuck.' Claire was quite rebellious.

'Him, fuck,' I said again, louder this time. I maybe sounded on the unhinged side, but Claire didn't seem to notice. She clinked my glass with hers.

∞

The flat I found was a nine-minute drive from the city, and I moved there during the school holidays. It had fresh cream paint on every wall, durable-looking carpet and a sticky sliding door onto a tiny concrete balcony.

Once I'd moved in, just to make sure I was not breaking any Personal Development After Your Breakup by-laws, I got back into ceramics and made a few pieces. If your hobby was ceramics, you had to call everything you made a 'piece' even if you just made cups. This was another by-law.

Maybe I could set up a business, I wondered, one Sunday. I was drinking out of one of my 'pieces' while trying to mindfully appreciate my early-morning coffee. Transforming my creative interest into zoemorelloceramics.com would be an uplifting activity, I felt. It was what an Ideal Woman would certainly do after a breakup. Definitely better than my plan of drinking coffee, shopping online for cheap fashion and eating toast all the sunny weekend long. Which, I might add, was exactly what I loved doing with my Sundays, and which, back when I'd had a partner, I'd always felt was a perfectly acceptable use of my time.

My phone rang, and it was Claire's special ringtone.

She asked me a few token-sounding questions about work and then she said, 'And how was your date?'

The night before had been my first post-Daniel outing.

'Uncomfortable, weird, dissatisfying.'

When we were little, Claire's mum used to pick us up from school two days a week, and she'd do this thing where she'd make us say three adjectives to describe our days. They weren't allowed to be 'good', 'all right' or 'okay'. 'Dumb, boring, stupid,' said Claire, once. 'Well done,' said Aunty Sheila. 'That's the spirit.'

'Actually, is dissatisfying what I mean?' I added. 'Or do I mean unsatisfactory? No, because satisfactory is—'

'Shut *up*, you loser. Why, why, why was it dissatisfying? Did you …? Couldn't he …?' Claire once had had a boyfriend with erectile dysfunction. Maybe as a result, she seemed to think it was way more common than it actually – at least in my experience – was. I always worried it might sound mean if I said that, though.

'Nope. There were none of those shenanigans,' I said. I remembered an article I'd read, about how, when you were single, your sex life became a fun topic for your partnered friends. 'Not that it's any of your business.'

'Sorry, Zoe.' She sounded very sincere. 'Of course it's not.' Being Claire, she didn't say anything like, *Shut up, we always talk about stuff like that, and what about all the times you gave me* way *too much information, because I still have images I can't unsee, including showers, for God's sake.*

'No. I'm sorry.' I picked up my phone from the table and turned off the speaker button. 'Sorry, sorry. It was just I didn't feel like it.' I stared frumpily at my almost-empty fruit bowl. 'Maybe two months is too soon.'

The date had been awful. I don't mean the man – Toby – had been awful, exactly. He wasn't ugly or stinky or rude. But he'd seemed so … *expectant*. As if he had an inner rubric – the sort of thing I used to mark essays – ick – and he was scoring me as soon as I walked in. And what made it worse was that he thought I was scoring *him*. I could tell. The way he moved his eyes. The way he said, 'I'm a big fan of the food here' and 'You're looking lovely' with a sort of polishedness. It made me feel as if dating was one of his hobbies, like social-league football, and he knew he was pretty good at it.

'Anyway, what are you up to?' I asked Claire. It was time to change the subject.

Claire said things about gardening and sourdough – sometimes she was so bloody wholesome you just wanted to puke – and then we said bye.

I stared at my phone for a few seconds, put it down, and tried to start thinking again about zoemorelloceramics.com. But for some unknowable reason, the conversation with Claire had ripped open the slippery-sloped hole of grief that was pretty much always right next to me, and as I hung up, I realised with terror that I was sliding right back into it.

It wasn't only – maybe not even mainly – Daniel.

It was a whole future. A whole other life, a whole other person – or people – who I already loved, loved like a waterfall, but who my body hadn't been able to make real. I couldn't hold my babies in my arms. They existed. They did; they were honestly so much *there*. But only as microscopic maybe-lives and huge chunks of my imagination.

I tried to get a grip.

But I left my coffee half drunk, lay on my bed and bawled until I had both a headache and an itchy face. I didn't feel any better, though. Even after I'd stopped crying, I had to keep lying there, because I knew that if I moved, all the pain stored up in my joints would somehow flow out around my body and make me cry again. In the end, I stayed still on my bed until it started to get dark.

At least with the lack of online shopping, I didn't spend any money that day. There was always something or other to try to feel mindfully blooming positive about.

Chapter Seven

ZOE

Winter

It would be nice to report that I first met Nick Kavanagh at a warm-hearted barbecue, on a honey-gold summer afternoon, while I was having a perfectly fabulous and feisty time of it and not even thinking about my relationship-slash-lack-of-it status.

But actually, the barbecue had an awkward, half-of-us-have-kids-now-so-nobody-better-drink-too-much feel, and the afternoon was not really warm enough to be outside, and – shame on me – I had put a lot of thought and time into my outfit. And no, not because I particularly liked creating beauty or celebrating my shape or expressing myself through fashion, but because it was now a solid three months since Daniel had left me and I wanted to look good, just in case my future life partner existed and happened to be at Claire and T-rex's house-warming.

When I first saw Nick, he was on the rickety old deck of their new house. It was a very run-down weatherboard, with green pelmet curtains and chipboard wardrobes in every bedroom. But it was on a street where all the other old weatherboards had been tastefully renovated, which, everyone seemed to think, was what mattered.

Nick glanced up as I was making my way out of the bodgy fly-wire door.

'I'm Nick,' he said. 'Since nobody's introducing us.' He took his hand off the deck railing, as if that was a mark of respect.

'I'm Zoe,' I said. 'Claire's cousin. And yeah, shabby introducing by our hosts.'

Nick put his hand back on the no-doubt splintery rail. He had light-brown hair and even teeth, and something about his posture – comfortable, observant – made me think of a pirate. In a good, story-book way. I was pretty sure that real-life pirates would not be at all attractive.

I swallowed some of my mulled-wine thing, told myself not to pull in my tummy and peered towards Claire's new garden. There was a tree trailing its branches against a fence, and a rectangle of scratchy lawn sloping towards weeds and berry bushes. Luckily, someone's puppy was rollicking about doing something or other, so I watched it as if I was riveted.

Nick bent forward. 'What's that you're drinking?'

I said something about it being pretty potent.

He said something about excellent day for it. Then he raised his glass to me, and we both sipped our drinks and made eye contact in the way that meant, *Yep, well, we both know what we're doing now.*

So Nick rested against the balustrade, and we talked about nothing much – football, live-music venues, Christmas-in-July puddings – and when we'd finished our drinks, Claire – bless her – brought us glasses of bubbles.

Every now and again, we were interrupted by somebody stopping by for a chat – a guy called Matt talking about mountain bikes, a girl called Imogen saying Oxford had been rewarding – but most of the time the two of us were alone, and I felt like all our questions about work and our answers about flats, our leaning-in laughs and our cute little stories, were nothing except the sewing of stitch after stitch. Or, put less romantically, I could tell he definitely wanted to sleep with me and was good at the moves. I knew the moves, too, even though I was extremely out of practice, and so a lot of flirty chit-chat had flowed under the deck when a guy I didn't know appeared and said he and Nick had to go to another 'event' now.

'No hurry, Damo,' Nick said. I could already tell Nick was the kind of man who everyone called 'laid-back' or 'chill'. 'Let me introduce Zoe Morello.' By now, the two of us were finding the whole old-fashioned, polite-introduction thing *hil*arious. 'And this is Damien Collins. Often known as Damo.'

Damo moved his eyes from one of us to the other as if we were clocks that were showing different times. 'Mate?' he said. Then he tapped his wrist, where a watch would have been if he'd been wearing one.

Nick said he'd better go. 'But come see this band with us, eh, Zoe?'

I was about to nod, but right then, Damo let the tiniest bit of pre-smirk cross his face. Goddy-god-god. Lucky I saw it, in a way. Because it was enough for me to know, enough for me to really *see*, just how much of a dab hand Nick was with the leddies.

I suddenly wished I was wearing a different outfit. Not this blue dress. And not this tight, 1950s-secretary business of a cardigan. I needed a loose cardy. Mohair. Sealed right up to the neck. Even though that would be very itchy.

'Wait, no, I already have plans,' I told them.

I was one hundred per cent lying. But I'd always been all for speak-your-truth-and-trust-in-the-Universe and random-acts-of-kindness and serenity-to-accept-the-things-I-can't and blah blah, and my lived experience told me that it didn't help you in the romance stakes. Claire was very big on the phrase 'lived experience'. As far as I could tell, it just meant 'experience', but it somehow made you sound both smarter and more down-to-earth.

'But have a good night, Nick Kavanagh,' I said. I adjusted my dress's neckline. 'And Damien Collins.'

Damo stared at me. He looked as if he'd just clicked that I had a lot of special needs and as if he was the type to find that weird.

Nick lowered his voice, tilted a fluid shoulder towards mine and angled his face near my ear. 'Maybe another time, then, Zoe?' he said. He smelled of beer, but also of clean clothes, and supermarket shampoo, and possibility.

'I don't think so,' I replied. Hot men, fuck. Smirking men, fuck. 'But thank you, anyway.'

And I don't mean to sound manipulative, or bitter, or – heaven forbid – anything negative or unlikeable or *spinstery*, but it was really very satisfying to see just how surprised the pair of them were.

∞

'Hear about that terrible crash?' I said. 'On the Midlands?'

'Let's not talk about it.' Claire was not one for dwelling on catastrophes. With Claire, it was all about controlling the things you could control.

The two of us were going for our sort-of-weekly early-morning walk around Waterworks Reserve. The weather was freezing, which was typical of June, although also of December, in all fairness, and we were wearing the matching down jackets that my mum had given us a couple of years before. Mum tended to buy Christmas presents in bulk.

'Okay, agenda item one: you and Barbecue Nick,' Claire said.

'Ha-bloody-ha.'

We moved to the side of the track and said hello to a jogger running past. To be honest, we said it in extra-friendly and extra-loud voices, because he was one of those very serious runners who didn't slow down, or smile, or nod thanks when we scrambled out of his way into the eucalypt scrub. You could tell he was just thinking about his heart rate or kilojoules or something, and that in his head the Waterworks track was the Olympic stadium and we had no place ambling two-abreast there.

'Well?' Claire lowered her voice. 'And what is it with leggings? Can men literally not run in shorts anymore?'

'Nothing,' I said. I watched an unidentified insect swirl around some rocks. 'I mean, I haven't seen him again.'

Claire looked over at me. The morning air was still and cold and damp. 'Still too soon?' she said.

It wasn't that it was too soon. In fact, I wished that everyone around me was saying things like, 'Zoe! You're about to be left on the shelf! The clock's ticking! Alert, alert, code red, May Day, Alpha Sierra Oscar, not a drill, stat, situation room, it's a go, we are in a countdown-to-old-maid *crisis* here, people!'

Because that was – privately, shamefully – pretty much how I was feeling.

But most people, such as my mum, said exhausting things like, 'I'm really proud of the strong and independent woman you've become,' or else they made comments about personal choices and/or playing the field and/or, once, and worst of all, that I probably saw enough kids at work, anyway. As if teaching other people's teenagers *helped*.

'It's just . . . Barbecue Nick seems like someone who wouldn't want to commit,' I said.

'I get you.' Claire looked like a meteorologist telling a farmer he was absolutely right, there was definitely no chance of rain. 'From what T-rex says, he does get around.' She was making her voice psychologisty and soothing, which was very annoying.

'I figured.'

I waited for Claire to ask me some more questions, but there was silence, so I asked how T-rex was. Not that I wasn't interested in T-rex. It was just that Claire generally replied: 'Sweet, busy, snorey,' or, 'Sweet, busy, hairy.' And I wouldn't have minded more of a Barbecue Nick versus finding-a-sensible-man-pronto debrief.

'Sweet. Busy,' said Claire. Then she paused. 'Clucky.'

'Really?'

'Yeah,' Claire said. In a very big rush, she added, 'Actually, Zo, I got my IUD taken out last week.'

'Oh wow.'

I hoped the shock in my voice sounded like excitement. It's not like I didn't know that Claire was thirty-three and that she and T-rex had bought a house together. But I'd been kind of assuming they were going to elope or have some sort of surprise-in-the-backyard wedding, and *then* have children. I'd thought that otherwise Claire would have talked to me about the baby thing.

Probably I just hadn't wanted to think about it.

'Goodness!'

I remembered going with Claire to have that IUD put in. I'd sat in the clinic waiting room listening to hits of the nineties on the radio. I'd driven us back to her place, and microwaved hot packs, and we'd eaten KitKats and watched old episodes of *Girls*. I'd been living with Daniel. T-rex had never been heard of. We probably muted the New York career girls and their lovers, and talked about whoever Claire was seeing in a less-involved-than-Daniel-and-me way.

'Guess we just decided it's about time,' she said.

We weren't looking at each other.

'I mean for us!' she added.

I wished another jogger would go past, to give me a few seconds to get myself together.

The sound of our feet on the gravel path became more noticeable than I could ever remember it being. I stared up at the mountain, and tried to think of a comment about whether the view from the top would be good today or how stunning the cloud-shadows were, but my mouth wasn't working properly.

'Well, that is *really* exciting,' I forced out, in the end.

'Thanks, Zo.' Claire put her hand on my back for a split second.

After a moment, she spoke again, and in a really timid – at least for her – way. 'Maybe you should just have fun? You know, for a short while? Say with Barbecue Nick, or—?'

'Oh, maybe.' I said it very airily.

'As long as,' she was back to her psychologist voice, 'you're careful with your feelings.'

'Maybe,' I said again. But I felt like saying, 'Gee, thanks, Dr Claire, because there's yet another thing I probably won't be able to do.'

Enjoy sex but set boundaries. Keep your heart out of it. Be sure you don't fall in love. Literally, billions of women had probably said that crap to each other over the years. Merry be thy coupling, oh saucy one, yet keep thy eyes alert for emotional red flags. Once that mammoth's slaughtered, go for it, by all means, as long as you esteem yourself first.

'If drug companies were run by women, there'd maybe be a pill that prevented falling in love by now,' I said. I thought that was the sort of smart thing Claire might like, and I wanted to change the subject.

'Men fall in love, too, Zoe,' said Claire, bossily. 'Women aren't always the ones who want—'

'Oh, right, yeah, good, fine, whatever!'

I sounded very, very upset.

∞

'Ms Morello?' said a little voice.

Pastoral care had finished, and most of the class had gone off to PE. At least, I hoped it was PE, because nearly everyone was in sports uniform. I was supposed to tell the kids off if they wore sports gear on their non-PE days, but the Lofton School uniform code was something I didn't really care to think too hard about, so I always sort of forgot to do too much noticing of when who wore what.

'Can I talk to you?'

In the almost-empty classroom, the newish girl – Emma Tierney-Adams – was standing behind one of the desks. She was neatening the stack of stickered laptop, shiny purple maths textbook and denim pencil case that rested in her arms.

'Hi there, Emma!' I said it way more enthusiastically than I needed to. I was in a bit of a daze, so she'd made me jump. Also, I was dying for another coffee: after the Waterworks walk, I'd been running ridiculously late, which I had to admit was not all that unusual. 'What's up?'

'I was just wondering if I might be able to ask you about something?' She gripped her things tighter and walked towards me. 'Something *personal*?'

They were always so sweet, the way they thought they were the first kid in the world ever to have one of about five Personal Problems. The problems were: body image, anxiety, depression, being bullied, confused about sexuality/gender, sad about breakup, or worried about a friend with one of these. I realised that that was actually *seven* problems, and that I myself was working through one of them, and that they were all important. It was just that they weren't *unusual.*

'Of course,' I said. I got up and walked around my desk so I could stand next to Emma. She was almost as tall as I was, but you could tell by her intense face that her mind snagged on every single one of life's twists and turns; she had none of that offhand, fuck-it bravado of some of the other kids. 'What's been going on?'

Sometimes I wondered if I was *too* approachable. I seemed to get more than my fair share of teenage girls coming to tell me about their issues. There was also a school counsellor – Ms Henry – who seemed very nice and very sensible, and who gave out free jelly snakes, but from what I could tell, she was drowning under the weight of self-harm and family breakups and Lord only knew what else.

'Well, I was just . . .' Emma laughed a tiny laugh, as if she was sorry not to be able to come right out with it. 'I've had some body-image issues, an eating-disorder-type thing, which I'm getting help with, but . . .' I waited. 'I just thought I should share that with you.'

The thing was that even though the stories were common, the kids were always so precious and so vulnerable. The danger was always so real.

'I'm really glad you told me,' I said. Presumably, Emma's parents had decided to keep things as private as possible, because there had been nothing about it in her enrolment information. Or maybe there'd been an admin glitch, to be honest. 'It sounds as if you've had a hard time.'

She made an oh-well waggle of her head. 'I have a psychologist, and you know, my parents and I have this management plan. And I take medication, and I have to not exercise too much and see my paediatrician. Last year, I was seeing her weekly, and um. Well, I had to go to hospital a couple of times. But now I'm down to monthly.'

'That sounds positive?' I said.

'Yep. I don't really talk about it very often. But I just thought? Since you're my pastoral-care teacher?'

It was on the tip of my tongue to say, 'Do your friends check in with you?' but I'd seen her a couple of times at lunch, and she'd been alone.

'Thank you so much for telling me,' I said, instead. It hurt to add the next bit, when she seemed so trusting and relieved and proud of herself, when she'd started to relax her hip towards the side of my desk.

'Hey, Emma? You know that if you ever tell me you're hurting yourself, bingeing, purging, whatever, then I have to tell your mum or dad, don't you?'

Her hip snapped back up to one hundred per cent straight.

'I know, Ms Morello,' she said correctly. 'Thank you for your time.'

I watched her as she pulled her pencil case, and her textbook, and her carefully-casually stickered Chromebook tight against her chest again.

'Bye-bye!' she said.

She was flushed, and careful, and sad, and nobody was waiting for her in the corridor outside.

CORONIAL COURT OF TASMANIA
INQUIRY INTO A DEATH
Pursuant to *Coronial and Other Act 1991*
Section 16(IV)

I accept police evidence that the road where the accident occurred had no obstructions and was dry, and that the border between northbound and southbound lanes would have been clearly visible to an alert driver.

Speed analysis carried out by the crash investigator indicates to my satisfaction that speed was not a factor in this collision.

Chapter Eight

GRACE

Winter

Emma had been surly after school again, snapping the edge of her uniform dress into the car with an enraged flick of her wrist and making a contemptuous, tormented click in her throat when Grace leaned over to kiss her hello. Grace had started off thinking about the stress of a new school and the reality of mental illness and feeling compassionate and concerned. That had lasted about a quarter of the way home. Then Grace had started feeling irritated. (How bad could Emma's life really be? She was a middle-class young person in a stable democracy, being driven to a nice home in a temperature-controlled car. Emma was wearing a goddamn Garmin!)

'Want some avo on toast with me?' Grace said, once they were inside and she'd put the kettle on. It had started to rain.

'Nah,' Emma replied, without raising her head. She wasn't using her phone. Her elbows were on the dining table, fingertips idling over the edge of the (carefully stocked) (by Grace) fruit bowl. Her half-open schoolbag was on its side by the window; her discarded shoes trailed their laces across the (recently vacuumed) (also by Grace) lounge-room doorway.

So, that was all *enraging*.

And yet.

At this time of day, Emma's average brown hair appeared mousy and straggly; the hopeful ponytail of the morning was flat; her upper arms were white and freckly and artless. Grace thought about the merciless Year Ten eyes of the cool boys.

'No worries, Ems,' she said. (But should she be asking subtle, probing questions – 'So, what are the girls in your art class like?' – or cutting to the chase – 'All right, Em, did you eat your lunch today?' – or making general 'See about Wimbledon?' conversation that broadened Emma's world view? She'd always trusted she'd be one of those brisk, confident mothers, someone who peeled potatoes and decided rules and fired off pithy reprimands without thinking too hard about anyone's *psychology*. Now she wondered whether those women even existed in real life.)

Grace reached for the bread, and found the bag was a crumby crumple, almost empty. She swallowed, she breathed, she told herself to be calm, she did every single bloody thing she was meant to do, and meanwhile she thought carefully about breakfast. They definitely hadn't had toast. They'd had cereal. Without glancing at Emma, she walked to the pantry and lifted the peanut-butter jar, testing its weight. She knew – because it was her job to know, because she was used to this now, twenty months in – exactly what had happened. The paper bag of sugar would be lighter, too.

'Emma?' she said (oh so very non-accusingly). 'Looks like there's less peanut butter and bread than when we went to bed last night.'

'Yep.' At least Emma didn't sound mad. 'There is.'

Grace kept her tone calm and friendly. She also noticed about four grains of caster sugar against the splashback. 'You have a binge?'

'Yep.'

'Do you know why, sweetie? Is there anything you want to talk about?' She went and sat next to her daughter. Reached out a hand, put it on Emma's arm, wished she could pull her onto her knee. 'Are things okay at school?'

'Yeah.' Long silence. 'Sort of.'

'Em?'

No answer.

'Emma, is there any more of that bullying rubbish going on?'

'No.' Emma stared down at her own knees. The kettle flicked off. 'I just ... the other kids have sort of already got friends.' Her voice sounded as if it had been allowed out through a tiny hole in her throat, and as if, on the other side of that hole, was a heartbroken roar.

Grace put her arm around her daughter, and Emma leaned her head against her mum's shoulder.

'Maybe it'll just take a bit of time,' Grace offered. If only there was something you could *do*.

'I'm sorry, Mum.' Emma straightened up. She was shaking her head, light and fast. 'I promise I've been trying.' She meant with the eating disorder.

'Of course you have.' Grace left her arm on Emma's back. 'We just have to keep trying. Long as you know I'm here for you.'

Emma said nothing, and after a moment she smiled at Grace in the way that meant the conversation had gone on for quite long enough thank you. She reached for an apple, stared at it as if there was a real chance it contained lice, and took a minuscule bite.

Grace sat and toyed with her own fingernails.

Maybe Emma's illness was due to genetics, but maybe it was at least partly because of Grace's choices. Grace had failed to shake off a self-destructive attachment to a man who couldn't commit to her. She'd had Emma with a perfectly nice man she wouldn't love, and had then refused to let the three of them be a family.

What if it *had* all had an impact? There was no amount of anything that would ever make Grace feel better about that.

∞

Grace was in her pyjamas, sitting at her kitchen table, sipping God-awful chamomile tea and waiting to feel tired enough to go to bed. There was a tap on her laundry door.

'I texted,' Ben said, as she opened it. 'This okay?'

'My phone's off,' she replied, by way of explanation. 'Gotta sleep soon. Come in.'

Once the door was shut, they hugged hello. He was obviously on his way home from work. Presumably, he'd had some sort of emergency.

'Want a wine?' she asked. 'Or are you on call? A water?'

He got himself a beer, in the end, and they sat next to each other at the table, her calf against the side of his leg. She sipped her tea; he scrolled his news.

'See about that Midlands crash last week?'

She nodded, wincing. 'Awful.'

He lifted his hand onto the back of her neck. 'Emma got off to Christopher's okay this arvo?'

'Yeah.' It had been Change-over Tuesday since Emma was young enough to appreciate the alliteration, if that even counted as alliteration. 'You really should go.' She let her head rest into his palm.

'In a minute.' He flipped his phone over, so it was facedown on her table. 'How's ... ah ... how's she going at Lofton?'

Grace thought about Emma. Her straight, hopeful back. Her anxious, smiling goodbye each morning. The leaning-in mums on the corner at drop-off; the dads with their phones and their brisk, nodding glances.

'I really think we'd better stop seeing each other, Ben,' she said. She sounded as dull and laconic as a bored panel beater. *We'd better take that door off, mate. We'd better replace that bumper, love.* 'Again,' she added. Not dull or laconic anymore.

Ben extracted his hand from her hair and turned his head. He stared at her until she looked at him.

They'd had a breakup conversation three times already. The first time was more than three years ago, after their first night together. They'd both meant it then. She'd believed they were making a tragic sacrifice and that she was, therefore, going to live in a sad but soulfully wise and ultimately contented way for the rest of her virtuous life.

But after that conversation – after each one of those conversations – they'd drifted back together. Four months was the longest they'd managed to stay apart. She reminded herself of an alcoholic. Four months sober. And she didn't care, to be frank, if alcoholism was a true addiction – a genetic problem, a chemical imbalance, a neurological glitch – and her thing with Ben was just plain bad behaviour. She literally could not care less, when it amounted to the same thing.

'People leave people all the time,' she said. 'Why don't you toughen up and *leave me?*'

He just shrugged – a *you know how it is with us* shrug – and tapped his fingers on the table. So forlorn.

'Oh, whatever,' she said.

She thought of the photo of his family that she'd once – once – seen. Ben was smiling modestly; the three kids were eyeing the camera with an on-trend sort of irony; Louise Buchanan looked clean-faced and wholesome, and – above all – beautiful.

Grace had seen that picture last year on Instagram (it was captioned *Saturday Morning Miracles*) because Louise Buchanan was one of those slightly famous people who created Instagram posts that were so very humble and so very relatable – All the juggling and chaos! The projects she was thrilled to be involved in! The casual get-togethers with attractively authentic friends! – that at first you didn't even notice the self-promoting undertow. Grace had scrolled through all the studious modesty with a guiltily crooked finger, and wondered why Louise Buchanan even needed to do self-promotion. Louise Buchanan already *had* everything.

In any case, that was the one and only time Grace had checked Louise's profile. Then she'd gone into the bathroom, had a very hot, very useless shower, and spent about half an hour working out how to stop having an Instagram account.

Grace glanced again at Ben's face. She could still see him as a young man, beer in hand, laughing at something one of his mates had said. His hand on the mate's shoulder, even then, back in the days when young men didn't touch each other much, because everyone was homophobic without even realising it. Except Ben. He'd always touched. He'd brushed his fingertips on doorframes and knocked his fist along handrails; he'd given gentle punches to forearms, stooped to nudge unremarkable shoulders with his own charmed ones. All in a well-judged way, in a way that drew people in. It had honestly seemed to her that everyone she knew loved him.

'You know I want the best for you,' she said. She made a genuinely self-deprecating wave with her hand. How dare she be mean about Louise Buchanan's perfectly understandable, business-savvy Instagram account? Louise Buchanan was just making something of her career, while she, Grace, was sleeping with Louise's *husband*. 'Probably I just need to go to sleep.'

At the door, he gave her another hug, longer this time, and said quietly, 'I wish things were different. I'll see you soon.'

'Yep. Take care.'

She wanted to scream at him that he was the one who could have made things different, so why hadn't he? But there was no point making him say it. She already knew why.

It was because Grace was always averagely pretty, but men – even now – pulled in their stomachs whenever Louise Buchanan was in the vicinity. It was because, ten years ago at a wedding, Grace had overheard one slightly drunk married man observe to another, '*Hell*uva pretty girl, that wife of Ben Hutchinson's, isn't she?' The other man had puffed out his cheeks in the way that meant: *Blokes like us can but dream.*

It was because everyone had always loved Ben, but only Louise Buchanan had seemed like a miracle.

∞

On the afternoon Ben first told her about Louise Buchanan, Grace was a newly qualified vet, and Ben was a twenty-something hospital resident, and Hobart looked like one of those magazines to do with expensive wine and expensive cheese and expensive getaways. Old trees were bare, their edges flushed with gold. The sky was a vital blue that faded to softness at the horizon, and the river didn't, for some reason, sparkle in the sunshine. It was a second blue plane, flat and deep at the same time, unmarked except for a single wedge of foam trailing a distant boat.

It had been Ben's idea to meet in the park. Grace hurried along the asphalt pathway in her new white top, tossing her hair and smiling at toddlers. Being so laughably full of pent-up charm and ideas and *assumptions*.

'Gracey,' he said, standing as she arrived. He was early, which was unusual, and he didn't reach out to kiss her. Kissing on the cheek was their standard greeting, now they were so mature. But today, he made a gesture towards the bench he'd been sitting on. It was on a slope; lawn ran down to play equipment. A mum with a trendily short fringe and espadrilles was pushing her toddler on the swing.

They sat. She was babbling in a way she thought might be enchanting about the lovely walk and the beautiful weather and the best ice-cream flavour combinations. She was reaching out to touch his black jeans.

'Gracey,' he said again. This time, the way he spoke made her suddenly aware of her facial muscles, and she put her hand back in her lap.

'What?'

His mouth was a little bit open, as if he was trying to suck air in through his teeth.

'What, Ben?'

'I've met someone,' he said. He was wearing a white shirt, open at the neck; his dark hair touched its collar. 'Someone to be serious about, I mean.'

And, instantly, for reasons she disliked but understood, her only objective was to appear casual. To maintain her 'dignity'. To reposition her rejected self as his *confidante*.

'This—' He hesitated, checked her face, and evidently decided she'd be able – keen, even – to share his good news, '—this woman I've met? Louise? She's really. She and I, we're just … It's like a miracle.'

'Good for you,' Grace said. 'Never thought I'd see the day.' She gave him a matesy punch on his arm.

He looked down at his trainers, flexed his ankle a few times in an oddly diffident way. 'You know, Gracey, obviously she knows I'm completely free, so—'

'Where did you meet her?' She sounded conspiratorial, not shrill. Not *unattractively* interested.

'My parents had that party.' A humble shake of his head, as if he was so hopeless with women he had to rely on his mum for introductions. 'Louise was there. From Brisbane? With *her* parents.' Grace mirrored his grin. *What a hilarious and unusual anecdote!* instructed the strings that pulled her face. 'Long story,' he concluded.

Grace had met Ben's parents and she'd known about the party. She hadn't been invited though. Ben had implied it was just a family thing.

And because Ben and Grace had really only ever been Just Good Friends, and because they'd never even slept together, and because her humiliation was all she could feel, she nodded, and she acted as impervious as one of the pretty, nonchalant high school girls she remembered never being. She said something about being happy for them both. She spoke as if his connection with her was just a line of fine print, a tiny, insignificant ripple that counted for nothing real in either of their lives. She spoke so understandingly. More than that. She spoke *supportively*.

'Goodo,' he said. 'Glad we're on the same page.'

It was the first time she'd heard that same-page expression, and she assumed he'd made it up. She also thought: *He's done nothing wrong. Not by me. Not at all. Not really.*

After a few moments of talking about God alone knew what, her legs managed to stand her up, perky and desolate, and she said she had to get going, that she had a ridiculous number of things to get done today, that honestly, she shouldn't have come out in the first place. He said he'd walk her home, it was quite a nice arvo, wasn't it?

So, he walked next to her, along the pretty footpaths to her gate, and then he touched her for the first time that afternoon. He put his hand on her forearm, and kissed her cheek, as easy as you like. As if the times when they'd nearly kissed, when they had kissed (properly, voraciously in fact, twice), when he'd almost but not come in, when he had come in and they'd slept in their separate, chaste beds, when they'd been drunk enough (once) to fall – clothed – asleep next to each other – as if none of those things had ever happened.

'Thank you for walking me,' she said. It was impossible to believe he'd forgotten, or even that he'd stopped remembering, all of that. 'Very gentlemanly. Well done.'

'No worries at all.' He glanced once along the street, as kind and distant as a busy daughter-in-law.

As he walked away, he was already flipping his phone open. Sunlight angled through the trees, throwing brightness onto his white shirt. The crumples he never bothered to iron out looked just right, as if they were supposed to be there.

∞

If she was someone else, she would think what an idiot this Grace woman was. So mopey. Such a victim. So pathetically lovelorn and teenagerish and *dumb*.

But it wasn't as if she ever decided: *I know, here's a great life plan! I'll fall in love with some man who doesn't love me, spend years throwing bucketloads of self-esteem-destroying emotional energy into the washing machine of my feelings for him, and keep doing that until long after I'm too old to start a family with someone else.*

She didn't do any of that.

When he walked away from her gate that beautiful autumn day, she went inside and ripped up the six photos she had of him. (Everyone had fewer photos in those days, so that at least had been labour-saving, in retrospect.) She deleted a message he'd once left on her answering machine, in which he'd said how much he was looking forward to catching up with her. She trashed every single one of his emails. Later, when people said, 'How's Ben?' in the slightly confused, slightly insinuating tone people used to ask her that, she made a vague face and said, 'Fine. Good. He's seeing someone called Louise, I think.'

'Ben talks about you all the *time*!' Louise Buchanan said, when the two of them met that winter. She turned and laughed into Ben's eyes. 'He's like, "Grace is so smart!" "Grace is so funny!" I was getting quite worried.'

'Ha-ha-ha!' Grace chortled, as if this wasn't in any way an insult. She sounded ridiculous, but it didn't matter all that much, because

Ben was busy watching Louise flip her golden hair. 'Ha-ha-ha-ha-ha-ha-ha!'

Anyway.

She learned; she worked; she jogged; she achieved. She became a heroine of the local wildlife park; she literally won a Young Tasmanian Premier's Award – five nights in Darwin and five hundred dollars – for her exceptional leadership regarding native animal rescue. She even found time to date two men (not simultaneously), and before she turned thirty, she set up her own clinic.

Ben married Louise Buchanan later that same year. There were hats on the older women; the guests' shoes all looked brand new; every single speech was as well-pitched and uplifting as one of those 1990s Coke ads where people danced on a beach. Grace smiled and drank a single glass of rosé. She said, 'I'm so pleased for you both,' and kissed his cheek, and she left on the early side, but only just on the early side.

When Dr Hutchinson and Ms Buchanan – no fusty old *Mrs Hutchinson* for Louise – moved to Sydney, Grace had just turned thirty-one. She told herself that their leaving was for the best, and she believed she meant it.

CORONIAL COURT OF TASMANIA
GENERAL INFORMATION

The coroner's role is to consider responses, training, policies, resources or other relevant factors, including historic factors, that may have contributed to or prevented the death.

Chapter Nine

ZOE

Winter

'Evening,' I said.

It was T-rex's thirty-sixth birthday, and I'd been invited to his dinner. The Blue Anchor was the sort of place that seemed average and unremarkable, until you went to a different pub. Then you realised that the Blue Anchor was actually really good. The menus were unlaminated; the floorboards were made of actual wood; the staff wore black T-shirts and knew a lot about music but were still friendly.

I gave T-rex his presents, which were a book he wanted about politics and a bottle of red wine, and after he'd given me a hug, I talked to Claire about the noisy roadworks outside her office until people started arriving.

'Happy *birth*day!' they kept saying.

'Hey, mate,' T-rex kept saying.

I barely knew anyone. I hadn't hung out with T-rex's friends much when I was with Daniel, I guess.

We all mooched towards our table. Garlic bread was ordered, jugs of beer agreed upon. The waitress was pretty young, and she had that nervous, how-can-I-possibly-be-expected-to-wrangle-such-a-big-group? look about her. She kept glancing at Claire, as if Claire would make people pay attention to the menus. Claire didn't believe women should have to take on responsibility for social situations, and she deliberately left that sort of stuff to T-rex, who was hopeless at it.

In my opinion, that was simply because he was a man, but in Claire's and Mum's opinion, it was because social pressure/conditioning/gender-role stereotypes/inequality/other things like that/also women didn't have enough superannuation.

Anyway, I was talking to Claire – about a shop assistant who'd been snooty with Mum – and deliberately not looking at T-rex's guests, because I was properly nervous about seeing Barbecue Nick again. I'd been hoping that having had my heart completely smashed by Daniel would sort of vaccinate me against that sort of thing, but no. Apparently not.

'So, we should never support that shop again, Zo,' Claire was telling me. I was saying things like *yes, good, fair enough*, and we agreed that Mum had been totally in the right, and what was the point of face-to-face retail if shop people were that rude?

'Totally,' said Claire.

Then there was a natural lull in our conversation, and unfortunately, just at that moment, Barbecue Nick came in. He approached T-rex, and I – because of the lull – had no reason to laugh merrily or flick my hair casually or crinkle my brow intelligently. I just gazed at Claire, feeling aware of every single atom in my face, nodding a gentle nod and saying, 'Hmm,' for absolutely no reason.

Next to me, Nick said happy birthday to T-rex, and they did some sort of hand-shake-and-pat-on-the-back business. He said hello to me.

'Hello!' I said. 'How about us, out on a school night!'

My voice was weird, and I could feel Claire thinking, *Fuck, what the actual is going on with Zoe?*

Nick took one of the few available chairs, which was across from me but three seats down. He gave a kiss on the cheek to the girl next to him, in that non-awkward way that meant they knew each other well.

I talked to the man next to me about things we liked on Netflix. We didn't really like anything the same. It was one of those conversations where you think: *This person is nice, and has excellent manners, and if we'd met ten years ago we'd probably be mates and I'd be saying things like, 'Of course I haven't watched that, your taste is crap,' and he'd be laughing and teasing me about my raunchy historical dramas and pouring me more wine without asking.* It was harder to make that sort of friend now, I felt.

I ate my chicken burger and hoped I hadn't just been invited to keep my jilted spirits up. On the edge of my attention, Nick was going to the bar and returning with a jug of beer in one hand and his phone in the other. He was leaning way back in his chair to talk to a man a couple of seats away. He was laughing.

I'd finished my dinner when he stood up, moved around the table and bent down next to me.

'Good to see you again,' he said.

I could barely hear him because it was noisy and his voice was soft, but at the same time, I was completely clear about what he'd said. I smiled, and in no way seductively. More like a seven-year-old with a swimming certificate.

'You too,' I told him.

Another friend of his – Imogen – I vaguely remembered her from the barbecue – came over too, and we all had a conversation about dinner and music and work, which felt both tinglingly exciting and way too long. The whole time we were chatting, I was becoming more and more aware that all I really wanted was to be alone with Nick, and I was also aware that that was making me feel ashamed. An Ideal Woman would have a healthy – an edgily adventurous, even – sex drive, but she'd never so much as *want* to sleep with someone who might be not in her long-term best interests. She would have some sort of special filter on her Ideal Libido.

The waitress made another stressed visit to the table, and found out that nobody wanted dessert, and then Nick pulled over a chair next to me while T-rex did a sweet little speech about how old friends were the greatest and then the surprise cake appeared. Everyone queued for ages to pay, and as I walked out, Nick was sort of hanging around by a fire extinguisher peering at his phone.

'Bye, Nick,' I said, as I passed him.

He straightened up and put his phone in his back pocket. The way he moved made me stop; it was as if he'd been waiting for me.

'Walk you out?' he said.

My Yaris, who I called Nina, was around the corner and quite a long way up the road – parking in that area was a nightmare – and I was aware of nothing as the two of us walked along. Not the sweet little houses, not the slight incline of the hill, not the lavender or the cat wee or the nothing-much smell of the air. Not even of what we were saying, which was some blahy thing about what made a good pub.

My head was too full of the idea of kissing him, and whenever it occurred to me that maybe he was thinking about that, too, then I would lose my place in life for a second, and I'd nod and say *Yes* or *No* or heaven only knew what, but in an enthusiastic, agreeing sort of way.

'Thanks,' I said, when we arrived at Nina-the-Yaris.

'My pleasure.' Was he really being flirty? Or just well-mannered? He was looking at me in a way that could honestly have meant either.

'Anyway, I better go,' I said. I had no idea where my car keys were – bag? Pocket? Pocket of bag? Hopefully, he'd walk off before I had to start muddling around. Sort of hopefully.

'Thought you might wanna grab another drink?' He gestured with his head towards Salamanca, where there were lots of bars.

I immediately thought something like, *Yum*, except not that actual word. It was more a feeling. Then I forced myself to notice his long limbs and his perfectly fitting T-shirt and his charming, but almost certainly fake, shyness. Without thinking anything much else, and maybe because I'd had a big glass of wine, I said, 'Probably not. To be truthful, Nick, I'm at the point where I want something long term.'

The words felt honest and polite in my head, but as soon as they were out of my mouth, they felt embarrassing and enormous. And it was as if the whole street could hear them, like they were all over the internet and everyone in the world was reading them and hammering at their phones to post things that meant *Zoe Morello Is Definitely The Most Ridiculous Person To Ever Live, Who Even Says That Sort Of Thing, Absolutely Nobody Ever, What A Disgrace She Is.*

Nick untilted his head and took an actual step backwards. He got his phone out of his pocket. All of those things took him less than a second.

'Fair enough,' he said.

He did look at me, but in a reserved, professional way, as if I was a customer who wasn't actually going to buy anything. He gave a single little nod. 'I better get going,' he said. 'Bye.'

Then he turned away.

∞

I sat in my car, and for no real reason scrabbled around in my handbag for my phone. My hands closed on my keys, my half-closed makeup bag, my sunglasses case, a hairy hair elastic, a petrol receipt. Finally, down the bottom, I found it.

There was not even one text. I checked my email. There was something about twenty per cent off at the Iconic tomorrow and a request to tell Dotti how my new purchase was going. The home screen was empty.

Goddy-god-god. No wonder social media was a thing. I'd stopped it all, because I was driving myself crazy over Daniel, but I suddenly missed Insta like a friend.

I put my phone in my handbag and started to drive home, with that feeling of sort of wanting to cry but not being able to. When I stopped at the second set of red lights, I realised my thighs looked fat. I tried not to have body-shaming thoughts, but then I decided I was bloody well allowed to think whatever I wanted. It was my body, they were my thoughts, and if I wanted to believe that any bit of me was too chubby then I was going to believe it. *Sake fuck's*, I fumed, with sudden rage. At least in the olden days, you could just hate your rolly thighs and leave it at that. Now you had to feel bad for being fat *and* for being upset about it.

The man in the car behind mine gave a polite little toot and I saw the light was green. My hand went up in a 'sorry mate' way as I drove off.

When I was inside my place, and showered, and in jammies, and drinking a cup of boiled water with a squeeze of lemon in it – sudden urge to cleanse – my phone pinged.

Unstoppable flush of hope. Maybe the text would somehow be from Nick, and it would say, *I want something long term with you, too, because I sense we have a really intense connection, and suddenly I'm ready, because you're obviously different from all the other girls, so let's have amazing sex that will then naturally and painlessly bloom into a steady, love-filled relationship.*

And then everyone would say, *Zoe Morello is the intelligent and beautiful and above all independent woman who finally made Nick Kavanagh fall in love, just by being herself.*

And then Daniel would find out about it and realise the error of his ways and be wild with jealousy and beg me to come back to him and I'd say no because I was happy and fulfilled, and possibly also pregnant now, and fiddle-de-dee.

But it was just Claire saying thanks for coming, and that she hoped I was far too busy having high-quality orgasms with Barbecue Nick to reply. Then there were three emojis.

All of them were crying, but with laughter.

Chapter Ten

IMOGEN

Winter

The day after the Blue Anchor dinner, I left for work before seven. There was a silver sheen on the river, and cold in every particle of the air. In the wash of sun on the mountain's eastern side, the dark columns were surprisingly clear, like when you saw your skin in a car's rear-view mirror. Not that I was driving to work. I'd decided to walk to the hospital. Moderate physical exercise could help the subconscious process ideas.

The evening before had been fairly enjoyable, overall. Nick sat next to me – of course – and gave me a loving kiss hello. But after his chicken-schnitzel plate had been cleared away, when he'd had a few beers, he began chatting to the Zoe woman he'd talked to for more than half an hour at Claire and T-rex's barbecue.

I went over to where he was squatting next to her chair.

'Hi, again, Nick,' I said. Just nonchalantly.

'G'day, Imogen. How's it going?'

I didn't get a chance to answer him, because Zoe smiled at me. Even though we'd met before, she said, 'I'm Zoe, by the way.'

She used her knuckles to tap Nick's shoulder, as if to tell him off for not making introductions. I thought it seemed overbearing – which he would dislike – but he smacked his own forehead and said, 'Shit, sorry,' and then they both laughed as if they'd done something funny. When he laughed, he touched her bare arm with two of his fingertips.

But it was only her forearm, and it was only for less than one second. You didn't want to read too much into these things.

In any case, I did a charming little giggle to join in. Then I answered Nick's question.

'Just, just going with the flow, now I'm back!' I'd planned that 'flow' line, because he used it a lot. It was helpful to mimic the verbal patterns of those with whom you wished to connect.

Zoe smiled at me again. She was wearing a white dress that I had seen advertised, but it was of a salacious style that was not to my taste. Also, the skin on my shoulders was temperamental, so I tended to opt for sleeves.

'Where have you been?' she said.

'Oxford, England,' I told her. 'Oxford University, that is. Researching molecular genetics.'

'And how do you guys know each other?' Possibly *she* felt somewhat threatened.

Obviously, I didn't relate the whole story, but I explained how Nick and I had been in the same high school homeroom from Year Seven until Year Ten, which was highly improbable, because students were randomly divided into new homerooms every year.

'Wow, that's a coincidence,' said Zoe.

'So serendipitous!' I said. I touched Nick's arm the same way he had touched hers. 'So crazy!'

Nick looked into his beer glass.

I explained how after high school, I went to university, and Nick did his carpentry apprenticeship. 'But despite all life's demands and challenges, we keep in touch,' I told her.

'Life gets sooo busy, doesn't it?' she said.

I told Nick about how on the go I was with my emergency-department residency. 'Not that it's as exciting as I'm making it sound,' I finished. Another giggle, which was a mistake. I realised later that evening that I might have sounded uncompassionate to emergency-department patients.

Zoe said that was very impressive, and that she'd been reading about women in science, and that she'd visited Oxford years ago as a backpacker, and while she was talking, one of the straps of her dress fell off her shoulder onto her upper arm.

Nick noticed the strap; his eyes flicked across to it three times.

I said, 'Oops!' and pointed and nodded towards her shoulder.

Zoe just smiled down at it, as if it was a charming puppy, and slid it into place while she was still talking. I was not one to criticise other women, but I personally did not indulge in that degree of flirtation, and especially not in public.

Right then, Claire – T-rex's girlfriend – asked for some shoosh, because T-rex was going to do a 'hopefully short and non-boring' speech. I took that as a hint to return to my seat, and of course I was wanting to have Nick more to myself again. But Nick didn't come back with me!

The next time I casually glanced his way, the strap was off Zoe's shoulder again, and Nick was sitting down now, in a chair next to hers. Her legs were crossed but pointing towards his pelvic area, and his knees were apart, and he was leaning forward, in a classic display of significant attraction. And the thing was, I'd seen him behave in that way before, but when that happened – like for example, the night he had sex with Charlotte Patterson, after Lila Nguyen's thirtieth – he usually caught my eye and I could tell he was thinking, *Don't judge me, Imogen. You know this is just me being me. This is nothing like it is with us.*

But that Blue Anchor evening, he didn't catch my eye.

Later, I walked past and offered to buy all three of us drinks. I said, 'I'm just on my way to the bar. I think the house pinot is popular!'

While Zoe was smiling and saying she'd 'already had more than enough', I looked at her ruched-up skirt – she was pretty fucking careless with her garments, I had to say – and her long, smooth legs.

From that moment, I saw how – just as someone who inherited a small amount of money could end up very rich – she was going to parlay her legs into a relationship with him.

She'd started with the legs, and she'd progressed to a long conversation, and soon she'd work her way up to texts he'd send just to her, and then favourite takeaways, and weekends at his place where they would probably have sex with each other more than once per day.

She was going to get to have a whole world with him. She wouldn't even have to *try* very hard.

It was so unfair, when they were just legs, and I was me.

∞

The carpark of the Blue Anchor was far too small for its purpose – it had twelve bays, when the venue could seat sixty-four patrons in the bistro alone – but I'd found a space because I'd arrived early.

I sat in my cold car, and was – I was sorry to say – not in the least surprised to see Nick leave the building with Zoe. I once thought that when he went through the male neurological-development surge, at around age twenty-four, Nick would develop behaviour and values that would be conducive to his long-term satisfaction. But here we were, a decade later, and he persisted with his addiction to instant gratification.

I assessed their non-verbal communication as they walked across the carpark and up the street. At the third cottage along, Zoe ran her hand lightly over the pickets of a dark-green-painted fence. At another, she literally stopped to smell some lavender. Nick simply walked with his hands in the pockets of his dark-blue jacket. I was unable to draw many conclusions.

It wasn't that I actually followed them, let me make that clear.

But I was going that way anyway, so I simply waited until they were almost out of sight before I turned my car onto the street towards them. When I caught them up, they were standing next to a parked car – a white Yaris, registration number AE 68 T – looking at each other. Loitering, in fact.

I thought of tooting and waving as I drove past, but didn't. I turned into a side street, did a U-turn, pulled over and watched. After less than one minute, Zoe got into her car and Nick trudged off. His ute would have been even further up the street, due to his chronic unpunctuality. Many well-credentialled psychologists held that people who were frequently late were conflicted about what they really wanted. That view was not just internet nonsense.

Zoe drove towards Macquarie Street, which coincidentally was sort of on my way home, so I cruised along behind her. She was a poor driver. She remained stationary after a light had changed to green, and the person one car in front of me was obliged to toot her. I wondered if she was intoxicated, so as a safety precaution, I followed her until she pulled into a driveway: 28 Maitland Close, New Town. The driveway led to a block of units. An inside light came on shortly afterwards. Second unit from the left, on the ground floor.

It was a nice area, the one she lived in. Not too far from my suburb.

That was why, since I'd left for work early that particular morning, I could take a fairly short detour past her place and still arrive at work on time.

I personally was very punctual, and also very clear about what I wanted.

CORONIAL COURT OF TASMANIA
INQUIRY INTO A DEATH
Pursuant to *Coronial and Other Act 1991*
Section 16(IV)
[EXCERPT] [DRAFT]

I accept the evidence of the Registrar of Motor Vehicles that vehicles the same or similar in appearance to Nicholas Kavanagh's white Toyota Hilux are very common.

Chapter Eleven

GRACE

Winter

Emma had asked her to come to the Grade Ten assembly, which you'd have to say was progress.

The latch of the gate was stiff, and Grace almost dropped her phone trying to pull it up. In a nest of thoroughly weeded gravel, a trio of dark-green signs with ends shaped like arrows read, 'WESTON HALL', 'SENIOR COMMON ROOM' and 'JUNIOR LEARNING HUB'. Grace followed the one towards Weston Hall.

There didn't seem to be any other parents (beautiful interior designers or otherwise) around. She had just quickened her stride – surely she hadn't messed up the times? – when behind her she heard someone say, '... gifted this really lovely bowl,' and someone else reply, 'Good on her! Because ...'

She stood aside as the women caught her up, and then followed them as they chatted their way past a glassed-in noticeboard and a sculpture of a Tasmanian devil with a browny-gold plaque at its feet. (She was so nervous she barely even registered the use of the word 'gifted', which generally annoyed her to distraction. '*Gave*,' she always wanted to say. 'No judgement, but what's wrong with *gave*?')

Walking into the enormous hall was like going into a TV store, one where every set was on and all the volumes were turned down low. Rows of chairs were even and beige and plastic, and the best seats were already taken. She felt conspicuous, excusing her way through all the 'How did Thursday go in the end?' and 'Don't let me forget that twenty bucks!' and eventually sitting down alone. But nobody was even looking at her.

And there was Emma, sitting quietly on the end of a row near the front. Most of the other girls were moving – turning around to smile and point, touching their own hair, leaning to whisper into friends' ears. When Emma briefly turned, Grace waved with a whole lot more confidence than she felt. Emma responded with a minuscule flick of her fingers.

Principal Corey Dankworth was holding a microphone. He looked to be having a great old time: if he was thinking about revenue issues or risk-management policies there was no sign of it. 'We've got the Year Tens this week,' he said. 'Take it away, Year Ten Leaders.'

Grace sat for Welcome to Country, and stood for the school song.

Louise Buchanan was sitting near the front. Even from this distance, Grace could tell she was wearing exactly the right kind of knitwear, that her hair was clipped up in the stylish, unstudied way that was only achieved with a lot of practice, and a lot of time, and a lot of products.

'We hope you enjoyed the visual media display in the foyer,' said a boy with black hair. 'Now, here are Millie Chung and Charlie Sermons to tell us more about our Ethics in Action fundraising and how you can help.'

Clap, clap, clap.

'Thank you, Charlie, that sounds great. Now, Gab Vanderley would like to play us a piano solo, which is a folk song arranged by Someone Someone.'

More clapping. Woo-hooing.

'And here are Jasmine Hutchinson, Caitlin Schultz and Evie Gullerova to play a guitar ensemble.'

When she heard Jasmine's name, Grace turned her eyes down until the clapping (and the louder woo-hooing, and the single, insolently long whistle) had stopped. Only then did she look.

On the stage, three girls were positioning black chairs. They were indisputably that handful who – at least to look at them – had bypassed adolescence, and had already blossomed – that was the only possible word for it – into beautiful young personhood. When Jasmine struggled to adjust a microphone, when she blushed and glanced first at her dismayed friends and then towards their teacher, her self-consciousness did nothing except charmingly demonstrate that, despite everything, she wasn't even smug.

'This is a nineteen ninety-five song by Jewel, which we have chosen because we like its melody, and because Jewel reminds us that women can do anything,' one of them – not Jasmine – said, after the microphone was fixed.

Grace remembered Ben talking about how Jasmine had sneaked out a few months ago. He'd mentioned a boyfriend who was in Year Twelve. Grace stared at the splay of the girl's golden hair and at her long, somehow-tanned legs. Surely, even if you assumed perfectly good intentions, there would *have* to be a lot of very complicated feelings in a lot of the dads right now. And in the mums. There came, after all, a point in life when you realised that you were simply never going to be conventionally beautiful, and that because of that brutal and unequivocal fact, certain doors would stay closed to you forever. Effort often *wasn't* what counted. It was not an easy truth.

Onstage, the three girls began to strum, and after a few only very slightly mistimed chords, one of them began to sing.

Grace was unprepared, that was the problem. For some reason, she hadn't expected songs from her youth to come at her in the middle of a school assembly. She'd thought it would be hymns (though of *course* it wouldn't be), or, or classical music, or, yes, traditional folk songs. School-assembly music was supposed to be like poetry. Unemotional, inert stuff that could be sweet, or clever, or even beautiful, but that pressed no real, wrenching button of feeling.

But this.

Grace bowed her head. She tried not to allow the tears to come, but they still came, few, and silent and – God, hopefully, because at least they didn't actually fall – invisible.

∞

It wasn't that that song was tagged with a specific memory. She and Ben hadn't ever danced, or kissed, or made love to those lyrics. (God, no. Not their cup of tea at all.) It was just that that tune had pervaded her twenties, and so it took her back to her younger skin, to her less-battered heart, to car rides that smelled of petrol and supermarket trips just for lollies and freezing beach swims where – at least in her memory's neat summary – there'd been nothing much going on except the two of them laughing.

The song was about a decade old when 31-year-old Grace met Christopher, and it was hard to say if she even heard it that particular day. She probably did. Even then, it was pretty much always around somewhere. Maybe it was playing in her hotel lobby, or while she ate narrow slices of honeydew melon between conference sessions, or in the marine-themed café where she ended up having a late lunch.

She'd just ordered when the man came in and asked for a pot of tea. He had a nice English accent – the friendly type, not the Royal Family type – and she must have been in a state of post-conference-presentation (*Harnessing Volunteerism in Native Animal Rescue: A Tasmanian perspective*) adrenaline. Anyway, she laughed and turned in her seat to look at him.

'What?' He smiled. He was at the table next to hers.

'Tea!' she told him. 'So English!'

If *she* was English, she would never order tea or chips or roast-anything; it would be like walking around in a beret saying, 'Oooh la la!' if you were French.

He said, 'I don't really like the taste of coffee.' In a friendly way.

She said she didn't think she could function without coffee, and he said his sister, Mimi, had once cried when she visited him and he had no coffee, and then they got into a conversation about Mimi's work (lawyer), and his work (also lawyer), and when his tea came the waitress sort of hesitated about where she should put it. So, it seemed only natural to say, 'Join me?' (Like in a movie. Miracle she didn't say, '*Care to* join me?')

The café was getting emptier, and her chicken-and-salad roll was finished, and he said he lived in Melbourne but was here in Sydney for a meeting tomorrow. He said he loved Sydney and its glorious harbour. She wrinkled her unpatriotic nose – Sydney Harbour did nothing for her, to be honest – and he laughed uncertainly, as if he thought being mean about national icons might be a standard form of Aussie humour, perhaps to do with all the famous self-deprecation.

Outside, there was an awkward pause, the sort where you tried to keep your face both pleasant and goodbye-esque while you hoped nothing was about to make you regret that you started talking to a stranger. She extended her hand – God knew why – and as they said their farewells, he dropped a kiss onto her cheek in that unselfconscious way even very diffident Englishmen could pull off.

Then he added, 'Unless you'd like to have dinner tonight?' He winced. 'Nothing ... not meaning ... I just thought ...'

She smiled in a way she definitely could not have managed if she'd found him particularly attractive. 'Sure.' Was she trying to sound like a New Yorker? Or just a proper Sydney woman? She was certainly tossing her conference-presentation blow-dry. 'Why the hell not?'

∞

It turned out – over dinner – that Christopher had recently broken up with his girlfriend, due to him wanting to get married and her not. The ex-girlfriend (Alexis) believed they'd got together too young.

'That old story,' Grace said unsympathetically.

'The very one,' he said non-defensively. His red cheeks went a tiny bit redder. He was one of those pale, reddish sorts of people.

Grace was feeling a rebellious type of semi-lust. Like: *I'm not even that into this man, and I hardly know him, but I can have a one-night stand if I want to, just watch me.* The post-presentation adrenaline must have run its course by then, so it was hard to say why she acted like that. Maybe it was just Sydney. The whole city was so sure of itself and transactional that you practically felt as if you had to have casual sex, just to fit in.

Or maybe it was – actually, who was she kidding? – of *course* it was because Ben lived in Sydney.

She hadn't even phoned him. She was scared he'd do an odd, 'Oh! Hi!' voice and then tell her he was sadly too overwhelmed with work to see her. *Overwhelmed* was exactly the word he'd use. And *sadly*. He'd sound regretful and grave; his tone would imply phrases like critical care and unspeakably demanding and lives in the balance. Grace would think: *There must be hundreds of cardiologists in Greater Sydney. You could sort something out if you really wanted to, no matter how* overwhelmed *you may be.*

And even if he said, 'Wonderful, Gracey, let's go somewhere spectacular and have dinner,' what was the *point* of seeing him? To marvel at photos of his beautiful, innocent toddler? To reminisce? To make silly jokes and have serious talks and exchange listening-telling looks until it was tragically clear that they still *got* each other? Or to realise that he was more flawed than ever – or that they'd both been worked on by life that little bit more – and so they no longer did?

Anyway.

Ben was the reason she went back to Christopher's hotel room, and it was because of Ben that when she saw the mini-box of cornflakes waiting on Christopher's counter, she said, 'Breakfast,' in an (ironic) suggestive voice.

Christopher said, 'Ah! Indeed!' and then – in case he'd misunderstood and overstepped – 'Good breakfast options here. For everyone. Not just in-house guests, as I understand it.'

Very sweet. So sweet and good and well-intentioned.

She put one of her hands on his waist and then kissed him. His mouth was cold. He squeezed her upper arm, not unpleasantly, but firmly, like he was a remedial masseur.

After less than a minute, they broke off the kiss and held hands, as if hand-holding while looking straight ahead and walking towards the couch would keep the flow going. They sat down and kissed some more, and then he put both his hands on her breasts, through her top. He had his eyes closed and his face tilted up towards the ceiling, and he was semi-frowning, like a child concentrating on a particularly delicious ice-cream. He started squeezing one boob and then the other. It felt as if he was sending a Morse-code message, and her body went more and more still, but she didn't stop him. In fact, she did an erotic-style moan, in case it helped the mood.

Christopher stood up quickly and undid his trousers. She lay on her back and scraddled her shoes off and got out of her jeans. By the time he turned around again, she was wearing only her knickers.

He didn't say anything, and he didn't look at her body. He met her eyes for one semi-tender, semi-shy second and then lay on top of her. He was gentle, but it also felt as if they were doing a dance routine he'd learned long ago, and now he was just going to run through it with her quickly.

It was hard to know what to do to make it better. (Perhaps she should have brought to mind an article along the lines of 'How to Get What You Want in Bed Without Being Too Demanding and Thus Putting Him Off with Your Nagging Ways'.) Instead, she closed her eyes and told herself to stop being silly.

She thought: *If this was Ben, I'd probably like it.*

But then she thought: *Ben would simply not* lick *my neck like that. And even if he did, if I moved my head that way, Ben would* know *I meant, Cease and desist with your weird licking!*

After a while, she realised the whole thing wasn't going to suddenly improve, and that she should fake an orgasm so it would stop, as otherwise she would end up nary the more pleasured and with cystitis to boot. So, she groaned – and she didn't overdo it; she knew what she sounded like when she had a genuine orgasm, after all – and then he had his orgasm. Then he looked down at her.

She gave a no-doubt pretty thin smile and said, 'Wow.'

And he said, 'I *know*.' (Happily.)

She gave his cheek a little kiss. It would have been nice if she had enjoyed the sex more, not only for her own sake, but so she could truthfully tell him what a great time she'd had. He seemed like such a sweet man.

'Um,' she said instead. 'I might just go to the loo.'

And it was as he obligingly reversed out of her, that they both felt the condom come off.

'Oops, sorry!' he said.

But she wasn't mad, or even all that worried. Emergency contraception was very effective, and he was being (as expected) caring and concerned and assuring her that he was most definitely not diseased.

They got dressed immediately, and took a 25-minute taxi ride (he paid) to the nearest open pharmacy. The morning-after pill was in her tummy within two hours of sex, which – as she understood it – would in almost all cases do the trick.

However. The whole time Christopher was using his laptop to google *Sydney CBD pharmacy 24 hours*, and the whole time she was in the bathroom wiping semen off her thighs with a still-folded white handtowel, and the whole time Christopher was speaking in a clear, self-conscious voice to the automated taxi-summoning service, and the whole time they were in the lift with him saying absolutely not, there was no way she was going alone, that whole oddly intimate, slightly adventurous time, there must have been one of her eggs lingering voluptuously in her reproductive tract, just waiting for his millions of sperm to bedazzle her with their speedy, mucous-penetrating agility.

In other words, she must have only just ovulated. And the morning-after pill – as she didn't know, and didn't consider – didn't work if you'd only just ovulated.

So, three weeks later, she was at work, blithe and efficient as you like. She picked up a shiny little packet of pregnancy test from the pharmacy across the road and then breezed into the staff toilet and weed a purely precautionary wee straight onto the undramatic white stick. She set the stick on a square of toilet paper on the cubicle floor, and when the two accusatory, you-*idiot* pink lines appeared in their tiny, huge window, she still had to work another six-and-a-half hours.

That whole afternoon, she kept forgetting about the teeny-weeny embryo, and then remembering it. A dog came in with an infected abscess. Lance. Antibiotics. Pregnant! A guinea pig with some sort of infestation. Weigh. Calculate dose. *Pregnant!* A cat who'd been hit by a car. Palpate abdomen. Check spine. *PREGNANT!*

She kept thinking – to be honest, hopefully – about miscarriage rates. Then about the merciless and inconvenient arc of fertility, and how she was single, and busy, and thirty-one.

She got home from work at just after eight o'clock. At eleven, she opened the fridge and stood staring at a recently cut avocado that was turning a surprisingly bright orange around its stone.

When the fridge-door alarm beeped she said, 'Will you *please* give me one single minute?'

But the alarm just beeped again.

'Well, fuck you, too, then!' she said, and slammed the door as hard as she could.

She looked from her fridge to the phone. She sat down on the floor. There was no one she could wake with her news.

∞

Grace rang in sick the next morning. It was the first time in her life she'd ever pretended to be ill to get out of work. (It was pretty easy, seeing as though she owned the business. She said she had 'a very nasty virus', and Maria said she sounded *just* as bad as her sister-in-law and that it was a *dread*ful winter they were having.)

Grace finished the call, left the phone off the hook and got back into bed. Her hands settled on her tummy.

She imagined Maria was her aunty. Aunty Maria would bring her chicken-and-corn soup in a scratched Tupperware container, and say something brisk like, 'You're not the first, and you won't be the last!' Then Aunty Maria would relate a family secret about the war and a soldier and a great-aunt who was really someone's illegitimate daughter by an American naval hero. 'But in this day and age, you can do as you please,' Aunty Maria would say, with a slightly disapproving sort of zest. 'Now eat your soup. I've put barley in it.'

Some people actually had aunties like that. Some people *complained* about those aunties.

Grace sighed. Everyone knew having a baby out of wedlock was nothing these days. Even if she had an aunty, there'd be no call whatsoever for stories about the war.

She let her mind go to her poor dead mother. What would Tess say if Grace called her up and told her she was pregnant? There'd be joyful tears. Admonitions to both rest deeply and strengthen her physical body. Talk of everything happening in divine right order. Something about Sagittarius rising.

She thought of Ben, and imagined for a brief and blissful moment that this baby was his and that it was planned. She imagined telling him and him nodding, all knowing and tender, and a grin suffusing his face and his voice trembling just the tiniest bit, in a way they both noticed and smiled at, as he told her how 'utterly delighted' – or maybe how 'deeply delighted' – he was. And then he'd say something wry about her still, please God, being able to have sex, and she'd say something droll and alluring about pregnancy making the female sexual response more intense, and they'd chuckle and have jolly, yet hot, multi-position intercourse for hours.

Ben.

She rolled onto her side and forced herself to remember that Ben had a toddler of his own and that Louise Buchanan had just been profiled in *Marie Claire*. Louise Buchanan had a flourishing interior-design business and believed in natural materials and natural light, and she woke up every single morning with Ben and their little girl in a house possessed of what the *Marie Claire* journalist said was a covetable double-height kitchen.

Grace made herself think about the computer-science boy she'd dated at university (Drew Bryan), and how much she thought about him (never) and she told herself that *that* was exactly how Ben felt about her.

That all took about half an hour, and it was not yet nine in the morning.

At just after ten o'clock, she rang Christopher.

'Hello, Grace!' Christopher said. 'Hang on a mo.' Presumably he was at work. 'How are you?'

'Pregnant.'

He gave laugh like a battery-operated teddy bear, and then there was silence.

'Christopher?'

'Sorry. Yes. I'm here.'

'Well, then, ah, in terms of weighing up options,' she said. 'I'm not sure if you're aware, but basically there's still quite a few weeks before I have to decide.'

'I see. That's ... well.' He sounded like he was blushing. 'Good.'

'And I know it's yours, because I haven't been with anyone else in the right timeframe.'

'Of course!' As if that line of thought hadn't occurred to him. 'Of course.'

'You could be involved as much or as little as you want. If we – I – went down that path.'

'I ... Right.' Even more embarrassed. 'That's very ... yes, I see.'

'I'm not feeling sick or anything, yet,' she added, and then regretted it.

'Er ... that's excellent.'

She'd thought they might talk about the critical stage her business was at, and the fact that she didn't have any family she could ask to help her, and her maternity-leave entitlements (none). But she couldn't seem to bring any of that up.

'Grace, I want you to know that the ball is one hundred per cent in your court.' He spoke like a conscientious financial adviser. 'One hundred per cent. Completely your call. Whatever you decide, you have my support.'

'Thank you,' she said. What did he even mean? 'Very much.'

She hung up. She wondered how he'd managed to sound so heroic, when he was leaving the hardest thing to her.

∞

Two weeks and a forty-five-minute counselling session later, she rang him and said, 'I want to have this baby.'

'*Well*, then!' Christopher said. Then he went quiet.

Grace was about to say something huffy, about *Obviously you have a life to be getting on with*, or even, *Have a nice life, then, Christopher!* but he cleared his throat.

He told her the 'recruitment gurus' felt he'd have no trouble finding work in Hobart, as long as he took a modest, 'perfectly manageable' pay cut. He told her he'd be 'in a position' to relocate down there mid-spring.

On the fifteenth of October, she picked him up from the airport. They shopped together for car seats and she helped him choose a couch and swap mobile phone providers. She took him up the mountain and to the market. Things remained entirely platonic, until one night – at a restaurant with very rude staff – he fished a little blue box out of his trouser pocket, and proposed to her the instant she'd finished eating something with mascarpone in it.

He was such a lovely man – so deserving, so *open*, somehow – that she had to tell him no, but thank you, and quite honestly without even thinking about it.

Which, obviously, was because of Ben, too.

The vehicles had mobile phones legally placed in commercially installed holders, and there were no obvious sources of driver distraction at the time of the collision.

Chapter Twelve

IMOGEN

Winter

My new route to work was that little bit longer, so I was feeling quite tired when I telephoned the paediatric registrar one afternoon. I needed to discuss a six-year-old boy with a suspected urine infection.

The paediatric doctor's name was Kurt Clements, and he said he'd come straight down. When I saw him, he was in the staff area talking to that non-team-player intern.

'… turns pink when you add tonic,' she was telling him. 'Looks like a soft drink, but very much isn't.'

'So, it's a gin bar?' Kurt said. He was leaning back against the bench, right next to her chair. 'Literally nothing else to be had?'

'I believe people do drink other things there. But it's frowned upon.' She twirled her pen in her ponytail.

'Where is this place? Maybe I'll order a beer and cause a commotion.'

The intern laughed and started explaining how to find a parking space near Gin Bar None. 'Anyhoo,' she finished up, as if she was Canadian, which she was not. 'Friday nights. Always fun.' She indicated her baggy scrubs. 'And sometimes I even go crazy and put on a dress.'

'This is sounding better and better.'

'I've been to Gin Bar None,' I said. 'You can have anything you want, actually. Or, not quite anything. But it's similar to most bars. Not just gin, is what I mean. Anyhoo, lots of people order beers.'

'Right.' Kurt turned away from the intern, stopped smiling and said, 'I'm here about the six-year-old with the suspected UTI?'

'Archie McRae,' I said. 'He's my patient. And you know, with the pinkness? They put a pH-sensitive botanical in the gin.' I was about to explain that tonic water was acidic, but Kurt spoke.

'So. Archie? What's going on with him?'

'Yes! Sorry!' Even though Kurt was about the same age as I was, he was my senior. 'Archie McRae is a six-year-old boy who presents with four days of lower abdominal pain, associated with—'

'So, what do you think's going on?' he interrupted.

'Well, I'm thinking that he may have a urinary tract infection.' Then I remembered to add, 'Kurt.'

'Vitals?'

I told him.

Kurt suddenly unfolded his arms. 'That kid sounds *crook*.' He looked at me as if I'd done something wrong, even though he'd been the one doing most of the socialising. To the intern, he added, 'Gotta go.'

She smiled. Her ponytail flicked and furled like a gymnast's ribbon.

I hurried after Kurt, whose legs were long and whose speed, therefore, was very fast.

∞

When we got to Archie's bedside, the nurse said, 'Ah, Kurt. Good.'

She already had the observations chart in her hand, and she passed it to him. I saw her tap a finger against the most recent measurements.

Archie was lying on the bed. He was wearing a school uniform – blue shorts, red polo shirt – and breathing fast, but not moving much.

Kurt introduced himself to Archie's mum, Tina. She was overweight, which I was mentioning only as a description, not as an insult, and was wearing a pale-pink hoody with a very small, reddish-brown stain on its left sleeve. Tomato sauce, perhaps.

Kurt asked her nine questions I could have answered – I'd already asked them! – and asked the nurse several things. He didn't ask me anything.

The mum watched Kurt's face, and Archie's. Every time Kurt spoke to her, she straightened her back. Then she gradually curled forward towards Archie again.

'No drip?' Kurt said to me. He continued staring at me for two seconds after he'd spoken. Maybe I was reading too much into it, but it felt as if his question was an accusation.

I swallowed and didn't reply. The cubicle was both noisy – from the surrounding department – and quiet.

'He's had bloods?'

'Not quite yet.'

I'd honestly thought about doing a blood test, but the guidelines around that were equivocal, and I hadn't wanted to interrupt Tristan to check. I knew he'd say, 'What do you think, *Doc*tor?' Tristan called most people by their first names, but he had taken to calling me '*Doc*tor'.

Kurt clicked his back teeth together without opening his mouth. I felt very Sick.

'His urine went to the lab when?' he demanded.

'I got the sample myself, around thirty minutes ago, Kurt.' The nurse would normally do that, but she'd been busy with Tristan and I hadn't liked to interrupt.

'But you say his dipstick showed infection?'

The dipstick was the preliminary test we did in the emergency department. The laboratory test was more conclusive. 'Imogen?'

I frantically tried to remember what I'd told him on the phone. 'I'll go get the dipstick for you!' I said. I'd left it by the sink. 'And I'll ring the lab. See how they're getting on.'

Kurt flicked his eyes across me towards the nurse and said, in a different tone, 'Let's set up for bloods. I'll put a drip in.'

'I'll get right onto that urine!' I told them.

But only the mum looked at me.

∞

'His urine looks clear,' I told Kurt, calmly. I'd given myself a short period of positive self-talk. 'Completely clear.'

Kurt held out his hand for the cardboard dipstick. As he checked it, his face went very still. He leaned in close to me and said, 'So. Where do we think this child's fever, this child's infection, this child's *sepsis* might be coming from?'

'Um? Abdominal pain is a well-documented presenting symptom of certain types of meningitis,' I said. 'Some studies mention it in as many as seven per cent of cases.'

'No shit.' He hissed it, so nobody else heard. 'He needs an LP.'

This meant a lumbar puncture, often known as a spinal tap, and important in the diagnosis of meningitis. LPs were not done all that often, though, and Kurt moved his eyes from side to side in an uncharacteristic way that may have indicated uncertainty. 'And we'll get blood cultures.'

The nurse said she'd set up. Tristan came in. If we were in a documentary, there would be urgent music playing. Viewers would assume we were all good, competent people who liked each other, that nobody was feeling Sick about their own stupidity, and that all of us were invited to the bar afterwards.

Kurt told the mum the plan, and the mum listened and nodded, as if she understood everything. I doubted she did. Kurt was using quite a lot of jargon, and most laypeople didn't know what the dura, the casing around the spine, was. Kurt was about to stick a needle through it, in order to siphon off some fluid for testing.

I said, 'This is a commonly done procedure, Tina. Hundreds of these happen every day.' I meant worldwide, of course. The mum's nostrils dilated then constricted. She gave her consent.

Kurt was frowning as he swabbed iodine all over Archie's back. I saw the silent, intense way Tristan was concentrating on Archie's airway, and the focused quiet of the two nurses. Kurt got out the four-centimetre needle, which he'd be inserting between the bones of Archie's vertebral column. The mum saw it and quickly moved her eyes towards the doorway.

'Don't be scared, Tina,' I told her. 'It's not quite as bad as it may appear.' I really hoped Kurt was good at this.

'Okay,' the mum said. She smiled down at Archie very brightly, even though he had been sedated and was curled up on the bed. 'Good to know.'

When Kurt had obtained the sample, he said, 'Let's get some antibiotics in.' He used a calculator and Archie's weight to work out what was needed. I saw how hard he had to concentrate, and that he had patches of flushed skin under his stubble.

'Thank you,' Archie's mum said to me, as I was leaving. 'Thanks heaps for looking after him, and for being so thorough.' She got tears in her eyes. 'I ummed and ahed about even coming in.'

'That's just fine,' I told her. 'And thank you for your positive feedback, Tina.'

∞

Archie McRae was admitted to the paediatric ward, and the next morning I caught a sticky-buttoned elevator up to see him. This was not standard practice, but I had been extremely worried.

'I just popped in to see how Archie McRae's getting on?' I said. 'Is he less crook this morning?'

Kurt was sitting at the ward desk, doing IV-fluid calculations. He told me Archie's lumbar puncture was all clear. 'So, it's a bit odd,' he said. 'We still have no idea where his infection was coming from.' He added a long sentence that meant a harmless virus was a possibility, but the diagnosis was uncertain, and the main thing was that Archie was improving. They were just going to continue the antibiotics and observe him.

I was immensely relieved, but I nodded with an appropriately professional blend of casualness and concern.

Kurt waved a hand in the air. 'He's in seven, if you wanted to go say hello.'

Room seven had a very high window you couldn't see out of, and beside the bed, a pleated curtain that hadn't been folded back properly. Archie was wearing navy-blue pyjamas with miniature trucks on them. The sleeves exposed the lower third of his little forearms.

I explained I wasn't officially caring for Archie anymore, but that I'd just called in to see how things were going.

The mum was sitting next to his bed. She said, 'Yeah, thanks. It's been a shaky old night. Say hello to Dr Imogen, please Archie.' She was wearing the same clothes as yesterday.

Archie looked at me and didn't say anything.

'That's just fine,' I told her. 'I'm sure he's feeling crook.'

I wondered if I could somehow go out in my lunchbreak and buy Archie some new pyjamas. But I didn't really get lunchbreaks, and anyway, it would be a breach of professional boundaries.

The mum was saying a lot of things about Archie's back and Archie's breakfast and Archie's teacher's opinion of his learning style. I nodded in a compassionate way until she stopped. I had worked hard to develop my clinical communication skills, and I had learned that, under appropriate conditions, such nodding could be a good way to convey empathy.

'Ah well,' she said eventually. 'I'm just so happy he's getting better?'

I put my hand onto her forearm. This was a similar technique to nodding. But the mum put her hand on my hand and nearly started crying!

'We're not real big fans of hospitals, but you've made it that much easier, Dr Imogen,' she said. After about five seconds, she turned away and put her palm against the tip of her nose.

I wasn't sure of the best thing to do, but in the end I counted to twenty in my head, and then said, 'Goodbye and good luck, Archie and Tina.'

I was nothing if not empathetic.

∞

That evening, I did not walk via Zoe's street, so I arrived home before it was dark. The stillness of all my rooms – the way the sound of my key in my front door travelled to their very edges – made me feel as if my chest, my abdomen, my physical self might float away.

I hummed while I opened a new packet of liquorice tea, because next door's television was irritatingly audible. I hated that stupid show. Pretty young people winning at everything but disingenuously pretending they were losing. I sat down at my dining table and put my fingers in my ears while the tea got strong enough.

On my living room wall, was a photo of me that Mum and Dad had organised for my eighteenth birthday. 'It'll be a lovely memento,' Mum had said. 'Nice to have something professional.'

The photographer's name had been Rye. He told me straightaway that he was just doing this job to save up to go overseas, that 'these kinds' of portraits weren't really his 'thing'. He had a tattoo on his forearm of a Maori symbol.

'Do you have an interest in New Zealand culture?' I asked him.

'Nah,' was all he said.

'Just, your tattoo made me think maybe you did?'

'Ah. Nah. If you could please bring your chin down a bit?'

His 'thing' would be taking photos of pretty, dark-haired women with sand on their thighs, lolling about near cliffs. He would think brunettes, and black-and-white film, made photos more artistically valid. He would talk about New Zealand with those women, about surfing and rivers and bands and parties. He'd segue from there into invitations, and then onto sex.

He would. He absolutely would.

Just not with me.

I took my fingers out of my ears. The neighbours' television rumbled on.

The photographer was not really the issue. The television wasn't really the problem.

But it wasn't as if I'd had a malicious intention. I hadn't been self-serving. It wasn't as if I was trying to terminate anyone's life.

I took a sip of the too-hot tea, so it burned my tongue. I hated liquorice tea. Even the smell made me nauseous. But I could still choose to drink it.

When I'd been providing care for Archie McRae, it had felt as if I'd had no ability to do anything except keep making quick decisions. But I had had choices. I was the first to admit that I could have made better ones.

I stood up, retrieved the remote control from its basket on the coffee table and turned on my own television. It only took six clicks to find Netflix, and then the program the neighbours were watching. *Friends*.

I took a big gulp of tea, enough to scour the whole middle part of my tongue. I clicked the volume up as high as it could go.

Penance was an interesting concept. How many days of liquorice tea would atone for endangering a child's life? How many nights trying to sleep with *Friends* season two up that loud?

I decided on twenty. Just a random allocation. I was operating in an evidence-free zone.

Key Principles of Emergency Medicine (2019 ed.)
W.J. Olsen et al.
Chapter 32

Human sources of preventable negative outcomes

- 'Slips' are often attributed to errors of concentration. Slips tend to occur when there are distractions, stress or fatigue. The minimisation of slips may be achieved with adequate breaks, adequate staffing, holiday leave et cetera.
- 'Mistakes' reflect incorrect decisions. These may occur due to inexperience or lack of training or knowledge, such as when staff are practising outside of their scope. Mistakes may be minimised by adequately supported professional development, and by the conscientious and competent supervision of junior staff.
- 'Misdeeds', in contrast, are rare, and reflect deliberately or wilfully harmful decision-making.

Chapter Thirteen

GRACE

Winter

'But chicken's a safe food, Em,' Grace said. She tried to keep the terror out of her voice. 'It's green.'

In their world, green food didn't mean kale or broccolini or lettuce. It meant the least challenging stuff, the things Emma could usually manage to swallow. In their world, potatoes were orange and cream was red.

'Will you just stop pressuring me?'

'Please try to eat your portion of salad.'

Emma put down her cutlery. 'I prefer to avoid discussing my eating habits,' she said loftily.

Oh, God. Emma was parroting one of several lines she'd learned before Christmas, lines that were designed to be used when kind, lucky, untutored people said things like, 'No ice-cream? Look at the size of you! You could eat whatever you wanted!'

She, Grace, had role-played the use of these lines with Emma. And Emma had barely needed to use them, because Grace had acted like a presidential advance party, making sure anyone with whom Emma came into contact knew to avoid references to weight, exercise, appearance or food. (Since then, anytime Emma happened to drop by the clinic, Maria refrained from conversation about skinny jeans and gluten-free caramel slice, and instead said things like, 'Emma, lovely to see you, darl, now tell me, what are you watching at the moment, because I'm desperate, really and truly desperate, for something Barry and I can enjoy together, and I'm struggling to find anything suitable, honestly and truthfully, even though we're very open to programs aimed at a younger audience, isn't it lovely the way so many gay characters are coming through nowadays?')

'We need to stay sitting here until you've finished it,' Grace said now.

'I need time and space.' Emma stood up. 'I need acceptance.'

'I can see you're feeling really upset today.'

'"I can see you're feeling really upset today,"' Emma mimicked. She was looking down at her mum. 'Mum, why don't you just be honest about how *you're* feeling? Why do you always pretend to be so calm and so *professional* when really you hate me the way I am?'

'You must be really hurting inside, Em,' said Grace. 'And I'm sorry for anything I've done to make that worse.' She paused. 'But as you know, it's your eating disorder that is—'

'Oh, shut *up*! You're not even sorry! You just want me to eat my salad so you can get on with your work without me dying on your watch!'

Grace turned her head away from Emma and pressed the heel of her hand between her eyebrows. She felt like saying, 'Fine, don't eat it, go to your room, purge away, I don't care, I don't even want to eat salad in fucking *winter*, and I actually do need to do some work, but I also need a rest and to go to sleep and maybe I will just leave you to it and in a few years, you'll have sorted yourself out.'

She might have said exactly that, if she didn't know any statistics.

'Please sit, Emma,' she said. 'Or I will need to confiscate your phone.'

Emma paused.

'You don't need to eat right away. We've got as much time as you need. But you do need to sit down.'

Emma sat. She gave Grace a look of contempt, one that extinguished, as effectively as water on a candle, any pleasure or pride or enjoyment that Grace might somehow still have had inside her.

Grace chewed her tomato and thought about what her own mother might have done. Honoured Emma's personal path? Diffused some cedarwood oil? Talked about totem animals or crystal healing or affirmations? Grace missed her so much. And she missed those pleasant, logical methods of healing.

'Just try for one bite at a time,' she said. She fucking *hated* Traffic Light Family Management Plans.

It was very, very much later that Emma finished her salad.

'Happy now?' she asked Grace. She slung her fork onto the table and walked away.

∞

'Sorry to pop in when you're just about to start, but you did say to let you know straightaway.' Grace looked up in something like terror. Was it the school? Was it Emma?

She would end it with Ben tonight.

'Wallie Chen's owner rang, and he's drinking well now, still off his food, though, and also, while I'm here, Renee wants you to call Derinya, it's urgent, she feels. A-*ga*-in.'

'Thanks, Maria.' Grace exhaled.

She would just finish with him. She just would. She just *would*.

The trouble was that whenever you put 'just' in front of a phrase like that, the phrase usually meant doing something either technically complex or emotionally impossible. (Just *catch* it. Just be your*self*. Just move *on*.)

She pulled the tourniquet a tiny bit tighter around the sick puppy's forelimb. Felt for a vein. Flipped gloves on. She could do this much almost without thinking, certainly without having to *decide* anything.

119

Breanna, the nurse, hooked up a bag of saline and passed Grace a syringe, and her mind became completely focused. Sometimes when she anaesthetised a dog, she remembered the first time she did it.

'This is an elegant way to induce anaesthesia,' her supervisor had told her. He'd been one of those quiet, handsome older men, the sort who wore new-looking navy-blue jumpers on weekends; she'd automatically believed every single thing he said. 'Not exactly standard methodology, but resolves the post-operative nausea issue nicely.'

Well. Surely, surely, surely, she could find an elegant way to resolve her issue with Ben.

∞

The most difficult thing, that 1990s day, had been keeping her eyes in the right place.

'He's milking it for all it's worth,' Ben's mum was saying. She was smiling, with the friendly authority of a woman who didn't mind drop-ins from Ben's new uni friends, who was in possession of every single thing required to handle drop-ins not only from first-year university students, but from *anyone*.

She led Grace through a kitchen, past a square china bowl of stone fruit, and an enormous pump pack of Aesop handwash, and three pristine grey tea towels on a brass rail. She waved a comfortable hand towards a set of glass doors that opened into what had to be the living room. 'You'll find him in there. Reclining in state.'

'Thank you, Mrs Hutchinson.'

'Call me Sue. Just don't encourage him now, Grace, whatever you do.' A twinkle, woman to woman: *men and their colds*. And there was no diffidence or deference in the twinkle, either, no concern that the young ones might not do that sort of thing nowadays. It was a long time later that Grace understood: Sue was simply certain of being respected and valued, and by all the right people. Her personal charm was based on the confidence that went with taking just about everything for granted, while being irreproachably kind to the many less fortunate.

Ben lay on one of three couches; thick socks stuck out from under a beige blanket.

'Chemistry notes,' Grace announced in place of hellos. She put the lecture pad – which felt like her admission ticket – onto the coffee table, next to a box of eucalyptus-scented tissues and a vase of poppies. 'As requested.'

He said a genuinely gracious thanks from amidst his kingdom of cream carpet, of framed photos on side tables, of paintings with their own downlights.

She stood, uncertain. (She'd imagined sitting at his bedside, taking his hand in a casual way – the way Rachel on *Friends* did that kind of stuff – and cheering him with a hilarious anecdote about ending up in the wrong tutorial or accidentally agreeing to a date with someone's estranged father. But nothing like that had happened to her.)

'I actually had a decent fever this morning.' Towards the end of the sentence, he realised how he sounded. 'You know, these common colds. Very common, but very nasty.'

She laughed and sat down on an empty couch's armrest. Hopefully that wouldn't seem ill-bred, or whatever its modern equivalent was. Ben was telling her he'd watched an old James Bond movie – Sean Connery – that afternoon.

'You into the new guy?' he said. 'Pierce Brosnan?'

She shrugged. 'I'm open-minded on the Pierce question.'

'We should see one. When I'm better.' Did he mean a James Bond movie? God, there'd be sex. Or another Pierce Brosnan movie? Were there any? Maybe he just meant a movie in general. And did he mean as a date? Or just a friendly outing?

'Okay.' It was so annoying, the way she was never spirited enough to ask any of her questions. Why couldn't she manage a simple, flirtatious, *Are you asking me on a date, Ben Hutchinson?* But no. Of course she couldn't. Those words would sound ridiculous in real life, or at least, in her life.

Sue stuck her head around the door just then. She had a tea towel over her shoulder and a clean apron on, and she asked Grace if she'd 'be joining' them for a 'simple dinner'.

'Oh! No, thank you, Sue.'

'Can't say I blame you.' Another twinkle. 'He's not exactly sparkling company at the moment, is he? Bad as his father.'

Ben smiled, and stretched, and then coughed. He looked so gorgeous that Grace nearly shot a lust-edged *isn't he adorable?* glance at Sue. Dear God. She had to get out of there, away from all that finely calibrated abundance, from these people who treated nectarines and apricots like apples and pears and who actually *used* their stain-free linen tea towels to prepare 'simple dinners'. She had to go home, to her mum, who shared a lawnmower with two friends and who wrote pleadingly positive affirmations about universal abundance on electricity bills, and whose bedside lamp involved an op-shop silk scarf and Blu Tack. She had to work out how to *be* somewhere like here.

'Grace should come for dinner when I'm better,' Ben said to his mother. 'Hey, Grace?'

'That'd be nice,' Grace said. 'Thank you.'

The thankyou was mainly to Sue, but also – undeniably and unfortunately – partly to him. That was the problem. It was just very hard, amidst all that was so beautiful and new, to keep her eyes in the right place.

∞

In a not-too-noisy pub, before the turn of the millennium and towards the end of her second year of university, Grace leaned both her elbows on the bar and looked into the mirror. Behind inverted bottles of Jack Daniels and Kahlúa were reflected the pale gleam of her own shoulder, the brown strap of her fake-velvet singlet top, several locks of her hair. Ben, next to her, caught her gaze in the mirror and raised his eyebrows.

'You look very nice,' he said. 'That top. Suits you.' She'd bought it from Supré for seven dollars. It would have been twelve dollars for two, except twelve dollars had seemed like a lot.

'Is that so?' She nodded – discreetly, euphorically – down at her beer.

Ben leaned closer. He said, 'Hey, Gracey. Three o'clock.'

Of course, he didn't turn that way. He sipped his own beer and stared ahead while Grace turned, flicked needlessly at the velcro-ed shut diary inside her calico bag, and then glanced up, towards three o'clock. The girl was long-haired and conspicuous in her synthetic attractiveness, and was wearing a tight aqua dress.

'Mmm,' Grace said, as she turned back to Ben. Their knees touched when she swivelled on the bar stool. Through the rip in her jeans, her skin touched his denim. 'Just your type.' The woman wasn't his *actual* type, not at all. His actual type could be not only summed up, but entirely described, as 'beautiful'. 'I'm sure she'd be very susceptible to your charms. Poor foolish girl. I should go warn her.'

She made to stand up, but Ben put three fingertips on the side of her thigh. Their knees slid an enormous inch, so that one of his was between hers. Into her ear, he said, 'But maybe she's waiting to meet someone.'

Grace manoeuvred her head so their cheeks were almost touching; he would be able to feel her breath – her lips, almost – on his ear. 'She'll be meeting her friends,' she said. 'Betcha. Girls' Night Out.'

'You think?' They were now touching at three points: their knees, their cheekbones, his fingers on her leg. They had spent that Friday afternoon in a chemistry lab, barely speaking. Even when she'd leaned a notebook against his back to scribble a random fact about sodium hydroxy-something, it would have been impossible to say whether or not they were flirting. But now it was after seven o'clock.

'I can tell these things,' she said.

Each of them had a free hand curved around a beer; each beer had about two mouthfuls left.

'The friends'll be here any minute,' she story-told, aware she was being bitchy, and aware she didn't like that, and aware she was doing it anyway. 'There'll be a Nikki and a Ricki and an Allie and a Sally. Then there'll be a Mel. There's always a Mel. Or a Bel.'

'But not a Grace,' said Ben. He let go of his beer and put his coldish hand on her hip, where her top met her jeans. 'Or a Gracey.'

'We've talked about this.' She insisted she was Gracey only to him, and only when they were alone, because, she said, Gracey sounded way too girly for everyday use. This was a ploy; she couldn't care less who else called her what. It was just she loved having a private custom with him.

'Gracey.' He put his forehead on hers. She didn't notice how he smelled; she didn't notice anything except what she wanted to do. 'Gracey. I like it when you're Gracey.'

'Oh, do you just?' She kept her tone exactly right: sardonic and clever and wry. She wasn't *that* tipsy. She also kept her hand on her beer, in her twenty-year-old self's best semblance of an enigmatic woman who was hard to get.

'Gracey,' he breathed. 'Gracey.'

A few beats passed.

'It's almost a shame I'm not completely stupid,' she said, in the end. She leaned away, moved her legs, sipped her beer. God, it took a lot of effort. 'You should go talk to her.' She gestured with her head towards the pretty-enough young woman.

Whatever it took to stand out from the crowd.

∞

At some point, one day during their third year of uni, they'd decided to use the word 'spectacular' every time they spoke.

'Or maybe just lots of times,' said Grace. 'Let's not be spectacularly pedantic.'

'It'd be spectacularly annoying.'

'Spectacularly so.'

He smiled at her and poured sugar into her coffee. The café had an impressive air of coolness on a shoestring; you got the feeling the owners had recently returned from Sydney or London or even Berlin. Ex-tomato tins held succulents; inverted milk crates were topped with stacks of *Cosmopolitan*s and *Gourmet Traveller*s; an enormous espresso machine pumped out steam and silvery noise in a way that suggested it was proud of itself and for very good reason.

'Seriously,' Ben said, nodding at her drink. 'The coffee's spectacular here.'

Grace took her first-ever sip of 'flat white', and waited to die of pleasure.

'What d'you think?' He was watching her face.

To be honest, she liked mugaccinos better. All those buoyant centimetres of choc-powdered froth. 'I think I prefer instant,' she said. 'And you look awful. What did you *do* last night?'

He made a little face at his serviette-wrapped glass, in the way that meant he genuinely didn't want her to know. 'Nothing much.' He'd already told her he was spectacularly hungover. 'What did you do?'

'Nothing much.'

They went back to their newspapers. A new study showed men

had more fatal road accidents than women. People were burning OJ Simpson memorabilia in front of a US courthouse.

'Thought you went out for dinner?' Ben said, looking up. He'd remembered. It was stupid, the stupid way that gave stupid her so much stupid pleasure. 'Last night. With The Baker?'

'He's not a baker. He's a pastry chef.' Too quick. Too defensive. She turned another page, and made herself see that someone somewhere was saying something about privatisation. 'Which is a spectacularly different thing.'

Ben made a silly, over-apologetic face. If only the pastry chef was a fire-fighter who worked part-time as a Calvin Klein model.

'So, how was it?' He'd closed his newspaper. 'Spectacular?' He was raising his eyebrows right at her.

'Certainly not. No spectaculating on a second date.'

Ben laughed. 'Because I'd be spectacularly jealous.' He rubbed his face and glanced around, and then asked a busy-looking waiter for another 'long black'. 'Christ, I feel like shit.'

He moved his foot so their ankles were touching. Only briefly. And maybe it was just an accident.

∞

Even by the end of that year, nobody seemed to know what was appropriate at someone's mum's funeral. After the service, Grace's university friends stood in ferociously polite clusters: the boys quiet and terrified; the girls talking and horrified, as if they'd accidentally arrived way too early at a party. And now, at the wake, they were all off in a bedroom that one of her mum's friends had designated 'Peace-Full Space'. Grace could hear them talking – in semi-restrained voices – about the World Cup.

Grace stood alone in her mum's kitchen. Well. Inside the kitchen of the house her mum had rented for the last three-and-a-bit years.

On the fridge was a pastel drawing of her mother's guardian angel, as visualised by a purportedly psychic artist. *For Tess*, the artist had written, in curly writing that made Grace think of the elves in *The Lord of the Rings*. She reached out and touched the angel's lemon-pastel heart with her forefinger.

Whatever anyone might think, twenty-one was far too young to lose your mother. It didn't matter that at least Grace was through her teens, or that at least she had a good solid science degree, or that at least she could support herself. Maybe there was never an old enough age – or a solid enough degree – but twenty-one was definitely far too young.

'You okay?' Ben was in his dark suit, his tie off, a mug in his hand.

'I'm—' She couldn't, of course, say how she was.

Ben crossed the little kitchen. He put his mug near the draining board and his arms around her. Ben, it seemed, *did* know what was appropriate. She let her head thump against his chest.

Sad laughter gurgled out of the womyn's sacred circle in the lounge, where her mother's friends were drinking cask wine from a motley collection of vessels. She heard Eve D'Alberto say, 'I always feel that song right here.' Eve would be indicating her heart, her fingertips – bunched together as if to pick up lint – pressed to the centre of her chest.

'Want to go outside?' Grace said.

The two of them sat on the cracked driveway, one on each side of a rectangle in which the concrete had been replaced with pebbles. Weeds were regrowing. Her mother had once weeded properly, with an old metal tool that made it easy to extract the roots. Down on her knees on her rented concrete, occasionally standing to counsel the neighbour about her challenging adult son. Tess had been doing that only four months ago!

'She was sweet, your mum,' Ben said. He passed her his mug. She drank (red wine) and passed it back.

Grace nodded. 'I just found out she gave twenty bucks a week to the women's shelter, even though ...' She made a gesture around the garden, the homemade circle of rocks, the leaning letterbox. Her poor, foolish, chemotherapy-refusing mum. 'She'd say she was blessed to have enjoyed all this.'

'Yeah,' he said. 'Really sweet.'

'She wasn't *dumb*.'

'I didn't—'

'She was not sweet or dumb!'

'Settle down, oh grieving daughter.' He screwed up his face and added, 'Sorry. Should I be nicer?'

She shook her head and held out her hand for the wine again.

Ben assumed a joke-serene expression and a joke-holy voice. 'Because I am here for you, Gracey. Should you need to release your sorrow or unburden your spirit or simply go out and drink large amounts of alcohol, I am here.'

'Thanks.'

'Seriously.' Normal voice. Meeting her eyes. 'Any time.'

'I know.'

She moved closer to him, onto the pebbles. He settled the mug between his feet and put an arm around her.

'What about your brother?' he said.

She explained that her brother was somewhere between here and Townsville. He'd said not to hold off the funeral for him in case he got delayed.

'I see,' said Ben, clearly not seeing at all.

'He's hitching.' That was part of it.

'Right.' To conceal his bewilderment, Ben handed her the mug. She drank, and imagined what Ben's own mother's funeral would –

one day – be like. The caterers, the champagne, the impossibility of a son not being present. The ease and authority with which airfares and suitable clothing would be purchased, the magnetic pull of that family's expectations on even the blackest of sheep. At Sue's funeral, there'd be a phalanx of siblings, of good suits and blow-dries and meticulously blended eyeshadow. Hard-cover guest books, ushers, maybe a children's choir. Not Eve D'Alberto singing a Native American song about soaring eagles in a too-passionate voice. Not someone shouting, 'Trust in the Universe!' into the ensuing silence. There'd be bittersweet anecdotes and admiring speeches, a shiny hearse, separate gleaming black cars for the family. People in the street would look. It would end up seeming as if Sue's life had been worth more than Grace's mother's.

'With my mum, generosity was actually giving *up* things,' Grace said.

Ben either didn't get it – why would he? – or decided to let it go through to the keeper. He kissed the top of her head. Her temple settled itself on his shoulder. Nice.

'What are you going to do?' he said. 'With your very impressive self?' She'd just won an award for biology.

She said she still wanted to train as a vet, but it seemed a funny time to move away – a one-hour flight away, an overnight ferry ride away, an *expensive* way away – to Melbourne.

'Maybe I'll stay here,' she said. 'Among friends?'

He didn't reply immediately. The vaguely uncooperative flywire door creaked as someone came onto the porch. The smell of a cigarette for a while. Then the door creaked open and closed again.

'Be-en,' she said. Woozy. She'd finished the wine. Cold skin and warm insides. 'It's nice here, Ben.'

Ben cleared his throat. 'Want me to get you some water?'

'Nah. Stay.' She tilted up her chin.

'You sure?'

'Mmm.' She leaned in closer. She reoriented her body towards his. This would be – should be, could be – the moment he kissed her. When that magical thing happened as their lips touched in the midst of tragedy and the floodgates of their passion opened, when all the confusion was swept aside by the force of their combined saliva, and afterwards they'd both know everything about each other and all that had to happen next.

'You're pretty drunk.' He squeezed her shoulder, then took his arm away and rested back on his hand.

'I know.' She said it in a jokey voice, and then leaned forward and brushed her lips onto his. He did kiss her back, but not properly, and only for a couple of seconds. *Politely.*

'Don't, Gracey,' he said.

'Seriously?'

'It's not that I don't want to.' Defensively, as if his virility had been impugned. 'But you're ... I'm not going to—' The whole catastrophe was too weird for him to even finish his sentence, apparently. In a squeezed-out voice he said, 'You're the last girl I'd have a stupid one-night thing with.'

'But it wouldn't have to be a stupid one-night thing.'

That hung in the air for a good few seconds.

'I'm not ready for a relationship.'

It came out very practised. Either he'd said it before, or it was just something men like him could say smoothly because all the other men like them were always saying it. (*Can I get a beer, please? My team's playing Saturday. I'm not ready for a relationship.*)

'Sorry,' he added. He actually put his arm around her again, but of course there was no ease to it now. It was more like they were ballet dancers smiling through agony.

'Don't apologise.'

Dear God, the mortification. She could already feel it, in the background, nowhere near as horrendously as she would tomorrow. She straightened, pushed her hair behind her ears and adjusted the hem of her black dress.

'I better be getting inside,' she said. *Things to do. Womyn to wrangle. Just as well you're not ready for a relationship. It would have interfered with the sharing out of Eve D'Alberto's pumpkin soup.*

'Gracey?' The grass looked dusty and pinched, and the driveway moved a bit as she stood up. 'We okay?'

'Yes. Fine!' She really had to get away from him. 'Thanks for the chat.'

She went off, towards the squeaking door, and towards Melbourne, and towards being a vet.

∞

Grace was suturing closed the muscle wall of the puppy's abdomen. The distant ringing of the phone from reception, the humble efficiency of the scissors and the satisfying sameness of her knots – all that was soothing.

After work, she would zip out to Derinya, text Christopher that Emma had left her blazer at his place, book her car in for borderline-unaffordable new tyres, try to work out what sort of tradie might consider fixing her kitchen rangehood, listen to a podcast about feline glaucoma and fold at least one basket of washing. Also put aside a few books Emma had outgrown that would probably work for Maria's oldest granddaughter.

Then, at seven o'clock, she and Emma would sit down together and eat a meal, as per Emma's Traffic Light Family Management Plan.

She could only do her best, and then try – somehow – and seemingly impossibly – to 'let go'.

But also, there was Ben. She had absolutely no management plan for him. There was no standard methodology. There were no elegant solutions.

CORONIAL COURT OF TASMANIA
INQUIRY INTO A DEATH
Pursuant to *Coronial and Other Act 1991*
Section 16(IV)

Standard methodology was used to investigate. This included the use of a drone for photography purposes, the impoundment of the vehicles involved, the taking of sworn statements from witnesses and the cordoning-off of the scene.

Due to the nature of this crash, sworn statements from multiple acquaintances and workmates were subsequently sought. These were also presented as evidence.

Chapter Fourteen

ZOE

Winter

'Just tre*mend*ous!'

'*Won*derful news!'

'I'm be*yond* delighted!'

One of the PE teachers – Adrian – had just announced his engagement, and everyone in the staffroom – led by my surprisingly insensitive friend Sophie – was carrying on as if it was the best thing that had ever happened to anyone in the whole world. There was a lot of talk about everybody putting in for some really nice cutlery, and when would the happy couple set the date, and how, yes, the pair of them had *seeeeeemed* serious at last year's Christmas drinks.

I found myself thinking about how I was, obviously, all for marriage equality, but now that we finally had it, where were my gay-man fallback options? I could have had a sexless yet affectionate lifetime union with Adrian, but now his boyfriend – also called Daniel, salt in wound – had popped the question while the pair of them were holidaying at Binalong Bay.

Happy bloody couples, I thought.

It was unlike me to be so bitter. I decided to put the lid back on my leftover curry and depart.

The Senior Library was built about five years ago, but everyone – at least, all the adults – still thought of it as new. My eyes didn't have to adjust as I went in, because even at that time of the year it was extremely bright and light, all high ceilings and skylights and colourful beanbags on dark-grey carpet. I wished it was dim and mahogany and poky. I was in the mood for solitude and dust and poetical brooding, not collaborative workspaces and posters about growth bloody mindsets.

Emma Tierney-Adams was alone at one of the light-grey tables that was meant for four people. She was reading a novel, her chin in one hand, her chair pushed way back. On the far side, a couple of the computer-loving boys were disobeying the no-personal-devices rule. Nobody else was in there apart from the duty teacher, and she was down the back hunched over the laminating machine.

Since I was in no state for students, their rule breaking or their problems, I went the other way, behind a display about women in science that the Grade Sevens had made. I wondered grouchily if anyone was making posters about men packing school lunches and cleaning bathrooms, or if women would be expected to keep doing all that stuff, too, as well as becoming marine biologists and coders and whatever. I sat at another table and opened the pristine newspaper so hard it made a noise.

My horoscope said I should be optimistic instead of pessimistic today.

Shut up, I told it, silently.

I turned to the Live Life section. There was a shouty double-page spread about healthy-eating essentials and – remarkable! – the benefits of thinking positive to beat winter blues.

Just shut UP, I told it.

Emma Tierney-Adams raised her head. I'd accidentally spoken aloud, apparently, and the library was very quiet, as even modern, skylit, growth-mindset-encouraging libraries tended to be.

'Um?' Loud whisper. Eyes like worried pearls. 'Pardon, Ms Morello?'

'Oh! Just talking away to myself over here. Don't mind me. Sorry!'

We smiled at each other, across a couple more laminated tables meant for four, and then we both returned to our pages until the bell rang.

∞

As soon as I arrived for my Thursday dinner with Claire, I knew she was pregnant. Not because she wasn't drinking wine, or because we weren't having soft cheeses – we hardly ever did – or because she looked tired, but because of something to do with the way she said hello. Far too enthusiastically. Also, T-rex was watching her bash ice out of the freezer trays as if she might collapse at any second. It didn't take a genius to put two and two together.

'Zoe,' she said, when we were all sitting down. We were having nice quiche, nice vegetarian shepherd's pie and a fairly shabby salad because we never got organised enough to decide what I was supposed to bring. 'We've got some news.'

I put my cutlery on my plate and tried to make my face open and receptive.

'I'm pregnant.'

It would have been all right, but as she spoke, T-rex gave her a little glance of such concentrated delight that it very nearly wasn't. I had to stare at my lap.

And I couldn't *believe* she'd told me in front of another person.

'Wow!' My voice managed to sound both excited and pleased, though. Perhaps this was now my lot in life. 'That's wonderful!'

I could imagine how Claire was feeling. How the never-before-used, but also somehow familiar phrase – *I'm pregnant* – had to taste in her mouth. How she was truly concerned that her news might be hurting me, but was still underestimating how very much it did.

We all smiled at each other for a moment, and then I picked up my fork. I saw the two of them exchange a smugly – or maybe not *smug*ly – concerned look.

The slimy warmth of the quiche made me feel sick.

I knew it wasn't as if her being pregnant made my situation any worse. Of course it didn't. Of course it *was* wonderful. Of course I couldn't *wait* to cuddle my niece or nephew, or second cousin, or cousin once removed, or whatever their beautiful baby would be to me. Of *course* all that was true.

It's just that jealousy was one of those things that made you not as nice a person as you wished you could be, and that was why, after we'd talked for a while about celery seedlings and sanding their floors and Amy Winehouse's talent, and before I'd even had any vegetarian shepherd's pie, I had to pretend I had a headache and go home.

Claire wasn't fooled, but it was one of those times when even she knew it was better just to pretend.

∞

'Not at all,' I said. 'Take your time.'

I was at the supermarket, looking terrible. Meaning: actually terrible. Not: like Julia Roberts with no makeup and a hoodie. I had a pimple and my three-year-old concealer had gone all cacky and caked, and I had cracked lips from having been swimming the day before. In a ridiculous bid to hide my face, I was wearing my hair down. It didn't suit me down at the best of times, and that day it had gone all split and wiry. I was also wearing a fancy-shop shirt that had cost so much – even on sale – that I felt I had to put it on sometimes even though it made me seem both no-waisted and stumpy-legged. I really shouldn't try to buy things from fancy shops.

The woman in front of me at the checkout kept asking the attendant to remove items from her order, and then saying, 'Oh wait! How much were they again? No, yes, I'll take them, sorry, dear, actually, how much? No,' and so on. I was keeping up a steady patter of, 'That's fine, no problem, I'm not in a hurry today.'

As she paid, the checkout guy made a face at me which meant, *Thank God we're normal, youngish people and this drama is almost over.* I gave him a blank stare which meant, *Don't be so judgemental and ageist, especially since you're getting paid to be here, Millennial Boy.*

'Zoe?' said a voice behind me.

Barbecue Nick was standing there. He wasn't in the queue. He was just passing, with a green plastic basket over his forearm.

'Hi,' I said. I reflexively glanced at his shopping, which of course I regretted before my eyes were even back to his face. Luckily, he just had non-awkward stuff, like apples and grapes and corn chips, rather than personal lubricant or anti-constipation powders.

I blabbed something or other about stocking up for the week. The Live Life newspaper article had actually been pretty good, and now I was doing the meal-plan, healthy-eating, budget-friendly, once-a-week-shop thing. This was also a by-law following a breakup. I was probably late to get on with it.

'Same here.' Nick straightened his arm, put the handle of the basket in his fist, and swung it around a tiny bit. No sign he was about to move away. The checkout man was not even halfway through scanning my stuff. Nick kept swinging his basket. There was a little silence.

'These ones passionfruit?' said the checkout man. He held one up accusingly, as if I was annoying for choosing fruit nobody normal could be expected to recognise.

'Actually, pomegranates. Thanks.' I turned back to Nick.

'Why are you buying *pom*egranates?' Nick said. He was smiling, as if we already had a private joke about seedy red fruit.

I said pomegranates were a key part of my health kick, which I just hoped was going to last long enough to use up all the fresh produce.

He laughed and said he'd been for a run every single night that week, which was guaranteed not to last. 'Running. So boring,' he said.

'Who would run?' I was very sincere. 'Unless to escape from a robber or something. Maybe then.'

He laughed again. 'Seen T-rex lately?' Standard small talk, but he made it sound like he was genuinely interested. I reminded myself that that was simply because he was *good at this*, and said I'd had dinner with T-rex and Claire on Thursday and they were thinking of sanding their floors. He nodded. Daniel would have asked who was doing it. Daniel always assumed you paid professionals to do jobs like that. Nick just said, 'Yeah. Right. Dusty.'

Another pause. He was wearing a blue T-shirt. I wished I could properly admire his shoulders in it, but he would have noticed.

A young woman in a backless cocktail dress and very high heels tapped past, carrying a cauliflower. Nick and I looked at each other, and I could tell we were both thinking: *Where could she possibly be going in that outfit that she would need to take a* cauliflower?

'I hope I didn't come across as too weird, after dinner, that other night.' I spoke without thinking much, but halfway through the sentence, I realised: *Sheesh, Zoe, that was nearly two months ago! He'd probably forgotten all about it!*

'Nah. Not weird.' An awkward smile. 'Good you set me straight.'

We both did very odd laughs, and then there was another silence. This one seemed to go on for about a decade. We listened to an announcement about dairy to register five please. Then we both laughed again. Nick still didn't walk off.

'Would you want to have dinner with me, some time?' I said. It came out of nowhere. As if I was on a Take Action in Your Personal Life kick, as well as the one about green smoothies and stuff.

'Yeah. That'd be good.' He sounded chuffed. 'How about if I text you?'

'Okay, then,' I said. Not very sparklingly.

'So, ah, if I grab your number?'

'Oh! Okay! Yes!' We faffed around with me for some reason digging in my bag for my phone and dictating my number to him, and him sending me a text so I'd have his number.

All a bit clunky. But as he moved away, he did a little point-nod-grin at my massive bunch of kale, which was sitting show-offily on the conveyer belt. 'Enjoy that, Zoe,' he said.

'I will.' I laughed. Cheery as anything. 'And happy running.'

Then I pulled myself together and glanced at the checkout man. I thought maybe he'd give me a look that meant: *You're very forward, aren't you? And eager! And pleased! Are you that desperate, you* spinster?

But he was busy trying to find the barcode on my economically large bag of basmati rice, and it was obvious that he hadn't noticed a thing.

∞

For dinner, Nick happened to book one of my favourite restaurants, which was as un-edgy as you get, and very popular. Dark-brown-maroon carpet, lots of round tables, decades' worth of photos of the owner – Ricardo – with his arm around football players and soap stars.

Luckily, we had a table down the back, out of the draft, because the door kept opening and closing as people in scarves collected their takeaway pizzas. Ricardo was up front next to the oven, saying, '*Ciao, bella*' to all the women, 'G'day, mate' to all the men and 'Here comes trouble' to all the kids. So nice.

'I'd like a very big glass of pinot,' I said to the waitress. Quite eagerly. 'Noir. And some garlic bread.' I was starving. 'I *love* this place,' I told her and Nick.

Mum always said you could tell a lot about a man from how

he treated waitresses, so I watched as Nick ordered his drink. I also tried not to think about the way Daniel had treated waiting staff. At first, I'd thought it was grown up; then I'd started to feel he was overly distant; now I realised he really had been quite the wanker.

Nick said, 'Can I please have a Boag's draught?' He closed the padded vinyl drinks list, passed it to the waitress and turned to me. It was hard to read too much into any of that, but he looked very nice. Ironed shirt. Freshly shaven. Product in his hair, but not too much. I appreciated the effort, and – could I just say – not only in a sweet-that-he-tried way.

I must be crazy, I thought. He was too handsome, and too charming, and I was too vulnerable, and would definitely get hurt and have nobody to blame but myself. But what else could I do?

'How was work?' he asked, after we'd talked about his day on a building site and the crime novel I was reading and his seventeen-year-old ute which had a broken heater. Also, it came up that he owned a dog called Rug.

I told him how the Year Twelves were trying my patience. A few of them had taken to asking really stupid questions, and yes, I knew everyone thought teachers should believe no question was stupid, but that was rubbish. Some questions were plain ridiculous, as all teachers realised.

'So, did you shout at them?' he said.

'Nope, I just used my strict voice.'

He made a face, as if he'd like to hear my strict voice.

'I said something like, "Would you please look for solutions, not problems!"'

'Stern, Miss Morello,' he said. One hundred per cent flirtily.

'*Ms* Morello.' But I was smiling.

'Stern in a very good way.'

I looked straight at him and sipped some wine. 'Well, that's very bold. Don't make me use my strict voice on you, Nicholas.'

He didn't reply. He just reached for some garlic bread, and made a face, and this tiny noise, like, *What are you* doing *to me?*

And I was *blushing*. Unheard of.

Meanwhile, Nick had started grinning at me so much, it was like he was only eating the bread to give his face something else to do.

God. God. God-god-goddy-goddy-god-god-god.

∞

'Zoe!' said a voice, the next morning. 'How *are* you?'

I turned around from shelves full of cookware to find someone I couldn't quite place.

'Hi there!' I used a very warm tone, to make up for my lack of knowing who she was. 'How are *you*?' Maybe she was from the gym. This was unlikely, though, as I never actually went to my gym.

'I am A-okay, thank you.' She took a step closer to me, and added that she was doing some shopping.

'Isn't this place a nightmare?' I indicated the frying pans. 'I have no idea which one to get.' That was the sort of friendly bonding thing you just had to say. Another by-law.

'I know!' she agreed, very enthusiastically. She was shorter than I was, with sturdy limbs and tense shoulders. Her light-blonde hair was scraped back from her forehead, and she had the kind of skin that would make Claire say irritating things about clean eating. 'Nightmare!'

I thought we'd both wander off, but she didn't wander, so I asked her what she was shopping for.

She said she needed coffee cups. 'Big time. Caffeine is a shift-worker's friend, Zoe.' She touched my arm. 'Last night I worked eleven in the pee em till eight in the aye em.'

Goddy-god-god. Who was she? Where would I have met a shift worker, even?

'Anyway, what did you do last night?' she said.

'Um.' I still hadn't placed her. 'I had dinner with a friend.' *With a gorgeous man who seems to like me, but who probably doesn't really, and since my ex left me I can never trust my judgement about anyone ever again, and after the dinner was finished I practically ran away when he tried to kiss me, and I cried myself to sleep, and I am very scared I'll be like this forever and die a lonely old crone who is not only childless but who never even gets to have sex*, was what I could have said. 'A date, I guess.'

'Somebody special?'

'Ah, you know, I don't know. Anyway.' I felt like crying again, all of a sudden. I wanted to be at home, at my real home, with reliable, pointy-arsed Daniel, and our Baccarat frying pan. 'I better, um, go to Woolies. This stuff's way more than I want to spend.' Daniel always said I talked far too openly about money.

'Totally!' the odd, unknown woman said. 'I hear you! Nightmare!'

At Woolworths, I bought a frying pan for fourteen dollars and gave myself a very strict-voiced talking to about strength, my good fortune and not being defined by relationships. It was only while I was eating my perfectly well-cooked egg dinner that I remembered where I'd met the woman before.

'*Im*ogen!' It was such a relief that I said it out loud. 'The Blue *Anch*or.'

Very satisfying. Even though, obviously, nobody was there to hear independent and feisty me.

∞

'Jeez, Zoe,' said Nick, a couple of weeks later. 'When you said "ceramics", I was thinking those brown jars from, kinda, Grade Three art.' He held up a cup, angling it. Evening light was coming in through my little kitchen window. 'Do you sell them?' He put the cup back, adjusted it so it was in exactly the right place, and leaned against the kitchen counter.

'Just a hobby,' I said. Lately I had noticed people calling ceramics my *passion*, which was going a bit far. Still, I spent probably far too much time arranging my 'pieces' on the 1970s shelves of my kitchen.

'Wine?' I opened the fridge. 'Crafty-type beer? And what are you cooking us?'

Nick rifled in a shopping bag – it was taking up at least half the bench – and held up a paper-wrapped parcel of fresh-from-a-nice-deli pasta.

'Mushroom fettuccini,' he said.

'Yum.' He no doubt had at least three varieties of fancy mushrooms, too, as he'd be wanting us to finally have sex. This was our fifth date – we'd had two lots of after-work drinks, and a Sunday-morning coffee – and the first time he'd cooked for me.

Between us the wine got sorted out, and then while I was supervising the pasta, which obviously wasn't a real job, and he was chopping basil, he said, 'So, what's on for you this weekend?'

The stove was making a soft, burring sound, and the occasional odd, loud tick. My new frying pan was doing fine with the mushrooms.

'Gotta mark some assignments. Movie with Claire.' I lifted an unnecessary fork through the fettuccini. 'That's on Sunday. What about you?'

'Not much, I don't think. Footy tomorrow.' He stared at the basil, as if it was an optical illusion he hadn't quite figured out. 'Not till the afternoon, though.'

There was quiet. I didn't care. I was watching his basil-chopping forearms and his grey shirt.

'Let me drain that,' he said, after a minute.

I had a moment where I couldn't remember where I kept the

colander, but managed to find it and put it in the sink. Nick came and stood near me. He tipped the pasta out. We were so close. When nearly all the pasta was in the colander, I touched the side of his leg.

I heard him clear his throat and then he put down the saucepan – there was steam everywhere from the pasta, and the last piece of fettuccini missed the colander and slathered across the sink – and both his arms around my waist. He leaned in and I closed my eyes, and after about two seconds we started kissing.

Goddy-god. The man could certainly kiss.

Nick said to wait a sec, and then he reached out one hand and shut the kitchen blind – good he thought of it; the lady next door often walked past at that time of evening. He turned off the mushrooms, and when he had both his palms back on my hips, he said, 'You're looking gorgeous in this,' and ran his hands up over me, lightly, as if he was just seeing what sort of cotton-rayon blend my top was made of.

And then we started kissing again, and every so often he'd say a nice thing, such as 'gorgeous' or '*so* pretty'. I put my hand on the front of his jeans, and he said, 'Ah,' in a jagged, delighted way and immediately started fumbling around with his zip.

And then I saw, in front of my closed eyes, that Damo guy from the barbecue doing his smirk. *Old Nicko's going to get his end in*, Damo would have been thinking. *On ya, mate. Before your fancy farken chanterelles are even on her table.*

It kept happening.

I took my hand away, put my fingertips on his wrists and held them by our sides. I intertwined our fingers, and then I slowed the kiss. He was breathing fast – so was I, for that matter – but by the time we actually stopped kissing we'd succeeded in settling ourselves.

I took half a step away and stared at his face. I knew I didn't have to apologise, and I knew everything else about consent, but I still felt funny. He didn't do that very annoying heroic and disappointed thing, though, and I checked him closely for any signs of irritation, but there were absolutely none to be seen.

He smiled, in fact, and said, with a good amount of wryness, 'Well. Pasta's done.'

There was really nothing not to like.

So, we ate our many-mushroom-varieties meal – it'd got pretty cold, but we didn't mind, even though cold mushrooms were horrible, including, it turned out, the ninety-dollar-a-kilo type – and we talked about music and his cryptocurrency-loving sister and the new apprentice he was taking on who was eighteen but looked about twelve.

I told him about my favourite curry recipes and work and how hard it was to help teenagers with anything that really mattered to them. He nodded and said, 'I reckon,' in a way that made me think he'd listened and understood.

We drank more wine, and I made us tea, and he offered to wash up, and I said no. Then I saw him to the door and we had another fairly thorough kiss.

'Talk tomorrow, then, Zoe?' he said, with his hand still on my waist.

'Okay.' I turned on the outside light. 'Bye, then.'

He did seem a little bit disappointed this time. A little bit surprised. Even a tiny bit impressed. Mainly just very sexually frustrated, though, of course.

∞

'First times,' I said. I sat up and reached for the half-empty glass of water on the bedside table. 'Go.' Call me nosy.

We were in bed, and it was Sunday afternoon. Football unplayed; movie unwatched. The water was stale – it'd been there since Friday –

and I didn't care. I was – we were *both* – in that zone where everything either of us did, or said, was gorgeous, and where things like stale water or running out of milk or even – not that we'd tried it – locking the keys in the car were fun adventures. And when I saw myself in the bathroom mirror, I felt as if I was sexily dishevelled rather than messy. Flushed, rather than blotchy. Voluptuous, not could-do-with-more-tone. Wouldn't last, I knew.

I'd called him back. Not telephoned. Called, as in, 'Hey, Nick, maybe come inside again for a minute?' The slanty plane of his neck when he turned around for one last wave had somehow squished all my Damo-smirk/unsuitable-man worries into a shrug about the size of a coffee ground.

'I was sixteen,' he said. He was watching me as I sipped the water, and I tilted my chin just a touch more than I needed to. 'She was older. Seventeen. Serena, her name was.'

'Older woman.' I put the glass on the table, stretching my arm right out, and started plaiting my hair, loosely. 'With a sexy name.' I was aware of how graceful my arms were, how straight my spine, how naked my breasts. When I lay down and slid my knee between his, he put his hand on my hip.

'So?' I said. 'How was it?'

'*Really* disappointing.' He laughed, but I got the feeling he really *had* been disappointed. It was like when an adult joked about their childhood dog dying and how they'd believed for ages that it went to a farm, and you could see they were still upset. 'Over very quickly.'

'Nothing's changed, then,' I said. But smiling. 'Kidding. Very impressive these days, Nicholas.' There were certain issues where you couldn't leave any doubt about whether or not you were being serious.

He made an attempt to hide his stoked grin, then said, 'What about you?'

'No need to look quite so proud of yourself. High school boyfriend.

Grade Eleven. Was nice, actually.' The boyfriend had had a very big willy – uncomfortably so, in fact, and not just the first time – but obviously, I didn't report on that. Even though it had been uncomfortable, and I definitely hadn't had anything like an orgasm, it had still been lovely. A few days later, he'd given me a red rose for my seventeenth birthday, wrapped in a clear cellophane tube, and with a plasticky red bow that I'd thought was the ultimate in luxury. I still had that bow somewhere, now I came to think of it. 'Then, you know, a few stupid uni things. Then I met Daniel – first real love – that lasted ages, till about six months ago. And then, um, I've been single since then.'

Nick studied the sheet. 'What happened with him?'

'He went off to Canada. To be an engineer. Lots of sustainable-energy opportunities in Vancouver. Apparently.'

'You didn't ... want to go?'

I shrugged, but kept looking at him. Thought I might as well let him see how it had been.

He got it. After a moment he said, 'First woman to break my heart was a girl called Layla. She was really good-looking and I was seventeen. So, you know, done deal.'

'What then?'

'Then ... well. I, you know, got around, couple of girlfriends, then I met this girl called Nova and we were together for ages, lived together, the works. Then one day, I'd just turned thirty-one, I came home from work and she said she wanted to get married, and I said all right, and then the next day I woke up and ... and ... and I'd changed my mind. So she left. She's married someone else now. Ring the size of a scallop. And since then, that was a few years ago, I've ah, you know, a few things. Been ... with quite a few women.'

'Being a heartbreaker, as my mum would say.' I really was getting more like Mum. It was freaky how *unavoidable* it seemed.

Nick looked as if, now that he put his mind to it, he wasn't sure about the brokenness or otherwise of various hearts.

'So, did you ever, you know, deflower a boy?' he said, after a while. 'And I seriously *can't* keep my hands off you.' He was sliding them up my body. He was doing this thing where he put his hands on my ribcage, his thumbs near my breasts, and gradually worked inwards.

'Um,' I said. It was *very* pleasant. 'Um. No. Even my first boyfriend – he'd already had a girlfriend before me. Oh, that's nice.' I loved kissing him. I knew I'd be thinking about his kisses while I was at *work*. In any lull. The Year Elevens would be busy getting out their Chromebooks, and I'd be reliving the moment when I was making coffee and he put his hand on my hip and said, *Back to bed, please, Zoe.* What would the kids think if they knew? What would the *parents* think?

'How about you?' I stroked his lovely shoulder. It was such a relief to be able to admire it to my heart's content. 'Were you ever the first one to sleep with any fair ... ummmm ... maidens?'

'Don't think so,' said Nick. His breath was getting quicker. 'Oh no, actually, once. Sort of. Or twice, maybe ... I think.' His lips all down my neck. 'Or, or something, I don't really ... God, this little freckle here ... I ...' He drew in his breath and then kissed it. 'Sexy. Sexy, sexy, sexy Zoe.'

Chapter Fifteen

IMOGEN

Winter

Nick's ute was outside the Zoe girl's house. Again.

It was definitely his. And there was dry asphalt underneath it, so it must have been parked there since before the rain started.

I stopped walking, on the other side of the street, for at least four seconds. The stressed drone of a garbage truck coming up the hill reminded me that I was in public, and visible. And the rain seemed to make me even wetter when I was standing still. There was no alternative but to keep walking.

On Zoe's street corner was a grey-painted café that seemed to pride itself on its vegan and dairy-free options. It had just opened, and a cluster of thin elderly men in lycra and cycling shoes were waiting for their takeaway orders. I sat by the window, ordered a milk coffee, which for some reason was known as a latte, and explored the Bureau of Meteorology site in detail. It was unclear exactly when the rain had started.

Nick, as usual, had not updated his social media.

Zoe had no accounts, as far as I could tell.

'You okay today, sweets?' The waitress bent right down as she put my coffee on my table. She was that stridently alternative type of woman whose religion involved being warm to everyone; possibly she believed I needed wellness coaching.

'Yes, thank you!' I was too busy with my phone to look at her properly. 'Thank you!'

On the Lofton School's web page, I read Zoe's one-paragraph staff profile again.

She grew up in country Tasmania.

I stirred one, then two, sugars into my coffee. I had not eaten, and needed to raise my blood sugar.

She had an honours degree in fine arts.

I licked my spoon.

She loved helping kids find their voice through ceramics.

The milk had been scorched.

She shopped at Woolworths. She left for work at or around 7.45 am on weekdays. She visited T-rex and Claire most Thursday evenings. She owned a lacy size-12D bra that she hung on her clothesline, bold as brass, not that there was anything wrong with that, even though I personally was not one for showy, tacky underwear as I had no wish to cater to male fantasies.

I wondered what Nick had explained to her about me. If he'd said, 'Imogen and I used to date,' and then, when she pressed him for details, if he'd said, 'Imogen and I had intercourse eight times, and twice she stayed over at my place, and once I stayed over at her place.'

I didn't think he'd tell her that I lost my virginity to him. I mean, she might have earned herself the right to know his sexual history, which – it was no secret – was very extensive. But of course, she wouldn't have the right to know mine, and he'd realise that. Anyway, sex with all his random women was one thing, but I knew the lovemaking with me – especially the virginity aspect – would be memories too tender for him to share, even all this time later. He never told Know-nothing Nova, his ex-girlfriend, a thing about me.

The middle-aged woman at the next table was looking at me. I stopped tapping my teaspoon against the table and sat up straighter.

Of course, Nick could be at Zoe's house to work. Her apartment was old, and it could be natural for her to ask a friend of a friend to renovate her kitchen. Except that she didn't own her unit. I'd already done a little check with the Land Titles Office. Zoe appeared to be renting.

And it was a Saturday morning. Nick rarely worked on Saturday mornings.

I hoped she didn't dry her underwear on indoor clothes racks on rainy days. Nick was a self-confessed breast man, and it was widely accepted that men in general were very visual in their patterns of arousal, although the evidential basis for this theory was unclear.

At just after 8.30 am, I finished my coffee and went to work. The mountain was dark grey. The sky was light grey. The river was medium grey. It was still raining. His terrible old ute was still there.

∞

Once you were inside the emergency department, you forgot about the weather and the scenery. In fact, if you looked at the big clock over the doors to the ambulance bay – at the smooth red second hand, at the Times-font numerals – you sometimes had to pause for a moment to ask yourself whether it meant 'am' or 'pm'. Inside the emergency department, there was no sky and no rain, no mountain and no river. There was just you.

'Tristan?' I said. 'Can we please discuss a patient?' I was treating a man with chest pain.

'Yep.' But he kept typing. 'Fire away, please.'

'Mr Greg Banakis is a fifty-four-year-old man, no, fifty-five, sorry, actually, who presents with three hours of chest pain that started on the right and—'

Tristan pressed the backspace key, hard. 'What do you think's wrong with him, *Doc*tor?'

'His pain commenced a few minutes before five o'clock this morning. But it settled spontaneously soon after arrival here, which was at 8.14 am, and he—'

'What …? Look.' He put his hands in his lap, and spoke to his keyboard. 'Can you please tell me what you think is wrong with this man?'

I was finding it difficult to order my thoughts. I was feeling Sick.

'Are this fifty-four-no-sorry-actually-fifty-five-year-old's bloods okay?' he said.

'Yes, Tristan,' I said. 'They are A-okay.' They were.

'ECGs?' He drew the 'G' out. Ge-ee-ees.

Mr Banakis's ECGs were what I needed help with. He had atypical chest pain, and multiple cardiac risk factors, and I was worried about Wellens syndrome. Wellens syndrome was life-threatening, but it was fairly uncommon, and the ECG manifestations of some of its variants had been shown to be subtle.

'I, um …' I tried to make all those words, which sounded logical in my head, come out through my mouth, into the air. The Sick feeling was happening to my throat, though.

I remembered a nice teacher I'd had once. When I couldn't answer questions in Grade Seven, Mrs Casamento used to smile and say, *Maybe write it down, and then you can read it out? I know you know it.*

Tristan just leaned closer into his screen. He typed at least three sentences while I stood there. One of the other residents came over and said, 'Am I right to send my lady in six home? In her twenties, nonspecific abdominal pain, five days, exam normal, bloods normal, not pregnant, I reckon she's constipated, GP follow-up?'

Tristan said, 'Yeah, goodo. Thanks, Eddie, mate.' He typed some more. Then, finally, he looked at me. '*Doc*tor?' he said.

I felt so very Sick.

The sounds around me hadn't changed, and it felt as if I could remember them, as if they had been playing in the background the whole time, like part of a dream. I was still in the emergency department. The light became much brighter as my eyes – almost without my instructing them – opened themselves. I found I had to think carefully about the best way to heave myself up into a sitting position.

Near my feet, in a clear plastic bag with a large knot at its top, were my clothes. I touched my shoulders. I was wearing a white, loose hospital gown. Just like anyone. Just like a normal patient. One of the medium-level nurses – Jemima – was removing a blood-pressure cuff from around my arm. She told me I had been discussing a clinical matter with Tristan and had then fallen onto the floor. Maroon gloss was congealing in the cracks of her lips.

'But you're safe, Imogen,' she said unnecessarily. She said a few more things, and then, 'We can call someone for you, if you want.'

'My mother,' I said. 'And a man by the name of Nick Kavanagh.' I gave a little chuckle, the sort Zoe had done when her strap fell down. 'My significant other!'

This was a slight exaggeration, but I did not want Jemima to stereotype me as a plain, clever woman whose closest relatives were her elderly parents. And she would. She absolutely would. And *that* wouldn't reflect the truth of me, either.

'No worries,' said Jemima. She scratched her maroon upper lip with the side of her little fingernail, and inhaled to say something else, but a woman in a grey cardigan was coming through the gap in the cubicle's curtains. She was the neurology registrar; her name was Lin.

'Imogen. You have had a generalised tonic-clonic seizure,' she told me. I had noticed before how Lin didn't abbreviate words. Everything about her was calm and correct and clear. She stood next to the bed, near my chest, and asked, 'Has this happened before?'

Her hands were still. Her name badge was unfaded. Her voice didn't change its pitch or its volume.

I shook my head. 'Never.'

Lin asked me some more questions and I answered them. I followed her instructions: *Watch the tip of my pen; keep your elbows straight while I try to bend them; relax your legs as I tap here, and here, and here.*

'Did I wet myself?' I asked her when she'd finished. 'When I collapsed?'

I was at *work*.

Lin didn't hesitate, nor did she look sympathetic. 'Yes,' she said. 'There was some urinary incontinence.'

Jemima smiled at me as if I'd been recently bereaved. 'Don't give it another thought, Imogen,' she said, most unhelpfully.

Lin's face did not move, but she sounded as if it was an apology when she said, 'As you would be aware, Imogen, we will need to scan your head.' I was aware. The scan would be to check for a tumour.

I nodded. I can't believe this, I thought. I can't believe this is actually happening.

Lin closed my chart. She ducked her shoulder past the curtain, and made her tidy way out of the cubicle.

'Try not to worry,' she said. 'Until we know for sure.'

∞

'Nick!' said Mum. 'How are you? Lovely to finally see you, even in these awful circumstances!' The whole time she was speaking, she was standing up and moving across the tiny space of my hospital room towards him. I had been transferred to the private hospital, but there was still not much space to be had. Mum had to sidestep her own chair and manoeuvre my table-on-wheels out of the way.

155

'Hi, Mrs Banks.' Nick leaned down and gave her a kiss, which she took in her stride. When he came to my bedside and brushed his lips tenderly onto my cheek, she sensitively looked away.

'Are you all right, Imo?' he said. 'Pretty full-on when the hospital called me.'

'I'm sure it's all a fuss about nothing.' I used a light-hearted voice. His hand lingered on my upper arm. 'It will take more than just a collapse at work to bother me!'

'Jesus.' He could be quite profane.

Mum said, 'I think I'll step out for a breath of air. If that's all right with you, darling?'

When I nodded, she picked up her coat off the foot of the bed. 'Lovely to see you, Nick.' She smiled at both of us, with her head tilted to one side. Mum had supported me all through my relationship with Nick. She knew it was only a matter of time before a man like him tired of playing the field.

'Enjoy your walk,' Nick told her. He sat down on the chair next to me. There was silence. 'Pretty good room.' He nodded towards the big windows.

'Yes! Which is great, since I'll be, er, chillaxing here for a while!'

Nick nodded, and there was quiet. I wondered if this was what people meant when they referred to sexual tension that could be cut with a knife. Tension of that nature was a nebulous concept.

Just as I was working out the best way to casually ask Nick about his weekend plans, he said, 'So ... ah, did you actually need me, Imo?'

'Well, that's a big question!'

'Just, ah ... I thought ... did you need me to bring you something? Or, ah, check on your place or anything?'

'Maybe a book?' I said. 'To while away the hours. Take my mind off the waiting.' My scan wasn't happening until the next morning.

He told me he had something on that night – it would be his football training – but that he'd come by the next day.

'That sounds perfect! A-okay!'

'Too easy.' Nick gave my arm a very loving pat and stood up. 'Guess I better head.'

When Mum returned, I explained that Nick would be back in the morning.

Mum said, 'What a lovely boy he is.'

'Oh yes,' I said. 'Yes, indeed.'

He really had seemed very concerned. Definitely more than he would have been if he was properly serious about Zoe Katherine Morello.

∞

Mum was looking out of the window. Dad was reading a Wilbur Smith book. Every unthinking noise from the foyer – the slam of a door, a politely hostile voice saying, 'Can you wait there, please?', a demanding phone – triggered a surge of feeling that, when it faded, left me more and more agitated. We were waiting for the results of my brain scan.

Out of the blue, I remembered how, in Year Ten, I had to give a speech to my English class. I wrote it out on pale-blue palm cards, except I ran out of palm cards, so I made an extra one out of a portion of manilla folder. I'd been worried I might lose points because it was a different colour from the others. The speech was about King Lear or Macbeth or Hamlet, or maybe even the mercurial Othello. So terrible of me, but I just couldn't recall which of Shakespeare's tragically flawed heroes I talked about!

I had of course practised in front of the mirror, and also to Mum and Dad. I walked across the front of the classroom, and double-checked I had the number-one card at the top of my stack. It was after lunch, so my classmates were mostly slumped on their desks and not talking much.

'Good afternoon, Grade Ten D,' I said.

I left a pause, as Dad had advised. Most people rushed when they did public speaking.

That's when I heard Damien Collins say – quietly – 'Wouldn't.'

Another boy, Cameron Barnett, next to him, said, 'Wouldn't.'

A third boy, Paul Sanders, said, 'Wouldn't.'

The teacher said, 'That's quite enough, boys.' To me, he added, 'If you'd like to get started, Imogen, please.' He sounded irritable with all of us, but he gave the boys the more displeased look.

I said my opening line, which I remembered was, '"What's in a name?" This question has indeed vexed many minds!' and then I went on with the rest of my speech. For completeness, let me point out that I was aware the 'What's in a name?' quote was from *Romeo and Juliet*. That play, while written by Shakespeare, was definitely not the topic of my speech. I was simply referencing some of the author's other work.

My talk went well, and I received a high mark even though that particular audience was not as engaged as some might have been. The boys who'd said 'Wouldn't' laughed almost silently through most of it. They honestly appeared as if they might wet themselves due to their suppressed mirth, and Damien Collins's face went unattractively red.

I didn't understand what the boys had meant until the next day.

That was when Tabitha Melrose got up to do her speech. Tabitha Melrose had blonde hair and the kind of skin that always looked tanned, and she had worn a bra since before Year Seven.

Damien Collins said, 'Would.'

Cameron Barnett said, 'Would.'

Paul Sanders said, '*So* would.'

Tabitha Melrose smiled at Paul Sanders and shook her head in a friendly, jokey way. She was even half laughing as she started her speech. The boys were rocking back on their chairs. All Nick's friends did that.

I focused on my desk while Tabitha Melrose talked nonsensically for the minimum possible time.

Let me be clear. That whole episode might have hurt my feelings, but I was strong, and gossiped about it with nobody, and I hardly even cried. That was because I was, luckily, never one to need the approval of every single male in the world.

In any case, all three of them changed their minds in the end.

∞

At just after midday, Nick wandered onto the ward with my book. He'd also brought me a glorious bunch of carnations and a card that said, 'Dear Imo, get well soon we are all thinking of you, Love from Nick.'

His grammar was still far from excellent, but of course it was so sweet, and it was yet another one of those serendipitous events that he was there when the doctor came in! I'd so very much wanted him to be present when I received my result.

'Good, good, here we are,' the doctor said, as she sat on the end of my bed. It wasn't Lin. It was a specialist neurologist called Dr Ashleigh, whom I had never met before. She had rather lank, greying hair, but you could tell she would have been moderately pretty when she was young.

Nick said he'd better be off and stood up to leave.

'Oh stay, Nick.' Mum used both her hands to pat the air in front of her, in a way that suggested Nick should sit straight back down in the chair next to my bed. She herself was sitting bolt upright, and so was Dad.

Nick obeyed. He perched on the front of his seat, and he couldn't meet my eyes. Poor man. He was always *terrified* of medical stuff.

'Good news,' said Dr Ashleigh. 'There is a benign' – she looked at Mum and Dad, and pronounced it 'be-nine' – 'I emphasise, benign, growth in your head, Imogen. It's an arachnoid cyst.' She said that last sentence only to me, and then talked on about how the cyst was not dangerous, although it may or may not be the cause of my seizure.

'No driving, I'm afraid. We'll need to start medication and consider surgical options. You can't keep having these episodes, far too inconvenient for all concerned.' She laughed, and told me I was fine to work as long as I was supervised, but no overnight shifts. 'Good, good. Questions?' She turned to Mum and Dad.

Dad said it seemed to be excellent news and he didn't have too many questions. That meant he had none.

Mum said she was a bit overwhelmed just at the minute, thank you, but she was sure she'd have a very long list of things to ask at my next appointment, if that would be all right.

I said, 'Thank you for letting us know so promptly.'

'Are you all okay?' said Nick, after Dr Ashleigh had stomped off on her stolidly heeled shoes.

'Oh, darling.' Mum had tears in her eyes. She reached very far forward to take my hand, and almost put her forehead all the way down onto it. 'I'm so relieved.'

I said, 'No driving!'

Mum took a noisy breath in through her nostrils as she straightened her back. She smiled – still teary – with her head tilted to one side, and turned to Nick. She said, 'Imogen, darling, I'm quite sure you'll find a way to get yourself about the place, driving or no driving.'

Nick nodded. 'Yeah.' His dear little face was so loving and so concerned! ''Course, Imo.'

∞

Obviously – in case you are a teeny bit fucking stupid and haven't already worked it out – I had faked my seizure. I was not proud of my actions. I was the first to admit they were less than ideal.

My arachnoid cyst was diagnosed in England, because a colleague there was concerned about me and suggested a scan and a number of other tests. Of course they were all clear, apart from the cyst thing, which even he conceded was not a factor in my behaviour. Anyway, my work performance in England was just fine. I'd heard that particular colleague was mildly anxious.

And – in case you also haven't worked *this* out – I chose Dr Ashleigh because I once overheard Tristan say she was 'brave'. That was code for 'bad doctor'. Decent neurologists would know that arachnoid cysts hardly ever caused seizures, especially when they were located in that part of the brain.

Still, having such a cyst was very handy if you needed to *imitate* a seizure disorder, and there was nothing wrong – as a great many people on Twitter have probably already explained to you – with being a resourceful woman who took every opportunity life threw at her.

CORONIAL COURT OF TASMANIA
INQUIRY INTO A DEATH
Pursuant to *Coronial and Other Act 1991*
Section 16(IV)

Samples taken at autopsy from the deceased's body were analysed. A small amount of caffeine, but no alcohol and no illicit drugs were found to have been present in those samples.

No prescription drugs were identified as being present.

Chapter Sixteen

ZOE

Spring

'Nick?' I said.

We were at his place. I liked it, which was good because I was sleeping there about three times a week. He had a lots-of-windows townhouse that had been built when townhouses were made of bricks and had tiled roofs. But he'd renovated it himself and inside it was your grey-and-white, luxe-features-throughout sort of place.

'Yes, Ms Morello?' We were drinking wine and he was searching the internet. He wanted to buy a little boat to go fishing in.

'Did you have a lot of friends in high school?'

I'd been thinking more about Emma Tierney-Adams and a few of the others. It was not like me, because, to be honest, I usually forgot about work as soon as I left the carpark. But I was making Claire and T-rex a patchwork quilt for their nursery – I'd decided it'd be therapeutic as well as useful – and quilting tended to give you a lot of time to think. And in between wrestling with acceptance of my own baby-related sadness and trying to be open-hearted about Claire's good fortune and all that jazz, I was also thinking: *Is it possible that these days I am uncaring and insensitive, while pretending to myself I am appropriate and firm-professional-boundariesish?*

'Ah.' Nick was a bit distracted. 'I pretty much got on with everyone.'

It was different with girls, anyway, I thought.

'You would've been one of the cool guys.' My scissors were slicing into heavy checked cotton that had once been a tea towel. I was probably too tipsy for quilting, truth be told. 'Good at footie and into wagging maths.'

'Not really.' He gave me a funny little smile.

'Oh, yes, you were.' I was teasing. I unfurled my tape measure.

'Dumb jock, eh?' There was a sharpness to his voice. He lifted up his hand from the iPad and took hold of his other elbow. More casually – forced smile – he added, 'That's what you reckon?' He was hurt, not angry.

'No!' I dropped the tape measure. 'Of course not, Nick.' God, I wasn't judging.

'Fair enough.' A nod. He turned back to the iPad and started scrolling. Then he looked up and used his index finger to make a circle in the air, in a way that showed the room we were in, his home. 'You know, Zo. This place is paid off.' He spoke very quietly, made it sound almost like a question.

'*Nick!*' I hefted up onto my feet, which was quite a business because I was sitting cross-legged on the floor and I had to move a lot of carefully arranged sewing kit first. 'I didn't mean – what are you even on about?' I plonked onto the couch next to him.

He was still staring at his iPad – there was an unfocused picture of a dock and an unattractive fibreglass dinghy – and I flipped the screen down so it was facing his lap.

'Nick? First thing, I seriously couldn't care less if this place is paid off. And I know you're not dumb. I've honestly never thought that.'

'Just, I wasn't some sort of loser.'

'I meant you would have been *cool*,' I said. 'Like, confident and sporty, and, you know, probably a bit of a smart-arse. But in a nice-enough way.'

He nodded. 'Yeah.' He put one hand up to his face and rubbed it, hard, so his skin stretched and then released again. 'Sorry, Zo.'

I waited in case he wanted to say anything else, but he just picked up the iPad again. I was about to restart my quilting when he said, 'That's how I got friendly with Imogen.' His friend Imogen had been sick; he was driving her around a lot. 'Her helping me.' Scroll. Scroll. 'The school stuff was so easy for her.'

It was still there, in his voice: the injustice, the stab of *Why did I find it so hard?* And with it, the flip side: *See my house? I never needed any university bullshit, anyway.*

'Right,' I said.

He'd stopped scrolling, but he didn't say anything else.

'So, Imogen helped you with your homework and you became friends?' It sounded more like one of those 1990s American high school movies. The girl would have shaken out her hair and removed her glasses and become a cheerleader. The boy would have found he didn't like playing football and won a poetry competition. Then everyone would've realised diversity was fantastic and cheered at the prom and lived happily ever after.

'Sorta. In Year Eleven.' He shrugged. 'Bit after that, Mum and Dad made me change schools, got me a proper tutor, all that.'

'Didn't you want "all that"?'

'Nup.'

'And?' I pressed. I thought he'd say more about Imogen and why they'd stayed friends.

'And what? If they wanted to waste their money trying to make me smart, let 'em.'

'Oh, you poor *thing*. Caring parents. *Fancy* parents. Imagine the *trauma*.'

Full credit, he laughed. He did a little shrug. 'All good.'

And that was all he told me about Imogen.

∞

I decided to set up a lunchtime poetry club. I literally got the idea from the American high school movie plot I'd been thinking about, which, as far as I knew, and pretty surprisingly, wasn't even a real movie.

I suggested the kids could write – or bring in – poems about art, or their artistic process, or whatever. No matter what the topic was, I was pretty sure the poetry would be all dark, personal pieces about feeling alone and not fitting in and fears for the future and so on. I knew that from my friend Sophie, who was one of the English teachers, and also from remembering my own high school journals, which were chock-full of my so-called poetry.

I was a bit nervous because I hadn't done anything with poems before, at least not since about Year Ten, and I thought probably nobody would come. But I stopped on the way to school and bought a packet of chocolate biscuits. Chocolate always helped. I would just eat them by myself if needed.

When lunchtime rolled around, Emma Tierney-Adams appeared, all brave and smiley and carrying some sort of wrap that she definitely ate. I'd mentioned the club to her a couple of times, but I only realised when I saw her how much I'd been hoping she'd come. I wondered if maybe my maternal instinct was directing itself towards my students or something, and decided that even if that was the case, bugger it, no harm done, and I was allowed.

Amy Petrovic, Brunella Lawson and a couple of other girls arrived in pairs. Amy Petrovic was this deep-thinking kind of girl; I knew her because she'd unsuccessfully lobbied the school to provide a bus for the student climate strike last year. There was one Year Nine boy I'd never met before, and a new boy from Year Ten who had pink hair, and another boy called Marcus Cunningham. Emma sat near one of the pairs of girls, angling her body so they could easily talk to her if they wanted to. They didn't.

It went pretty well. Two of the girls read out poems. I read out one, too – not one I'd written, I wasn't *that* touchy-feely – and then we said what they meant to us or why we liked them. The kids surprised me, actually, with their enthusiasm, and at the end Brunella wandered off with Pink Hair Boy and so Emma was near the door at the same time as Amy Petrovic.

Emma smiled and said, 'Thank you for the poetry club, Ms Morello.'

Amy Petrovic said, 'Yeah, thanks, Ms Morello.'

'You two need a hot chocolate,' I told them, casually. 'It'll be cold in the yard.' Even though it had clicked over into spring, it was still freezing.

Emma glanced at Amy Petrovic, and Amy Petrovic shrugged and said, 'Okay,' without really moving her features.

Off they went towards the canteen.

It was my absolute favourite thing that happened at work that week.

∞

'So nice to get to hang out with you properly!' said Imogen. 'I've heard so much about you!'

We were in a pub – between the ceremony and reception bits of someone called Lila Nguyen's huge wedding – and Nick had gone to buy us drinks. The pub was packed full of people I didn't know, most of them wearing suits and dry-clean-only dresses. Over by the black-painted fireplace, I saw Smirking Damo, more than halfway through a pint and smirkily chatting up a woman who was never going to sleep with him. I knew that sounded brutal, but it honestly could not have been more obvious.

I smiled at Imogen. 'Good things, I hope?'

Of course I had to say that – it was another by-law – even though

I wanted to ask, '*What?* What has Nick actually *said*? In detail, please! Has he really talked a *lot* about me? Does he seem as if he's *serious*?' I knew I was a hopeless, too-busy-thinking-about-relationships-and-babies-to-think-enough-about-my-career idiot. What was worse, I did not even care.

Imogen looked at me. 'Oh,' she said. 'Yes.'

I sipped my drink, waited another second, then said, 'So, you work in the emergency department?'

'I do,' said Imogen. 'I'm a doctor there.' She emphasised the 'doctor' a bit more than I probably would have.

'That must be quite stressful?'

Imogen nodded her head in an exaggerated, eye-rolly way, how the Grade Eight girls did sometimes. 'Yes, Ms Morello, we're all sooo exhausted!' 'Yes, Ms Morello, it was sooo super freezing that we practically got frostbite!'

I nodded sympathetically, and when she still didn't ask me anything, I said, 'Nick tells me you've been under the weather, lately?' The pub was getting louder. I had to lean forward to be heard.

'Did he?' She seemed delighted. 'Isn't he sweet? To think of me?'

'He's a sweetie, all right. He—'

'It's been such a stormy time, Zoe.' She shook head. 'I've had to dig deep.'

It was honestly hard to tell whether she was being silly or not. I didn't laugh, just in case. 'That's a good, roomy handbag,' I said, instead.

I saw that Nick was ordering. For some reason, he turned around to point out our standing-up table to the stylishly grungy and pulling-it-off-so-well-it-almost-made-me-want-to-get-my-hair-cut-short woman behind the bar. When he caught my eye, he gave a really pleased smile. Goddy-god, he was gorgeous.

'It *is* roomy!' said Imogen. 'I am someone who likes to invest in classic pieces.'

'I always try to do that, but then I see things on sale and get them and never have enough money left over for anything "classic".'

'Really?' said Imogen. She sounded genuinely shocked, as if I'd told her I was orphaned and only had gruel to eat from ages four to seven. 'That must be sooo hard for you.'

I wasn't too sure where to go from there, but Nick was on his way back. He was carrying three drinks, and as soon as he'd plonked them on our little circle of table, he wrapped his arm around my shoulders. Behind me, I could hear a woman asking whether warm cider was still available. It wasn't, and I felt for her, because you could tell by her voice she'd been really looking forward to it, and the glass-collecting guy was not being at all sympathetic.

I glugged my sauv blanc straight down onto my almost-empty stomach, and settled into the muzzy pleasure of Nick's arm around me in all the noise and the strangers and Imogen telling him about a 'follow-up' medical appointment she was due for.

'Just regarding the cyst,' she said. Hell, bloody. 'I might need brain surgery.' Thank *goodness* I hadn't laughed.

Right around then, a woman with fabulous eyebrows, a hoarse voice and a martini came over. She introduced herself as Susannah, the bride's cousin from London who had literally no friends within a thousand miles, and then she complimented my 'outstanding' necklace. 'I'm so jealous of it I could barely concentrate on the vows,' she said.

Somehow Susannah and I got ourselves into a very funny conversation about *Fifty Shades of Grey*. I did try to include Imogen – partly in case Nick wanted to go and talk to his other mates – but she seemed awkward about it, and anyway, the pub was too loud for a big group chat about sado-thingy, or bondage, or whatever you called it. There were certain words you just didn't want to yell.

When Susannah went to get the two of us more martinis, Imogen looked over at me and said that lately, she'd been thinking of doing a ceramics course.

'I love ceramics!' I said. It was quite a coincidence, and we had a nice talk about clay and personal creativity and poetry until Susannah arrived with my drink.

∞

Later that night, Nick said, 'You and that Susannah girl were having a good old chat.'

I laughed. 'Yep.' We were in his bed, about to go to sleep.

'I nearly couldn't think straight,' he said. 'Poor old Imo was going on about God knows what, and you're right there, in that *dress*, saying spank and fuck and blow job and . . . well. Jeez, Zo.' He stretched one of his arms along the pillow.

I smiled in the dark. Halfway through the second round of martinis, Susannah and I had got . . . not exactly flirty, but at least not one hundred per cent laughy. I'd known Nick'd been listening. I'd leaned against him and he'd moved his hand down from my shoulder to my hip. It had all been a bit drunken and woozy, and I'd forgotten, until now.

'Do you like that kind of . . . what's it even called? Sado-maso-whatever? That kind of sex?' I said.

I made an effort to keep my voice non-judgemental, even though I was thinking, *I certainly* hope *not*. In real life, ick, there's no way I could do it, not even with him. I would definitely get the giggles, apart from anything else.

'Nah. Just liked hearing you talk about it.'

'Bit enjoyable, was it?'

'Had to go have a wank in the toilets,' he said casually. 'Took me about five enjoyable seconds.'

'Nick!' I was shocked – unheard of – and I was about to say, *Nicholas Kavanagh, that was* way *too much information.* But then I decided not to.

I actually liked that he'd told me. Daniel would never have done anything like that, or at least, he would never have let anyone find out about it. In fact, if Daniel had been next to me in that pub, I would never have talked the way I'd talked to Susannah.

Daniel would definitely not have enjoyed it. He would have thought it was cheapening. He would have thought it was tacky. He would have thought it was vulgar, obvious, embarrassing and *slutty*. Not, of course, that he would have used those words. Daniel was far too progressive for that.

Conversations like that were totally fine, but they weren't really for women who expected to be taken seriously, was how Daniel would have put it. 'Call me choosy,' was what Daniel would have said.

For the first time, I realised just how hard I'd worked to keep him happy. As if I had to make up for my silly old womb that couldn't give us what we wanted.

Chapter Seventeen

GRACE

Spring

The best thing about this school was that Emma seemed just that little bit happier, and the worst thing about it was its ridiculous pick-up arrangements. One-way streets. Huge cars, small cul-de-sacs, tense intersections. Grace manoeuvred her car past a hatchback being piloted by a teenager, and wondered if, next year, and depending on her health, Emma could perhaps start catching the bus home every day.

'How was school?' Grace asked when Emma got in, and for perhaps quite literally the ten-thousandth time. (At some point, she'd have to do the maths. How many days, multiplied by how many weeks, multiplied by how many years, had she been asking Emma that question?)

Emma peered down at a hair elastic she'd found in the side of the door. 'It was okay,' she said.

In fact, Grace wondered why she *still* felt disappointed when Emma replied, '*Fie-yun!*' or 'O*kay*' or (at best) 'Good, thanks, Mother-dear.' What was Grace expecting? 'Well, Mum, even though I appear to be coping with maths, it's reducing my self-esteem because I'm worse at it than some of the others, and also I wish I was in the cross-country despite the fact that I didn't try out for it, and on a scale of one to ten I'm hovering at about six-point-five in terms of accepting that I'm not one of the prettiest or most popular girls in my year group, but I suspect I'll develop better self-acceptance and more wholesome priorities as I mature, and in terms of having my actual, legitimate needs met, such as making some friends, there's not much progress on that, but at least I'm still eating and menstruating and my BMI is almost back in the healthy range'?

'How was poetry club?' Grace tried again. She kept her voice casual, the way she'd done since Emma was small. 'How was maths?'

'Ha! Good,' said Emma. 'Maths, we're doing trigonometry, *so* crap, and English was good, and we found out about the end-of-year production, and yeah, Ms Peters says I can be in the ensemble. Which will be good. Because Amy is probably going to be the stage manager or at least the assistant stage manager.'

'Really?' said Grace. Emma hadn't told her she was trying out. More sedately, she added, 'That all sounds pretty good.'

'Yeah, and her mum could drop me off,' Amy said, 'if we have late rehearsals, and I could maybe have dinner at her house sometimes. What *is* for dinner?'

'Roast lamb.' Grace had to work to keep the delight out of her voice, for so many reasons, but mainly because Emma had forgotten. A few weeks ago, they would have been negotiating about the fat content of the meat, about the kilojoules in potatoes. Emma would have been saying, *So, Mother-dear, about this roast lamb you're suggesting?* and then, minutes later, screaming, *How can even* you *think that's reasonable?*

'With salad? Or steamed veggies? What do you reckon?' Grace said.

She shouldn't have mentioned salad. Any minute there'd be an irritated shrug and a 'Calm down, Mum, just whatever you already *decided.*'

But Emma said, 'Um, salad? *If* we've got cherry tomatoes. And I could maybe make a dressing?'

Grace gripped the steering wheel harder and clenched her pelvic-floor muscles with the effort of not saying, 'Please, Emma, please stay like this. Please hold onto this feeling and don't go, don't fall back into that other place, back where I can't get to you. Please. *Please.*'

'You've done so well,' she said. 'So well. My strong, brave Emma.'

'Ummmm,' said Emma. She turned her head slowly to face Grace, and inspected her mother as if Grace was a desiccated historical specimen: interesting, and somehow sort of cute, but all in a slightly gross way.

'Thanks?' she said.

Chapter Eighteen

ZOE

Spring

'Wanna go to bed early?' said Nick. He was on the couch with his – clean-socked, fortunately – feet on the coffee table.

We were at his place again. The kitchen smelled nicely of the spanakopita he'd made for dinner. Rug the Dog was asleep on Rug the Rug.

'Sure.' I was also sitting on Rug the Rug, pinning more patches of fabric together. 'Soon as Imogen's dropped that stuff off.'

'Shit.' It was like he was a balloon that the air had been let out of. 'I forgot.'

At the wedding, Imogen had offered to bring around some old ceramics magazines she happened to have. They were 1970s ones, which tended to be inspiring and useful, and were also very hard to come by.

'It's a weeknight.' I was holding up two squares next to each other to see how they matched. 'She probably won't stay, you grumpy old man.'

Nick threw a cushion at me, and I threw it back at him, and after a bit there was a knock on the door.

I said things like, *Hello, busy day? Week's whizzing by!* and all that.

Imogen said things like, *Yes, just fine thank you, sooo busy, wasn't it always, though!*

Then I held out my arms for the magazines, which were in a heavy-duty supermarket bag. 'Thank you so much,' I said.

'Is this still a shoes-on house?' She pointed both her forefingers at her feet.

'No! I mean, yes! Shoes are fine. You come right on in!' I sounded like Carol Brady, for some reason.

'I hope I'm not imposing.' Imogen was undoing, one by careful one, the metal pop buttons along the front of her black puffy coat.

'Not at all!' I blabbed on about a cold day and snow on the mountain. 'We'll make some tea.'

Nick had wandered over. He shut the door and gave me a look, like: *Why did you say that, when we were supposed to be going to bed?*

I gave him three quick looks that together meant: *Because it's basic good manners, you no-social-skills sex maniac, now hurry up and take her coat for her!*

Imogen sat down at the dining table, Nick found a chopping board and cut up some cake, and I made over-my-shoulder conversation about a new bicycle lane while I faffed around boiling the kettle and getting out cups.

We drank tea and talked about Lila Nguyen's wedding, Imogen's job, my job, Nick's job. I told them about the poetry club. Imogen asked me again about my ceramics. She had a lot of interested, technical questions to do with why different glazes were suitable at different temperatures, and I had only a vague idea about what the answers were. I wasn't a very science-oriented person.

Nick watched me while I was talking. He kept rocking back on his chair. In between answering Imogen's questions about oxides and Fahrenheit, and listening to her answers about a challenging job and a heavy workload, I was giving him secret, silly, sit-on-your-chair-like-a-good-host-or-you'll-be-in-big-trouble looks.

'Wow, that cake was a*maz*ing, Zoe,' Imogen said, when she'd finished. 'The way to a man's heart is through his stomach.'

Now, I wouldn't call myself particularly woke, but even I wouldn't come out with something like that. And, seriously, thank *God* Claire wasn't there.

'Nick made it,' I said. The great baker himself was tipping his head from side to side, like he had a crick in his neck.

'Nick!' Imogen turned her whole body towards him. 'I didn't know you cooked!' She tapped him on the shoulder with her fingers. 'Amazing! Multi-talented! Chef Nick!'

'Just sometimes.' He shrugged – multi-talented Chef Nick was humble, too, clearly – and pointed to the magazines. 'Want me to put those with your school stuff, Zo?'

I smile-nodded, and when Nick returned, he stood behind me and rested his hands on my chair. The very tips of all his fingers touched the skin just above the neckline of my top.

Imogen asked him if he knew whether Tyrone Doyle's wife had had her baby yet.

Nick said he hadn't heard.

She asked him whether he'd been invited to Mikayla Warren's house-warming.

Nick said he wasn't sure.

Then there was a pause. I considered Imogen's carefully scraped-back hair, and her interested, upright posture, and all her makeup, and I thought about offering to make more tea, but didn't. I sat in the silence, and wondered about the line between boundaries and selfishness. We'd been sitting there for about seventy-five minutes.

After a few seconds, Nick said, 'Ah well, early start tomorrow.' Maybe all that boundary stuff was easier for men.

'I better leave you to it,' Imogen said. 'I wouldn't want to impose.'

'No hurry!' But I spoke with that half-hearted, high-pitched type of enthusiasm that I usually hated.

Finally – after Imogen told a longish story about a meme someone called Helen Maher had shared – her coat was on.

'Thanks again, Imogen,' I said.

Nick opened the door.

'My pleasure! Thanks for the cake, Chef Nick!' She gave him a wink. 'You coming now, too, Zoe?'

'Oh, no. Not yet.' I mean, what else could I say?

Nick smiled at her and waved his arm around so the outdoor sensor light came on. From his dining table, we'd looked out at the black river and a somehow-exciting forest of lights. But from this doorway, we saw parking spaces with faded paint lines and a squadron of wheelie bins.

Imogen said goodbye and thank you and the cake was a*maz*ing some more times. I was getting pretty cold by the end, and when she walked away, I shut the door and snuggled up against Nick. We stood quietly until we heard her Uber drive away.

'Poor old Imo,' he said, then. He sounded sad. 'Was nice you invited her in, Zo.'

'Mmm,' I said. Then I thought I'd plough ahead with the obvious. 'She likes you, right? As in, *likes* you.'

'You think?' But he knew it was true.

'You and she ever ...?'

'Once or twice.' He sounded staggered that I'd been able to tell – whatever Claire reckoned, men were around a million times denser than women about these things – and he leaned back so he could see me. 'Or ... you know, I was a dickhead when I was younger. Probably more than that. But not for a while.'

'High school thing?'

'Pretty much.' He zizzed his eyes across my face. 'Or, no. No, actually. Not just high school. Much more recently than that, Zo.' More concerned eye-zizzing. 'When I was under the influence. When I was single.'

I gave a slow nod. 'You're not doing that now, are you?' I said. 'Sex with other people?'

'Shit no.' He looked flatteringly horrified by the idea. 'Are you?' Even more horrified.

I shook my head and put my cheek against his chest.

'You should be careful,' I said to his jumper. 'About leading her on, or whatever.'

'I know.' Not with any irritation. Just as if he understood what I meant. He tightened his arms around me.

'Because the thing is,' I said, after a minute, 'that we all know you are *so* multi-talented!' I realised I was being pretty mean to Imogen, but I had the giggles, and once the words were in my head, I really wanted to say them. 'Just oh-so-*amazing* at oh-*so*-many things!'

Nick started laughing too – I could tell he was pretty chuffed, even though he knew I was just mucking around – and he picked me up in this big, wrestley sort of hug. We were tickling each other and I was squealing in an enjoying way, and liking how easily he could carry me, and of course, the whole thing turned into sex on his couch.

That part of the evening really *was* amazing.

∞

I set up a poetry club sweet-treat roster, and at some point, I said the next session's poems should be about something to do with the letter H. This was a random idea that everyone accepted: I just had to keep saying, 'You can interpret it however you want,' to all their questions. We now had seven regular kids; we had lost two girls but gained a girl and a boy.

That week, Amy Petrovic somehow got us onto talking about Hideously Humiliating moments – I managed not to tell them about when Daniel was supposed to propose but broke up with me, *Ha-ha-ha, Hilarious, Heartache!* – and when that discussion was finished, the room emptied. Except for Emma. She was doing that thing where she took a lot of time shuffling around with her laptop. Holding Her Horses, perhaps.

'How are things, Emma?' I said. Out the window, I saw Sophie heading for the staffroom. She had a few laminated posters under one arm and a mug dangling from her other hand. In ten minutes, the end-of-lunchbreak bell would ring.

Emma gave me a big smile – she had this sincere smile that made you want to tell her to be careful of all the nasty people out there – and told me she was going well, thank you, and also did I want to see a photo of a baby echidna her mum was caring for?

'Mum's a vet,' she said. 'She does wildlife volunteering in her spare time.'

We looked at a few photos – baby echidnas were ridiculously cute – and then she said, 'Um.' She was drawing a line on a desk with one corner of her phone. 'Um, with the end-of-year production? *Pirates of Penzance*?'

'Yes?' Because of something or other to do with the pandemic, a dialled-down version of the usual extravaganza was being put on later than normal. One of the maths teachers was predictably up in arms about the impact on exams.

'Did you, I was just wondering, if you knew that I got in?' A proud, shy little glance. 'Just into the ensemble. And I don't have to dance if I don't want to. But I was just checking.'

I said a very real and very excited congratulations, and Emma prepared to leave.

Right then, Amy Petrovic reappeared in the doorway, all nonchalant and fiddling with her blazer sleeve. Emma turned her smile towards her, and Amy curled a flick of hair behind one ear and said, 'Did you still want to get hot chocolates?'

The two of them walked away together, their hips level, their arms in identical embraces around their laptops, and without speaking to me again.

I picked up my keys and my own empty coffee mug.

It was all just Hugely and Humongously excellent.

Pursuant to *Coronial and Other Act 1991*
Section 16(IV)
[EXCERPT] [DRAFT]

It was the testimony of all parties interviewed that, at the time of the collision, Imogen Banks was a platonic friend of Zoe Morello's. Multiple parties conjectured in evidence that Imogen Banks wished for an intimate relationship with Nicholas Kavanagh.

Chapter Nineteen

GRACE

Spring

'Mum?' said Emma, appearing in the doorway of the lounge room.

'Sheesh!' Grace jumped and nearly spilled tepid ginger tea all over both her laptop and her brand-new foam-contour laptop tray. 'I didn't know you were there.' It was after ten. She put down her tea, adjusted her glasses and looked properly at Emma. 'Can't you sleep?'

Rain was falling hard. Grace had been half listening to the weather and thinking about her gutters.

Emma was possibly on the scrounge for food. There wasn't much in the house that could be used for a binge, though. Grace kept their small supply of bread in the freezer. She had to cut it all up first, because she bought the healthy, bakery kind that you sliced yourself. *My daughter may be managing a life-threatening psychiatric illness, but see what nutritious sourdough she purges*, she'd thought as she'd sawed through its crust.

Probably she was being too negative. Emma hadn't done any of that for quite a while now, at least as far as she knew.

'I just found this,' Emma said, proffering what appeared to be a bookmark. 'Who is Ben?'

'I beg your pardon?' Grace put both her hands on the edges of her ridiculous cushiony 'desk' and felt herself lean further back into the couch.

'Who's Ben?' said Emma, again.

'I thought you were in bed!' Grace spoke with a snappy combination of good-parenting righteousness and late-night tiredness. Not to mention adultery-related horror. 'What were you doing going through my things?'

'You *said* I could look on your shelf! For a *poem*. For my *poetry club*.'

Yes, she had told Emma that. *See what you can find, sweetie.* She'd been checking the bloody BASs. *Poetry? Um. Try that shelf thing under my bedside table.*

'Sorry.' She swallowed. 'Sorry. What have you found?'

Seriously, what could it possibly be? She possessed no photos of him. She kept nothing connected with Ben; even his texts got deleted as soon as she read them. He was in her phone as 'Ben The Electrician'.

Emma was holding the strip of card in one hand, and a little green book in the other. Grace recognised the book straightaway. Her mum had found it in an op shop and had given it to Grace, just before she'd been diagnosed, and around the time a bandicoot they'd rescued from the side of the road had died.

It was the sort of book Grace herself would never buy: small and almost square, with a shiny floral cover, and (worst of all) called *Embracing You*. It was filled with supposedly self-esteem-building quotes, some of which were by people who clearly hadn't had very good self-esteem (Marilyn Monroe, for one, and Othello, for another), and many of which were contradictory. (*The coward's life is not worth living.* A stern full stop. And then, on the very next page, the cheerily exclamation-marked: *Accept your faults and live as you are!*)

Grace hadn't looked at the book in ages. In fact, she'd been very mildly offended when her mum had bought it for her. Did Tess think she needed that kind of psychological boost? She would have preferred a Mars bar. But of course, whenever Grace did a cull she would reread her mum's inscription (*For my treasured Daughter, with love on this journey of Life*) and smile and get tears in her eyes and lean on her knees away from the charity bag and back towards her bookshelf.

In Emma's other hand was the strip of card, and Grace saw now that it wasn't a bookmark. It was in fact a set of those photos that young people had once squashed into booths at railway stations to take. For some reason, photos like that had always seemed hilarious and daring and original, designed for people more popular and more sophisticated and more *right* than herself.

'Show me?' Grace said. Emma sat down next to her, and Grace held out her hand.

On the reverse side was written in slightly smudged blue pen: *Me & Ben!*

Her writing was round and neat, the letters mostly unjoined. Her ampersand was a backwards '3' with a vertical line through it. There was no date. No location. She turned over to the photos.

'Oh,' she said. 'That's right. That day. 'Oh.' She'd thought there were no photos left. And certainly none that showed what they'd felt.

There was a long quiet, the kind where you didn't even hear the fridge, or the heater, or the overgrown leaves scraping paint off the guttering. She touched her own younger face with her forefinger.

'Was he your boyfriend? Ben?' Emma was settled and warm against her side.

'No. Not really.' He'd had that funny sort of bowl cut. She'd forgotten.

'You look happy,' Emma said, nodding towards the photo.

'Yeah.' She did. *They* did, with their requisite silly, cheeks-pressed-together faces, then their helpless, laughing scrunches, then a sort-of kiss. Their eyes were closed. Ben's hand was a blur near their shoulders; he seemed about to curl it into her hair.

'Was he? Your boyfriend? How old were you there?' Emma often asked questions like that. *How old were you the first time you got drunk?*

The first time you tried a cigarette? Stayed up all night? Grace got the feeling Emma was worried she herself was taking too long to get a boyfriend, too long to argue about going to beach parties, too long to start being a proper teenager.

'Not much older than you.' Unbel*iev*able.

'How old?' Emma turned her head, interested.

'I was eighteen when we met.'

Emma grunted and put her head back on Grace's shoulder, as if everyone knew that eighteen was *worlds* away from fifteen. Which, in fact, it was.

'Soooo, Mother-dear. Who was he?' Emma took hold of their ancient grey couch shawl and pulled it over her legs.

'Um,' Grace replied.

She thought of a documentary she'd recently watched about friendly, relatable middle managers who'd been secretly pilfering for years. Women were more likely than men to commit that sort of small-business fraud, apparently. And women in their forties were the absolute worst.

'We were really just friends. Maybe you could even say we dated. But nothing serious. It was all back when I was young and silly.' She squished her elbow into the couch so she could stroke Emma's hair. 'Before you were born.'

It was oddly nice to talk about him like this; it was as if she finally had him in the proper context: *Yes, sweetie, Ben was this handsome, sexy boy I kissed a couple of times, oh years before I met your father. He had dark hair and green eyes, you can't really tell from the photo quite how green, but, my, they were* green. *Now, hmm, let me see if I can remember his surname. Hewson? Huxley? Ah, I have it! Hutchinson. Never a long-term prospect, you know the type, but so* much fun.

'What happened?' said Emma.

'Oh, you know. He got married and they moved away, and there you go.' *I wonder what he's up to now. Let's hope he married someone nice. He was a lovely boy, as far as I remember.* Or even, *Oh dearie me, yes, I thought my poor young heart was broken!*

'So, that was before Drew Bryan?'

'Guess so.' Drew Bryan was the university boyfriend she'd told Emma all about. She'd 'seen' Drew Bryan while Ben was off on some elective jaunt, once – apparently accidentally – cc'ing her into a barely punctuated group email that contained a photo of a Thai beach where his medical training did not appear to be going forward with particular zeal. The photo took minutes to load, but Grace's patience was rewarded with a pixelated image of an unknown woman in bathers and a sarong, holding two bottles of Singha beer. Grace had taken desperate, hopeless comfort from the fact that Ben usually drank Corona.

She looked again at the strip of photos in front of her. She'd forgotten all about that blue cardigan of hers. She used to wear it often. It had been useful: thick and soft and not itchy.

'Fun times,' she said. *What a crazy youth I had! Op-shop cardigans! Cute boys! Hysterical!*

She'd started to relax. She glanced at Emma and managed to sip her tea.

After a bit, Emma spoke again. 'Hey, Mum?'

'Yeeeees?' Friendly voice. Coaxing out the question.

'Do you think ...?'

'Yeeeees?'

'That I'm pretty?'

'I think you're beautiful outside and in,' Grace said promptly. She had read in a psychologist's book that that was what you were supposed to say to that question, although she had her doubts, frankly.

'Humph. Thanks a *lot*,' said Emma.

'It's true.' And it *was* true. Emma *was* beautiful, with her pallor and her hesitancy and her wide blue eyes. The strands of her brown hair were shot with copper; they were shiny and always clean and soft on her shoulders; her teeth were white and small.

But Emma wasn't beautiful in the eyes of the world. The world's brutal answer was: *Emma, now that you're not horrifically thin you're more or less good-looking, but not eye-catchingly so. Probably not pretty enough for a boy as handsome as Ben, although you'll be attractive enough if you work at it. And maybe you'll blossom spectacularly later; that occasionally happens, but don't hold your breath.*

Those answers were awful. Grace would *never* give those answers. (Especially considering she herself had just been reflecting that *she* didn't look all that great in those photos, even though she was at the age where she was supposed to have stopped beating herself up for imagined imperfections. But all she saw was that her eyebrows had been even more out of control than currently, and her temples were too pointy.)

'You're beautiful, outside and in, and whoever gets to date you one day will be very lucky,' she said firmly.

'Yeah, yeah, Mother-dear, whatever.' Emma kissed Grace's cheek – dry and quick – and picked up the book of quotations off the couch.

'Did you find a poem?' Grace thought to ask, as Emma stood up.

'Yes. Something about stars.' She flipped through the pages. 'Hang on, I'll find it – oops.'

Another photo was drifting onto the carpet.

Smaller, passport-sized, as if it had been chopped from the first strip. It landed face up, near Emma's ugg-booted foot. Grace had a quick impression of Ben. Clearly, it was from the same day, but in this picture, he was alone, staring at the camera with a serious, self-conscious smile. *Imagine that*, she thought, as more of the memory – a Sunday, a government form, a booth at a chemist – slid blurrily around. *He was allowed to* smile *in a* booth *for a* passport *photo.*

Emma had bent down. Now she straightened with the little oblong in her cupped palm, the book dangling from her other hand. She stared from the photo, to her mother, and back again.

It took a couple of seconds for Grace to register her daughter's new face.

'Em? You okay?'

'Fine.' But Emma was standing oddly still.

'Are you sure?' What was happening? What was wrong? What on earth could she say? 'You seem a bit upset.'

'I'm fine.' Emma didn't make eye contact. Her dressing gown clung bulkily to her legs as she turned slowly away. 'Night-night.'

'Emma?' Grace half stood up. Her laptop and its tray fell sideways onto the couch. Her tea wobbled dangerously on the armrest.

'I'm *fine*, I said! I just need *rest*!'

And after a few seconds, Emma's bedroom door opened and then shut with a non-dramatic click that was much, much worse than a slam.

∞

Grace didn't sleep. She lay in bed and looked at the orchid on her bedside table, which no doubt would die soon, despite her best efforts with ice cubes and natural light. Twice she padded along the corridor, knocked uncertainly on Emma's door, and walked unanswered back down the cool polished boards to her own room.

She was a sinner and a liar and she would be made to pay. Emma knew something, and she would feel lost and confused, and she'd start with the purging again, and Grace would be unable to reach her, and Emma would waste away and die, and it would all be Grace's fault. Her beautiful daughter was going to suffer for her wrongdoing, which – conveniently for God, for basic human decency, for karma and/or for the Universe – would be the worst possible punishment for Grace.

She asked herself if she really believed all that, and found that she pretty much did. It occurred to her to pray for redemption, or forgiveness, or just for help, but probably nobody would hear her prayers, and it was ridiculous to start asking the benevolent Universe for things at this stage. And even if there was a God, S/He'd be quite justified in thinking that S/He had other priorities, all things considered. 'First World problem,' God would say briskly. 'And what's more, it's of your own immoral making. No judgement,' God might add, kindly. 'It's just I'm gifting you with the opportunity to sort it out yourself.'

Why on earth had she even told Emma anything? She should have said, 'Oh, er, yes, some boy or other. Anyway, it's late, school tomorrow, off to bed.'

But Grace had been swept up in the moment, as if it was *romantic*. They'd looked so happy in those photos. They'd looked in *love*. She'd felt ludicrously proud of herself and Ben; she'd wanted to show him off, and more than that, she'd been feeling all those reckless youthful feelings about openness and serendipity, because honestly, she still had no idea how those photos could possibly have ended up there.

'Give me that book!' she could have said. 'And those photos! That's private, thank you very much, young lady!' Lots of mums would have done that. Proper, married mums would have done exactly that, invested as they were with all the authority that came with their solid, nice-guy husbands.

When it was almost light, Grace got out of bed and knocked more assertively on Emma's door.

'Emma! Are you okay?' she called. Then, 'What's going on? Can I please come in?' Tears were in her voice.

'No.' The false brightness was gone. Emma sounded as if she was hungover.

'Shall we go for a drive? A walk?' Grace leaned against the closed door with both hands and the side of her head. 'I could take the morning off? Please, Em?'

She thought her obvious anguish might count for something, but apparently not.

'I already said, no,' Emma replied. 'Can you please just go away!'

1.

By being a friend, you befriend yourself, so treasure
your friends – they are like seashells, washed up
upon the shore of your life!

2.

Cull from your days people who don't make you feel
good about yourself …

36.

No matter what, your first real love shapes your destiny.

(Due to the first two, Grace had never read as far as that last one.)

Chapter Twenty

IMOGEN

Spring

'Oh, thank goodness for that!' Mum said.

'Yes! What a relief!' I said.

Dr Ashleigh was sitting with her elbows on her desk and all her fingertips together. The pose did not really suit her. She had just finished telling us that she'd had my brain scans reviewed at a team meeting.

'We even got the neurosurgeons involved,' she said. This was a joke about the undesirability of neurosurgeons; such so-called humour abounded among neurologists.

Apparently, the 'overwhelming view' was that my arachnoid cyst was 'most unlikely' to be causing my seizures. They weren't going to give me any surgery. Not even a biopsy. No fucking procedure at all.

'You're positive?' I said.

'The cyst was an incidental finding. That's the consensus.' It was the third time she'd used the word 'consensus'. Of course, she had not managed to use the word 'sorry' regarding the ridiculous baloney she'd waffled on with the last time.

'And she hasn't had any more seizures, which is wonderful, isn't it, darling!' said Mum, apparently talking to both me and Dr Ashleigh, simultaneously.

Mum sounded as if she expected Dr Ashleigh to give me a prize, but Dr Ashleigh just nodded once and said I should stay on my medication, advise her of any side effects and have some more blood tests in six months.

'I've been so worried,' Mum gushed. Dad had told me that Mum had been crying in the mornings, which was not ideal, but was also an example of why women her age needed to let go of their adult children.

Dr Ashleigh said, 'And how's work going, Imogen? You coping all right?'

'Yes, thank you.'

'Not too tired? Concentration's okay?'

'I mean, I do get tired, but I'm only human!'

'Ah, yes, I know how busy you residents are.' She went rambling off into a story about the olden days and sixteen-hour shifts. People of her generation pretended to think that culture was terrible, but it was very obvious they were proud of themselves, and they did nothing to advocate for change. 'But nothing untoward?'

'No.'

'Good, good. Now, regarding driving . . .' Dr Ashleigh said a whole lot of things I already knew, about precipitants and EEGs, and then finished with, 'So, assuming you remain seizure-free, you can drive again in another five months or so. I know it's a pain.'

'That's just fine!' I said. Nick was so attentive, and in any case, the probability of my being stopped for a random police check was extremely low.

'*Thank* you for understanding,' said Dr Ashleigh. She turned to Mum and Dad and said, 'You wouldn't *believe* the carry-on I get from some people.'

Mum tutted and shook her head. Dad hmmed and nodded his head.

I opted to frown, thoughtfully, and scratch my head. I said, 'We have to consider public safety, don't we?'

I was nothing if not responsible.

∞

One day, as Nick was driving me home from the supermarket, he said, 'So, um, how long till you can get your licence back?'

I truthfully said about six months – I was rounding up – unless I had another seizure.

'Shit,' he said. 'Not that I mind, but a pain in the arse for you.'

'I'm going with the flow. But I hope it's not too annoying to spend time with me?'

'Of course not.' Nick spoke with gentle emphasis. He glanced out the window, at a young woman walking along. That was just the sort of thing he did, no doubt due to cultural conditioning or to biological factors.

'Nick?' I sat up straighter and adjusted my handbag on my lap. 'It means a lot. The way you've been so worried about me.'

Nick made a serious face and didn't say anything for one-and-a-half blocks. We were going past a children's playground when he spoke.

'Imogen, I'm really sorry if I was a … you know, not a nice guy. In high school, and …' He took a very deep breath and turned on the windscreen wipers, even though it wasn't raining much. 'Or if I haven't been able to give you what you maybe might want.'

'Don't be silly,' I said. 'Just because you're not ready for us, it doesn't make you a bad person.'

He made a dear little face. 'Yeah, but—'

'I hold onto the sweet things you said,' I told him. 'And those wonderful moments. You know, Nick, that's what everyone has to do. You have to look to the future, not dwell on the negativity.'

'Mmm.' Nick rubbed his face, then after almost one minute of very loud, scratchy windscreen wiper noise, he said, 'You met anyone nice yourself? I thought maybe in England you'd—'

'Oh no! I'm super busy with work, anyway.'

'Fair enough.' After that, he had to concentrate on changing lanes, and a short time later, he indicated towards my street.

'Remember our pact?' I said. He'd pulled up in front of my house, but he hadn't turned off the ignition or put on the handbrake. He was very competent and confident, but also mildly careless, as a driver.

'Um. Which one was that?' he said.

'About, if we don't meet anyone by the time we're thirty-five? How we'd get married?'

'Ha!'

'Thirty-five just seemed so *old* then!' I said.

'I know, mate.' Nick laughed delightedly. 'Where's the time gone? Anyway, I better—'

'I hear you!' I laughed right back. 'Thirty-five! It's less than a year away!'

'Jeez, don't say that.' He'd stopped laughing.

I was still composing my goodbye when he said, 'Ah well, see you at the altar, then, Imo.' He gave me a really beautiful, warm smile. 'You right with that door?' His caring words were as tender as any caress.

I returned his smile, and said goodbye to Rug, who was unsecured in the back. Then I got out into the sunlit rain. Nick sounded our special toot-toot. He also gave me the most intimate of waves. It was rainbow weather on so many levels.

I went inside and made some coffee. When moments like today's happened, I knew that I wasn't foolish to believe that he would, eventually, wake up to himself.

'My secret recipe,' I said, as a joke. 'Special delivery!'

I had made a lasagne for Nick, to thank him for all the driving around he was doing and because I had an inkling that he needed a little push in the right direction. The lasagne was still warm, which was nice, because it was cold on his doorstep and I'd decided not to wear my gloves.

'Oh.' Nick's hair was wet, and his shirt wasn't done up all the way. He grasped the dish. 'Thanks, Imo.' He held the lasagne on his forearm; his other hand rested against the doorframe. This represented a classic non-verbal display of dominance and openness. Or, in simple parlance, it was a come-hither pose.

'Nice and warm inside.' I blew onto my bare, velvety hands and shivered.

'Yeah,' Nick said. 'Yeah, got the heat pump on.' He lifted the lasagne up several centimetres. 'Okay, Imo, well, thanks heaps for this.' With his other hand, he took hold of the doorhandle. 'I'll see you soon.'

He gave me another very special smile. I was the first to admit that I could misunderstand people sometimes, but the conflict in Nick's eyes on this particular occasion was very clear.

'Goodbye.' We stepped forward, and I kissed his stubble-roughened cheek.

'Nick!' yelled a voice from his living room. 'Invite Imogen in! Goddy-god, sorry, Imogen.'

I was so surprised that I almost asked where her car was.

Inside, the TV was silently playing commercial news, and Zoe was wittering about how she'd just been getting changed and she'd been to the gym for the first time in about a decade and I was a total life-saver who of course had to stay for dinner. She spoke as if it was *her* house.

I stood next to the dining table, and wished I'd done my hair more casually. Zoe's was in a ponytail, but falling down around her face and onto the back of her neck. I was unsure of how to stand, and so I gave Rug a little pat on his head, but then I needed to wash my hands. It was a relief when Nick pointed me towards a seat and offered to make a salad.

'Nah. Talk to Imogen,' Zoe said. She'd already taken some rocket from his fridge.

'Sure?'

'Yes. Go away.'

Nick laughed. He used a remote control to turn off the television and turn on some music. After we'd finished my lasagne and Zoe's salad, he went off to hang up some washing. I was still only halfway through my bowl of ice-cream.

'Washing, washing, washing!' I said. 'It's always around, isn't it? Clothes. Towels. Sheets, and I don't know what all! And then Nick's work clothes. Smelly work socks! Those boxer shorts, if he still wears them? Total nightmare!'

'I know! You been busy at the hospital?'

'It's always busy. Nightmare!'

She just smiled. She was so self-satisfied, with her intimate knowledge of Nick and his underclothes. Well.

'Zoe?' I said. 'I wouldn't want you to feel that I personally hadn't been honest with you. Now that we're becoming so friendly.' I lowered my voice to a whisper. 'Nick and I were once involved, and I think you should know that he has a tendency to ricochet from woman to woman.' I assumed an empathic expression. I also touched her arm. 'I just thought you should know.'

Zoe burst out laughing!

'Good of you to tell me.' She licked her spoon. 'He did mention you and he had a little thing. Had a thing, I mean.' With ice-cream on her lip, she said, 'Ricochet, eh? I'll have to tease him about that.'

'If you think that would be appropriate.' I spoke with great dignity.

Zoe wiped her mouth and reached both of her tackily nail-polished hands across Nick's table towards me. She rested her palms near my plate.

'I just think, you know, everyone has a history.' Another smug smile. 'But thanks for telling me. Seriously. I appreciate it.' Then she stood and started stacking the dishes, despite the fact that I clearly still had ice-cream in my bowl. 'So, are you, you know, seeing anyone now?' she said.

'No.' I laid down my spoon, quite pointedly, and stood up. 'Which is just fine with me. I don't think old-fashioned rules about needing to be in a relationship apply anymore.'

'Good for you, Imogen.' Zoe laughed and picked up my bowl. She proceeded to ramble on about her own purported loneliness when she was single for about two fucking milliseconds. 'I mean, gosh, Imo, just how passionate about ceramics is a woman really supposed to be?' she giggled.

'Totally!' I said. There was no way she would be able to meet his long-term emotional or intellectual needs. 'Nightmare!' I added.

Nick came back right then, and they began to stack his dishwasher, and he offered to get me an Uber.

I told him I would source my own ride, since he was obviously too busy for old friends like me that evening, and I said my goodbyes very soon afterwards. I kept them elegant and brief, and I left them to their weekend, and their washing, and their stupid, cookie-cutter, leg-and-fucking-breast-based infatuation.

Likewise, I can find no evidence that the deceased at any time made threats against any party.

Chapter Twenty-one

ZOE

Spring

'What did you think? When we first met?' Nick said.

It was Saturday, and the two of us were lying in the soft green bowl of St David's Park. For the first time in ages, you couldn't feel any chill even at the bottom of the breeze, and we were watching clouds and feeling far too tired and far too pleased with ourselves.

'Hot, I thought.' I said it straightaway. 'You reminded me of a sexy pirate. What did you think?'

'I dunno.' But I could tell he did know. He seemed pretty keen to have this conversation, actually. 'Hot, 'course. At first, I just wanted to ... you know. You were in that blue dress.' He nodded like a tennis coach whose player had just pulled off a match-winning backhand. 'And I liked you. I thought you were really fun. You know, Zo, how you're so ... friendly?'

'Yes, I'm well known for my bubbliness.' I pointed to my own face. 'See? Very warm and bubbly smile.'

He smiled his own pleased smile back. 'Yeah.'

We turned again to the sky. Above us was a cloud shaped like a teddy bear.

'I said to my mate, straight after, "That Zoe girl's cool." And Damo said—' He stopped. He'd put the brakes on hard.

'What?'

'Well, I can't remember the exact words, but it was along the lines of, she's ... she ... she's very attractive.'

'Big boobs?'

Apparently so, if his face was anything to go by.

'Well, they *are* very nice,' he said. 'And they weren't exactly ... hidden. In that blue dress.'

'I beg your pardon?' I was suddenly propped up on one elbow, frowning down at him, aware of the tightish jumper I was wearing and not in a good, sexy way.

Nick swallowed. He had a face like a man who'd accidentally scratched his boss's Ferrari. 'They were – *you* were, I mean – looking superb. I just meant. In that particular dress.'

'Oh, they were, were they?' I moved so that I was lying on my tummy, leaning on arms that were crossed in front of me. I focused on the grass. '"She had her nice big tits out." Very original. Well done, the two of you.'

'Hey. Zoe. That was all just at first.' He put a very respectful hand on my shoulder, and his voice was so different from his trademark laidback-Nick tone that I felt a bit better. Better enough to make eye contact with him.

'You're so sweet, Zoe. Pretty. Friendly. Kind. I'm ... I'm really into you now.' His voice was soft and shy when he added, 'It was very much worth the wait.' He presumably meant the 'wait' between when we met and when we first had sex.

'Three months.' My voice was brisk. I was still annoyed – and *hurt* and even, somehow, scared – about the big-boobs thing. It made me feel weird in a way I didn't quite understand. Daniel wouldn't have talked about me like that. Daniel wouldn't even have had *mates* who talked about me like that. 'Less! Not exactly forever. People used to wait years. Years and years. Until they were *married*.'

Nick crossed his eyes, as if to say that that system was *obviously* terrible and thank *God* we lived in a more civilised world nowadays. He was so genuinely horrified that I laughed, and – probably because we'd just had such a nice night together – lay down again. He did too, so we were facing each other. He used his palm to flatten the grass blades near his face. 'I was nearly out of my poor old one-track mind,' he said. 'By that night with the mushroom pasta.'

'Tell me about it.' I had no truck with the I-only-go-along-with-this-sticky-lovemaking-business-to-please-my-man caper.

'Why did you? Not come out with me?' he said. ''Cause I felt like a massive tool when you turned me down.' He smiled and pretend-slapped my hip. 'Twice.'

'Your trusty mate Damo *smirked*.' I gave him a jokey-grumpy glare. 'The very first time you asked me out. I wasn't going to be smirked over.'

'Damo's kind of a dickhead.' But he spoke as if dickhead mates were just a part of life, like having to put petrol in your car. 'And I'm going to kill him. Seriously. That little … *smirker*.'

He leaned in and gave me a quick kiss on the mouth. I thought it would turn into a long kiss – which would have been more than fine with me, to be honest – but then his face went all serious.

'Night of that barbecue, he – Damo – he did say you had great …' He screwed up his face and squeezed his eyes shut. '… tits. Sorry. And I did just sorta laugh along. So, um. I'm sorry. Yeah.' His eyes got bigger in his face, as if he was about to be sick. ''Cause I reckon I'm really in love with you now, Zoe.'

Goddy-god. *God*.

It felt almost too nice to be true, especially with the spring breeze and the sunshine and the blossomy trees and all.

'Same here, Nick.' But it also felt like the most natural thing in the world. 'Me too.'

By now, we both had completely unmanageable smiles – he'd

stopped looking vomity – and after about ten seconds we pretty much had to flop onto our backs just to give each other a moment. We held hands, and stared up at the soft blue, feeling no doubt more annoyingly pleased with ourselves than ever.

I noticed the teddy-bear cloud again. One of its paws had started to fray.

∞

I invited Imogen around for dinner. Partly to say thanks for the lasagne, but also because I'd clicked that she might be lonely. While in the pit of my Daniel-related despair, I'd promised myself to be kinder, and I didn't want to trip at an early, smugly in-love hurdle. I had also been to the gym twice that fortnight and had excellent sex six times in one week. Was acing life on many levels, although I did mess up the cheese sauce and so dinner was late.

After we'd finally eaten, Nick was finishing his beer and Imogen and I were drinking a yummy bottle of wine that she'd brought. The conversation was slowing down when Imogen asked how Claire was.

'I heard they're starting a family!' she said. The pregnancy was now public. In fact, Claire was having her first scan any day. She'd sensitively not been talking about it much, and I'd kept meaning to ask her for details, but not quite being able to find the way. At least I was still making the nursery quilt.

'That's right!' My voice was probably a touch too cheerful. 'Isn't it great?'

'I hope that can happen for me.' Imogen dabbed something invisible off her lip with her little finger. 'With seizure medication, things can be very difficult.'

I somehow kept my voice normal while I said I was sorry.

'Yeah, mate,' said Nick. 'Sorry.'

Imogen shrugged and looked at her lap.

She was really brave. And very generous with the fancy wine.

I needed to stop being so bloody full of myself just because I was making a perfectly ordinary nursery quilt and had invited someone a tiny bit odd over for dinner. Also, I needed to stop being so self-pitying. And while I was at it, so secretive.

Chapter Twenty-two

IMOGEN

Spring

'Isn't it great!' Zoe was beaming like a loon, if that expression was still permitted, about her cousin's pregnancy.

She'd invited Nick and me to dinner, where I'd learned that she followed the interior-design trend popularly known as shabby-chic but more aptly described as visual cacophony. Plants were cluttered along the top of the bookshelf, with their leaves hanging so you couldn't see some of the book titles. Pictures leaned on walls. One engagement party, two wedding and a christening invitation, plus at least two bills, obscured approximately sixty per cent of her fridge.

We'd had a late meal, due to what Zoe said was a 'total cheese-sauce debacle', and I was leading the conversation towards health concerns, when there was a lot of noise at her front door.

'I'm leaving T-rex!' It was her cousin, Claire. She barged straight into Zoe's kitchen. 'I've been calling you. *And* it's fucking *twins!*' She looked as if she'd been crying. 'Oh, hi, Imogen,' she added.

Claire did not appear the slightest bit embarrassed about her shouting. She used her sleeve to clean her nose and sniffed very loudly. No judgement, but some basic manners would not have gone astray!

'Hang on, sit down, I'll put the kettle on, what?' Zoe did not offer a tissue. In fact, there were none to be seen. Nick gave me one of our secret, very respectful nods, and walked off towards a bedroom.

Claire didn't sit. She wailed that she'd had her ultrasound that afternoon, and she was having twins, and she was upset by that rather than thrilled, and T-rex had not been supportive, but had told her he was surprised she was being so negative about a happy event.

I had to say, I entirely agreed with him. And at her age, I personally would have been getting myself an ultrasound scan much earlier on, no judgement.

'I'd like to see *him* push them out!' Claire said. 'Him, fuck.' As she said the f-word, she sat on the dining table.

Zoe was at the teacup shelf. 'Stop getting all how you get,' she said, without even turning around to Claire.

'Two kids hanging off my boobs!' yelled Claire. 'And a pelvic floor that'll be a hundred per cent stuffed!'

This was not necessarily true. I also sincerely hoped poor Nick was out of earshot.

Zoe glanced over her shoulder at me and waved a hand, as if to say, Don't worry, everything's fine. Only the kind of woman who wore yellow nail polish would wave a hand in that manner during an episode like this.

'He said he was "overjoyed"!' Claire was still using a loud voice. 'That was his exact word!'

'Oh, right,' Zoe said. 'Well. You know.'

'Zoe, stop doing that thing I told you to do!'

'No, because I promised I'd do it. What tea do you want?'

'Just normal, please, Zoe. With milk.' I used a calm, conflict-defusing voice.

'Sake, fuck's, just give me whatever.' But Claire was making no effort to control herself. 'Idiotic, fuckwitted, male!' she said, for some reason.

Zoe made the tea and nobody talked. I timed it by my watch and four minutes went by. The kettle had clicked off. The teabags were steeping.

'Sorry.' Claire spoke all of a sudden. 'Very sorry, Zo. God. Sorry, sorry, sorry. Shit, I'm sorry. Jasmine tea, please, if you have it.' She got off the table and sat on a chair, like a normal person. To me, she said, 'I'm just really shocked. Although, goddy-god, twins. Tell me we've got biscuits here, Zo?'

Zoe smiled and turned around, and sort of crouched down on the floor in front of Claire. 'Do you need to call T-rex right now?' she said.

Claire shook her head, and then leaned into Zoe's shoulder, and whispered, 'I'm so sorry, Zo,' and they hugged for more than thirty seconds. I watched because they both had their eyes closed, and they both had tears on their eyelashes, and I felt something very sad inside myself. I had never hugged anyone in that way, at least not since childhood. And I knew I would never hug anyone in that way, because of the creatinine lady and my pretend seizure and Archie McRae and now the other thing. People like me could never hug like that. Maybe if I'd had a cousin, or a sister, or even just one single proper friend, I would have turned out differently, without the rottingness inside me. That was what I thought.

When they finished hugging, Zoe put three cups of tea and an unopened packet of chocolate biscuits on the table, and took tea in to Nick.

'He's hiding,' she said, when she came back. 'From all the heart-to-heart drama. He said if we could please try to leave him just one single biscuit.'

Claire laughed as if Nick had been joking, and Zoe started explaining a 'deal' she and Claire had had since high school, about how Zoe was supposed to 'handle things' when Claire was upset.

'She hardly ever gets cross, Imo, but when she does, she just loses it.' Zoe had her mouth full. 'Usually for no reason.'

Nobody except Nick called me Imo. I actually didn't mind it all that much.

'Twins,' said Claire, dipping a biscuit into her tea, 'are not "no reason", thanks very much, lovelies.' But she sounded calm now. She was smiling.

'Sometimes it's for no reason. Like when you failed that French test? Remember? Adult Learning French.' Zoe turned to me. 'Not even school!'

'I've never failed any tests,' I said. 'But I think it would make me very upset, too.'

That was not a joke, but they both laughed, and Zoe held the packet of biscuits towards me again.

It was really all quite nice.

I wasn't ashamed to say that I felt very severely conflicted.

Chapter Twenty-three

GRACE

Spring

Emma had been at Christopher's for almost a week. She hadn't emailed to complain about her dad's cooking. She hadn't texted to see how Eric Echidna was. She hadn't replied to any one of Grace's four casually friendly check-ins.

Christopher said Emma was eating her dinners but not her lunches and seemed 'on the quiet side'. ('But then, she's an adolescent,' he'd told Grace. 'She's unquestionably an adolescent.')

'Are you all right?' Maria said, as soon as Grace walked into work on the Monday morning.

Grace said she was very well, thanks. She put her handbag on the hook and asked Maria about her own weekend.

'And is your lovely Emma all right?'

'Yes.' Grace bent over, opened the drawer and extracted a vitamin-supplement catalogue and something or other about tick protection in a single tasty chew. She knew without looking exactly how Maria would be standing. 'She's well, thanks.'

Grace straightened up, and true to form, Maria's arms were folded and she'd turned her whole body away from her computer screen. Now, she raised her trendily pencilled eyebrows and let a full two seconds pass.

'I'll bring you in a cup of tea, Grace, this morning,' she said finally. 'And I'm going to tell the Francises sorry but you just can't see them today, I'm quite honestly up to here with you bending over backwards, they take advantage, those two, plenty of house cats manage to get to appointments on time, and it's not acceptable, I'm afraid, when you're only human.'

Maria's eyes were so worried and so motherly that Grace had to frown down at the tick-protection flyer.

'That'd be good, Maria.' She managed to say it fairly briskly. 'Just this once.'

Maria gave two slow, silent nods. She raised her immaculate eyebrows again, adjusted her headset and pressed a button on the telephone as if she was launching a missile.

∞

At nine o'clock that evening, Ben knocked on the laundry door.

Maybe it was all the emotional stress – or her hormones, or her age, or just a natural thing because who didn't like really nice sex? – but that evening it *was* like a proper love affair. Instantaneous kissing. Frantic, or at least *hasty*, shoving away of clothes. Clonking about the very noisy laundry – her washing machine was the old and reliable and loud sort, and it was in the middle of its spin cycle – and then clonking about the bedroom.

'Thanks be for that,' he said afterwards. Sometimes it felt as if they couldn't talk properly until after they'd had sex. 'How are you?'

They were in bed (things hadn't been *that* hasty) with the doona right up around their shoulders. She'd forgotten to put the heater on.

'Um.'

'What, Gracey?' He turned towards her. All concerned.

'Ben.' She'd been longing to tell him. Unable to text. Hating to ring. But now, she found she was dreading saying the words. (Perhaps she didn't want to 'make it real'. Everyone seemed to find doing that problematic, despite constantly exhorting everyone else to speak up, ask for help and share problems.) She looked down at the disorganised sheet. 'I think maybe Emma knows.'

'What?' Ben's face was loose and uncomprehending, but then it snapped alert. 'What do you mean? How?'

Grace remembered when she'd heard about September 11. She was getting ready for uni, buttering raisin toast, wondering why all the others had overslept. *What do you mean?* she'd asked her boxer-shorted flatmate, who for once wasn't trying to sound like Chandler from *Friends*. *How?*

'She found a few photos. Of you. I told her you were some boy from my ancient past, but I don't think she believed me.'

And now, she's gone into that unreachable place and she's acting as if I'm nothing and I don't know if I'm ever going to be allowed back in and what sort of person am I that I wanted to have sex with you, that I have had sex with you, that I enjoyed having sex with you, when I've maybe harmed my beautiful daughter?

Ben moved closer. 'Just tell me exactly what happened.'

Grace recapped the whole thing as best she could. Outside, the next-door neighbours – a young couple of physiotherapists – were shrieking happily on their deck. Maybe they were having a water-fight. They seemed just the radiant types for a spontaneous water-fight on a weeknight.

Ben shook his head. 'A teenage girl, with her friends, or mad at you, or needing some leverage ...' Further words appeared to have failed him.

'Yeah, all that hasn't escaped me, Ben, and excellent and constructive fun though this is, I might go and make myself a cup of tea.'

'Hey. Hang on.' He put a hand on her wrist 'Sorry. Are you okay? Jesus, is Emma okay?'

'I don't know.'

She waited for him to start doing the much-vaunted masculine problem-solving thing, but he still didn't speak, and anyway, she already knew what the options were.

She could tell Emma and expect her vulnerable fifteen-year-old daughter to live with the whole, secret truth.

Or she could lie to Emma.

They could tell everyone, and have Emma and Louise and all three of Ben's children suffer.

They could break up.

Or they could just continue. They could keep calm and carry on.

'What photos?' said Ben, after a minute.

She leaned over him, awkward but unselfconscious, and retrieved *Embracing You*. She'd slotted the photos back in.

'No idea how they got there,' she confessed. 'I don't remember ever seeing them before. Sorry.'

Ben took the book and flipped out the photos. A quick smile when he saw them, in spite of everything. Then he rubbed his face and said he had to very deeply apologise, but he'd put those pictures in there months ago and forgotten to tell her.

'Jasmine found them,' he said. 'In an album from Dad's house. Wanted the one of me for some art project about images. How people "represented themselves" back in olden times.'

'Right.'

'Yeah. And when Jasmine'd finished, Louise said presumably I didn't want to keep those old snaps, and I said, nah, I'd put them in the bin. But you know.' He gave her a tender look. 'I put them in my pocket. Wanted to show you.'

Grace nodded. Had Louise been droll and sweet and innocent? Or testing and shrewd and vicious? 'That must have been a weird conversation,' she said.

Ben shrugged. Maybe that sort of weirdness was the least of his worries. Probably, he had to lie so often it had become natural. Unbearable to even think about.

'And you were asleep when I left and I didn't want to leave them in the open in case you missed them and then Emma ...' Another shrug. 'Obviously, I didn't want to take them home again, so I put them in there. And that was the week Jasmine snuck out and there were major ructions, and then I was on call or away or something, and I kept thinking of it when you weren't there, and forgetting when I saw you, and you know how you don't like me texting you much. Sorry,' he said.

'You forgot?'

'I said I was sorry.'

'Fuck, Ben.'

'I do have quite a bit going on.'

'Yeah. Thanks for fitting me into your busy double life.'

'Don't do this.'

'You're the worst offender in all this, Ben, and I have quite a bit going on, too.'

'I know. I really am sorry.'

His tone was so chastened and sincere, and she felt so ashamed and so alone, that when he put his hand on her waist she didn't snap it off.

They lay for a long time, listening to the bright young things shrieking about outside. Thinking forward and back.

∞

12 September 2001

Dear Gracey,
I hope this is the right email address still.
Just wanted to get in touch. What a day.
How are you? How is Melbourne? You a vet yet, pet?
Ha-ha I should go onstage. Comedy gold in times of international crisis.
Otherwise, everything has been pretty good here.

Cheers, Ben Hutchinson

. . . .

12 September 2001

Hi Ben,
Nice to hear from you.
I know. There's a girl from my tute group whose dad was in LA. He is okay, but airport's crazy and he's struggling to get home. I hope you and your family are all right.
Hope Hobart is good?
How is med going? You must be all done?!
I'm living in a share house in Richmond. On weekends, lots of football people walk up our street in their scarves. You would like it.

Cheers, Grace

. . . .

13 September 2001

Dear Gracey,

Great to hear from you.

Yes, everyone is fine. Thanks.

Intern now. Thank God 51% gets you called doctor. How about you?

I'm much the same as always. Need to improve my work ethic etc. What you doing with yourself? Min Callaghan is pregnant. That Frank guy from Commerce. You always liked his glasses.

Footy street sounds spectacular.

Ben

··

18 September 2001

Hi Ben,

Oh wow! Is Min okay? I have emailed her.

All good here. Just reading about horse parasites. Thrilling! But cool people, dinners, parties, kayaking trips to Lake Eildon, nearly dying when kayak tipped over and I forgot how to get out, et cetera.

I went out last night, for laksa. Very yummy (the food). The guy I went with is a computer sort of boy. He told me he is designing a computer game, but he wouldn't tell me what about, in case I copied his idea. (!!!) I said I didn't know how to program and had never played a computer game in my whole life (obvs), so his secret would be safe. But he said it was a very unique premise and he had to keep all details in the vault. In a serious voice! Pretty funny.

Gracey

··

22 September 2001

Very unique. Jesus. I thought computer guys knew how to talk.

Ben

....

2 October 2001

Didn't mean to upset you. Did you like him?

Ben

....

3 October 2001

Hi!
God, no, not upset at all. Sorry. Busy. Studying. Working. You know those things? All well. How are you?

G

....

3 October 2001

OK, good. And good luck with all your dedicated vetness.

Ben x

PS Since when are you too busy to actually type 'Gracey'? How much time do the five extra letters take? Because I checked and I can type BEN in less than two seconds and you were always a faster typer than me.

PPS Also – obvs????

....

3 October 2001
Shut up, Benjamin.

G

....

9 December 2001

Dear Gracey,
Are you okay? I know it's the anniversary. I thought of you
today and I hope you are all right.
I just went to the pub with the boys, for Andy Ng's birthday,
he annoyed you by talking about a girl's bottom once, at that
21st, you told me his bottom was not itself of the highest
calibre, which was funny in the good way, I kept laughing in
the speeches thinking of it, you told me off.
I toasted your mum in my head tonight. Rest in peace, Tess,
I said.
Gracey, I know you were mad at me that night. But I hope
you aren't anymore. It wasn't that I didn't want to. Just
you should be with someone proper, not the very unique
computer guy, though, that would be the most depressing
thing in the world. Although, comic potential at times,
obviously. Or obvs.
Nobody much to laugh with here. Girls act weird. Remember
that time with the pretend high jump?
Ok. Am spectacularly drunken tomfool. Going to sleep.

Love, Ben

....

10 December 2001

They act weird because you've slept with half of them.

Educated guess. And made with a smile.

Thanks very much, Ben, for all that. And for the toast. Mum would've liked it.

I am okay. Hard but getting by. Grieving but not depressed. Down but not out. Et cetera.

Don't worry about that night. You saved me from myself. Well done. Very noble of you.

Gracey xo

PS Those jeans are still grass-stained from that high-jump day. Have to sort of hold a bag over my right knee if ever I wear them. Is a tripping hazard.

....

10 December 2001

Hi Gracey,

That's spectacularly good.

Spectacularly hungover.

Are you coming home to be a vet soon? Been missing you all these years.

Ben xo

....

∞

Then there was this other memory.

It was the night before Ben's wedding. Grace was home alone, in the house she'd just bought. Her dinner dishes were washed, her old carpet was vacuumed, and she was about to apply her first-ever face mask (or 'masque', as the packet said). She was reading the instructions when her doorbell rang.

'Ben!' Thank God she didn't have her mask/masque on yet. 'Come in.' This was only his second visit. 'What's wrong? I'll get us a drink.'

They arrived in the kitchen. Wine from cupboard. Glasses from shelf.

'I just came from Louise.' He half sat on a stool near the bench. 'We had this fight.'

'Right.'

This was like an ethical-dilemma exam question in real life. (How would you approach a domestic pet in severe pain whose owner declines euthanasia? List three KEY considerations.) (What advice would you give the person you love the night before s/he marries another? Answer in UNSELFISH dot-point format.)

However, no immediate answer was required from her (luckily) because Ben's narrative was in full and factual swing.

He'd gone to the hotel where Louise was staying, just to say hello, and her bridesmaids were there, and her mum, and her married sister, who didn't want to be a bridesmaid because of her children, and they were all having champagne, and at some point, right as he was leaving, Louise had mentioned the photographer.

'Some guy who's coming to take photos of me getting ready. Louise wants one of me with my bowtie on but undone?' He didn't even seem sheepish. In fact, he put down his wine and made a concise, matter-of-fact gesture to indicate how an undone bowtie would lie around his collar. 'Whisky with the groomsmen. The cufflinks in their boxes. And so on.'

'All pretty standard, Ben, as I understand it.'

'Apparently. Everything quite casual and authentic.' God, not even a shred of irony! 'So, I said I'll probably have a beer, not a whisky, and Louise said something about not drinking out of bottles in front of the photographer, and I said, well, what do you mean, and she said she could not be*lieve* she had to tell me, and I said, sorry but you do, and she said *nothing* looks worse than men drinking out of *bottles*, and I said but I always drink beer out of bottles, and then she just, just lost it, and said if I trusted her judgement and if I loved her then I'd do this one single tiny thing for her, and slammed the door, and I heard her crying and her mum calling her *Precious*.' He swallowed half his glass of wine.

'Ben?' Despite everything, it was a little bit funny. 'That is just your typical pre-wedding fight. From what I can tell. It's, you know, all the heightened emotion.' She paused. 'So, you simply phone Louise, and you say, of course I'll drink out of a glass in the photos, darling, anything for you, love you, et cetera, see you tomorrow, can't wait, bye.' She swallowed quite a lot of her own wine. (And she would get an *excellent* mark for that answer.)

Ben shook his head. 'But I don't want to drink beer out of a glass tomorrow.'

'Ben. It's one day.'

'When I see the photos, I don't want to be thinking, *There's me, drinking out of a glass like Lou screamed about.* I want to be thinking, *There's me, having a beer with my mates.*'

'Your dad drinks beer out of glasses,' she said reasonably, even though she knew that wasn't the point.

'Yeah, because Mum *makes* him.'

He was wretched. Grace stood next to him and put her hand

on one of his shoulderblades. His jumper was thick; she had no impression of his skin.

'It's just a silly fight,' she said, in the end. 'I don't think you want to read too much into it.' She smiled at him. 'You'll probably hardly ever look at the photos, anyway.' (*Another fabulous answer there. Top marks, Grace.*)

He put an elbow on the bench and rubbed his face with one hand. To his wine he said, 'Just heightened emotion, you reckon?'

'Sure.'

Long pause.

'Like … you after your mum's funeral?' His voice was very quiet.

'Well. Um.' She'd been stroking his back consolingly. Now, she took her hand away.

Outside, a group of young people were leaving the house next door. *Aww, that'd be right!* one of them yelled above the hubbub.

'Do you sometimes wonder why we never …?' he said. Still quietly. 'In all these years, Gracey.' He met her eyes.

'Is that what this is about?' She leaned her shoulders away from him. 'Last hurrah?'

He made an uninterpretable gesture. *Sort of* shook his head.

'Because that'd be a very, very bad idea.' She drew her wine closer towards her, in a way that made her think of a prim Victorian lady with a shawl. 'I'm not the girl to "have a stupid thing" with, remember?'

Her feelings were still pretty close to the surface; that conversation was her clearest memory of her dead mother's wake. God, she was pathetic.

'Gracey?'

And the idea of her as a serious partner apparently still hadn't occurred to him. *God.* She was so *pathetic.*

'Gracey?' He said it again.

'Ben, can you please, *please* stop calling me that?' Her voice came out loud and jangly. 'God's sake.' She made a fist and knocked on the centre of her chest, twice. Tears pressed on the rims of her eyes. 'It is salt in the fucking wound.'

A long beat. He stared at her.

She didn't turn away. Maybe now he'd say something about how much he loved her, about how it had *always been* her, of course it had been, and so he was calling the whole thing – the whole clichéd extravagance of a tasteful wedding to a beautiful, 'miraculous' woman – off.

He didn't. After a moment, he tightened his face muscles and examined his shiraz.

'Jesus, Ben.' She swiped one cheek with her palm. 'You and Louise had a dumb fight. It's nothing. You need to go home, ring her, make up and get on with it.'

He still said nothing to correct her.

'Ben.' She sliced at the air between their faces, so that her wine sloshed in its glass.

He nodded two, three times. At some heart-breakingly final point, he stood. He left his drink unfinished on the counter, and he remembered the knack of her tricky front doorhandle first go.

And presumably, he followed her impeccably unselfish – but in hindsight, spectacularly bad – advice, because he married Louise Buchanan about sixteen hours later.

∞

When she was thirty-six and Emma was five, and on the afternoon of someone else's wedding, Grace had performed the tricky art of making herself appear as fabulous as possible, without it being noticeable that she was putting in any particular effort. (It was much harder than it sounded.)

She'd bought seventy-dollar foundation and she stroked that on, thinking it didn't seem that much better than her usual twenty-twoish-dollar foundation, but that the lid made a very nice click when she closed it. She sighed at the mirror. Her new hobby was stretching the skin around her eyes and reflecting that she had not metamorphosed into one of those stunning thirty-something women who was so witty and so stylish and so capable of producing razor-sharp turns of phrase that thinking men of all ages were driven wild with lust by her crows' feet.

She frowned suspiciously at her very old blusher. She was still just an ordinary-exterior, ordinary-interior female. Not particularly feisty. Not particularly funny. Not even particularly bubbly or hospitable or full of life. Hard-working would be her only claim to fame. And meticulous. *Grace, now I see how Meticulous you are, I realise I was wrong all those years ago and I do actually love you.*

Perhaps Ben had got fat and bald and unintimidating. It seemed unlikely.

Going through the oddly high doors into the reception, she was surprised to find that her pupils weren't magically sucked towards his. She had to look for him – of course, without appearing to – amid the flotilla of twenty-one round tables and 168 perkily white-bowed chair covers. This was not so she could greet him, obviously.

But there he was. He was already sitting down, next to Louise, who was wearing a perfect grey dress, and *laughing*, and being so brutally and unequivocally beautiful that Grace – despite the fact that she was braced for this *exact* moment, for this *exact* feeling – still felt a vicious stab of anguish, even worse than it had been at the church. Seventy-dollar foundation was for pathetic fools. She'd known that all along.

Obviously, Ben wasn't fat. Nor bald. Older, of course. Taller than she remembered, if anything. It took her a few seconds to recognise the man next to him – the one Louise was laughing with – as Tom Mullins. Tom Mullins *was* much fatter and quite a lot balder.

'Grace. How are you?' Ben said, when – an entree of seared scallops and an alternate-drop plate of pan-fried chicken breast later – she found herself in a group that included him. He did not extend his hand, thank God.

He'd agree with her about the chicken (*What except pans could it possibly have been fried in?* he would definitely also have thought) but now she couldn't find a way to laugh about that. Instead, she spoke as per middle-class, grown-up-lady protocol.

'Fine, thanks, Ben. And you?' Her nice watch in place. Her earrings affixed. God, it was sickening.

'We're all well,' he said.

We're, she thought. *Oh, fuck you, Ben.*

'How *is* the family?' Her voice had a placid sort of jauntiness. 'How's ...' She half pretended she was trying to remember his wife's name. 'Louise?'

He said something or other about how Louise was. She thought: *Louise Anne Buchanan. I wonder what she's like, apart from beautiful and tasteful and humorous and good at interior design. What is she actually like?*

'Christopher's sorry not to be here,' she replied untruthfully.

'Would've been good to meet him.' Ben was half leaning across two other people, raising his voice a tiny bit, using a profoundly interested tone to exchange these banalities.

'Yes. Pity.'

There was a pause. She smiled in a way that she hoped implied: *I am only being polite because Christopher has more important, more exciting and above all much* sexier *things to do than be here, Ben, and it is of absolutely* no *consequence whether either of us ever sees you again, and by the way, we are* extremely *happy with our edgily modern arrangement, and also, although I may be single I am* utterly *sexually satisfied.*

'And how's your daughter going, Gracey?'

She saw the wince in his brain, even though he kept it off his face.

'I mean, *Grace*,' he said. For the first time in his married life, he met her eyes properly. It felt as if she'd accidentally splashed her own face with boiling jam. 'Sorry. About that. Grace.'

'That's okay.'

She was not a modern, strong woman. She was not even good at making sensible choices. She was pathetic and stilted and flushing, and – most pressingly of all – she just couldn't think of anything to say. She could only gaze down at her handbag as if it was an incredible work of art, and think mortified thoughts about her expensive foundation.

Then a man called Phillip Lacey said something about paella upskilling that made everyone laugh, and after a few more minutes, the group started to dissolve. She left the wedding without talking to Ben again.

Some more years went by. Every now and then, she went for a whole day without thinking of him.

∞

Just after Emma turned ten, Grace started googling Ben, maybe once every six months or so. It was around the time googling people you knew was segueing from something slightly unsavoury to normal due diligence. And she felt safe: she was settled and *forty-one*; he was in Sydney, far, far away, and so no harm could come from just checking up on him. Of trying to tell by squinting at the professional head-and-shoulders shot ('Meet Our Caring Clinicians') whether he still thought of her, and what he remembered, and if – above all – he was *happy*. She'd zoom in on his picture, feeling that by peering closer she might be able to see what was going on behind his eyes, but they would just turn to odd-coloured pixels.

Afterwards, she would feel both sick and ridiculous. She would comfort herself with the fact that she had never once searched for

Louise Buchanan: obviously *that* would be a breach of moral code and just plain stalking.

One day – it was very late; she was very tired; that was often the way of it – she typed his name in. It was after she'd paid her car registration, as if seeing Ben's picture was just another briskly standard part of single-mother housekeeping.

There was a new entry, near the top. Google's familiar blue writing now listed – bland and invincible – the website of a *local* practice. She clicked Tasman Cardiology Group. It felt as if suspenseful – or maybe nostalgically uplifting – music should be playing in the background, but the only sound was of a truck rumbling in the distance.

Ben's profile – ('Our Experienced Team') – contained the same (experienced) photo, and said Dr Benjamin Hutchinson had a professional interest in something or other and was highly skilled at blahing, and that he and his family had returned to Hobart for the lifestyle. They couldn't wait to enjoy the very best Tasmania had to offer!

Grace immediately clicked the little red 'x' to collapse the page, and walked away from her desk. Her heart was going faster than usual, as if she was trying to smuggle drugs – or even mangoes – through customs. She wondered why the Hutchinsons had come back. Was this a career opportunity? Or to do with grandparents or house prices? Or – with a very shameful flicker of hope – because their marriage was in trouble?

Either way, she was not going to try to see him around. She would pay no extra attention to her clothes. In fact, as a sort of penance for having designs on a married man, she deliberately didn't get her hair coloured for a few months, until Maria said, 'Grace, are you doing that thing, which I know is quite popular now, where you grow your greys out in a loud and proud way, because that's fine, if that's what you're choosing, and you know me, I'm all for female empowerment, but maybe you're not quite at that stage yet?'

More than two years later – she'd had some foils by then – after a day dealing with a dying guinea pig, a dog with a tumour in its mouth, a puppy who'd swallowed a coin and a cat who needed desexing, she went to reception to call in her next patient. She was walking quickly because she was still running on time, but getting smug about that and relaxing her grip on her pace never ended well. Her Crocs made a squeaky noise on the corridor floor; she could hear Maria saying, 'But if you can just stop, please, yes, I hear you, stop and think for a quick second, would Cola have had that done here at our clinic?' into the phone.

'Minor,' Grace called to the waiting room. A small boy with a Shih tzu-cross on his lap looked up. The man next to him made a brief, just-one-second gesture with his hand. He was typing, urgently, single-thumbed, into his phone.

It was Ben.

∞

The thing was, it didn't feel at all awkward. There were no embarrassed explanations about *Louise made the appointment, so . . .* Or, *Just, it's a common surname, and I didn't . . .*

He said, 'Ah, Grace, lovely to see you,' and she said, 'Yeah, you too.' There was no question of kisses on cheeks. There was just a really nice smile, quick, and full, most of all, of humour. *How about us, all grown up! Children, professions, pets. Can you* believe *us?*

While she checked over Minor, she talked mainly to Ben's son, who seemed like a perfectly sweet little boy, sandy-eyebrowed and fairly polite. Ben had put his phone away. He watched her. At the end, he said, 'Say thank you, Tom, to Dr Grace.' He nodded an affectionate nod, and walked his son and their dog off down the corridor.

She found herself things to do in her office until she was sure they were out of the building. These things included: staring into the mirror for about thirty seconds, sitting at her desk and resting her forehead in her hands for about seven seconds, standing up and doing laps of the examination couch for about two hundred seconds.

It was later that week that he contacted her. She was at home, blamelessly emailing someone about a CBC she thought their cat really should have that week, when she noticed his message.

Hi Grace,
Thanks for your care of Minor. He's doing much better.
It was really nice to see you.

Cheers, Ben Hutchinson

....

Hi Ben,
Yes, you, too.
I'm glad Minor is doing well.

Best,

Grace

He wrote back straightaway.

Hi again,
We should catch up properly?

Ben

Catch up. It was one of those phrases. Catching up could mean anything. He presumably wanted to 'catch up' in a perfectly respectable way, one that involved the bringing of families and the discussion of good schools and trustworthy plumbers. Maybe he thought she and Louise could make friends and be in the same book club or something.

Then she thought: they weren't *that* new back to Hobart anymore. And people like them always knew how to fit in. Louise Buchanan probably already had friends here; she probably went on girly weekends away where she and these friends drank expensive wine, and shared squealing *what-was-I-thinking?* type memories, and made the occasional, tearful confession about a perfectly ordinary issue that seemed like a huge splodge of horror on someone's meticulously curated life.

She spent about ten minutes typing:

That sounds nice. Just let me know what suits. Say hi to Louise!

That couldn't possibly expose her to any claims of pushiness. Or any claims of . . . anything. She pushed 'send' and thought of his long-ago, now-deleted emails. Not that many. Their relationship had been more about landlines and answering machines and creamy-yellow Post-it notes.

Great. Can I grab your number?

She sent it, and to her surprise her phone rang immediately. After a bit of nothing hellos and nothing how-are-yous, he said, 'So, are you busy Show Day weekend?'

'Oh! Well, Christopher will have Emma.'

She blabbed on as if she was oblivious to the fact that they hadn't spoken on the phone in years. 'I was going to repaint the lounge room. I'm going with this nice sort of dark blue.' She reached for the colour chart on the counter, like she thought someone might be watching her. Look, see, she really *had* been planning to repaint her lounge room. Look, see, she really *did* have a life. 'Nicer than it sounds. And apparently, the world's stressful realities will fade as I transform the space into a lustrous realm of my own creation with a patented low-sheen formula.'

They both laughed. Then there was a pause.

'Because the family'll be away, and I was thinking you and I could grab a lunch,' he said.

She might or might not have tightened her grip on the phone, but she certainly sat down on the floor (paint chart still in hand). Ben was talking on, telling her, in a very casual tone, that Louise was taking their children to Noosa to see her parents, because the kids needed some sun. He made it sound as if the two of them having a meal together was an equally obvious thing to do.

'My treat, Grace.' As if who *paid* was the most important thing. 'Keep me company.'

Grace frowned. She suddenly remembered him in her waiting room, legs outstretched, throat open, phone in hand.

'What were you typing, the other day, when I called in Minor?' she said. 'So very busy and important and, you know, absolutely insufferable?'

'Ah, nothing much.' There was a smile in his voice. Then he hesitated. 'Nothing at all, in fact. It was just – I'd just seen you. Been a long time. I was taking a moment.'

She looked at the paint chart and felt. His words, his tone, this conversation: it all seemed too much to fit into a single evening. It would be better to have just a little portion of this feeling every day, not such a whole big whack of decision and surprise and – undeniable, overriding – delight all at once.

'I see,' Grace said. 'Right. Well. I mean. We can easily just have *a lunch.*'

Of course she was going to see him.

∞

Just inside the door were enormous displays of flowers, and a man with a fashionable haircut. She arrived eight minutes late – by genuine accident – and made her way past the matte timber panels and under the discreet black downlights, through all the minimalist decadence and between all the surprisingly ordinary patrons, to their table. Ben stood to greet her. Kissed her cheek. Navy shirt. Black pants. Requisite stubble. He'd given her the seat with the best view.

'This all right?' he said. Behind him were fairly unpleasant pieces of original art and tubby leather chairs. Behind all that was water and sky and boats.

She sat. 'I never come here,' she said. Ordinary restaurants, with their nine-dollar wines and normal salt, always seemed more than indulgent enough. 'This is so bloody typical of you, Ben.'

He laughed. 'How are you? How's Emma?'

'Emma's great.' They had a conversation in which Grace enquired after Louise, or Ben referred to Christopher, or one of them mentioned the children in every single sentence. That went on for about twenty minutes, while they shook out their heavy white napkins and chose a bottle of wine, while he ordered panzanella salad and she asked for grilled flathead. After the waiter had slapped the menus back together and strolled off – waiters seemed so much more *casual* than they once had, even in places like this – she looked at her bread roll.

'Is this a comfortable silence?' Ben said. 'Because I thought we should be catching up on good movies or important books or something.'

'Shame on us. And what terribly insightful podcasts should we chat about?'

'Ah, Grace.' All affectionate. 'What are *you* up to?'

She said something brief about the wildlife park and the little hospital they'd set up. He said that all sounded terrific and added something even briefer about cardiology.

'So, you basically strut around in a good suit and yell "Clear!" every now and again?' she said.

'Oh I have residents for the yelling. Nowadays, it's mainly the strutting.'

Then he stopped smiling and made a dismissive gesture, as if to say it was just a job and not all that interesting, but perfectly fine.

Behind him, a woman in a green dress blew out what looked to be a candle on a birthday cocktail. Her friends took photos of her holding up the drink and smiling. Grace thought: *Of course, it's going to be like this. There is no other way it can be.*

'I actually did listen to a good podcast the other day,' she began. 'It—'

'My mum died.' He leaned a little bit forward, so the light fell differently on his face. 'You remember my mum?'

'Of course I remember Sue.' It felt right to use her name. 'I'm so sorry, Ben. I hadn't heard.'

'She had a heart attack. Ironically.' He cleared his throat. 'Just sitting on our deck one Saturday. We were all there.'

'Oh, Ben.'

He was staring straight at the dinky wooden pepper grinder.

'Hey,' she said quietly. She leaned forward and curled her hand over his knuckles. 'I'm sure you did all you could.'

'Yep.' He rested his other hand on the back of her forearm.

'Everything possible was done.' They sat like that for a moment, then looked at each other and let go.

'Louise feels,' he said, touching the tines of his fork, 'that it was very traumatic for the children.'

'I imagine it might have been quite confronting.' She hated that word. Why had she used it? And *might have been*. What was wrong with her? 'It must've been awful.'

'She feels we perhaps did too much. That perhaps *I* did too much. With the CPR and so on.'

'Oh?' Grace said. Very neutral.

'"You always have to play the doctor," is what she said. She feels I should have been a son and a father. Whatever that would have entailed.'

'I see.' Not *exactly* neutral anymore.

A brisk forearm curved their meals in front of them, topped up their water glasses, refilled their wine. A voice asked if they would like anything else. Ben murmured they were fine, thank you.

'Sorry.' He said it as soon as the interruption was over. 'It's all good.' He picked up his water glass, took a sip and asked her with a straight, interested face what podcast she'd been going to tell him about.

'Oh, Ben. God. It doesn't matter.' Heaven's sake. 'Are you all right?'

He made the same gesture as the one he'd done about his job. *Not great, but getting by*, the gesture said. *Can't complain, mustn't grumble. Misery's a pathetic First World problem, to which, at the same time, I have no right.*

She looked towards the windows and tried to think what best to say. An elderly man on the other side of the restaurant was standing at the glass wall, craning first his head, and then his whole torso, to watch a yacht being moored.

'I was twenty-six when I got engaged,' Ben said.

Grace put down her fork.

'Stupid boy,' he added.

Grace recalled his engagement party. Square white platters, sundried tomatoes. Dozens of gleaming hired glasses. *Not risking my good stuff on this lot*, Sue had whispered to her, jokily. Grace had tried so earnestly to appreciate the real champagne. She'd been so sincere when she'd told herself she was *fine*. And she'd thought she would be fine.

She'd assumed she *would* forget him, and that from this distance of time (forty-three!) her inner life would feel as carefree and nicely groomed as her tensely smiling outer life had looked. Stupid, stupid girl.

'You made me laugh, on the phone.' Ben was watching her as if she was a penalty shoot-out. 'About the paint brochure.' He leaned forward again. 'Remember how much we always laughed together?'

Of *course* she remembered.

'I don't think—' She'd been going to say she didn't think he should talk like that, but it sounded too ridiculous and repressive. She adjusted her knife along on the edge of her plate, and rested all her fingertips on the table.

Should she suggest he talk to a psychologist? Or to a mate? (A straight, *male* mate. They could drink beer and listen to Midnight Oil and discuss annoying wives in a non-adulterous way that used terms like 'me missus' and 'giving me grief'.)

'Ben,' she said, to her wrists. 'If you need to talk about your marriage, then you probably should see a counsellor, or I don't know, talk to a friend or something.'

A beat passed. Then he lifted up his palms in a humble, hurt gesture. 'I thought I *was* talking to a friend.'

Grace straightened her back. She picked up her knife and cut off a small piece of fish in one stroke. She inserted it into her mouth, chewed a reasonable number of salty times and swallowed.

Fuck's sake, she thought, very clearly. *For fuck's* sake.

'Is that right?' she said. She used the tone Maria did when someone gave an extremely bullshit excuse for having kept Grace waiting. 'You thought you were just having lunch and just talking to your just good friend?' Every time she said 'just' her pitch changed, like an opera singer going up the scale.

He put his stupid question-mark hands back into his lap. 'I didn't—'

'You know exactly what you're doing.' Low and definite now. She touched the air between their chests with her pointer finger. If she was a different type of woman, she'd stand up and leave. As it was, she leaned forward and lowered her voice. 'And it's not okay. All this. It's not *friendly.*'

'Grace—'

'You think if you never *fuck* me that makes everything all right?' It seemed she actually *was* standing up. 'You think it makes you *noble*?'

He'd always hated scenes. He appeared to meld his spine into the back of his chair.

'You made me feel so stupid,' she said. 'All those years. You made me feel as if I was misreading every single thing, every single day.'

He apparently didn't have anything to say in his own defence. His mouth was literally open.

'You *always* knew how I felt,' she said.

She sidestepped her chair, held her handbag close against her chest and walked towards the doors.

∞

Grace sat in her driver's seat, looking at seagulls (who absolutely had their bums in butter) and wondering whether she'd done the right thing. In her rear-view mirror, she saw him scanning the carpark. She flicked the glass down and stared hard into her own eyes.

'Ben.' Her door felt light as air as she opened it. 'Ben.'

The wind pushed his hair into something like a keel while he walked – chin down, shoulders up – towards her. She sat back in her car before he reached it, and once he got in, they were still for a while. He could bloody well talk first.

'Look. Just so you know,' he said (eventually). 'Louise and I . . . we don't . . . We're really not properly married anymore.'

'Does she know you're here? With me?'

'Well.' He shifted his cramped legs. The passenger seat was very far forward. 'But it's not really a secret.'

'Exactly.'

He said he'd cheated 'only' once before. Three years ago. With a woman he met in a bar, at a conference, in Adelaide.

'How original.'

'I did tell Louise about that. She said, "Ben, believe me, I don't want, and I certainly don't *need*, any details."'

'Wow,' Grace said accidentally. (Although, seriously. *Wow*.)

'She expected me to cheat. She was glad to have another reason to be mad with me.'

Grace thought of Christopher. How she felt a complicated combination of irritation and pleasure on the rare occasions he was a bit late to pick up Emma. How, one time when he'd forgotten to take Emma to a Grade Four birthday party, Grace had caught herself feeling glad she had such a good excuse to be properly cross with him. And she and Christopher weren't even *married*.

'I really do think you should be talking to Louise about this,' she said.

'We've talked.' He set that down like a little bundle of cash. Quiet and emphatic. 'She says we should stay together until Tom finishes Year Twelve.'

Sweet, sandy-eyebrowed Tom. Tom who apparently liked football even though he wasn't cut out for it, who was really very good at drawing, who had struggled socially in early primary school, but who was now loving Grade Five. What would Tom think if he knew what the nice lady who'd looked after Minor was up to?

Ben turned in his seat towards her; he was holding his face in the smooth way he did sometimes. 'I was such a stupid kid. Don't think I don't know. Vain, superficial—'

'You can't just waltz in now, Ben. You can't just, *email* me, and then presume ... assume—'

He was still listening; it was only she couldn't shove the words out through her chest. She struggled on while a seagull landed outside and flew away. Then she managed: 'Fallback option.'

Each syllable was a trembling droplet.

'Ah, Grace.' He reached out a hand towards her, seemed to hesitate for a second, and then wrapped it across her forearm. He took a deep, levelling breath. 'You're a gorgeous, gorgeous woman.'

'Don't *patronise* me.'

She stared through the windscreen. Two young men stood in the wind, peering at a fish-and-chip boat's menu. They conferred, then walked on.

Ben said, 'I did really love Louise.' As he said the word 'did', he put his other hand on her arm, too. 'But the last few years. Decade, even. When things happened, anything, something sad with a patient, or, you know, a rude bloke in a carpark, I'd find myself telling you. In my head.'

Grace nodded. She knew exactly what he meant. (And in almost any other circumstances she would have asked him: *Well? So? What happened with the carpark man?*)

Ben was still talking. 'And one day, we were getting ready to have people for dinner, and Jasmine was on at Lou to buy her a print about one true soulmate for every person, and Louise was saying wasn't she too young for quotes like that, what about the dancing in the rain one, and Jasmine said she was old enough to know it was *true*, and I was checking on the ice, and I thought: Jesus Christ, I *hope* it's not true, because—' A small shrug, incredulous, irritated, like a diligent student being shown just where he'd gone wrong in a maths problem. 'I've missed my one.' As if it was a dumb rooky error, the most obvious thing in the world once he finally *saw* it.

'Yeah, well.' She grumped down at the steering wheel. 'That's just a massive cliché, Ben.' But she didn't sound entirely irritated.

'I'm not sure that clichés can be *massive*,' he said. He let a beat pass. 'As such.'

She sort of laughed. He'd *known* that'd make her laugh.

Their eyes met and they had another laugh together. Not the sort where they snorted, or wet themselves. The sort where they just glanced at each other for about half a wonderful second.

When it finished, he focused on her dashboard. She let the silence roll on.

'I'm sorry.' His face, when he turned, was tangled. 'Grace. Gracey. I'm so sorry.'

His hands were still holding her arm. And forgiveness, love, history: they were all there in her skin, whatever else.

After a moment, she turned her wrist, so now her palm faced up into his. They interweaved their fingers.

There was nothing logical about it. It wasn't that it was magically the right thing. It was just that she couldn't stop herself.

63.

Your soul mate may not be your only romance, but they're the one person you want to tell, about everything, about every moment, about anyone else you ever loved.

Chapter Twenty-four

IMOGEN

Spring

The night of our heart-to-heart drama regarding the twins, Zoe and Claire invited me to go to the movies with them! I tied my hair in a double-bubble half-up style and bought a new, casual-wear top. The saleswoman assured me it would be perfect for a midweek get-together. I also experimented with yellow nail polish. Trying new things might help stimulate dopamine, although the mechanism was not well understood.

'Imo! How are you?' Zoe smiled at me as soon as I arrived. She was wearing a white cotton singlet with lacey fabric near the neckline and the cardigan she'd had on the first time I ever saw her.

'Oh, I'm just fine! A-okay! Busy, but not too busy, you know. Just a good level of busyness!' It was not the answer I'd practised, but I'd been caught off guard. The sight of her, so pretty and so smiley, made me think of Nick, and of what he would be contemplating if he saw her in that outfit. 'But fine! Thanks for asking. It's good to be here!'

We watched a film about a man who lived in an apartment and made money, and a woman who wore crumpled shirts and painted murals. There was a party where the man talked to many conventionally unattractive, formally attired women, at least two of whom were romantically interested in him. He watched the painter over their shoulders.

'So gorgeous,' said Zoe, as soon as the film finished. She had even been crying!

I said I thought it was very predictable. And that the man did not love the painter because of her casual clothing or her avant-garde values, even though that was the film's implication. He felt attracted to her because she was the most beautiful woman in his social circle and was in her reproductive prime. Relationships based on that sort of lust often did not last, I pointed out.

Zoe and Claire agreed that mine was a very interesting perspective.

After that, we ordered hot chocolates and sat down in the foyer. In the ironic manner of upscale entertainment venues, our table was next to an exposed brick wall and an ostentatiously weathered timber beam.

Zoe opened a bag of chocolate-coated nuts. 'Protein in the peanuts, right?' She laughed as if she'd made a joke. 'How did you find the subtitles, Imogen?'

I explained that I was fluent in French, so I hadn't read the subtitles except when a lot of colloquialisms were being used. Claire and Zoe were impressed.

'And I couldn't even pass Adult Learning One!' Claire and Zoe were laughing, and Claire was hiding her face with her hand.

'You would have been one of those model students, Imo,' Zoe said. She'd stopped laughing and was sort of throwing the peanuts into her mouth. 'Acing every single subject.' She turned to Claire. 'Have I told you I'm getting worse at cheese sauce?'

'I most certainly wasn't!' People often didn't like model students very much. 'I got into a lot of trouble! In Year Eleven.'

Zoe made a sad, friendly noise. She took another small handful of chocolate-coated peanuts and pushed the packet far away from herself. She and Claire were still looking at me, and although I was a self-sufficient person, I thought I would enjoy having another heart-to-heart. So, I told them about how, when I was sixteen, I had done some homework for a few boys at my high school.

'Bless your little heart.' Zoe made an amused, pretend-shocked face. 'That'd be blooming right.' She crunched a few more peanuts with her molars.

I also used to give them oral sex. And then Nick and I began our romance, and so we made full love. But the teachers found out about the schoolwork I was doing, and Nick was so protective of me and so jealous of the others that he confided the whole story. Everyone got into trouble. Even Nick! Even me!

My parents and I were called to a meeting with the Year Eleven coordinator, Mrs Rickman. First of all, Mum and Dad had to go into her office. I waited in the foyer outside. There was an orange public phone with square white buttons, and a vase of fake flowers on a fake-antique table.

When Mrs Rickman eventually called me in, Mum and Dad were both looking serious. Mrs Rickman appeared mainly to be overtired. She also smelled repugnantly of cigarettes, despite the school's no-smoking rule.

'Now, Imogen,' she said, before I had even finished taking my seat. 'All we care about, is finding out what happened.' I was next to Mum. Mrs Rickman was behind the desk.

'You can be quite open about the situation, Imogen,' Dad said. He adjusted himself in his chair, and ran his thumb and finger along his tie. He was embarrassed, not Cross, luckily.

Mrs Rickman leaned forward with her hands spread flat in front of her and one ear closer to me than the other. Next to her elbow was an empty, dirty coffee cup made out of smoky-brown glass.

'Could you maybe just tell me what this is about?' I honestly didn't know.

'I understand you've been producing work for Nick Kavanagh.

And some of the other boys.' Mrs Rickman used both hands to hold up a printout of Nick's essay about Macbeth.

'Oh,' I said. 'That.'

'How did this all start?' said Mrs Rickman. 'You just tell me in your own words.'

'I knew Nick had been struggling with his work, and so I've been helping him.' We'd had the most beautiful afternoon together while I worked on that essay. 'He does understand Macbeth's motivations, though.'

Mrs Rickman asked me what else I had helped Nick with, and I answered her honestly about the maths quizzes, and the geography presentation, and the Working with Wood – Theory Module One. 'But I'm just helping out my ... my good friend.' Nick was someone who was uncomfortable with the term 'boyfriend', and I had to respect his wishes. 'We are very, very close.'

'Imogen, I'm glad you've told us the truth. As you see it.' She asked if I'd been doing work for any of the other boys, and I told her I had, in the past, but had stopped doing that. Nick was my priority now.

Mrs Rickman nodded and frowned unattractively. She looked at my parents, then back to me.

'Sometimes,' she said, 'certain people are very charismatic, and very charming, and they can make us ... make us feel we'd like to become close to them?'

I nodded.

'We might feel we'd like to – a person might feel, I mean, that they would like to – be *very* close to them?'

'Yes?'

'Imogen, it's extremely important that you're not being coerced into doing schoolwork, or doing ... anything, for another student, against your will.'

'I'm not!'

'You would tell someone, I hope, if you were feeling pressured into any of that side of things? Nobody's ... pestering you? No unwanted ... intimacy?'

I shook my head. 'No.'

Everyone sat silently for a few moments.

Mrs Rickman said we'd need to have a talk about how much help was appropriate to give friends, and that perhaps I could speak to a counsellor about personal boundaries, but that that was enough for today.

Mum was looking at me. 'As long as you know Nick cares for you, darling,' she said. She reached out and patted my hand. 'He's a very lucky boy!' She added that I should invite him around to our house for dinner. In actual fact, I already had, three times, but he could never come due to his football commitments.

Mrs Rickman was staring down at her papers, and I saw her give a little shake of her head. It was exactly the shake she did at assemblies sometimes, right after she told everyone off for not singing the school song, and right before she said, 'Sometimes, Senior School, I really do wonder why I bother.'

∞

The thing Mrs Rickman didn't find out about until quite a lot later, was that one of the boys involved gave me a nickname, which was Rooter-Tutor.

And in schools, everyone always knew everyone else's business, so I was called Rooter-Tutor often throughout Year Eleven and Year Twelve. Someone yelled it out on the bus to Year Eleven camp. I was up the front and the boy who yelled it was down the back, so a lot of people laughed. It was moderately embarrassing, and the teachers in charge made every single boy on the back seat write me a letter of apology. But what the teachers failed to understand, was that we were a big group of friends, and in any group of individuals there would be eccentricities of personality. It was honestly not that big of a deal.

'So, anyhoo,' I finished. The cinema foyer was still fairly busy. We all had a lot of hot chocolate left. 'It was quite a challenging hiccup.' I looked up from my saucer. 'Adolescents do need supportive peers.'

Zoe still had her peanuts in her hand.

'Imogen?' she said. 'You're not talking about *my* Nick?' She pointed the peanuts towards the door, as if that was where Nick was. Chocolate was starting to melt onto her palm.

'Nick Kavanagh. Yes.'

'Nick called you ... that name?'

'No! Nick never! He wasn't ... Nick would never call what we had a ... "root". It was just his mates. Damo and Cameron Barnett and those boys.'

I saw Claire and Zoe looked at each other.

'I'm so sorry that happened to you,' Claire said. 'Nobody deserves to be treated like that. It wasn't your fault.'

'Imogen, how are you still *friends* with them?' said Zoe. 'That's just ... you don't have to stay *friends*.' She still had the peanuts curled up in her hand. 'Does T-rex know about this?'

'Probably not,' I said. T-rex met us all later. He and Lila Nguyen's ex-boyfriend played rugby in the university years.

The two of them still looked quite shocked.

'It's really not that big of a deal,' I said reassuringly. I was nothing if not considerate.

They asked me other questions, about what my parents had said, and if it was even legal, and if Nick was definitely the one who'd told the teachers. Zoe asked twice more whether Nick had ever called me Rooter-Tutor.

'We're here if you ever need to talk,' Claire said. But I noticed it was Zoe's hand she touched with her own.

'Of course we are.' Zoe let the nutty mess she was holding fall onto the table. She pushed the packet of peanuts towards me. 'Have some.' Then she walked around and put her arm across my shoulders. I hoped she wouldn't get chocolate onto my new shirt, but it actually did feel pleasant. 'That is just awful, and I can't even say how mad I am at them.' She really did sound significantly upset.

It was all very well meant but of course unnecessary. It was approximately eighteen years ago, and it wasn't that bad. Just locker-room-type behaviour from some young lads, back when we were all somewhat naïve and indulging in natural adolescent experimentation. It wasn't like terrible cyberbullying, or like sexual assault.

Women who looked like Zoe often had expectations that did not align with the real world. When Nick finally came to his senses, she would be in for a rude awakening.

And not before time.

Nick's letter of apology to Imogen (she kept it all these years)

To Imogen,

I am very sorry if what my friends said on the bus yesterday upset you, nobody meant it to. Because you are a very nice person who deserves to be treated better, and they will not call you names like that again.

From Nick Kavanagh

Chapter Twenty-five

ZOE

Spring

I didn't trust myself to drive, so I left my car at the cinema. Claire was going to take me straight home, but at the last minute I asked her to drop me off at Nick's place.

'Love you, Zo,' she said, when she leaned over the gearstick to hug me goodbye.

Now it was after midnight. Nick and I were in the third hour of a fight-talk.

'But how could you *let* her?' I had at some point started a random, angry sort-out of my handbag. Petrol receipts and cacao-bar wrappers and lipstick lids were all over his dining table. 'That poor girl!' I snapped open my sunglasses case, inspected it like it mattered and snapped it closed again.

'Because I was a sixteen-year-old boy! Not your partner. Not ...' He was literally waving his hands in circles in the air and looking at the cornice, the windows, the floorboards. 'Not *me*.'

'You and your disgusting "mates".'

'We were *sixteen*.'

'Who you're still "mates" with, I notice.' On the way home, Claire had told me that Damo was never setting foot in her house again.

'Only with Damo.' Miserable. 'Zoe, I did tell the teachers in the end.'

'When they found out she was doing your work. As well as everything else you ... ordered.'

He didn't deny that.

'Did you call her that name?'

'I swear I never.'

'Just "laughed along", did you?'

No answer.

I picked up a random lipstick lid, sneered at it, and suddenly remembered myself at sixteen.

The decision about whether to have sex with my first proper boyfriend, Sean Harvey. The surprise, the relief, the *disappointment* that he wasn't at all pushy. The unnecessarily secretive visit to the doctor for the pill, the thrill of the serious, adult questions about menstrual cycles and allergies. The multi-sleepover *so-should-I?* discussions with my girlfriends, all virgins, all of us in our carefully chosen, almost-identical pyjamas. Their respectful delicacy; their massive curiosity; their shy comments and self-consciously mature questions. Shrieking giggles and corn chips.

I could see, now, how they had all made an effort to hide their envy, and in return I had made an effort to both conceal my delight in it and also to increase it.

'No, I *tot*ally trust him, it's not that,' I'd said, as if I was a famous actress giving a rare personal interview. 'And I'm *def*initely attracted to him.'

I'd known that one of those girls had a crush on Sean. While I admitted in a possessive, fake-shy voice that I just *loved* watching his hands when he played guitar for me, her face held itself still and she searched Bronwyn's mum's baking bowl for exactly the right corn chip.

I'd known that. I'd *liked* that.

I hadn't really ever thought before about just how very awful and cruel I'd been, what a fucking bitch, actually, with all my stupid, pretty, I'm-such-a-nice-girl condescension, all my olive-skinned good luck.

But, also, I'd been sixteen.

Most of those girls were still friends with me.

'When was the last time, Nick? You and Imogen? Exactly?'

He shrugged both his shoulders way up to his ears, let them fall, and then said, 'New Year's.' He cleared his throat. 'Eve.'

'*This* year?' The Blue Anchor dinner had been in June. 'The last New Year's?'

'I was drunk. Really drunk! And she wasn't. Zoe, I swear. I promise, Zoe, I *swear* she wasn't drunk. She – look, Damo was smashed, reckons he cracked onto her and she turned him down. But she wanted to, with me, she was just back from England, she kissed me, she … she … kind of took me home to her place in her car. And even the next morning, I told her, listen, sorry, I'm not ready for anything serious, and she was fine, and we … you know, she still wanted to, and I … was a horny dickhead. But she had not one single regret, she said.'

I stared down at my vomiting bag. My phone charger, with a swish of blusher on the cord. A random paintbrush. A single used tissue.

'Just so you know – it's not that I'm jealous.' I flicked a few protein-bar wrappers onto his floor. Then the tissue. 'It's that I'm disgusted.'

'Of course.' Rug the Dog was watching us with a perplexed little face. 'Of course, Zoe.'

'Why "of course"?' And I was pretty much screaming again, because I knew exactly what he meant, and exactly why I *wasn't* jealous, and I hated us both for it. 'What do you even mean by that?'

Nick shrugged and did the hand-wavy thing again.

'I'm going home,' I told him. I picked up my handbag, and without thinking started putting most of the rubbish back into it. The cheap, blingy gold zip closed as neatly as it always did.

'Okay, Zoe, sure. Whatever you want.'

He opened the door, like that would help, and on came his trusty sensor light. I remembered the night we'd stood right there and talked about Imogen's feelings for him. How we'd laughed at her, as an aphrodisiac, and then fucked so proudly, so *impressively*, on his couch.

I hadn't really even believed I was being all that mean.

'Do not touch me,' I said, as I walked past him.

∞

I was eating lunch at my desk, and thinking thoughts about my boyfriend just as heartrendingly and confusedly as any teenage girl ever had. More heartrendingly, in fact. More confusedly. These things apparently got worse, not better, with maturity.

'Ms Morello?' Emma Tierney-Adams was standing in front of me. 'Um?'

I put down my salad roll and looked at her. I was exhausted.

'Ms Morello,' Emma said again. 'Just, um, haven't we got poetry club?'

Oh fuggery, fuggery, fug.

'Sorry, Emma.' I stood up. 'I forgot.'

We walked together along the corridor, and found Amy Petrovic and a few of the others lounging around in the English room. Every time I saw a teenage girl, I imagined someone calling her Rooter-Tutor. That morning, I'd told off one of the smart-arse boys, Jayden Nielsen, about swearing, to the point where he'd said, 'Ms Morello, sorry. I seriously won't say it again.' He'd hunched his shoulders up inside his *Pirates of Penzance* hoodie as he'd walked off.

'I've got no chocolate biscuits,' I told the poetry kids. 'Crazy week. But what's our theme today?' We'd long since moved on from poems about art, and I couldn't remember what they'd decided. Hopefully not Past Mistakes, Toxic Relationships or Poor Choices.

Someone said it was First Love, and a few of them made *wooo-oooooh* noises.

I didn't really take much in while various people read out their poems. I was thinking about how Nick made me coffee in the mornings. *Wake up, gorgeous Zoe, good morning, sweet Zo*, he would sort of sing as he put it on the bedside table. Not that morning, though. No coffee in bed or cuddles or singing for stupid, spinstery me.

Marcus Cunningham was telling the poetry kids about his boyf cheating on him, when I tuned back in.

'It's not just the cheating. It's the infidelity I can't stand,' he was saying. 'The breach of trust and the infidelity.' I had a feeling he might be confused about what 'infidelity' meant, but didn't have the heart, or the energy, or even the concrete knowledge, to raise it with him. I'd finished my salad roll and was thinking about how I could wind the whole thing up, when Emma Tierney-Adams spoke. She seemed to be talking mainly to Amy.

'But do you think cheating's ever okay?' she said.

Amy absolutely did not. Marcus Cunningham definitely did not. Three other kids totally did not. Nobody thought it was ever okay.

'But if two people really loved each other?' Emma said.

'How do you mean, Emma?' My voice was suddenly adult: probing and unteacherly. Because I was thinking now, and from out of nowhere, about Daniel and Rhianna. What if Rhianna had had a variation on this conversation with one of her sustainable-engineering colleagues? Y*es, yes, Daniel* is *with someone else, but they got together so young, she wears nothing but on-trend synthetics, consumes resources like you wouldn't believe, poor Daniel, she'd can't even get pregnant, it's all very toxic, and* we *really* love *each other.* 'I mean, sorry, that—' I put down my ball of cling wrap and cleared my throat. 'What do others think?'

Daniel had not been a trustworthy man who loved me. Nick wasn't a sweet guy who cared for me. He was an evil person, and I was just a dumb, big-boobed girl to have smirky fun with for a while.

253

'Marcus?' I said more calmly. 'Emma?' How had I even got myself into this inappropriate conversation? I needed to pull myself together and be a more boundary-conscious person.

'I think good people can do bad things.' Emma spoke very clearly.

There was a small murmur of agreement, but Marcus Cunningham said, 'It's still betrayal,' and Amy Petrovic replied, 'Betrayal is the worst.'

I nod-frowned as if I was a wise adult who knew everything but was just going to let them work the answers out for themselves, out of charity, and due to my good teaching methods.

'Well, great discussion this week, everyone. Sorry about the biscuits, and I'll see you all next time.'

There was a general filing out.

I leaned against the edge of a desk, staring at my ball of cling wrap and feeling the absolute impossibility of teaching a double print-making to the Year Eights that afternoon. It took me a couple of moments to realise Emma was still fiddling around with her water bottle. I saw that her face was full of the quiet, slidey kind of tears, her shoulders curled forward towards her heart.

'Emma?'

She pressed on her cheekbones with her palms.

'What's wrong?'

Her face was like an injured Olympian.

'My mum,' she said. She started crying louder. 'My mum-my.'

'Oh, darl.'

Obviously, I gave her a hug. She began whisper-sobbing about *Pirates of Penzance* and how there were certain people she really needed to avoid.

'I can't tell Amy, and I don't have a psychology appointment this week, and I don't want to tell Dad, and I just … my mu-um.' A big, gasping breath. 'She's *not* a bad person.'

The penny dropped while I was sort of shepherding her over to a chair. And then, when we were sitting down, a whole long story about photos and Jasmine Hutchinson's father and infidelity – Emma seemed to properly know what the word meant – came lurching out.

My skin held me straighter and straighter, and tighter and tighter, in my own seat. Her mum had seemed so nice in those echidna photos. So *ordinary*. If I'd seen her at assembly, I would have thought she was as upstanding and harried and harmless as the next forty-something lady. I would have thought she was too busy saving wildlife to have an affair! But even wildlife-rescuing mums couldn't be trusted, apparently. I was suddenly horrifyingly close to crying myself.

'Emma, I think perhaps you need to talk to the school counsellor.' I was speaking in something that sounded like Claire's most annoying psychologist voice. 'I don't think I'm well placed to help you work through this issue. Now, would you like—?'

She snapped up her head. 'No!'

Her hand reached out for the edge of the desk; her little face was so hurt and disillusioned and *young*. I could tell she was fighting off more tears like mad.

'Emma, we—'

'Please do *not* tell.' She stood, picked up her water bottle and stared down at it for a moment. Made a movement with her neck, as if she was sucking everything back in. When she spoke again, she'd gone all cold and dignified.

'I'm not "at risk",' she said. 'So, you don't need to worry yourself about your "duty of care".'

'That's not what I—'

'Not that you *actually* care anything about me, Ms Morello.'

We looked at each other for a no-frills, no-roles second.

Then she turned around, paused for a millisecond to remind herself where the door was, and walked away.

Chapter Twenty-six

GRACE

Spring

She could always tell when Emma had been crying. It wasn't that her eyes were red or swollen. It wasn't that tears ever 'clung' tragically to her lashes. It was something about the muscles of Emma's face. A tightness in the skin, a change in the contours – the ones that would, in a decade or so, become the light-line first drafts of wrinkles – near her eyes.

So, even though Emma was rinsing noodles and emitting syllables regarding the Japanese quiz tomorrow, and even though Grace was busying herself patting dry bok choy and wondering cheerily and aloud about the viability of the coriander, she knew both that Emma had been crying and that she herself was desperate (*unhealthily* desperate, no doubt) to know why.

'So, how was the rest of your day?' Grace asked, when they were eating their stir-fry. She swirled noodles onto a fork and used a dessert spoon to marshal them towards her mouth.

'Fine.' Emma was preternaturally good with chopsticks. She picked up a tiny rhomboid of chicken.

'And your rehearsals are busy next week? Performances really soon, right?'

'Mmm.' A shrug. A gap. '*If* I stay in it.'

Grace left a long, receptive pause, then – with nerves like those of a crime-fighter in a warehouse stepping out around a corner – she hazarded a mild, 'I thought you were all set?' (She herself had received around seventeen thousand emails regarding no responsibility for students outside of scheduled performances and obligation to fellow cast members and any necessary medication being carried AT ALL TIMES.)

Emma picked up a corn kernel and dropped it again. As if she was starting a whole new topic, she said, 'A girl called Jasmine Hutchinson has a main part.'

Oh, God.

'I … who? I … I didn't know you knew a-a-a Jasmine Hutchinson?'

Emma looked up from her bowl and stared at Grace. Her face was neutral: mouth closed; eyes open. Maybe it was the tilt of her shoulders that conveyed the contempt.

'Emma?'

Emma flicked at some obviously woefully inadequate broccoli.

'Why are you worried about, ah, this Jasmine Hutchinson person?'

Emma raised her chin and piloted a small, straggly bundle of food into her open mouth. Chewed. Swallowed.

'Because.' A beat passed. Another one. Emma laid down her chopsticks. 'I am not fucking stupid, *Mum*.'

'Don't speak to me like that!' There, at least, was something she could say. Yes, she might be guilty of infidelity and lies, but see her take a righteous stand against teenage swearing, just as firmly as any respectable person on this planet.

'Why not? *You* talk like that.'

'I just—' But she had no moral high ground on which to stand. 'I'd like to hear more. About how you're feeling.' This was what Dr Claire suggested, for when you didn't know what else to say. 'Em?'

'I'm sorry I ruined your life, *Mum*,' she said. 'Sorry you ended up alone, and lonely, and what*ever*, because of me.'

'I never—'

'Such a terrible *shame*.' All sarcastic. 'I was such a terrible *accident*.'

'Emma!' They'd always been – if not exactly loud – at least *open* about Emma's conception being unplanned. It honestly had never seemed as if it was an issue.

'I've known for ages you had a boyfriend, Mum.' The way Emma spat out 'Mum' reminded Grace of an elegant Frenchwoman. Icy and contemptuous and adult. But then she seemed to lose her bearings. 'You expect *me* to tell you about every little thing. What I eat. Where I walk. If I use the *bathroom*.'

'How did ...?'

'I bet you wish *he* was my father!' Emma was shouting and crying now. 'And then I'd be like Jasmine Hutchinson, and not like stupid, annoying, ugly ME!'

'Emma, that is simply not true.'

But it was true that in some barely acknowledged place, a seed version of that thought had existed. It was also true that she would not swap her complicated, precious Emma for the blessed, swishy-haired Jasmine. Not for anything, not on pain of death, not ever.

'You know you weren't exactly planned, and that your dad and I aren't right for each other. But we both love you very, very much, and having you was the most wonderful—'

'Oh, whatever, I don't want to talk to you anymore.' Emma shook her head, fast, then shoved her tears away with the soft sides of her forearms. She picked up her chopsticks again. 'Just let me eat my dinner, will you? We all know how much you *love* that.'

'Of course. Let's, um, let's eat. It's pretty nice, actually, isn't it?'

'Oh, seriously, Mum,' said Emma. 'Honestly. Just fuck you.'

CORONIAL COURT OF TASMANIA
INQUIRY INTO A DEATH
Pursuant to *Coronial and Other Act 1991*
Section 16(IV)

Evidence suggests that the deceased was in a distressed emotional state on the morning of the collision.

Chapter Twenty-seven

IMOGEN

Spring

Zoe wanted me to go for a walk with her!

I stood and waited near the turnstile of Waterworks Reserve, watching threads of pink cloud dissolve in the tops of the gumtrees and across the face of the mountain. Her Yaris became audible before I saw it. As it approached, magpies and kookaburras stopped vocalising.

Almost as soon as Zoe parked, I began to cross the slippery grass. I walked quickly and quietly, and within a few moments, I could hear what she and Claire were saying. Cold air was an excellent conductor of sound.

'All I mean is, it's a very tricky situation—' Zoe was talking at a normal volume as she got out of the car.

'And all I mean is . . .' Claire was out already, and zipping her phone into a pocket. I couldn't hear the next bit, but then she said, 'It's a complex condition. Complex, serious, treatable. And you can't just blame the mother.'

'I'm not blaming anyone!' Zoe slammed her door. 'I just said it can hardly help. Jeez, Claire, stop doing your psychologist voice. I was just—'

'Well, I am a psychologist, Zo.' Claire shut her own door. 'Who has a special interest in *eating disorders.*'

'I would never've guessed!' Zoe sounded angry, and it occurred to me that she needed a new friend, or 'bestie', in her life. She saw me then – I was approaching from their left – and her face absolutely lit up.

'Imo!' she called. 'Hi, lovely!'

She knew I'd intended to come in an Uber, and she pantomimed looking around for my vehicle. I pointed back towards the public facilities in a way that suggested I'd been visiting the toilet.

Zoe spoke to Claire again. 'I'm honestly not blaming anyone. But imagine. Year Ten, new school, and it's *Pirates of Penzance* one minute, and your mum's cheating the next. Nightmare.'

By this time, I'd arrived next to them, so we all said hello and how are you and things of that nature. They both appeared very concerned about my wellbeing, because they used my name twice each, and drew out the 'are' when they said, 'How are you?'

We took the damp path alongside the reservoir, and ended up on a stony track through the bush along its northern side. I asked Zoe about Nick, just nonchalantly, and she said, 'Oh, you know. He's fine, I guess.'

The path became narrower. Claire fell behind. Zoe chose to keep going with me. I let my hand trail over the smooth white bark of a eucalyptus tree as we passed, just the way I had seen her do.

'So, how's your love-life, Imo?' she asked me. 'Anybody on the horizon?'

'That side of things is just fine, thank you,' I told her. 'But my endometriosis is playing up. Total nightmare.'

'Oh, do you have endo?' Zoe said. She sounded sympathetic and delighted, and the two of us had another heart-to-heart, this time about living with endometriosis, all the way back to her car.

She gave me a very long hug when we said goodbye. At least seven seconds.

Claire had remained well in the rear. And once she'd had her babies, she wouldn't have as much time for walks, or movies, or things of that nature.

Zoe would really need me.

Chapter Twenty-eight

ZOE

Spring

My car chugged up Nick's very steep hill – there was always a touch of drama about whether or not Nina-the-Yaris would make it, but Nina-the-Yaris never got flustered – and after I parked, I decided I'd better mindfully appreciate the view.

It was just on dusk, and white lights of different sizes seemed to pin the city to the edge of the Derwent. In the distance, out past the Peninsula, you could only just tell where the empty water finished and the empty sky began. I ended up just soaking it in for quite a while.

Amongst all the female supportiveness and natural serenity and so on at the Waterworks that morning, I'd realised it was time to try to sort things out with Nick. We hadn't seen each other for eight days, which was the longest we'd been apart since our first dinner date. To make up for all the nice sex and nice meals and nice laughing, I'd been spending marvellous hours writing him texts and then deleting them.

I'd also realised that I needed to tell him the truth.

'I've been calling,' he said, when he answered his door. His voice was all pleased and relieved. 'Really good to see you.' But he didn't try to kiss me.

As we went into the kitchen, I noticed he was wearing a very battered T-shirt. I'd never seen it before, and it occurred to me that maybe he wore his better T-shirts when I was around. That made me feel surprised and sort of tender, as if I'd stumbled upon a really dorky photo of him as a little boy.

He turned off his TV while I sat on his bench, and then he handed me a glass of wine. All without talking. The only sounds were of some birds raising the alarm about something or other, the squeaking brakes of a bus in the distance, and burbling from a pot on his stove.

He stood in front of the bench opposite me. The beer in his hand was half empty.

'Really good to see you,' he said again, and with more emphasis on the 'really' that time.

'You too.'

And it was. He was so gorgeous that I honestly wished I could pretend – or maybe accept – that things people did when they were teenagers didn't count, or that, even if they counted, they should be forgiven. But no.

I made my voice come out brave as anything. 'What's the go, Nick?'

He set his beer on the counter.

'I know I did the wrong thing, by Imogen, in high school,' he said. It was obviously rehearsed, but also, obviously sincere. He took a step closer, and I had the feeling he wanted to touch me, but he didn't. 'I would never do something like that now, and I've tried to be a friend to her.'

'What about New Year's Eve?' I said. Not angrily though. I *wanted* him to explain it.

'We're both grown-ups now.'

I stared at him, hoping for more, but he shrugged. It was a sad shrug, one that meant: *I was drunk, and it was easy sex, and what do you want me to say?*

'I'm gutted, Zoe.' He was still standing there with his arms by his sides. 'Gutted it makes you think badly of me.'

'Yeah.' There were no other truthful words for me to say. But I took in his shoulders – they were so droopy – and after a moment I put a hand on his wrist.

He stepped in closer and reached his arms all the way around my body. My cheek was against his collarbone, and I heard myself make a soft, glad sound. We stayed still. The traffic noise was quiet, and far away.

'Nick?' I said, after quite a while. My heart started beating so hard I could feel it. 'I've gotta tell you something.'

'What?' He dropped his arms and stepped back, moved his chin a tiny way towards his chest, stood his feet a bit further apart. 'What?'

'So, you know how, before I was ... with you, I was with Daniel?' I said.

He gave a single firm nod.

'So. Yes. We did break up. He got together with this woman from his work straightaway.'

'Rhianna.' Another nod. 'You said.'

'Yes. So.' I didn't know where to begin. 'So. Before Daniel and I broke up, he and I had been having IVF. To have a baby? For about twenty-three months.'

'Right.'

Nick looked towards the microwave for a second, as if he and it were agreeing that this Zoe person was a whole different kettle of fish from who they'd thought she was. But then he turned to me with a very sweet expression.

The curry made a loud blopping noise into the quiet.

I could tell that even though I'd been feeling okay, as soon as I had to actually say the words, I would start to cry. That always happened, even when I thought it definitely wouldn't *this time*.

'And the reason we had to have IVF was because of me.' The tears arrived right on cue. 'I have this thing. This problem. Endometriosis, it's called. I . . . it's hard for me to get pregnant.' Shaky breath. 'Daniel'd – we'd – he'd spent more than ten thousand dollars. When he broke up with me.' I probably had mascara down to about my nipples by now. At least my jaw.

Nick nodded, a slower nod this time. He used bare, warm fingers, and both his kind palms, to wipe the tears off my face. Rug the Dog gazed up at us. He lifted his front paw.

'Ah, Zo,' Nick said, really gently. He held my face.

'Hardly anyone knew.' I leaned into his arms. Daniel had wanted it kept secret. 'It's not a *social* event,' he'd said, of the first egg harvest. 'It's not *entertainment*.'

And he'd been all pernickety and grossed out about providing his sperm, as if the doctors were practically violating human rights by asking it of him. As if locking a door and looking at porn and splodging into a plastic cup was the most horrible and difficult mission that any poor man had ever had to put himself through. Afterwards, he'd take the rest of the day off work. As paid sick leave!

'Just so you know,' I told Nick's shoulder. I still didn't think about the egg harvests. Or the frozen maybe-lives the whole thing had resulted in. All those embryos were gone now. My body hadn't been able to hold onto any of them.

Nick hugged me, hard, until I let go. Then he stepped to the side, and after a second picked up a chopping board with a pile of raw pumpkin chunks on it.

'Glad you told me,' he said, as he moved over to the stove. 'In case we, you know.' A big scrape with the blunt edge of the knife. 'Ever wanted to go along the kids road.' He frowned professionally at the suddenly oh-so-important saucepan. 'Together. Some time.'

'That's sort of what I thought,' I said.

He managed to tear his eyes away from the curry, and we smiled at each other. He looked absolutely stoked.

When Daniel had found out about my diagnosis – when it became clear, at least, that it meant babies were going to be hard for us – he'd sighed and said, 'Not to worry, Zoe. I'll stand by you anyway.' He'd added something about the cost of IVF being manageable because of his 'relatively well-paid' job. I'd felt grateful, and I'd thanked him, but also, I had never, ever told anybody he'd said that.

I slurped my wine. Nick asked me if I'd be staying for dinner, and I said yes, please. Nick said no worries, that I should just drink my drink and look pretty till everything was ready.

'So.' I swung my legs and spoke very lightly, as if I was just continuing on with our happy-couple banter. 'No other secrets in the cupboard?'

Nick stopped stirring and faced me.

'None.' He wasn't acting casual anymore. He was being serious and gorgeous and gentle and kind and sexy and capable and loving. He was being the kind of man who wouldn't make me feel like shit even if he had to sploodge into a billion plastic cups. 'Honestly, Zoe. I promise.'

'Okay.' I nodded. 'Okay, then.'

The curry simmered away. It smelled deliciously of ginger. Nick was humming something unrecognisable. He topped up my wine, and asked me what music I felt like.

It should have been – it almost was – such a wonderful moment.

∞

Tuesday evening arrived, as Tuesday evenings generally did. I was quilting like a maniac, and telling myself everybody had a history, and nobody was perfect, and Nick was a different man now, and feeling desperate to have a proper morning-walk chat about the whole thing with Claire the next day. But then she texted that she couldn't make it. She had to squeeze in a patient, she said, and also was feeling depleted.

I made an effort to push aside bitter and unfair and unlikeable thoughts about pregnancy being a watertight excuse for getting out of whatever you didn't feel like doing, and I was just texting back something along the lines of who in the world puts 'depleted' in a text message, when my phone pinged. It was Imogen.

Just confirming what time we're meeting for our Waterworks Wednesday Walk tomorrow morning ... we could share an Uber? Or if it's not too much of a nightmare, I could maybe even grab a lift with you? Or are you staying at Nick's? And thanks again for the amazing heart-to-heart last time! xox

We must have told Imogen at some stage that our walk was a weekly thing. I toyed with the idea of simply explaining that it was off this week, but there were so many reasons I needed to be a friend to her.

I texted that I'd meet her at the Waterworks carpark at 6.45 am. Even typing those numbers made me feel exhausted. So bloody early.

For some reason, I thought: *At least this time of year, it won't be at all dark.*

∞

The Waterworks was beautiful that morning. The air was zingy – it felt as if just breathing made you healthier – and the indigo mountain and the light-fizzed sky were in stunning cahoots, like a beautiful famous couple everyone loved looking at but could never really get to know.

Almost as soon as I opened my car door, Imogen came strolling towards me.

'Just you and me, Zo, lovely?' she said.

I explained about Claire and her patient while we walked down the bitumen path towards the grass. Nobody else was around, apart from a jogger man who was a long way up ahead. His high-vis vest made wobbly blips through the trees along the far edge of the water.

'She must be feeling exhausted! Although, often the fatigue does settle in the second trimester.' Imogen talked on. Her voice was loud; I felt like it would rumple up the sleek, dark surface of the lake, or scare the wallabies. 'And Claire's so busy! She must look after some very complex conditions. As must you, Zo? I have the greatest respect for the tricky situations you teachers manage. Eating disorders, depression and so on.'

'Oh, well, I don't really ... I'm not a counsellor. I just try to sort of get a connection going with them.'

'But family dynamics. They can definitely make things worse, or at least not *help*, can't they? Mothers, for example? Or fathers or siblings! Whoever!'

'Mmm. Yeah.' I thought of Emma and reassured myself that she was already getting the help she needed. And she was still smiling and still turning up. She was just not making eye contact with me anymore. 'Stuff with parents is the hardest. And *between* kids' parents. Nightmare.'

'Zo, if there's anyone you ever want to chat about, anyone particularly tricky ... just go for it!'

A kookaburra was making a racket. I waited till it all of a sudden stopped, and then said I'd keep that in mind. I was thinking about how Claire and I sometimes walked along pretty quietly. But Imogen seemed to want to talk about endometriosis again.

'So, why didn't the progesterone implant agree with you?' she said, at some point.

'Beg your pardon?' I might tend to overshare, but I definitely didn't remember sharing *that*.

'Just! Lots of us women with endo have those. So, did you try one? Such a nightmare, aren't they?'

Then she started talking about how busy Claire would be very soon and how babies were so time-consuming and how Claire would probably make at least three new mum-friends. I was pretty ready to say goodbye, but as we hugged, Imogen suggested having dinner.

'I'm free tonight or tomorrow night,' she said. 'But after that, I'm on evening shifts for ten days.'

I explained I already had plans for that evening, and didn't mention the plans were watching TV and eating leftover spaghetti bolognaise.

'And tomorrow night I've got a family dinner. But let's do it after your evening shifts,' I said.

'Ages away!' she said. '*Night*mare! But it's been soooo good to see you!'

Her Uber arrived, and I hopped into my car. As I turned out of Dynnyrne Road, I rubbed my thumb over my left arm, where the horrible progesterone bar had once been. I realised I felt funny.

I felt exactly the way I used to when a certain sort of man would start talking to me in a pub, back when I was younger. I would worry about seeming unkind, and so I would stand there, smiling and nodding, and watching the man's tensely eager face, and his much-bigger-than-me body, and feeling a really complicated mixture of awkwardness, and sympathy, and an odd, surprised type of power.

But also fear.

Chapter Twenty-nine

IMOGEN

Spring

Zoe and I had a delightful walk, and I believed she might have contrived things so it was just the two of us. I made sure to empathise with her tricky work situations just the way Claire did, and we had another lovely heart-to-heart about endometriosis.

Since Zoe had a family dinner the next night – her parents lived on the other side of the river – I decided to take Nick another 'thank you' meal. But neither he, nor his dreadful old ute, were there. And Zoe's shiny white Yaris was in his carport.

I deduced that Nick had gone to meet Zoe's family. It was not the first time he'd done something like that. When he was living with Know-nothing Nova, they had often helped her parents with their landscaping and then purchased takeaway Thai for dinner, even though Thai cuisine would not have been Nick's first choice.

I stared at Zoe's car in Nick's neatly swept carport, and it occurred to me that she must be missing out on her regular Thursday-night get-together with Claire and T-rex. And as soon as I had that thought, I started to feel Sick.

I ran back down along Nick's road to my own car. I was puffing because I was carrying lamb shanks in a heavy pot.

Surely, I'm wrong, I said to myself. I was having palpitations due to my emotional state. I put my car into reverse.

The so-called Moroccan lamb shanks slid sideways on the passenger seat as I turned a corner. At a roundabout, a man in a silver car hooted me. It was fortunate we didn't collide, considering that legally I was driving unlicensed.

I was so upset that I didn't even remember to park some distance from Claire and T-rex's. I drove directly to their house.

I'd so hoped I would be wrong. But I was right. There, smack bang in the middle of their driveway, was Nick's ute. And although there were six cars parked along the street, they were solely the neighbours' usual vehicles.

The so-called 'family dinner' was a fallacy. Zoe had been referring only to her regular catch-up with Claire, who, yes, might technically have been a cousin, but who was clearly being visited in the context of *friend*.

And I had been left out. Even though I'd specifically said I was free. Even though I'd known Nick and T-rex for longer than either of them.

They were all inside together, laughing and having heart-to-heart conversations, and calling each other 'lovely', and looking nice and sharing food and making jokes, and the next time I saw them they'd have even more history together that I wasn't part of, more threads of knowledge and experience that I would have to struggle to weave myself into.

I wouldn't be able to. Even though I tried my hardest, people never gave me a chance.

I contemplated my Jamie Oliver version of Moroccan lamb shanks. The meat alone had cost $32.99 per kilo. And I'd personally risked twenty driver-licence demerit points to deliver it to my beautiful Nick.

Nobody could say I didn't make the effort.

I was not ashamed to admit that, thanks to their sheer fucking selfishness, I sat in my car and I cried.

Chapter Thirty

GRACE

Spring

They were on the phone, going over it all yet again.

'Louise mightn't even care that much.' Ben was driving home from work. 'But if she, if Louise, was to find out by accident. From someone other than me. Very much worse.'

'Yes,' Grace said.

'And I don't want the kids to find out chaotically. If I ...' This was always where his expertise seemed to run out, '... tell Louise I want to, uh, end the marriage. If I just ... tell her, and don't mention you? And then, after a while, you and I can ...'

'Ben, don't you think she might know already?'

'No. Well. Maybe. But even if she – if Louise – does know, she certainly isn't ready for it to become public.'

'God's sake,' said Grace. 'She's not Jennifer *Aniston*.'

It was an unprecedented jab of hostility, and there was quiet for a few moments. Grace rubbed a remorseful forefinger back and forth over a curved scratch on her dining table.

'Sorry,' she said. 'It's only ...' It was only that her days were now ugly beads on a hopeless tangle of knotted necklace. 'Whatever we do. Either way. The kids.'

The kids.

Emma had decided she would stay in the production, after all. She was barely speaking to Grace, who only knew that via Christopher, and because Emma had taken to wearing her *Pirates of Penzance* hoodie (with the hood up) at the dinner table.

Grace woke every night with her feet cramping on the sheet, and her thoughts racketing down the stairwell of exactly what Emma knew, or *thought* she knew, and how on earth she knew it, and what the consequences could be if they told her, or if they didn't tell her, or if Ben simply asked for a divorce. (The consequences of *that* started with the Year Ten student body taking scandalised sides when Emma Tierney-Adams's mum was revealed as the evil woman behind Queen Jasmine Hutchinson's parents' separation.)

Every single one of the options led to Emma's funeral, and it was all very well for Grace's inner grown-up to declare that that was melodramatic, but Emma was fragile, and anorexia nervosa was a potentially lethal illness, and Grace's terror was like a screaming baby.

'What a shit show.' And Ben sounded so defeated and confused.

'Sorry.' She was so desperately sorry. Not only for and about Emma, but for loving him and for not growing up properly and for being so pathetically available that they had to make this awful decision and cause people they loved so much pain. 'Sorry.'

'Ah, it's my fault.' She could hear him pulling himself together. He'd be rolling his shoulders back a tiny bit. 'Entirely, Gracey.'

Admitting mistakes made men like Ben more likeable, though. She was the one everyone would hate. The one who was a traitor to women, who was conniving and duplicitous and selfish and pathetic and who must, also, be laughably horny. She suddenly missed her mum.

'*Jee*sus!' Ben spoke over the blast of his horn. '*Christ.* Sorry, Gracey. Some idiot in a VW about to get someone killed.'

'Well, excellent.' She was trying for lightness. 'Perfect.'

But then her tone changed back to sombre all by itself, as she said she'd try to talk to Emma again.

CORONIAL COURT OF TASMANIA
INQUIRY INTO A DEATH
Pursuant to *Coronial and Other Act 1991*
Section 16(IV)

In this setting, I find that the deceased's own actions were likely causative of this tragedy.

Chapter Thirty-one

IMOGEN

Spring

The wind blowing west across Murray Street was chilly but not fresh, and as I walked to work I smelled only exhaust fumes from the afternoon traffic. In the bus mall, disconsolate-looking teenagers who should still have been at school were milling around, their faces and uniforms worn out and unappealing.

I thought about the Lofton boy with pink hair and the girl who wanted to fight climate change. Zoe had told me they both attended a 'poetry club'. Then there was the Year Ten girl with the adulterous mother and the eating disorder, who Zoe had been wittering about with Claire before they deigned to notice me at the Waterworks that Wednesday.

Zoe really shouldn't have been discussing her student's health in public.

I had opened my heart to friendship with her, and invested dozens of hours in trying to understand her, but I recognised that ours was a toxic relationship and I needed to remove her from my life. Which would mean her leaving Nick's life, too.

There were no easy solutions, that was for sure.

I was nothing if not realistic.

∞

It was approximately halfway through my shift that I saw Kurt, the paediatric registrar. Being around him always made me feel Sick, even when he was just sitting at the staff station, writing up fluids.

Tristan was also there, so I had to click on the first patient on the computer's list. Generally, I bent the rules and chose the least unwell-sounding patients. For example, I'd just finished treating a laceration. I was exceptionally good at stitching.

Without warning, Kurt put down his pen and turned towards me.

'Hey,' he said, 'remember that little boy with the LP? Archie McRae?'

I smiled at him, sat on a stool and said, 'Yes. His mum was Tina.'

Kurt moved his face the way Nick always did when his football team lost a game. 'He's got Wilms,' he said. This was an abbreviation for a type of kidney cancer.

'Oh. No.'

'I had to tell them yesterday.' Kurt shook his head and bulged out his lower lip so it covered his upper lip.

'That's so sad!' I kept my tone businesslike, even though I felt Sick. 'How was it picked up?'

'Blood in his urine. Lump in his belly.' Kurt shook his head again. He said he'd been back through all Archie's results, and Archie had had a urine infection very recently, but the urine test 'we'd' done that first time Archie came in had definitely been absolutely clear.

'No blood. No sign of anything amiss at all. Can't see how we could have done anything different.' He chewed, once, on his pen. 'We can't scan every single kid with a fever.'

'Of course we can't! It's nobody's fault this happened!'

'Yeah. Thanks.' He leaned his elbows onto the desk and looked at his paperwork. 'The dad's a labourer. About our age. They were just—' He did the thing with his lips again and shook his head. 'Ah, well.'

I stood up. Tristan was now taking a phone call, which was a rare lucky break, so I went and rested in the bathroom for a few minutes.

I felt very, very Sick.

Chapter Thirty-two

GRACE

Spring

'So, sweetie, how was school?'

'Fine.' Emma deposited salt onto her chicken fillet with three fastidious little shakes.

'How're rehearsals going?'

'Fine.'

'You have maths?'

Silence. Emma turned her unfocused eyes to the dining-room wall.

'I've just been wondering if you're all right, Emma?'

'I'm not.'

'Well, I'm so glad you told me!' Grace tried to keep calm in the face of such major progress. She wrenched her vocal cords back into serene-mother mode. 'Because I've had the feeling, since we looked at those photos that night, that you maybe had a few questions, or some concerns, or something like that, about them?'

'I told you I'm *fie-yun*.'

'But, Ems, you just said you're not!' Grace was leaning forward, her cutlery discarded. 'You have to tell me what's *wrong*, so I can explain, or just help you, or ...' Her steady voice had ripped wide open. 'Sweetie, I know sometimes things grown-ups do can seem very confusing, or be very difficult to understand, and we don't always get everything right. But if you would like to ask me anything, anything at all, then I'll ...'

God. What *would* she do?

Emma just gave a contemptuous shake of her head.

'I at least understand what "condescending" means, Mum,' she said. 'And also "liar".'

Chapter Thirty-three

IMOGEN

Spring

Inside the emergency department, behind its horseshoe-shaped desk, between its noisy trolleys, under its unassailable clock, the ratchet of my evening shifts ground forward. The rest of the time, I researched. I also restarted my penance.

Just before the sun rose on the seventh morning, the neighbours asked me to turn down my television. They were one of those anxious, well-meaning couples who recycled even peanut-butter jars correctly. The man said they knew I was a shift worker, the lady interjected that they truly felt for me and the man concluded they needed me to please be reasonable. Then they went home together.

I was left alone. I was up to *Friends* season six.

It was the morning after my final shift when Zoe roused herself to text. It was a long message, with multiple emojis and flowers and hearts. But actions spoke louder than emojis. Maybe she could have made another fucking artisan mug and painted that on it.

I texted back that I had had a very demanding time, and also added a few well-researched remarks about hand-crafted tableware and endometriosis. It seemed to work, because she replied she just needed to check something out with me, and invited me to meet her for a drink that very day.

Just the two of us. On a Monday evening. It was something, at least. I began to feel that perhaps our friendship deserved another chance.

We met at a pub in Salamanca. Ironically, the prices of the drinks there were now such that the convict-built storehouses could be frequented only by the middle classes. But this concern did not appear to bother Zoe. Even though it was not quite five o'clock when I arrived, she was already sitting under a lifeless outdoor heater, watching traffic and plane trees and drinking white wine.

I purchased myself a glass of South Australian sauvignon blanc and sat down next to her.

'How did your late shifts go?' she said. Moderately caringly.

I was extremely tired, and she was behaving receptively. That combination was my downfall.

'A patient of mine is very sick,' I said. 'I should have looked after him better.'

Zoe was eating a salt-and-so-called-balsamic-vinegar chip. 'Have you ever heard of imposter syndrome, Imo?' she asked me.

I replied that I had.

'And?' She was smiling. She bit into her chip, chewed, and then started using her tongue to clean her teeth.

I said that imposter syndrome didn't apply to me, because sometimes I *really* was not very good at my job. Due to the sleep deprivation, and the wine, I got pathetic tears in my eyes.

Zoe rubbed her hands once on her skirt and put both of them on my arms, near my shoulders.

'Imo,' she said. 'Sweetheart. I'm sure that's not true.'

She kept looking at my face. Then she leaned closer and put her arms around me properly. Zoe never stuck her bottom out backwards, the way most people did when they hugged in social situations. Zoe and I hugged like friends did on television.

Sleep deprivation impaired judgement and reduced an individual's ability to inhibit negative emotions. And her breasts were so soft I could lean properly into her and feel comforted. That was probably why I started crying.

'What on earth's happened?' she said.

I was the first to admit that I spoke without adequate thought.

'There's a six-year-old boy,' I said. Music was playing. Nobody else could hear us. 'Who had a fever of unknown origin. So we did a spinal tap.'

Archie McRae. Archie McRae, with his skinny little back and his huge tumour. At the very least, he'd lose his whole left kidney. He might die.

'Okay. Imo, just letting you know, your work details sometimes go a bit over my head, to be honest.' Even though she'd stopped hugging me, she still had her hands on my arms. 'But I'll do my best.' Her brown eyes appeared to be kind. She acted like I should trust her!

'I made an error with one of his tests.' I whispered it very quietly.

'Well.' Zoe was looking at me the way the nice school teachers often used to. 'Nobody's perfect, right? What happened?'

A tradesman-type person shuffled past our bench, and we had to lean forward to make room. He said, 'Sorry,' to Zoe, in a saucy tone that implied he was not sincerely sorry. She didn't even seem to notice him.

When we were effectively alone again, I went on with my story.

On Archie's very first trip to hospital, I had organised a urine specimen from him. And I had taken it to the sink area. I had tested it with a dipstick, and it had indicated a likely urine infection. But then I'd been distracted by a request to order some morphine for a different patient, and I was trying to be efficient, so then I'd decided to ring Kurt. And while I was doing that, I saw Tristan frown towards me, and so I thought I'd better get on with my next patient. And then Kurt was chatting away about gin bars.

So, in summary, I forgot to send Archie's urine to the lab. I left it sitting, unlabelled, by the sink, with the dipstick on a paper towel next to it. When Kurt finally finished socialising and asked for it, it had gone. Some busybody nurse had probably thrown it away.

I stood at the sink and stared at the yellow sharps-disposal container. I washed my hands, and while I was doing so, I looked all along the shelves and the benchtop again. I really felt so Sick.

'Hands clean enough there, *Doc*tor?' Tristan asked, from right behind me.

I wondered, briefly, if this issue with Archie's urine was one of the Clinical Dilemma situations where I could consult a senior colleague for guidance. But I knew it wasn't. It was just a terrible thing to have forgotten, and Tristan would be confirmed in his view that I was bloody stupid. Nobody would respect me, and I would never progress in my career or be invited out for casual after-work drinks.

'Yes siree, thank you, Tristan!' I dried my hands, picked up a clean urine container and walked away.

In the staff toilet, I stared at a sign on the cubicle door. It was about how clinicians could access confidential support from qualified counsellors. There was a photo of a beautiful woman – with a ponytail and minimal makeup, so she looked 'relatable' – in a white coat. She was holding a stethoscope and gazing into the distance, as if she was overwhelmed by the illnesses of humanity and therefore needed some qualified counselling.

Doctors in Australia didn't even wear white coats.

I sat down on the toilet and passed some urine into the container.

I thought: *If I told a counsellor what I was doing, they'd have a legal obligation to report me. I would probably be deregistered. My photo would be on the internet, as if I was a dangerous criminal. My mum would cry. Dad would get Cross. Then Mum might become unwell again.*

I screwed on the container's lid.

I thought: *If I looked similar to that model-doctor, Tristan wouldn't mind so much when I interrupted him, and Kurt would talk to me about wearing dresses, and I'd have a proper boyfriend – Nick – and a great many friends, and they would invite me out to gin bars, and we'd exchange anecdotes about acceptable, amusing slip-ups we made at work.*

I thought: *If I was even half as pretty as that model-doctor, then I wouldn't need to* be *like this.*

ARCHIE MCRAE, I wrote, on the urine container's label. URGENT.

I opened the cubicle door and washed my hands. Back at the sink, I dipped a cardboard testing stick into my own urine, and then sent the sample, with Archie's name on it, to the laboratory. I showed Kurt the normal, all-clear dipstick.

You might judge. But believe me, there was nothing else I could have done.

∞

Zoe still had her hands on my arms. 'What do you mean?' She loosened her grip. 'Sorry, *what* do you mean?'

'I didn't want to get into trouble for losing his urine sample. So, I did some of my own and sent it to the lab with his name on it.' I took a shaky breath. 'If I hadn't done that, then his cancer would almost certainly have been diagnosed earlier.' I tried to smile.

'But. So. Imo, you've told your boss *now*, right?'

'I'm just confiding in you.' I wiped my tears away with my hands, the way Claire had, although of course I had tissues in my handbag. 'Having a heart-to-heart!' I managed to smile properly. Maybe my authenticity would bring us closer together. 'As a friend.'

'Imogen. Seriously?' She gestured with her head towards the

street, in the general direction of the hospital. 'So. Like, recently? At your work?'

I nodded and leaned forward for another hug. But Zoe had her teeth together and her mouth closed. She had an unattractive line between her eyebrows.

'Have you done anything else like that?' She took her hands right off my arms and moved her torso backwards.

'No!' I said.

But she was shifting further away from me. She was not making me feel at all comforted. She was making me feel fucking worse!

'Imogen, you ... are you going to tell your boss about this?'

'Certainly not!'

'But, Imogen, sometimes we all make errors. I'm sure if you—'

'Don't be so stupid,' I told her. I kept my voice down. 'Ruining my career would solve nothing.' That was entirely true. That was why I had elected to do penance!

'But I think people do trust health workers. And you know ... If Archie was my little boy, then I'd want—'

'But you'll never even *have* a little boy!'

'That's not—' Zoe looked up at the heater and then back at me. 'Imogen,' she said. 'You know I'm going to have to tell the authorities about this, don't you? If you won't?'

I told her again not to be so stupid. She wouldn't even know which 'authorities' to tell.

But she talked at some length about her rationale for making that decision, and how 'we' couldn't risk this sort of thing happening again, and how I needed help, and how she was not the person who had the skill to provide it. She said a number of other phrases which really meant that she had my Nick, and her precious Claire, and a fridge loaded with invitations, and I would have to pay somebody to *talk* to me.

'I better get home,' she told me. 'Nick's coming over soon.' That was a big lie. He had indoor cricket until at least 9.30 pm. 'You're going to be okay, right?' Pretending she cared.

'Just fine,' I said. I didn't feel Sick anymore. I felt very Cross. I touched the edge of her packet of chips, and thought for a moment about what to say next.

'Give my regards to your Year Ten female student with the eating disorder,' I settled on. 'I hope her adulterous mother enjoys watching her in *Pirates of Penzance* next week!'

Zoe made an interesting jerking movement with her thumbs. She put her back to me while she flipped her legs over to the other side of the bench. Then she walked away.

I'd *known* she wasn't a true friend.

I finished off her chips while I considered what to do. People like Zoe were so insufferably stupid. It was always left to people like me to work out how to fucking handle them.

DAY OF THE ACCIDENT

Chapter Thirty-four

IMOGEN

The Lofton School's carpark was dark and empty, and the random perfection of the stars made its rutted asphalt and dusty boronia even uglier by comparison.

I stayed in my car until Zoe arrived. The stars had disappeared by then. It was a sunny morning.

'Zoe,' I called. She stopped with her hand on her car's door. 'I need to talk to you.'

We were facing each other across the carpark. A moderately handsome teacher shut his door and glanced at us. He adjusted his bag on his shoulder and headed towards the school.

I crossed the carpark and faced Zoe, so that the two of us stood between her car and the one parked next to it.

'Have you changed your mind?' I said. 'Have you informed on me already?'

I predicted she would not have. It was less than sixteen hours since she had left the pub last night.

'Imogen.' She made a sickly-sweet face, as if she was about to offer a reasonable explanation for her disloyalty and betrayal. 'People put a lot of trust in health professionals, and you—'

'Emma Tierney-Adams,' I interrupted her. I sounded just as suave and calm as I'd hoped. 'She trusted *you* with private information.'

Zoe looked as if she wanted to step backwards, but due to

wing mirrors, there wasn't enough space behind her.

She didn't ask me how I knew. This was disappointing, because I was proud of my sleuthing. The evening before, I'd photographed one of the Lofton student's *Pirates of Penzance* commemorative hoodies, which was moderately easily done at approximately 5.15 pm in the Hobart bus mall, and which had every cast member's name printed in full on its back.

There were thirty-one female or indeterminate names on the cast list. I cross-checked with the online school newsletters. These of course rarely used students' full names, due to the privacy conventions schools were so anal about. But I was able to rule out seven girls as being in either Year Nine or Eleven. That left twenty-four female potentially Year Ten names. It would not be feasible to check twenty-four hospital files.

Then I remembered Zoe wittering about the adulterous-mother girl being 'new'.

I had already obtained last year's Lofton yearbook, back when I was first researching Zoe, and by the simple expedient of walking into the virtually unattended school library and removing a copy.

Two female cast members were missing from that publication. One was a girl called Olivia Chang, and one was Emma Tierney-Adams. The new girls.

I took some brownies into work at just after 9 pm, and looked up Olivia Chang's and Emma Tierney-Adams's hospital records. This was, of course, very risky for me.

Olivia Chang had been seen in 2016 for an appendicectomy, and Emma Tierney-Adams had had several presentations with dehydration, electrolyte disturbance and anorexia nervosa. I refrained from clicking through and reading details, as I did not wish to invade patient privacy, and that level of access would also be more difficult to explain. As a side note, and just in case you are extremely slow and hadn't already worked it out, this was also the methodology I had used to research Zoe's endometriosis.

'The only thing I'm not sure of,' I told Zoe now, 'is who the mother's cheating with. But you told me "stuff" between kids' parents is very difficult. I suspect it's one of the dads. Or the mums, for that matter.' I was nothing if not open-minded.

Zoe didn't answer. On the street, a line of vehicles was approaching the drop-off zone.

'I think we all have a duty to keep things people tell us to ourselves. You could argue that it's my duty, as a doctor, to make sure Lofton is aware that you don't adhere to the basic principle of confidentiality. Especially when it affects student wellbeing.' I paused.

'And not that I'm one to gossip, and nobody would accuse me of being salacious, but the school community will insist on knowing the full story. I am familiar with a number of social media platforms.'

I had already joined the Lofton Uniform Buy/Sell Facebook page. It was completely public, and more than six hundred people followed it.

'Nightmare for Emma,' I said.

Zoe was looking at me and at the carpark behind me. She said that I should let her out.

I told her a few long-overdue home truths about her so-called relationship with my Nick, and then I stood aside.

'Let me know,' I called after her. It sounded as if we were girlfriends arranging a catch-up after work. Maybe if she'd been a genuine friend to me, she wouldn't find herself in this position now. 'If I don't hear from you, I'll pop something up on Facebook after lunch. And ring Corey Dankworth.'

It was 8.14 am. I was nothing if not generous.

∞

Imogen was standing near the boronia bushes, with her arms down at her sides.

'Zoe,' she called, through the shade. She drew out the *oooo* and the *eeee* in a way that made my name sound really creepy.

When she came closer, I saw that her eye shadow was perfect, and her white shirt had sharp creases along the length of its sleeves. She looked so normal and so *conservative* that I honestly couldn't believe what was happening. A part of me was thinking that she was unhinged and nobody would believe her, and another part of me was just thinking, *Shit. Emma.*

As soon as she left, I called Nick. No answer. I should've called him the night before. I almost had. But I couldn't bear to have to talk to him again about anything to do with Imogen. Sometimes you just really, really want to keep one precious, tender part of your life sealed off from another horrible bit.

I texted: *Imogen's here at school. Something weird going on. Can you call me?*

I called Claire. Also no answer. I texted: *Can you call as soon as you can?*

The sun was slanting under the blinds when I dumped my bag on my desk with one hand and started logging in with the other. I checked my phone. Nobody had called back. I was rubbing my teeth together, the way I did when I was very tense.

At 8.23 am, I began the multiple-password-requiring process of locating Emma's mum's phone number.

∞

'Not even eight twenty-five!' said Grace, brightly. 'We're in good time today!' She released her accelerator to take the corner into the school's street, and slowed almost to a stop as she hit the usual traffic. 'Beautiful weather!'

Emma said nothing. Emma did nothing.

'Ems?' Grace spoke over the idling motor. 'How are you this morning?' There was a pleading note in her voice, which was bad. Everyone knew you were never supposed to plead with teenagers.

'Fine.' Emma had not eaten breakfast. She had refused to sit down with Grace.

'You got your lunch okay?'

'Can you let me out here?'

'Um ...'

'Can you please let me out *here*!'

'Okay, sweetie, it's just it's hard to park right this minute, so—'

'What*ev*er.'

Grace glanced at Emma's face. Emma stared straight ahead, as if the whole fiasco of her mother was light years beyond anything a person could reasonably be expected to suffer.

'Ah! Perhaps there!' said Grace. She manoeuvred around a 4WD with a P-plate on its rear window, indicated and pulled over. A sizeable portion of her bonnet was blocking someone's meticulously groomed driveway access. 'I think we can get away with that for a sec!' Grace never parked like this. And she'd never heard herself *sound* like this. So falsely upbeat, so like a flailing, ratings-starved game-show host.

Emma didn't say thank you. She didn't look at Grace. She opened her door.

'Bye-bye, Ems.' Grace started a sentence about how of course it was Change-over Tuesday, and so she'd see Emma in a week, and that she loved her.

Emma didn't reply. She still didn't look up. She slammed her door while her mother was speaking, jerked open another, and wrestled her ludicrously heavy schoolbag from the back seat.

Grace turned, watched, made a long, final attempt at eye contact. 'I love you, Emma,' she said.

'Yeah, right.' Emma's reply was exhaled towards the slamming car door.

Grace began a grimly mortifying U-turn. It was very, very difficult.

∞

An extremely unwise woman was attempting to make a U-turn despite the traffic congestion, and I decided to give way to her. I was nothing if not polite. She held up her hand in acknowledgement, which represented a sadly unusual display of basic courtesy.

I smiled as I waved back. She would probably assume I was one of the school mums.

I wished I was. I wished I had just delivered my daughter to school, and that now I was going to call Nick on speakerphone and inform him that 'drop-off' had been just fine.

Nick and I would not mind if our daughter had some sort of special need. We would not tell her she was an ungrateful young madam if she experienced separation anxiety, or if certain foods made her feel nervous. And if she cried, Nick wouldn't smack her once to give her something worth crying for, twice for her own good and thrice just for luck.

The traffic was almost at a standstill, barely moving. I looked at small oblong hedges that lined paths. At custom-built letterboxes with matte-silver numbers. At wedges of black mesh trampoline barriers that rose behind fences.

I wondered if Nick and I might one day live in this street. If and when Nick came to his senses, our child could play on a trampoline. Perhaps we would somehow stay friends with Zoe and Claire and T-rex. They could come over to our house for a casual barbecue. Claire's twins, who would be a few years older, could take my little ones onto the trampoline, and Zoe would have met someone else and started a new career and all these hiccups would be in the past.

The U-turn woman's car preceded me down the street. The traffic was barely moving.

For the first time in a very long time, I watched students walking towards school. It was possible to determine who were the socially powerful students, and who were the nervous ones, and who were the average-looking, mid-range pupils who were moderately skilled at sport. I hoped Emma Tierney-Adams was one of those, or even better, one of the cool, mean girls. I hoped Emma Tierney-Adams wasn't one of the girls with careful posture, who walked along by herself, listening to something she didn't care very much about and pretending not to mind being alone.

The unwise woman's car reached the T-intersection as the 8.30 am news started. She turned left, into the faster-flowing traffic towards town. I felt like giving a little goodbye wave, but it would not have been socially appropriate.

I waited for my own chance to turn. It was going to take a long time, as that section of road was a nightmare, as Zoe might say, and I was not one for pulling out without due caution.

What if Emma Tierney-Adams *was* one of those terrified girls? What if almost every day, nobody except teachers asked her how she was? What if one time someone threw an old schoolbag-apple at her head, when the teacher was out of the room, and she never knew who did that?

If Emma Tierney-Adams was already facing any of those hiccups, then it might be mildly or moderately difficult for her when the school community was informed of her mother's actions.

∞

Unfortunately, I had to log into three separate bits of database to find Emma's mum's phone number. *What actually even was a server?*

I wondered, while the casual-seeming computer asked me to Please Wait A Sec.

I dialled the office and asked if someone could please find Emma Tierney-Adams and send her to me. The surprised-sounding office man said he could try, but attendance had of course not yet been taken, and to the best of his knowledge Emma Tierney-Adams was not yet on school property. He was quite a lot more eager to please than Sandra.

I typed in another password, and wondered why the screen now said 'Guest Remote Access' when I was right *there*. At the actual *school*. Where I was a *teacher*.

Those were the random things I was thinking to keep my mind off questions like: *What exactly had I said? When had I said it? How could I have let this happen? Would anyone even believe Imogen? Should I try to find Emma myself? Or Jasmine Hutchinson? Or phone Jasmine's mum? Or her dad? And if so, what words could I possibly use? What was I even going to say to Emma's mum? And how could I limit any of those conversations to a reasonable time, because I'd just realised I was on bloody supervision duty and I had to try to control a Year Nine maths class at 8.50 am and it was already 8.31?*

But really, and most of all, I was just feeling sick, and scared, and more and more certain that Imogen was one of those people who could do anything.

∞

A nice school mum in a VW had waited patiently while she did her multi-point U-turn, and now Grace was driving along Wellington Avenue. The traffic wasn't too bad; she was doing just on seventy; she was trying very hard to compartmentalise the horrible situation with Emma. She told herself all about how she was going to drive out to Derinya that morning after she'd given a few vaccinations, and that that was doable; that was fine; it was not even twenty-five to nine.

She slowed down for a cyclist. Then her phone rang.

When she saw the screen, she forgot all about Derinya and vaccinations and stabbed a completely straight finger at the green circle.

'Ms Tierney?' A female voice filled up the car, the bouncy sort of voice that went with pina coladas and bangles. 'It's Zoe Morello here. I'm Emma's pastoral-care teacher at Lofton School?'

Ms Morello. The harvest goddess. The poetry-club woman. Emma liked her.

'Yes?'

'Emma's fine.' Reassuringly. Yet not.

'Okay. Yes?'

'I just, ah ...' Ms Morello sounded slightly less bouncy. 'We have a bit of an unusual situation here this morning. I, well, Emma's *fine*, as I say, there's no danger to her, as such. But. Look, Grace. I think I just—' Ms Morello stopped. Had the connection dropped out? Then she said, 'What might be best would be if you could meet with me? I need to have a talk to you about some personal matters that have come to light that might affect Emma. Or her schooling.'

Grace heard herself make a small, odd noise. 'Is Emma there with you?' she said.

'We're just in the process of establishing that she's here. On school property. So, yes, if you could maybe come in? I know it's—'

Grace was already trying to pull off her second ridiculous U-turn for the morning.

∞

It was 8.36 am, and I'd semi-forgotten about the Year Nines and their maths supervision. I knew they'd just sit around the classroom, doing no work but not coming to any harm. Worst-case scenario: Rosco Wilson would set off the fire extinguisher.

I'd told Emma's mum, Grace, to meet me at the main office. I was walking up there and trying my best – but failing – to do slow, mindful breathing when Nick called me back.

'You okay?' I could tell he was driving. 'Just saw your text. Zo?'

He'd be on his way to work. He'd have his phone in this dusty little well thing next to his handbrake, slanting into a couple of takeaway squirty-packs of tomato sauce and some ancient five-cent pieces.

'Imogen was here.' I talked louder than normal and hoped he could hear me. 'I think she's kind of unhinged.'

'What?' He said it in the way that meant he couldn't hear me. 'Sorry, Zo, nowhere to pull over. I'll—'

I suddenly felt as if the whole thing was his stupid fault. 'IMOGEN WAS HERE. SHE SCARED ME!' I yelled.

'What?' He'd heard. But now I could hear buzzing and echoing louder than his voice. 'IS SHE STILL THERE?'

'Yes, no, I DON'T KNOW. I think she left, I'm at WORK, or, I don't KNOW, maybe she's still in the CARPARK.' I felt like crying. 'She really SCARED me, Nick.'

'Are you …?' More buzzing and echoes. 'ZO?'

I called 'HELLO?' a few times. No response. My voice was probably squished up against his grimy loose change. 'HELLO? NICK?'

Two Year Eight boys came walking up the path and looked at me. I stopped yelling. I really had to get it together and go and meet Grace Tierney.

I texted: *Please call me when you get somewhere we can talk properly? xo*

But he texted back: *wtf ner lofton on way lov u*

300

∞

Let me be clear.

I knew that I could potentially harm Emma Tierney-Adams. But the principles of utilitarian ethics recommended choosing actions that resulted in the greatest good for the greatest number. And as a doctor, I had the potential to do great good for a great number of people, as long as the business with Archie McRae never came to light.

Still. It might be difficult for Emma Tierney-Adams when her mother's misconduct was revealed.

That was what I was thinking about as I drove past the lighting shop with the digital clock. I saw it was 8.41 am, and then I saw that Nick's terrible old ute was approaching through the sunshine, coming towards me up a long, shallow hill on the other side of the road.

There was no median strip in that part of Wellington Avenue, and I would know his vehicle anywhere. I made oral love to him in that ute once, at Cameron Barnett's going away party.

Of course, I couldn't see Nick himself, but I could imagine him. He tended to swivel his chin to check his rear-view mirror. He almost always held the steering wheel with one hand, his palm facing up, his fingers loose.

Why would Nick be driving in that direction, when he was supposed to be renovating a semi-retired audiologist's kitchen that morning? And why he would be moving to the right of his lane, as if seeking an opportunity to overtake?

Oh.

Zoe must have *summoned* him. She would be 'shaken' due to my revelation, and she would have clicked her fingers and he would be rushing to her aid.

I veered a tiny bit towards his side of the road, towards a motorcycle. Oops.

Nick would skip work to help Zoe. Even though she already had Claire! And a job she was good at, and beautiful breasts, and beautiful skin, and beautiful hair, and Sophie Carnahan and Adrian Duffy and Susannah from London who had stopped replying to my Insta messages!

What if Nick never got over his infatuation with her? What if this episode brought them closer together? What if I got deregistered, and Dad got Cross, and Mum became unwell, and Zoe manipulated things so that Nick didn't even want to be my *friend* anymore?

We were about to pass each other.

I started waving, but of course he didn't fucking notice me.

I didn't think about ethics. I didn't think about anything. If I didn't know it to be both physiologically and physically impossible, I would say that my steering wheel deviated towards his vehicle without any intervention whatsoever from me.

Nick swerved. He was always an amazing driver. But then I saw the other car.

∞

The office man told me Emma was in one of the science labs. I semi-hurried through the student-art-lined hallway, then along the wide, locker-lined corridor. It was empty under its internal windows. The insects on the skylights made tiny half-shadows on its floor.

'Let's go to my office,' I said, after I'd extracted Emma from Mr Hammell's explanation of velocity or acceleration or some such.

Emma didn't look at me as we walked back past Year Eleven oil paintings and Year Ten screen-prints. She was doing a humiliated-teenager-trying-to-be-icy walk, because she was still mad at me. Poor Emma.

My office was just a cubicle within a big room, but nobody else was in there. Emma sat on the chair I'd left ready for her. She had the soles of her feet flat on the floor, her knees pressed together with her hands between them, her eyes on the shredder in the corner.

'Emma.' I tried again to make eye contact. For once, I had tissues at the ready. 'Your mum's been in a car accident.'

Chapter Thirty-five

GRACE

It seemed to Grace that the sounds of crunching metal and skidding tyres and the serious, agitated voices of strangers had always been lurking just ahead of her, as if she'd been waiting a long time – perhaps since Emma got sick, perhaps even since Emma was *born* – for those noises to become real.

It was almost a relief, now they had. And it was a relief to lie there, without trying to understand anything, and to have, somehow, Christopher there, too, and he was doing all the understanding, and were these clean sheets she hadn't had to wash?

Where was Emma?

'It's all right, Grace,' she heard Christopher say.

A sound had come out of her, but now she couldn't make another one. She just kept her eyes closed and didn't answer. Nobody seemed to mind, which was nice. A strange male voice started talking again to Christopher.

Spleen, she heard. *Blood count … pain relief … something … something. Spleen.*

Where *was* Emma?

And who was that other important person? Ben. Where was Ben?

Some sort of beeping started. Did it come from her? Longer beeps. Not stopping.

Emma, she thought. *My beautiful Emma. And Ben.*

Sorry, she tried to say. *Sorry. Sorry. Sorry to be causing everyone so much trouble.*

∞

Grace had never thought too hard about the afterlife. It was just that her mum had always done so much of that. Reincarnation and karma and the Universe. Destiny and crystal healing and psychics. No conversation about souls had ever held any glamour for Grace; mortgages and new-car service agreements seemed way more exotic.

And who really knew what her soul was doing, while she lay in her intensive-care bed, and the doctors exchanged sentences about splenectomy and blood loss and renal failure? But if it was true that a bit of her sort of hovered above her cubicle, gazing down at the obscene breathing tube coming out of her mouth and at the boxes of S/M/L gloves near the sink, then that bit of her also saw Ben as he beeped himself into the ICU, as he nodded professionally at one of the doctors on duty, as he stood very still at the foot of her bed until her nurse looked up and asked him, in quite a stroppy voice, if he needed something.

'Nothing!' he said. 'Thank you.'

Poor Ben. He wasn't swinging his arms properly. And he was going to have to go somewhere private and get his face normal.

In the family room off the corridor, on funny old chairs (much too low for people with bad knees) (and much too deep for people with bad backs), were Emma and Christopher. They seemed to be coping all right, under the circumstances.

When Ben went in, Christopher dropped Emma's hand and stood.

'Yes, Doctor?' he said. He put his body in front of Emma's, as if he planned to take the bullet of news for her.

He was really such a lovely man.

'I'm ... I'm ... I'm just here as a friend this morning.' Ben's

305

movements were hastier than usual. He flipped off his hospital ID, shoved it into a pocket and extended his hand. 'Ben Hutchinson.'

The men shook, sizing each other up.

Emma said, 'Hello,' with a self-conscious sort of recognition, like Ben was famous.

Ben smiled and said hello, but he'd started tapping his forefinger against the tip of his thumb, the way he used to when he was a young man. Exactly the way he had at that long-ago wedding when he'd accidentally called her Gracey.

'Would it be all right if I just sat in here, with you both, for a few moments?' he said.

Outside, a trolley juddered along the corridor. The ICU doors swooshed open and snapped closed around it. (They were really getting annoying, those doors. So officious and bossy, as if they knew best what was good for you.)

Christopher said, 'Yes, Ben. Certainly! Of course.'

But Ben was looking towards Emma, who gave a series of quick nods. She was trying very hard not to cry, and virtually succeeding, when she said, 'My mum might maybe like that.'

Beautiful Emma.

∞

The vending machine had a habit of making an occasional noise like a tiny bit of velcro being ripped open. It sounded (somewhat unnervingly) (particularly in view of all the lifesaving apparatuses nearby) like an electrical fault.

'Doesn't seem terribly healthy, does it?' Christopher said, after an especially long *bzzzzh*. He nodded towards the machine.

Ben shook his head. 'No.'

Ice thus broken, Christopher went on with a probing sort of conviviality. 'And how is it that you know Grace, Ben?'

'Very old friends.' His tasteful silver wedding band would have to be feeling like a volcano-scale beacon. 'University.'

'And you work here now?'

Ben launched into a long and relieved explanation about science tutorials and veterinary studies, and then proceeded to expound on the medical education program past, present and future.

Christopher nodded a number of times, as if all that was critically relevant, and then reciprocated with an even longer analysis of the duties of legal officers in state government departments.

Emma stared from one to the other, as if she was trying to understand tour guides who were speaking about something vitally interesting and in a foreign language.

'Excuse me,' she said, when Christopher had just about flogged the life out of something called a change-process framework. She was speaking to Ben. 'But do you think Mum's going to be all right?'

Ben held his face in smooth professional lines while he said he very much hoped so, but that he wasn't involved in taking care of Grace himself.

'Because I was mean to her this morning. And last night. And ... lately.'

So hard to see, the way she held in her tears. Even the watching men could barely keep it together.

Ben managed a little shake of his chin. 'Don't worry about that now,' he said. Something else seemed to occur to him. 'You know it wasn't your fault, what happened, don't you?'

'You think?'

'I'm certain. One hundred per cent. Absolutely.'

Christopher chimed in with sentences about there being no way in the world that Emma should blame herself, that these things happened from time to time, that car accidents were tragic but sadly and unfortunately a part of life that we all had to come to terms with.

He really was such a sweet man.

A few moments later, Ben's phone burred in his pocket, and, without looking at it, he murmured that he had better get going. (Obviously. How on earth was he planning to explain his absence from the clinic he was supposed to be running?)

Emma told him he should come back later. 'Perhaps when you take your afternoon coffee break,' she said, in her best attempt at adult-to-adult graciousness.

'Sounds good,' said Ben, levelly.

But on his way down the corridor, he had to roll his shoulders back, the way he always did when he was reminding himself that people needed him, and he was a grown man, and so he had better keep acting like one.

∞

All that afternoon, just two floors up and a hospital wing to Grace's left, Ben read ECGs and interpreted echocardiograms and dispensed advice with his usual competence. It was almost enough to make a girl feel a bit miffed.

At just on five – he hadn't finished before six in at least a decade – the hospital cafeteria was closed. He waited at the traffic lights, walked fast across the road and ordered three pretty dodgy-seeming flat whites. Carried them back along long fluorescent-lit corridors. Nodded at a ridiculous number of people he appeared to know.

He beeped himself in through the doors that led towards intensive care and raised a casual hand to the security guard. A departing ICU nurse gave him a shrewd corridor assessment. It was clear from Ben's face that he had no professional reason to be there.

The family room was empty. He didn't sit down, but stood alone, using both his hands to hold the cardboard coffee tray in front of him.

'My dad's just parking the car.' Emma spoke from the doorway. She was now dressed in jeans and a hoodie; her hair was damp.

They took chairs across from each other. Established there was no news.

The coffee would have been colder than tepid, but they drank it anyway. Emma held her phone but didn't look at it. No strangers went in, even though there were six other patients in the ICU and only two family rooms. For ages, there was quiet.

'So, you go to Lofton?' Ben said, in the end.

'Yep.'

'My kids go there.'

'I know,' she said. They looked at each other, then looked away. 'Jasmine's in my year.'

The pause went on long enough for the vending machine to make two fizzes of noise.

'Just, um? I saw you, coming out of Mum's, one night.' But Emma spoke as if she were making a confession rather than an accusation. 'I was staying at Dad's and I used to sometimes, um, this was last year, I'd just stretch my legs by going to Mum's and back, and, um, and so on. In the evenings.'

Ben nodded. He'd remember that particular strand of Grace's anguish. When Emma finally got sprung exercising – halfway along the steep slope of Grace's street – she'd pretended she was on her way to retrieve a vital piece of homework. It had been after 10 pm.

'And then, Mum didn't tell me anything, but you know, this year, I saw the collage – Jasmine made this visual-media collage? It's in the science foyer, there're like fifty prints of your passport photo – and I kind of, for ages, I was trying to remember where I knew you from. Every time I had science.'

'I see.'

'Yeah. So, when I found Mum's photos and she said your name was Ben Hutchinson, I clicked. Figured you were probably Jasmine Hutchinson's *dad*.'

Ben met her eyes and nodded.

'And then I searched you up, and ... and ... you know. There's your *wife*.'

Ben didn't look away, but something about the lines on his face changed.

'So. Yep. I was pretty mad.' She still sounded apologetic, though. 'Plus, no offence to my mum, but it was like, *sooo* obvious she still liked you.'

Well.

Ben said, 'Please try not to be too hard on her. She loved – *loves* – you so much.'

Emma gave her quick little nods.

'Jesus Christ,' he said. 'You poor kid.'

Emma stopped nodding and clasped her hands like an adult.

It was now after seven o'clock in the evening. He must have missed calls from Louise, and he should be getting home. But he was staying in his chair.

The two of them were looking together towards the doorway from which news might issue, and beyond which lay their Grace.

∞

Probably even Grace's mum would not have believed it was possible for Grace's astral form to follow Ben home to Louise Buchanan. And Grace herself would not have considered it okay to invade their privacy, even as a waftily disembodied wisp.

So, when Ben finally arrived home at just before midnight, with a shattered face and no explanation except the truth, Grace definitely didn't witness their conversation.

AFTER THE ACCIDENT

Chapter Thirty-six

ZOE

I stood on my tiny concrete balcony, watching them get out of their car. The policeman had a shiny head and a nice build. The policewoman had one of those sculpturey grey bobs, not even due for a trim. I wondered if it was true, all the good-cop, bad-cop stuff.

Their knock wasn't particularly loud, but I suddenly wished Daniel was with me, and that the police were visiting us in our old apartment. Daniel had a certain way about him – respectful and businesslike, but also a tiny bit dismissive – that would have made me feel more confident. If I'd been sitting next to Daniel in that schmancy white kitchen, or holding his hand on that immaculate modular sofa, then I'd have felt completely respectable and law-abiding. Not that I was in trouble. And not that I had plans to lie.

They sat down at my dining table and I offered them coffee. The policewoman, Annette, said yes, please, she could do with some caffeine. The policeman, Paul, moved his eyes around my living room. He wasn't acting shrewd and calculating; it was more like he was interested in my décor.

'Nice flowers,' he said. A normal man would never say that, though.

'From Nick.' Of course, they'd already talked to Nick, both straight after the accident and again yesterday. It was hard to believe it had been a week. 'I was upset.'

They did matching sympathetic nods, but in a brief, professional way. Annette's bob swung forward and back, once. Paul's scalp hit the morning light from the window, and retreated. I thought: *Maybe they're both medium-friendly cops.*

I brought us all coffees, while Annette said they were investigating last Tuesday's crash. They knew, she said, that Imogen Banks had been at Lofton that morning. 'Can you tell us, Zoe, in your own words, about what happened?'

So, I told them. I told them the truth and nothing but the truth, and then they started with the questions.

Right, so, how did Grace Tierney seem on the phone that morning? How well did I know Emma Tierney-Adams? A poetry club? And what did that involve? Emma seemed quite vulnerable, did she? And had I ever met Grace? Had we ever socialised? Definitely, never? Not friends on social media? What prompted my call to her that morning?

'I ring parents pretty often,' I said truthfully. 'Lofton's very big on pastoral care. Emma had been a bit withdrawn, lately.'

'Did you ask Grace Tierney to come to the school?' said Paul.

'I did, yes. But from memory, it was Grace who decided to come straight away.'

There was a silence.

'Rightio.' This was Paul. 'How would you describe your relationship with Imogen Banks, Zoe?'

I told them I'd met Imogen through Nick. 'They were high school friends,' I said. 'They'd been, you know, romantically involved. In a casual way.'

'And now ...?' That was Annette.

'Just friendly.'

'I understand he'd been driving her around recently? Due to her licence suspension?'

'Yep.'

'Some women mightn't like it, if their partner was driving an ex around?'

I shrugged, very genuinely. 'I didn't mind.'

'And that morning? How did Imogen seem to you?'

'She was unhinged, like I said before. Really upset.'

'What words did she use?'

'Well.' I remembered her poor little face. 'Um. Nick and I always thought she still had kind of a crush on him.'

'You and Nick had talked about that?'

'Couple of times. We'd laughed about it, mostly.'

'Mostly?'

'He didn't treat her that well. Which he regrets. I got mad with him.'

'That so?' Paul said. 'Treated Imogen badly in what way, Zoe?'

'Casual sex.' I looked at Paul. *Ms Morello's strict look*, Nick might've joked once upon a time. 'It meant a lot more to her than to him.'

'Rightio,' said Paul, in a tone that was the neutralist version of neutral in the whole wide world. I would have bet a thousand dollars he was on Tinder.

'Thinking back to that morning ...?' Annette prompted. 'The words Imogen used?'

'She talked a lot about Nick. That he'd see through me in the end. That I was stupid and didn't deserve him. Stuff like that.'

'How did it make you feel?'

'Uncomfortable. A bit scared, even.'

'She threaten to hurt you, at all? Or Nick?'

'No,' I said. 'Definitely not. She just seemed really upset.' Tears filled my eyes. 'She was all mixed up. She said she'd needed me to be her friend but I hadn't stepped up. She said good looks didn't last forever.' *Nice breasts don't last, you fucking idiot* was what she'd actually said. *Nick and I have so much more than leg-related infatuation.*

315

'She said I wouldn't even be able to give him children. I'd, um, talked to her a bit about that side of my health.'

'I see,' said Annette. That earned me two nods. 'Had you given Imogen informal permission to access your medical record?'

'No!'

'I see.'

They didn't say anything for a moment. I wondered if I was supposed to be reading between the lines.

Paul cleared his throat. 'After you were so upset by Imogen, Zoe. Upset enough to telephone Nick. Scared enough to phone your cousin, Claire. You went to your office and *immediately* telephoned Grace Tierney? And arranged to meet her? Even though the Lofton roster had you on duty elsewhere that morning?'

'Um,' I said. 'Not exactly.'

'No?' said Annette. No more nods. No more woman-to-womany sympathy.

I swallowed. They were both looking at me.

'Imogen had threatened to tell details about a student's personal life. Her health. One of my students, Emma. And Grace was her mum. Imogen reckoned she'd found things out, about Emma, from me, but I don't know how. I honestly didn't tell Imogen anything.'

They didn't even ask me what Imogen knew about Emma. Paul just said, 'But I'll ask you again: did Imogen threaten to physically harm anyone? Did she mention Grace, at all?'

'No.'

A little while after that, they picked up their phones and their folders and said things about appreciate your frankness and sorry for your loss and we'll be back if we need to. They gave me a blue card in case I needed counselling, and a white card in case I remembered anything further. The exact same cards were already on Nick's fridge.

'I just want to put it behind me,' I said. Even though I already knew that Nick could never, ever make me as happy as he had the first time he'd oh-so-politely ordered a beer and then joked about my strict voice.

Paul nodded. It was a normal nod now. 'Very understandable.'

After they left, I leaned against my door and remembered what Imogen had said about Archie McRae.

I had never told Nick about that conversation. I would never tell Claire. Nobody would have to lie. And everybody else could tell the whole truth.

A heart-to-heart, she'd said. *As a friend.*

I felt I owed her that much. Look at what my perfect boyfriend had done to her.

And if that Archie McRae conversation ever did come to light somehow, if Imogen had written it down or told someone else about it or something, well, it was plausible that I'd been drinking wine, and that I'd been concerned about Imogen's feelings towards my partner, and then scared and upset, and that I'd been so preoccupied by all of that, that I'd clean forgotten a few technical bits and pieces she'd mentioned about some slip-up at work that I hadn't even properly understood.

Or maybe I'd get in trouble with the police. I was even prepared to risk that.

Because I was hoping that if I kept her secret, then it would somehow make me feel okay about also keeping Nick.

∞

Nick drove us home from Imogen's funeral. On the way, he rested his hand on my leg. Not sexily. Comfortingly.

He'd cried properly during the service. Hands on the back of the pew in front of him, arms straight, head bowed. People had looked.

His carry-on seemed to make them all think he was a great, sensitive bloke.

'Terrible for Nick,' a man I didn't know told me, while I took tiny, respectful bites from a curried-egg sandwich afterwards. Apart from that, nobody had mentioned a thing about the fact that Nick was right there when she died.

I looked out of the car window. We were in this industrial-type street I didn't remember ever driving through before.

'Can you take your hand off me, please?' I said.

'Sorry.' He put it on the steering wheel. Very meek.

'No. I'm sorry.' I adjusted my face into something softer. 'Just feeling kind of claustrophobic today.'

'Fair enough.'

'I *know* it's fair enough!'

Nick turned on his indicator and checked his wing mirror and pulled very carefully over. He'd already bought another ute. Airbags and fancy brakes and Bluetooth and all that. The super-clean upholstery smelled of cigarettes from the last owner.

'Zoe?' he said. There was a photocopier shop and a mechanic's. A small takeaway place with signs about chips, sandwiches and ATM/EFTPOS AVAILABLE. 'Are we okay?'

'Um,' I said. The car was so quiet with the engine off. 'I don't really know.'

'It's ... it'll be ...' He reached out to my thigh again. ''Cause what I think, Zo, we just need—'

'I said, don't *touch* me!' I jerked my legs away from him.

He flipped his hands into the air and stared down at them. Took hold of the steering wheel. Then he put his palms together in his lap.

'Sorry,' he said again.

I looked at him, in his perfect-for-the-occasion black suit. My handsome, popular boyfriend. The sweet man who'd fallen head over heels for me. I remembered back before, before that night at the movies when Imogen told her story. So much of the time I used to feel as if I was just waiting stuff out until we could finally be touching.

'It's fine,' I said fake-calmly. 'It's just that—'

It was just that Nick had shaken Damo's hand at the funeral. It was just that all I could hear in my head was Imogen's little voice, chirpily explaining how being called Rooter-Tutor was really not that big of a deal. It was just that my head knew Nick had only been sixteen, but the idea of the hands that had exploited Imogen being anywhere near me made my skin feel like slimy mud, as if I was part of the whole revolting thing.

'Zoe, is this because of Imogen? Or is it, you know, just me? Because if – shit, Zoe, Zo, Zo, please, please, don't cry, it'll be all right.' He leaned forward to hug me, remembered I wouldn't want him to and stopped with his arms half out.

I leaned into him. I cried and hugged him hard. He stroked my hair, and said sweet things, and I could tolerate it then, for some reason. The relief was wonderful. I thought: *No, see, it's fine, we're okay, I just have to relax and accept him for what he is, and then it'll all be back to normal.*

After I calmed down, he drove us to his house. Pulled into his carport. Glanced over at me.

'You right now, Zo?' he said, before he got out.

I was thinking about how I didn't need to panic, because things could still work. I simply had to get my skin to obey me.

'I'm fine!' I told him. I gave him a very big smile and then opened my door before he could touch me again.

Babies, I thought, as I went inside.

Chapter Thirty-seven

GRACE

She'd always sort of assumed that people woke up from comas all by themselves: that they squeezed a beloved hand, or whispered a treasured name, or fluttered open eyelids that had no unromantic bits of tape in the way.

But it seemed that people usually woke from comas after their intravenous sedatives were withdrawn, when a bunch of other people had had a morning meeting, and had navigated the slight annoyances and mild pleasures of being at work, and had discussed whether the withdrawing of those sedatives, and the pulling out of the breathing tube, were sensible ideas.

At that particular morning meeting – after her chest X-ray had been reviewed, and her oxygen saturation considered, and when it was established that her haemoglobin was trending up and her creatinine down, and without any of the eleven people present making any extraneous – let alone humorous – remarks at all – the decision was made.

Grace Tierney in bed four. Forty-six, splenectomy, yep, settling, yep, straightforward. She could be extubated this morning. Everyone happy? Okey-doke, good. So, the 62-year-old man in bed five ...

Which seemed to mean that Grace was all right, and that she was going to wake up.

Chapter Thirty-eight

GRACE

Two weeks after she was discharged, Grace peered out of the car window while Christopher drove towards, and then far out of, the city. He was playing God-awful music (he had an incongruous liking for 1980s-era heavy metal), but he'd clicked the volume right down. She didn't have the heart to ask him to turn it off.

After a crossroad, a sign read: 'Zero Toll Should Be YOUR Goal.' Catchy.

They passed a roadside stall selling rhubarb seedlings on an honesty system. Beige hills, dried-out fences. At an empty, white gravel carpark, one with tea-trees crowding its edges and a shouty yellow sign about rips, Christopher turned off the engine. Grey sea chopped around under an equally choppy sky.

'Is this exactly the place you meant, Grace?' he said.

She nodded, and manoeuvred her body out of the car like an old person. Emma bouncily extracted scarves and a bottle of water. Grace couldn't help but feel that the modern urge to rehydrate all the time was a little bit over the top.

'You sure you're up for this, Mum?' Emma said.

'Yep.'

'I'll wait right here,' said Christopher. He was joining them, he'd said when they planned the expedition, solely as a chauffeur. Ben was at work.

The long, long stretch of sand was wide and pale and skimmed with wind, and even though it was allegedly summer, and definitely school holidays, it was freaking freezing and nobody else was on the beach. She zipped up her coat and smiled at her daughter, and the two of them walked along in silence for a while.

'I thought we should talk about Ben,' Grace said when they were about halfway to the first headland. 'I wanted to make sure we – you – are okay. And to apologise, I guess.'

She stopped for a moment. Her energy ran out ridiculously quickly. They watched a couple of oystercatchers prance around on the sand, black feathers dull, cylindrical beaks like bright-orange cigarettes. In the far distance, two tiny figures appeared.

'I'd known for ages, Mum,' Emma said. Gently, though.

'It was just that other people were involved, sweetie.'

'You still should have told me.' A flash of hurt. Of that specific type of childishness that so furiously resented being treated like a child.

'I'm so sorry you had to find out the way you did.'

But for the first time, it occurred to Grace that even at her deceitful worst, she'd been simply a person, loving, being loved, soaking that up when she could, accepting her own agony – without question – as background noise. 'I really was trying so hard to do the right thing by everyone.'

Emma nodded. They started walking again. The oystercatchers ignored them.

'Why didn't *you* get married to him?' Well, there was the question.

'He didn't ask me.' And there was the answer. 'He always had other girlfriends, sort of, and then he fell in love with his wife, ex-wife, with Louise, and they moved away. But we'd see each other now and again and we …' She paused and looked at Emma. Was even that too much? What girl wanted to hear these sorts of details about her *mother*? 'Sweetie, things like this are very complex.'

'Well, *I* will never do that.' Emma spoke with the air of a teacher who could make even very complex concepts accessible. 'Get with someone who's *married*.' Her cheeks were confident, with their vast reserves of undiminished collagen.

'Good idea,' Grace said humbly. 'Do not do it.'

She tried to allow the wind to blow away her confusion about what else to say – God, she was turning into her *own* mother – but it didn't work that well.

'It's not like I didn't know it was wrong and stupid,' she tried.

'Yeah, I know.'

'It's not like I wasn't ashamed.'

'I get it, Mum.'

'I just always really loved him. And, well, him me. That was always the main thing.'

The two tiny figures were coming closer, and now she saw they were a brisk, elderly woman, throwing her Labrador a ball from one of those ball-throwing contraptions everyone had these days. A young woman, a jogger in a black visor with a white tick on it, had also appeared from somewhere.

'Hey, Mum?' Emma said. She took off her beanie and ran her fingers through her hair. 'You know I'm not, like, cured now, don't you?'

'Of course,' said Grace. Although, it had actually crossed her mind that all this might help a bit. All the openness and release. Not to mention all the subtext about shame and imperfection and forgiveness.

'I really wish I was.' A sweet little glance, leaning forward, tilting her head under a slant of sun to catch Grace's eye. 'Cured.'

She spoke the word the way Grace's mother used to sigh 'John' whenever a Beatles song came on the radio. So loving and longing. So aware of carrying a sorrow that uncounted, unknown others carried too.

'I know, sweetheart. I wish that as well.' Grace bit back the urge to add an anxious, *Although, I love you whether you've recovered or not*, and instead said, 'But it's probably going to be a pretty long, hard road.'

'God, Mother.' But Emma was smiling, and she gave Grace's arm a friendly, woolly flick with her beanie. 'You sound exactly like *Embracing You*.'

Grace started laughing. And in a way that really, really, really hurt her chest.

Chapter Thirty-nine

ZOE

Nick and I lasted until the autumn.

For Christmas, he organised a trip to Cairns for us. I said, 'Wow, that'll be great.'

Towards the end of February, he said maybe I should move in with him when my lease ran out. I said that sounded lovely.

About a week after that, he made my favourite dinner. Spaghetti bolognaise. Nick's spaghetti bolognaise was the best. Full of bacon and garlic and pre-roasted onion.

'This is amazing,' I told him. I'd put on earrings, even though we weren't going out, and a black top I knew he liked me in. I'd rubbed vitamin E cream into my legs and I'd caught myself thinking: *Well, I'm going to have to have sex with him at* some *point.* 'So nice and garlicky. Really amazing!'

'Good. You look beautiful, by the way.'

I glugged wine straight down onto my feelings. 'You're not too shabby yourself.'

We smiled at each other, both of us so brave and so hopeful. Nick touched the inside of my wrist. I moved my hands and picked up the salt.

'Zo?' he said, after a few seconds. I had the salt grinder sort of poised over my food. Not grixxing any salt out. 'What's the matter?'

I put the salt onto the table, and rested my forehead onto all my fingertips. My feelings were impossible beasts, but my thoughts were as clear and hard and finished as a diamond ring.

'I don't think I can really do this,' I said. I rubbed my knuckles across my mouth. 'Be with you, I mean.'

'What?' He stopped chewing.

I knew I wouldn't be able to bear lying there, later, waiting dully for him to finish the whole thing. And if I let his hands and his mouth and his jagged breath make me forget – if I got into it – then that would be so very much worse.

So I said something stupid about how I was sorry for all his trouble with the meal and that I'd get an Uber now and maybe I could come and grab my stuff in a day or two, and while Nick was telling me how he wasn't pressuring me, and he was sorry, and I could take all the time in the world, because he loved me, that was the thing, he loved me the most he'd ever loved any woman, I suddenly and irrelevantly understood why Daniel had gone on about financial disadvantage and hydroelectricity and the spare room being *spacious*.

You said that kind of stuff just to give yourself something normal to say.

∞

It was worse than Daniel. So much worse, and for so many reasons.

I didn't date. I didn't do ceramics. I just went to work, and came home, and when April rolled around and Claire had her babies, I cooked casseroles and cleaned her house. I burped Django, who guzzled like crazy and then sicked half of it back up, and rocked Stella, who fell asleep while she was feeding and then woke after twenty minutes. Not that any of those details were endearing. They were just life-facts, like that petrol was more expensive than it used to be and you were better off wearing sunscreen every day.

The twins weren't even particularly cute. They were *odd*, the way their heads were so lolling and their eyes were so googly and their skin was sort of mottled and purple.

I thought: *Nick and I would have had prettier babies.*

I didn't really believe that. I was just trying the thought on, like a dress you know you'll never buy.

∞

We basically had only family at the twins' naming ceremony, but a couple of months later, on a Sunday, Claire was having a nap and T-rex was off somewhere or other. I was in the middle of cleaning their bathroom, and I opened their front door to find Nick. He was holding a microwave. A bare tree behind him looked like it was growing out of his head.

I was pretty sure from his face that he hadn't expected to see me.

'Come in,' I said. He'd put on the tiniest trace of weight. 'Maybe just pop it on the table.'

Turned out he was swapping microwaves with T-rex and Claire for a while, because of something to do with night feeds and the dinger on theirs being too loud. It occurred to me that maybe Nick visited them and had coffee, or a beer, or dinner, when I wasn't there.

'Okay!' I said, when he'd capably unplugged their microwave and capably wiped the bench under it, and then capably plugged his own microwave into their wall. 'I'll tell them. Thanks!'

I opened their front door for him.

Claire found me sitting on the hall floor crying. She had Django in her arms already, and she stood, rocking him, and looking at me.

'I think it might be time you got some help, Zo,' she said. Not in her psychologisty voice. In a worried voice. 'With, you know, grieving.'

I didn't know what else she expected from me. I was celibate and hobbyless and barely getting through the motions at work. I was wearing bathroom-cleaning clothes and sitting on her floor with snot hanging off my chin.

She knelt down in front of me, still being careful to keep Django upright. 'I mean,' she said, 'about the baby thing.'

'Did you *know* Nick was coming today?' I sounded much angrier than I meant to.

She said no, that she'd never do that to me.

'Okay. Well.' I wiped my cheeks with my hands and my nose with my sleeve. 'I'm fine, Claire.' I sniffed a very loud sniff. 'And isn't that Stella waking up?' As if she was a terrible mother.

Claire lowered her chin so we were eye to eye. Her knees must have hurt on the boards, and she had pale criss-crosses on her temple from the pillow.

'Stella's not your concern, Zo,' she said, very gently, and with tears in her eyes.

∞

One lunchtime when the staffroom was nearly empty, I asked Sophie what she reckoned. I thought she'd say Claire was being bossy and looking for psychological problems where there weren't any, but she said, 'Sheesh, Zo, aren't you seeing anyone?'

It took ages to get in, and I expected it to be rubbish, but the psychologist was called Martin, and even though it took me a while to warm up to him, partly due to his German accent, he was pretty good. There was not a speck of dust in his office, and he had a peace lily that was thriving, and his certificate glass was polished. I liked all that.

One day, I talked about how, when I was a teenager, I'd thought I'd never do anything as pathetic as want a *partner*. How I'd assumed the grown-up me would be flawed, but only in a careless, lovable, too-authentic-and-self-reliant-for-my-own-good kind of way. Fending off fulfilling job offers and hilarious friends, and far too busy to care about men. Just having excellent sex with a few gorgeous ones who worshipped me, so as to fulfil my passionate needs.

'Do you know anyone like that?' he said. There was a vase of wattle on the shelf behind him, that day.

I said I didn't. Martin nodded. He said he liked to call that kind of thinking a heroine fantasy.

Then I told him how I'd also imagined the grown-up me in a frumpy coat, cheering embarrassingly at under-ten footy games. Stressily spraying little ballerinas with far too much hairspray. Putting my foot down with teenagers about homework and parties, and with my husband about having his cholesterol checked. I'd believed I'd do all that, but also, I'd thought I'd be kind of eye-rolly about it.

'You wanted it, but you didn't know how much?' Martin said. 'Is that what you mean?'

I started crying then, for some reason. 'I know it's not the same as losing a real child,' I said-sobbed.

'It's still a loss,' he said. 'A potentially huge loss. I can only imagine.'

The way he said that, at first in such an expertish voice, and then the last sentence in such a human voice, made me feel very sad.

'I don't want people *not* to talk about their kids.' I was crying too much even to blow my nose. 'But I don't want them *to* talk about them, either.'

Martin said, 'That's a very common feeling.' He patted my arm. Hearing him say my feelings were common made me feel annoyed, but better, too.

At a different session, when he had no flowers on his shelf, we talked about Nick and Imogen.

I talked about how I loved Nick, so much, and how I had this feeling that maybe we *could* have made a family together, but that my mind hadn't been able to get past the whole Imogen high school thing. I didn't say anything about the police. They'd asked for a sworn statement, and then never come back.

Martin nodded. He seemed to think I had taken on some of Imogen's trauma, and that because of her death, and the manner of her death, the taking-on had been heightened.

'Do you think I did the right thing?' I said. 'Breaking up with Nick?'

Martin said that depended on what I wanted. 'The question is probably not whether or not Nick could have made you happy. It's probably whether or not he could make you happy now, knowing what you know about his past.'

I knew, very clearly, that he couldn't. I'd scrambled against that reality since the night Imogen first told me about Rooter-Tutor, while I sat there with chocolate peanuts melting all over my hands, and a slippery sort of terror crawling from my ears down to my pelvis.

I told Martin about the time Nick made that delicious lamb curry, the evening we did our happy-couple banter and talked about my IVF and going along the kids road together. We'd had sex, later that night. He'd been so loving and so into it, and I'd felt so pretty and so sick.

I said, 'I'd honestly rather be miserable without Nick than sort of sick-happy with him.'

'Well, then.' Martin made a face, like: *So, there's your answer. Sorry I can't gussy it up any better for you, even though I've got a lot of certificates.*

'Life goes on, though,' I said, after a minute. 'I guess?'

'Life goes on,' Martin replied. He had a nice twinkle in his eyes, as if he agreed it was pretty funny that I was paying ninety-eight dollars out-of-pocket to have him confirm that. 'It certainly does.' Then he added, 'And you probably already know the one about fishes and seas.'

I felt quite a lot better that day.

And it's not like I was suddenly cured of the pain, or of wanting kids of my own, or of anything. It's not like a hero came galloping in and made everything all right, either. But the next Thursday, when Stella tipped a bowl of pumpkin moosh over her own head and did a really proud grin, I at least didn't have to fake my laugh in the slightest.

Chapter Forty

They were sitting at the breakfast table, as if they were in a play.

Whenever Grace said, 'Can you pass the jam, please?' or, 'Want more juice, Em?' her voice came out sort of absurd, like she was a bad actor trying to imbue ordinary words with deep inner motivation. (*But how does my character* feel *about this fancy croissant?*) It was as if she was pretending to be a happy, relaxed bride, despite the fact that she *was* a happy, relaxed bride. At least mostly.

She was about to be married in her – their – garden, even though garden weddings were an extremely high-stakes proposition at any time, but especially in autumn. And yes, the poplars across the way were a glorious yellow, and yes, the mountain was glowing like a luminous deity, but the pale-blue sky had grey smudges at its edges, and now that it was too late, Grace saw that Ben and Emma and Christopher and Maria had been right all along. They should have hired a hotel or a winery and let a professional boss them around.

('You're being too self-deprecating, Mum,' Emma had announced months ago, with her mouth full of vegetarian pizza. 'It's like you think you don't *deserve* a proper wedding.' 'Don't give me that crap!' Grace had snapped through her mozzarella, even though she'd been wondering along those very lines herself.) (Emma had just started university; she wanted to be a psychologist. It was going to be a long few years, Grace felt. In a very delighted way, obviously.)

All three of Ben's kids were coming today, which was a triumph. Jasmine had been warm and adorable almost from the beginning – smiling at Emma and making conversation about music in a way so full of seriousness and *understanding* that Grace had been deeply ashamed of her beautiful-mean-girl assumptions – and Tom had been so malleable and so into Minecraft that his opinion of Grace kind of hadn't mattered. But Lauren had done everything Grace had feared. That first year, she'd returned Ben's Christmas gift and birthday card unopened. But time had passed, and when Lauren had RSVP'd that she would be 'able' to attend their wedding, Ben had read out her entire text to Grace and then added, 'And she's put an "x" at the end.' (His eyes had filled. Heightened emotion, presumably.)

She brushed croissant crumbs off her dressing gown, peered at her disappointingly already-empty coffee cup and then frowned out of the window at the clouds.

'It'll be fine, Mum,' said Emma. 'Forecast's good. Go get dressed.'

She had allowed Emma to talk her into a whitish dress, and Jasmine had made suggestions about shoes and earrings and hair with *exactly* the easy authority Ben used on work calls. Grace had gone along with her advice out of politeness – she secretly thought Jasmine was too beautiful to understand how clothes even worked for normal people, and she had no idea what was meant by 'a nod to metallics' or 'an undone vibe, only polished' – but she had to admit that her outfit was much better for Jasmine's input.

Anyway, now she was ready.

In the garden, coin-sized leaves drifted like confetti, and the fresh gravel pathway she'd last-minute decided on was dark grey and clean. The man who'd delivered the stones had said, 'For a wedding, yeah?' with at least a small amount of interest. 'Have a good one.'

People seemed so *excited* for Ben and her, so genuinely pleased. Off near the recently zhoozhed-up roses, Emma's bestie, Amy, had set up a white-clothed bar for cocktails afterwards; Amy'd sent Grace at least six texts about the menu. She was chatting brightly to Maria, who was wearing the darker of the two new dresses she'd bought. ('So as to be flexible with the mood, and the weather, you know autumn, I'll want to get it just right.')

Grace held Emma's hand, and as they arrived at the little knot of people under the biggest tree, the violin's tune seemed to travel slowly to her ears. The air was cool and still on her neck, and the morning light gentle on the grass.

Emma squeezed her fingers, shot her a complicit smile, and went and stood next to Christopher. (Christopher was beaming. He had a spotted handkerchief in his upper pocket. Dear Christopher.)

And here was Ben, in what appeared to be a secretly purchased new black suit. He had a tenderness on his face, as if he thought the two of them already remembered today in just the same way, and as the preposterously young celebrant drew in her breath, Grace was seeing not only this Ben with his deepening dimples, but Ben as he was in her memories.

The very first time she spoke to him, puzzling down at a *paper* university timetable; their second proper kiss, how he'd stood back from her, wiped his mouth with the side of his forearm and looked so young and so stricken; him walking away from her gate the day he told her about Louise; urbane and miserable at that aborted lunch; standing by the fancy hotel's sink holding his toothbrush by his side after the first time they slept together; half kneeling next to her hospital bed, messy-haired and (once again) stricken; just a few weeks ago, while she grumped around getting ready for work, and he told her for no apparent reason that he loved her 'a truly sickening amount'.

She saw how in memory, *feelings* didn't blur. They became clearer, if anything, more inescapably obvious.

And now Ben was smiling at her. On their solidly – and also ludicrously – happy wedding day. Everyone was smiling, in fact, for them and with them.

Which was why she didn't care that much about her hair, or her shoes, and why the photos didn't matter to her in the slightest. Because when she looked back on today, Ben would be there, and Emma. All the people who meant the most to them would be there, and through memory's clear lens, her inner life would feel exactly (or at least *almost* exactly) the way her outer life looked.

And both of those lives would be smiling.

A report

CORONIAL COURT OF TASMANIA
INQUIRY INTO A DEATH
Pursuant to *Coronial and Other Act 1991*
Section 16(IV)

I, Janet Sethby, Coroner, having investigated the death of Imogen Camilla Banks, find, having regard to Section 18(2) of the *Coronial and Other Act 1991*, that:

1. The identity of the deceased is Imogen Camilla Banks.
2. Dr Banks died as a result of multiple blunt traumatic injuries sustained in a motor vehicle crash on Tuesday 29 November in Hobart, Tasmania.

Background
Imogen Banks was aged thirty-four years at the time of her death. She suffered from a seizure disorder, for which she was prescribed the medication sodium valproate. She lived alone and was employed as a resident medical officer at the Southern Tasmania Hospital, where she was regarded as a conscientious, punctual and knowledgeable staff member.

Dr Banks had completed nine evening shifts (2 pm to midnight) approximately thirty-two hours prior to the collision. She had been noted by neighbours to have difficulty sleeping after these shifts.

On Tuesday 29 November, at approximately 8.40 am, Dr Banks was driving her white 2018 Volkswagen Golf hatchback in a southerly direction on Wellington Road, Hobart. Her destination is unknown.

Grace Tierney, a 46-year-old veterinary surgeon, was driving her red 2016 Mazda3 hatchback on the same road in the opposite direction. She was on her way to the Lofton School, where her child, E, was a secondary student. This followed her having received a phone call from a Lofton School teacher, Ms Zoe Morello, expressing concern as to E's wellbeing.

Both drivers were alone in their vehicles.

As Dr Banks approached the southern end of Wellington Road, her car travelled wholly onto the incorrect (northbound) side of the road.

One northbound vehicle veered left onto a grass verge adjacent to its lane. This vehicle was driven by Mr Nicholas Kavanagh, a 34-year-old self-employed builder, who was well known to the deceased. He was driving a white 2004 Toyota Hilux and was uninjured.

Dr Banks's Volkswagen briefly continued in the northbound lane, where it collided with Grace Tierney's Mazda.

Dr Banks died at the scene.

Grace Tierney was transported by ambulance to the Southern Tasmania Hospital with significant injuries.

Standard methodology was used to investigate. This included the use of a drone for photography purposes, the impoundment of the vehicles involved, the taking of sworn statements from witnesses and the cordoning-off of the scene.

Due to the nature of this crash, sworn statements from

multiple acquaintances and workmates of the deceased were sought. These were presented as evidence.

Key events preceding the crash

It is the testimony of Zoe Morello and Nicholas Kavanagh that Dr Banks was a former intimate partner of Nicholas Kavanagh, and, at the time of the crash, a platonic friend of both his and Zoe Morello's. Both (and other) parties conjectured in evidence that Dr Banks wished for an intimate relationship with Nicholas Kavanagh.

Shortly before the crash, Dr Banks attended the Lofton School carpark where Ms Zoe Morello was employed. The two had a brief conversation, the substance of which was that Dr Banks expressed significant distress at Zoe Morello's close relationship with Nicholas Kavanagh.

Dr Banks also divulged knowledge of Lofton student, E's medical history, which she threatened to disclose, with the apparent intention of discrediting Zoe Morello. Dr Banks alleged Zoe Morello had breached student confidentiality with regard to E. I can find no evidence to suggest such a breach occurred.

I accept police evidence that the evening before her death, Dr Banks attended her workplace at the Southern Tasmania Hospital and accessed the medical record of E, of one other Lofton School student (also a student of Zoe Morello's) and of Zoe Morello herself. Dr Banks was not rostered to work, but deposited a plate of baked items in the staff room before 'logging on' to the relevant database.

A Lofton School yearbook, several photographs of unidentified students in Lofton School uniform, and an extensive internet search history of persons and places associated with Zoe Morello and her family, were found among the deceased's effects. Evidence suggested Dr Banks had purchased costly ceramics magazines for the express purpose of lending them to Zoe Morello.

I note that the deceased was professionally acquainted with Dr Benjamin Hutchinson, also known to Grace Tierney. Dr Benjamin Hutchinson, by acting as referee, had assisted the deceased to obtain a prestigious research position at Oxford University.

I can find no evidence that the deceased otherwise knew, wished to know, or had ever approached either E or Grace Tierney or the other Lofton School student whose medical record was accessed.

The deceased was repeatedly described as a kind and caring woman who was somewhat socially isolated. I can find no evidence that she at any time made threats to physically harm Zoe Morello, Nicholas Kavanagh or any other party.

Traffic investigation

I accept police evidence that the road where the accident occurred had no obstructions and was dry, and that the border between north- and southbound lanes would have been clearly visible to an alert driver. Speed analysis indicates to my satisfaction that speed was not a factor in this crash. Likewise, I am satisfied that both people involved were wearing correctly adjusted seatbelts. I note that the airbags fitted to the vehicles of Grace Tierney and Dr Banks deployed. Both vehicles had mobile phones legally placed in commercially installed holders, and there were no obvious sources of driver distraction at the time of the collision.

I am satisfied that at the time of the crash, Dr Banks's

vehicle was in the incorrect lane. The vehicle driven by Grace Tierney was in its correct lane. The fatal crash occurred wholly within Grace Tierney's lane.

I am satisfied that Dr Banks was driving unlicensed at the time of the collision, having had her driver's licence revoked on the grounds of her unstable seizure disorder.

Biopsychosocial investigation
Samples from the deceased's body were analysed. A small amount of caffeine, but no alcohol and no illicit drugs were found.

No prescription drugs were identified as being present.

This suggests that Dr Banks had *not* ingested her prescribed anti-seizure medication for some days, and its therapeutic effect would have been non-existent on the day of the crash.

The state pathologist was unable to determine whether or not a seizure took place immediately prior to the collision. No other medical cause for any lapse of consciousness by Dr Banks was apparent at autopsy.

The evidence suggests that Dr Banks was significantly fatigued at the time of the collision. I accept the medical evidence that fatigue may, in general, trigger a seizure of the type from which Dr Banks suffered.

Evidence suggests that the deceased was in a distressed emotional state on the morning of the collision.

I am unable to determine whether Dr Banks identified Nicholas Kavanagh's vehicle before her own vehicle left its lane. I accept the evidence of the Registrar of Motor Vehicles that vehicles the same or similar in appearance to Nicholas Kavanagh's white Toyota Hilux are common.

I can find no evidence that Dr Banks had any means of identifying Grace Tierney's vehicle, nor can I find that she had any motive for harming Grace Tierney.

I can find no evidence that the deceased was suffering from suicidality. I note her medical records do not suggest any history of mental illness.

There is thus insufficient evidence to conclude that Dr Banks's vehicle moved into the incorrect lane voluntarily.

Conclusion

I find that neither Grace Tierney nor Nicholas Kavanagh were in any way responsible for the collision.

I cannot determine, on the evidence, why it was that Dr Banks's vehicle crossed into the incorrect lane and thus into the path of Grace Tierney's vehicle.

I cannot rule out that her vehicle crossed into the northbound lane voluntarily.

However, I find that:

- Dr Banks's non-compliance with medication and a consequent seizure,
- and Dr Banks's non-compliance with driver's-licence restrictions

are *likely* contributing causes of her death.

In this setting, I find that the deceased's own actions were likely causative of this tragedy.

I extend my condolences to her family.

A final little message from Imogen

Ah well.

Not everyone gets a happy ending, and there certainly wasn't one for me!

I was not a heroine. The reason I know that, is because heroines are effortlessly beautiful and effortlessly wonderful, and even their flaws are lovable.

In hindsight, I would have saved us all a lot of trouble if I'd realised that I wasn't heroine material right from the get-go. Heroines' mistakes have to be relatable. Their authenticity has to be *fun*. And heroines have to be at least somewhat pretty, and all that without trying too hard.

I was always destined to be one of the women in the background. You know the sort. We are the ones in outfits that don't quite work; we have nervous smiles and painstaking posture and not enough hobbies of our own. The hero deals with eager women like us politely, while he watches the heroine. Just like in that movie I saw with Zoe, the night I told her about Rooter-Tutor. I really didn't mean to upset her quite as much as I did.

But there is something else you might like to know, because unless you are an utter cretin, you've probably been baffled about why a person of my calibre was still an emergency-department resident at thirty-four years of age.

And why I would go off to Oxford to fiddle about with mice in a molecular genetics laboratory, right around the time Nick finally got rid of Know-nothing Nova.

Well.

That's really quite a story.

But in summary, some years ago, a certain Hobart cardiologist took it into his head that I was unsuited to specialist training. Because of his toxic backbiting and interference, which he tried to pass off as 'concern', my clinical career was stymied. It was so humiliating! Dad was so Cross! And I ended up being forced to leave Nick at such a crucial time!

Our love eventually drew me home, despite the fact that it meant I had to putter about in a lowly little job that, as mentioned, was also extremely stressful.

I was not out for revenge or anything of that nature. But I am sure you know me well enough to guess that I kept my eye on that cardiologist. Benjamin Hutchinson.

Turned out, he had a particular house he liked to visit, one that always had a red Mazda3 in its driveway. He would park his own vehicle three blocks away and walk to a side gate in the dark, even though that involved a very steep hill. Once, after he left, he sat in his car and rested his head on his steering wheel for seven minutes. It was impossible to say for sure, but he might have been crying. I felt sorry for him, actually.

It would have been moderately easy to identify whomever lived behind that side gate, but with everything else that was going on, I simply didn't have time for the research. Life got soooo busy, as Zoe would say.

So, it was a big surprise that the side-gate woman's daughter turned out to be Emma Tierney-Adams. I didn't make the connection until things came to a head with Zoe. Then, when I was researching the

Lofton students' hospital files, I realised Emma and her unwise mother lived at the side-gate address.

So serendipitous! Up to two birds with one stone! For any idiots, the 'birds' were: protect my career from Zoe, or discredit Zoe and disgrace Benjamin Hutchinson.

Of course, I hadn't planned the ending. Nobody could possibly plan for that.

But you know me. I simply saw that red Mazda3 behind Nick's ute and seized my opportunity, even though it involved significant self-sacrifice. I was not a vengeful person, but at the same time, I was nothing if not resourceful. And fortune favours the bold.

Poor Emma Tierney-Adams, losing her mother so young. That was my very last thought.

I may not have been a heroine, but I was nothing if not compassionate.

A letter

Dear Mr and Mrs Banks,

My name is Tina McRae, and your daughter, Dr Imogen Banks, looked after my little boy, Archie, when he was in hospital. I saw in the news about her, but at the time of her accident, I was not able to write because Archie was so very sick.

But he is all better now, thanks to amazing luck and to people like your beautiful daughter!

Dr Imogen looked after my Archie early on, and she was just such a kind, lovely, caring, sweet and nice doctor. She came and sat with me and Archie in the children's ward, even though that wasn't part of her job. She knew I was worried and she took the time to answer all my questions thoroughly, even though there were so many other sick people needing her help, and I could tell that she was extremely dedicated and smart, and she was trying so hard to help all her patients. Not everyone is like that, just so you know.

I hope you don't mind me writing.

With very best wishes, and all our sympathy for your loss, and love,

From Tina and Aaron McCrae, and also Chloe, Declan, and most of all, ARCHIE

Acknowledgements

Thank you to Tegan Morrison, Katie Meegan and Alexandra Nahlous for their editorial expertise. Thank you also to Juliet Rogers, Diana Hill, Lizzie Hayes and the rest of the wonderful team at Echo–Bonnier who helped produce and promote this book, and to Christa Moffitt for the fab cover.

Thank you to Katie Daniels for her always-insightful comments, and (with her doctor hat on) for answering my nit-picky questions about brain scans. Thank you to Leonie Elizabeth for telling me all about running a small business like Grace's. I'm indebted to Chelsea Harris for her long-ago dinner-table remark about mascara down to nipples, which Zoe appropriated. Thank you to the extraordinary Farida Khawaja for telling me about life as an emergency department specialist, Anthony McMahon for advice about cars and much else, Ian McMahon for editorial opinion, Robert McMahon for football know-how, Dave McNamara for information about violins at weddings and Finnian River for reviewing the high-school scenes. Thank you to Nerida Warburg for so kindly telling me about working as a vet. Any mistakes are mine, obviously.

Not everyone who helped with this book wanted to be named: deep gratitude to those people as well.

I spent a lot of time reading (harrowing) coronial findings as handed down by the Magistrates Court of Tasmania, in order to understand what such reports do and the tone and language used. The coronial court and legislation alluded to in this book are made up; poetic licence has been taken with the format and scope of the fictional coronial report. Similarly, *Embracing You* and *Key Principles of Emergency Medicine* are fictional books, although they each have quite a lot of non-fictional cousins.

Hobart is a cosy city; it really does have only a handful of hospitals and secondary schools. That is part of what makes it fun to write about, but I also worry that readers might think I'm having a crack at particular individuals or places. I'm not. All the institutions and people in this book are entirely fictional. Mt Wellington-kunanyi and the Waterworks Reserve are real (and lovely).

The following publications were helpful in my research:

Everymind (2021) *Guidelines on reporting and portrayal of eating disorders: A Mindframe resource for communicators*. Newcastle, Australia

Janet Treasure, Grainne Smith and Anna Crane (2017) *Skills-based caring for a loved one with an eating disorder*

Various publications from the Butterfly Foundation, a support and advocacy group for those affected by eating disorders, were also helpful.

Thank you to the writers and readers and booksellers who have supported my work. It means a huge amount.

I'm very grateful for all my wonderfully encouraging and fun, funny friends, in particular Katie Daniels, Claire Donohue, Lianne Haddad and Gillian Tsaousidis.

Thank you to all my beloved, warm, wonderful extended family. I truly am so fortunate.

And to the kids and Phill: you know what I mean already. Hashtag verybigthanks.

People living with or affected by eating disorders can access help.

In Australia, contact the Butterfly Foundation at butterfly.org.au or ring the national helpline on 1800 33 4673

In the UK, support is available from the UK's eating disorder charity, Beat. Head to beateatingdisorders.org.uk

If you enjoyed *The Accident*, why not try
the author's debut . . .

The Mistake

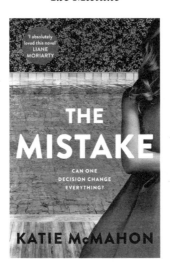

*I couldn't believe that Bec would, after all these years,
bring the whole thing up so … casually.*

Bec and Kate are sisters, but they couldn't be less alike.

Bec lives the domestic dream with her surgeon husband Stuart and
three perfect children. So why is she so attracted to free-spirited Ryan?

Kate's life is hardly a dream. But when she meets Adam – tall,
kind, funny – things start looking up. Until she finds
out he's been keeping secrets from her.

Then there's the incident both sisters are desperate to ignore . . .
Will they discover that some mistakes can't be put right?

Available now, read on for a sneak peek …

Bec

I never thought of myself as smug. That's the really humiliating bit.

I didn't plaster a BRIARWOOD: INDEPENDENT AND OUTSTANDING sticker on our car's back window. ('Not everyone needs to know where you go to school, darlings.')

I wore my engagement ring – of course I was going to wear it – but my wedding band was as discreet and unassuming as a light switch.

I was careful never to mention how easily I fell pregnant (yes, all three times) or that, after twelve years of marriage, Stuart and I still had sex at least once a week. I didn't say things like, 'The kids are doing long-haul so much better these days' or, 'My dermatologist is excellent, but I'm too much of a scaredy-cat for filler before forty'. (Those are actual quotes from the school gate, by the way. You can see where my baseline was.)

I thought I was way too humble and sensitive and *grounded* for any of that sort of talk. And anyway, I felt the opposite of smug. I felt like someone who had to try really hard just to manage the minimum.

But I was smug. Insufferably.

Lots of people probably think I got exactly what was coming to me.

And I agree with them.

Kate

Mum once said Bec was the easy one. Even when we were little, she was one of those people who never put a foot out of line. At least not deliberately.

But when she makes a mistake, it's a really, really big one.

Chapter One

Kate

Eventually, I decided to try online dating.

'So,' I said, casual as anything, 'I'm going on Tinder.'

It goes to show how strong the urge to procreate is, because just about everything I'd heard about internet hook-ups was bad. Stories about ghosting and photos and genuinely frightening weirdos. It was almost enough to make you look back with fondness on the days of smoke-filled nightclubs where your bottom was pinched by simple, honest menfolk with beery breath and heads like red capsicums.

'Oh right,' Bec said. 'Aren't you on it already?'

We were talking on the phone, and I could tell she was cooking dinner. She sounded a bit distracted: probably worried she'd accidentally put non-organic kale in the kids' frittata.

'Well, if you meet someone nice, you can bring him to Stu's fortieth. As your plus-one.'

Hearing Bec use the term 'plus-one' without irony was almost enough to make me cry. I loved my sister, but honestly, there were moments when I felt I didn't know her anymore.

In any case, I didn't want a 'plus-one' for social events. I also didn't want: walks along the beach, red wine in front of fires, or even sperm for my (no doubt rapidly dwindling) 39-year-old supply of eggs. I was just yearning, absolutely yearning, to have sex. (Intercourse, to be more specific.)

Of course I know – believe me, I know – that intercourse is Just One Of The Many Ways Human Beings Can Enjoy Their Sexuality. But I felt I'd fully explored my personal sexual identity – if you catch my drift – and it was well past time to involve someone else. A man, in my case.

Anyway, the yearning. For skin and touch and eye contact and that quiet, concentrated breathing. For the way some men know how to look at you and say – all level and effective – 'God, I want you' or 'Been dying to get you alone' or something like that. It hardly matters what they say. It's all in the tone. And I wanted to wake up with urgent hands on me. I wanted to be undressed. I wanted to be dragged across a bed. But you just can't say stuff like that to someone who uses the term 'plus-one' in general conversation.

'Ha! Maybe,' I said instead. 'Listen, I'd better go.'

I hung up, feeling a bit sad, as if I'd given someone a really thoughtful present that they hadn't bothered to open. But it was hardly Bec's fault she didn't know what was going on with me.

Far below my apartment windows, Melbourne gleamed. Lights were starting to come on: they snaked along the coast, all the way around Port Phillip Bay. So many headlights. So many houses and banks and football grounds and beaches and delis and trams and apartments and offices and building sites.

I will go on as many dates as it takes, I thought, until I find one man to have sex with. The only criteria are that I must want to have sex with him, and he must want to have sex with me.

I would give it three months, then reassess.

I wasn't optimistic.

∞

'Kate!' said Juliet. 'There will be right-swiping a go-go! You'll have so much fun!'

Juliet – my main Melbourne confidante, given Bec lives in Hobart

357

– is enthusiastic about most things, especially if they have to do with me. She is extremely kind.

'I'm putting just my face in my photo,' I said, looking at my cauliflower salad.

Juliet chewed a cherry tomato. (We were having lunch at a café with second-hand chairs, butterscotch walls and a we'll-accept-you-even-if-you-eat-gluten vibe.)

'Whatever you're comfortable with.' She used a strident tone, as if someone had suggested I should do something I was uncomfortable with, and pushed her hair out of her face. She has curly red hair, like Nicole Kidman's was before Hollywood.

Just then her phone rang. Juliet is a travel agent. You would think that travel agents would have all perished of the internet, but a few of them hang on, battered and defiant. They are like survivors in a ye olde English village after the Black Death has galloped through. (The reason Juliet survived is the high-end retiree market. Her clients are elderly, but not sweet, easily-fobbed-off, grateful-for-any-old-rubbish-because-at-least-it's-not-The-War elderly. More like: 'I'm paying top dollar for this Northern Lights helicopter jaunt, so why is the Moët non-vintage?' elderly.)

'So when's your first date?' said Juliet, when she'd finished explaining to the man on the phone why he didn't want a balcony the size of a postage stamp.

'You sure? About just my face in the photo?'

'You don't owe anyone anything.' She gave me a sweet smile, then started eating fast. She would have an appointment to talk about Copenhagen, Iceland or Budapest at two.

'All right,' I said.

'Just don't show your bazookas,' she added, with her mouth full. 'Tinder would actually burst into flames.'

That's Juliet. Exceptionally kind.

∞

Two weeks later, both Bec and Juliet had texted to ask me if I had met any 'cuties' (Bec) or 'contenders' (Juliet).

No luck yet, I texted back, to both of them. I sent the emoji with the crossed eyes, as if the whole thing was a hilarious adventure.

I didn't know how to tell them there's a certain look men get. It's the look that probably crosses your face when you think you've spotted an amazingly good deal and then realise you missed a zero on the price tag, or when you grasp that the $14 is per oyster, not per six oysters. And that's the look from the *polite* men – the ones with nice mums and dads, the ones who weren't the coolest boys in school.

The others – the ones used to getting their own way – look annoyed, as if they've been duped by a shoddy naturopath into buying herbs that do nothing. Date Number Seven fake-yawned as I said, 'Hello.' So I'd know it was a fake yawn, he raised four straight fingers to his wide-open mouth and gave his lips several slow taps. Date Twelve – cuffs flipped back revealing tanned wrists – looked at his watch as I sat down and said, 'I need to be elsewhere.' He gave his head a little shake, the way you might when your team loses because the referee made a stupid decision.

On the way home that night I remembered the time David Hillman – the film producer – invited me out for Italian and I said no. I told him it was because I was off to New York in the morning, but really it was because he pulls his shirt collars out over the necklines of his jumpers. (That's a really bad look; I stand by my judgement there. Even he couldn't pull it off. And he still wears them like that, too; I saw him interviewed recently. Handsome as ever. He's aging well.)

I listened to a podcast the other day, about aging. Some women thought it was easier to age if you hadn't been good-looking to start with. You would have based your self-esteem and your sense of identity on your intelligence or your sense of humour or your kind heart or whatever. But other women thought that it was easier to age if you'd been hot in your youth. They said that hotties, having been hot for their allotted two decades (late-teens to late-thirties, or thereabouts) inevitably realised the limitations of hotness. They saw through it. Understood hotness never buys happiness.

I wondered if I would, eventually, have come to believe that.

∞

Adam Cincotta was the seventeenth date. No one can say I don't persevere.

We met at a newish restaurant with good black-and-white drawings on the walls and sensible – by which I mean dim – lighting. It was crowded, but not too noisy. Well-designed acoustics. I was wearing a pale-green mohair sweater, black skinny jeans and my favourite black ankle boots. Also the earrings Bec and Stuart gave me for Christmas. They were dangly and sparkly and, having been chosen by Bec, much more tasteful than they sound.

I was first to arrive, partly because I wanted to get it over with. I waited, facing the door, watching plates of gnocchi go past and thinking I'd definitely stay and have dinner even if he left straight away. When he arrived I was reading the menu.

'Kate?' he said.

He was standing behind the chair opposite me, one capable-looking hand resting across each of its polished wooden knobs. His black polar fleece was the sort of thing I'd wear for a bushwalk, if I were to suddenly become the bushwalking type. He was skinny, but not in a bad way, and at least as tall as me.

'Adam?' I said . . .